THE SNIPER,
THE SHOPKEEPER
AND SAMI

Geoff Daplyn

First published 2021

Publishing partner: Paragon Publishing, Rothersthorpe

ISBN 978-1-78222-846-2

Maps: https://palestineawarenesscoalition.wordpress.com/the-maps/
Book design, layout and production management by Into Print
www.intoprint.net
01604 832149

Preface

THERE ARE, SADLY, still many conflicts between people groups and nations in our world today. Some hit the headlines for a few months then disappear from public view and we are left wondering whether there was ever a resolution, just or not. For others, the hostility of both sides becomes a stalemate and an international running sore seemingly destined never to be resolved.

This is one such story – the Israeli-Palestinian conflict. For those who watch the news, it is sometimes wearying to continually read of either Palestinian rockets fired from Gaza on to Israeli houses, or Israeli military and settler aggression towards Palestinians on the West Bank in the form of stolen land, house demolitions and indiscriminate shootings. That is, until you visit the place and see ordinary people on both sides trying to live their lives and bring up their families in peace. Then the poignancy of the status quo hits home powerfully.

This particular conflict has passionate supporters on each side, passions that derive from both human rights and religious concerns. For Europeans, it is mostly the human rights dimension considering the endless anti-Semitic pogroms, deliberate discrimination and broken promises of past centuries. It was a terrible history of 'Christian' European states confining Jewish people within ever tighter boundaries, identity cards that shouted 'second class' citizen, military rule, restrictions on movement, jobs, housing etc. A dehumanising policy of which the vast majority of us are totally ashamed. It culminated in that horrendous episode – the Holocaust.

American support for Israel derives more from regional political concerns and evangelical religious beliefs. Whilst the former revolves around oil and Iran, the latter is about biblical prophecies concerning the physical return of Jesus Christ and Armageddon. Together these forces form powerful, almost overwhelming, electoral pressures on all US administrations.

Support for the Palestinian cause, however, is more patchy and constantly rubs up against the charge of anti-Semitism. This drum has sounded in both continents when any criticism of past or current Israeli government actions has been made. But this cannot be right for a supposed democratic country. Whilst I wholeheartedly support Israel's right to exist, criticism of the policies of such a government must come with the democratic territory and should be tolerated, if not welcomed. Similarly, the Palestinian Authority should also be subject to comparable scrutiny, though its democratic credentials are far from clear.

So let the story begin.

Main Characters

Israeli

Medad	IDF Sniper then a civil servant in the Peace Process Division
Shana	Medad's wife and freelance journalist-in-the-making
Akiva	IDF friend of Medad and later Shin Bet officer
Hirsh	IDF friend of Medad and later IDF commander
Seth	IDF friend of Medad and later PA to Knesset member
Dan	Head of the Middle East and Peace Process Division
Natan	Senior aide to Minister of Defence
Shai	Senior aide to Major General Hersch

Palestinian West Bank

Hani	Shopkeeper and Fatah representative for Bethlehem area
Ayshaa	Hani's wife and founder of Bethlehem Women for Peace (BWP)
Ethar, Israa & Rabia	BWP leadership team members
Zeyad and Kamel	Part of Hani's Fatah team in Bethlehem
Ghalia	Hani's mother
Omari	Founder and CEO of Ghu-sin Zay-tun, a Palestinian mediation charity
Lara	Omari's wife and leading Bethlehem counsellor
Mariam	Leader in the Bethlehem Christian Institute (BCI)
Jamal	Hani's superior based in Ramallah
Abd Alraheem	Hezbollah mole with Palestinian Authority
Ahmed al-Fahd	Radical Shi'a Imam based in Jenin
Safi	Teenager suicide bomber from Jenin

| Nada | US informer, turned Iranian informer |
| Parwez | Nablus founder of Al-khabaz |

Palestinian Gaza

Sami	Gaza teenager and author of influential vblog
Rachel	UNWRA employee in Gaza and friend of Sami
Khalid	Hamas 'fixer'

American

| Chuck | State Department Under Secretary |
| Larry | CIA freelance in Jerusalem |

Iranian

| Angra Mainyu | Member of VAJA (the Ministry of Iranian Intelligence) and a part of the Quds Force – a unit of the Revolutionary Guards based in Beirut. |

1

SAFI WAS JUST sixteen. Not a bad lad and never been in trouble with any authorities. With two older brothers and three younger sisters, he had lived all of his life in Jenin on the West Bank. Tall for his age and a bit overweight, he had experienced some bullying at school but found refuge in his religion. School, thankfully, was now over for him, but there was no prospect of a job let alone a career. Not a bad lad: to some he would forever be classed as a hero but to many others, a terrorist. And so he was, for this is what he had chosen to become. With the help of the Imam, he could see no future for himself where he was.

"Perhaps," the Imam had said after another mid week meeting of teaching, "you could still make some mark with your life in this world." The comment was left hanging in the air. Others had gone home and Safi was moaning about his father, his sisters, his boredom, his life. He had that 'half-empty' view of life and who could blame him, Jenin was not exactly teeming with opportunity.

"What's the point of it all?" he had asked again and again to no-one in particular. The Imam made no further comment. The group he had joined often talked about martyrdom and revered those who had made their mark and were now living in paradise. It had been exhilarating to hear about men who had become his heroes but he had never thought of himself as a man and so it had all been history to him.

Tonight however was different. Maybe the Imam had had enough of the moaning or maybe there was more of an intensity in Safi's emotional turmoil. The youngster looked at the older man with a flicker of interest in his eyes. "Make a mark with my life?"

The Imam continued, "…and at the same time begin to enjoy a better life in the next." Instantly Safi knew what he was talking about. He turned away unsure of himself.

"Perhaps, a boy would prefer to stay at home with his mother," chided the Imam. Safi didn't need much persuasion after that. He weighed it all up in his adolescent mind and decided. What was there to lose?

He had been given clear and precise instructions. This was necessary, he was told, so that his mind could be clear and no doubts or hesitation would deflect him from Allah's will. So he willingly determined to keep to them. The Imam had deliberately not told him that the Quran specifically prohibits suicide bombing – that *whoever kills themselves will be punished in the same manner of death on the day of judgement*. However Ahmed al-Fahd, the Imam in question, had explained that whilst murder was forbidden, killing in self defence was not.

He explained, "If an oppressor lays violent hands upon us, are we not obliged to cut them off? If he writes ill of us, do we not sever the tips of his fingers?" Safi had responded, "If it is the will of God."

Ahmed al-Fahd confirmed, "It is the will of God, and are we not the chosen instruments of God?" "*Aywa*" replied Safi, and that was it.

It was a Tuesday. He had got up at his usual time – six o'clock – important not to vary his routine, not that he had much of one, after all he was a teenager. Something to eat, a quick goodbye to those still in the rooms they rented and he disappeared into Jenin. He had been instructed to take a roundabout route to avoid anyone following, before making his way to a pick up point. Apparently he was going to be taken to Bethlehem initially and it was going to take most of the day. Why Bethlehem? He had no idea and to ask any questions was to exhibit fear. So he tried to keep his mind clear and let the driver do his job. It was a long ride and soon the forty degree heat outside the car was penetrating the inside and completely out-powering the meagre air conditioning unit. Both were perspiring freely such that the smell of body odour was almost over powering. Sweat poured off their bodies, down their legs and into their socks, except that Safi didn't have any socks. The little Mazda was not the latest model by a long stretch and the driver not too good at avoiding holes in the road. It was obviously not his car which went some way to explaining the terrible driving.

Although he had never been outside the bounds of Jenin before, the countryside wasn't much different to that he already knew. Scrub, dust, heat, the occasional Palestinian village which looked out of the nineteenth century and brand new Israeli settlements being built on the tops of hills right out of the twenty-first. His driver wore sunglasses to protect his eyes against the power of the sun, but Safi didn't possess any. They probably thought he wouldn't need them shortly anyway, so why bother. After just one toilet and fuel stop at some God-forsaken place, they arrived at the Dheisheh refugee camp. It was now about six o'clock in the evening.

Dheisheh was a Palestinian refugee camp located just south of Bethlehem established back in 1949 on a very small piece of land originally leased from the Jordanian government. It was established as a temporary refuge for over three thousand Palestinians from nearly fifty villages west of Jerusalem and Hebron who fled during the 1948 Arab-Israeli War. The car stopped outside an anonymous-looking building and he was almost pushed through a door into a single room.

"This is where you will stay tonight," his driver told him, then left. Safi had never been on his own before. He ate the food that had been left for him, drank the water and lay down on the mattress that was in the corner. This is where he would spend his last night on earth. He felt miserable. During the journey he had kept himself strong in his mind with hardly a word shared with his driver, so focussed was he. But now he was on his own and he felt tears forming in his eyes and within a few minutes his face and shirt was wet. He tried to give himself a real talking to, but inside he was aching and perhaps for the first time really wondered what on earth he was doing. He wanted his mother. He wasn't a man like the others, he was just sixteen.

In Jenin, his mother had already raised the alarm that he was missing and had begun wailing. His father had come home and shouted at his wife to shut up saying that he was probably be with 'that Imam' and would surely be home soon. Neither his brother nor sisters seem to be bothered either, but by the evening mealtime, still no Safi.

In Bethlehem, Safi was struggling to overcome his emotional state and so he took the ragged cloth on the floor as his prayer mat and began his *salat al-'isha* prayer routine to be done between sunset and midnight. He had been well taught and knew the set prayers were not just phrases to be spoken for Allah's benefit. For a Muslim, prayer involved uniting mind, soul, and body in worship with a whole series of set body movements that went with the words of the prayer. Safi took time to make sure that he was in the right frame of mind before he began. He tried to put aside all everyday cares and thoughts so that he could concentrate exclusively on Allah. If he prayed without the right attitude of mind, it would be as if he hadn't bothered to pray at all. But he singularly failed and felt even more miserable. He went back to lay on the mattress and after tossing and turning for what seemed hours, eventually fell into a broken sleep.

The next morning, Wednesday, he had to be woken up by the driver. He had missed his s*alat al-fajr prayers* (dawn, before sunrise) and felt really bad about it. His driver had brought some more food for breakfast and, whilst Safi wolfed it down, explained that he had a work pass which would get him through the military checkpoint into Israel. This would be the first time Safi had attempted to go through any formal IDF checkpoint.

He started to ask the driver, "what if I don't get…" The driver interrupted him. "No questions, just do what you have been told."

He got into the car again and the driver headed towards the checkpoint. Safi was dropped off about four hundred meters from the building and he made his way, along with many others, towards the checkpoint. It was a long narrow corridor built with scaffolding and corrugated iron sides and roof. Cameras monitored the slow moving, down-trodden inhabitants as they walked in single file towards the turnstiles at the end. Once he was in the queue, he looked back to see his driver still watching him. He waited until Safi was well into the queue and unable to turn back before lifting his phone to his ear and reporting in.

Although he had overslept, it was still early in the morning. Men, he was told, had to queue up from four o'clock in the morning to make sure they got through for their minibuses on the other side, otherwise they would miss a day's work and a day's money, which they could ill afford to lose. The young Palestinian boy was not sure what to expect and thus was quite nervous. As he shuffled forward in the queue he continued to tell himself that there was no reason that entry would be denied. His pass would work.

After an hour or so in the queue, he began to calm down. He was under no time constraint, so he contented himself by observing the men around him and shuffling along in the queue with them. He was one of them. Unknown to Safi there was a man three places behind him in the queue whom he had never seen before, but was ready to report on his progress and to make sure the youngster didn't bolt. Twice he was asked by other men around him how old he was. Eighteen was his answer.

Apart from that, he had no conversations with anyone else. In fact, he was quite happy to be left alone, but as he got through into the turnstile area before the face to face encounter with Israeli soldiers, he began to sweat. What if they don't let me through? What if I get arrested? It was nearly seven thirty when he eventually reached the end of the queue and faced an Israeli soldier through the steel grill. His legs were aching, his mouth dry and he was wishing there was a toilet nearby, but there wasn't. He passed the documents he had been given through the gap and looked up. He saw a girl only a few years older than himself, dressed in military fatigues looking fed up and bored. When she saw him, her attention returned.

"How old are you?" she asked. "Eighteen," was his reply. She looked closer at him, then at the documents and paused. Safi's heart was racing and his adrenalin pumping. She said nothing for what seemed an age and for the first time Safi got a close up of an Israeli soldier. He was amazed that such a young person, a girl, was trusted with such a job and get to carry a sub machine gun. In any other context she could have been one of his cousins, except she had blond hair poking out from under her military beret. No make up or lipstick that he could see, but quite pretty though with stern blue eyes. She looked up at him as he was staring at her. His face now turned red with embarrassment and he looked down submissively. He blurted out that it was his first time, then desperately wished he'd kept his mouth shut. He'd been strictly told to offer nothing but only answer any questions put to him as briefly as possible. But his mouth seemed to have a mind of its own. Still she said nothing.

Then he was free to go. He was through. He walked away from the military buildings and looked for the silver Honda Civic which would be there to pick him up. Nowhere in sight, so he sat by the side of the road, not quite knowing what to do. Again, unknown to him the watcher behind him had seen his exit and was calling the car. It took another ten minutes for it to appear and Safi began to wonder whether it was all a set-up, a test. Perhaps he was the dummy, to be picked up by the Israelis as he sat by the roadside so that they would be otherwise engaged when the real activist came through. But as soon as the Civic appeared, he pushed such thoughts out of his mind and got in.

The new driver said nothing. Safi said nothing. There was nothing to say. He knew he was being driven to a safe house where he would be fitted with his vest. All the bits necessary had been smuggled into Israel separately he was told and, having had his one question answered, was ordered not to ask any more. After only a short ride, they arrived. To Safi's eyes, the safe house was a mansion. It was detached, in a leafy street and was furnished with more stuff than he had seen in his lifetime. This must be how the Israelis lived, he thought. He recalled the poverty of where he had come from, how he lived. Now there were no second thoughts.

He was fitted with his vest which took a lot longer than he envisaged. Initially, he thought they had made a mistake with the vest since it was too big for his chest size. But those in charge didn't seem to be too concerned. It was only as they added a package to each pocket and then wired him up, did he realise that they clearly knew his chest size because once loaded up, it felt really comfortable. The last thing he was given was a *kippah* to wear on his head. At first he objected, but was quickly told that it was part of his disguise. He was reassured that they all knew what they were doing; they were a team.

It was about midday when he left with his driver in the back seat of the Honda for Jerusalem, a beautiful day with blue sky and a powerful sun. They headed towards Route 50 with Safi looking out of the window at the metropolis which was Greater Jerusalem, a mixture of ancient and new. He had never seen anything like it, and never would again. They stopped near Jaffa St with its busy tram lines, lots of people and most importantly lots of pavement cafés. Their umbrellas were up shielding customers from the sun's rays; a perfect day for old and young to stop for coffee and maybe lunch.

Safi admitted to himself that he was feeling rather strange, an odd mixture of fear and excitement. Up to now he had been concentrating on each step as it happened, as he had been instructed to do. He had not really given much thought to what was going to happen when each step was done and it was time to die. His imminent departure now caused him to think about his mother again. As he began to picture her distress, his eyes began to well up just for a moment. He had never wanted to hurt her but he couldn't tell her what he was about to do because she would have tried to talk him out of it. Safi was absolutely sure he was doing the right thing, after all the Imam had said so and Imams were right, weren't they? He glanced across to the driver to check if he had been watching him in the mirror for signs of weakness. He didn't think so.

Safi had been told the name of the café that had been earmarked and that the driver would drop him off a few minutes walk away from the target. The car couldn't be associated with the divine task so was kept well away from local street cams. It was needed to be used again, and they certainly didn't want the safe house to be identified. Safi started his walk, concentrating solely on his assignment. They had given him a cotton vest underneath the suicide belt for comfort, and an *abaya* or cloak over the top that completely covered the device. His right hand was free and outside, but his left hand was firmly inside the *abaya* with his thumb over the ignition button. He ignored the bustle of the Jerusalem streets, the tourists, the markets. All his attention was now on his mission and his faith. As he walked to his death he was muttering *Allah u Akbar* over and over to himself, following his instructions to the letter. His head was clear and his thoughts were exclusively on doing Allah's will. He knew the job he had to do.

Suddenly the designated café was just there, right in front of him. He saw some women, his mother's age, sitting on chairs outside having lunch and chatting. Suddenly he woke up. What was he doing? There was the café, but he walked straight past, full of confusion. *Allah u Akbar* sounded in his mind. This was his task, his destiny, his route to paradise. He turned and walked back slowly trying to make up his mind. Out of the corner of his eye he saw his driver on the other side of the road watching and he knew the vest should have been detonated by now.

Abruptly, he felt the pressing need to relieve himself and was thinking he might go into the toilets of the café before he completed his task. But it was too late. As he hesitated, he could hold his bladder no longer and a warm stream of liquid surged down his leg and onto the pavement where he was standing. The driver made no attempt to come over and ask for an explanation or urge him to complete the divine task. As if in slow motion, he watched as his driver dropped his own left hand into his pocket…

Safi was no longer there to see police and ambulance crews screaming through the streets to do their job. His remains were scattered over the pavement, the road and into the doorway of the café. The women, finishing their lunch with lemon tart and coffee, received the full blast. Windows all around blew out and into the café scattering their vicious shards everywhere. The owner, at the back, wasn't badly hurt but all of his customers at the front of the shop were either killed or seriously injured. The driver was unhurriedly making his way out of the area whilst rescue services were urgently making their way in. These were men and women who had seen it all before. It wasn't that they weren't compassionate, more a dispassionate professionalism allowing them to do an atrocious job. Although they were used to such massacres, it would still take a personal toll on them once they got back to their homes that evening.

The drill was well rehearsed. Shin Bet followed by collecting all the CCTV footage and taking away the various bits of human flesh retrieved for DNA analysis. By Wednesday evening they knew the bomber had passed through the checkpoint which separated Jerusalem from Bethlehem. The suicide bomber, it seemed, had come from the city of peace just down the road from Jerusalem, or so they thought. A forty-eight hour curfew was immediately slapped in place across the whole Bethlehem region to run to Friday midnight and detailed plans for a house to house search of the city were dusted off and an IDF unit dispatched to implement it with specific names to arrest.

2

"O Jerusalem, Jerusalem … how often would I have gathered your children together as a hen gathers her brood under her wings, and you would not!"

(Matt 23:37 RSV)

IF ONLY THEY had taken the offer, it might have saved years of bloodshed. Over the centuries, Jerusalem had become one of the most blood-soaked cities on the planet. It had been conquered, re-conquered and conquered again. There was always some empire, religious, political, or both willing to send young men to their death for the fame and riches, it was said, the city would bring. Wasn't it Muqaddasi, that medieval Arab author, who said that Jerusalem was a 'golden goblet full of scorpions'? Yes, there were plenty of riches in Jerusalem, the churches were full of golden goblets. Scorpions? Well if they were once in the goblets, now they were out alive on the streets of the city seeking victims and wreaking havoc on the inhabitants.

Another *"Allah u Akbar."* Another blast. Another young man persuaded that killing others was the cause of Allah. Maybe he thought it was for the freedom to move around the West Bank without hindrance or humiliation. Maybe for the return of the land and home that had been stolen from his parents and grandparents. Maybe for revenge against an occupying and oppressive regime which constantly targeted young men of his age. Maybe even for release from the concentration camp that Gaza had become. Who knew?

Gaza. What a hell hole! A land wall on one side, no way through. A sea blockade on the other, no way through. Even its air space was occupied. The birthplace of Goliath, that towering giant of a warrior who, although clothed in full armour, was famously or infamously slain by a young Israeli lad with a sling and a stone. But now who was the giant with full armour? Now who was the young lad with stones and the occasional suicide belt? The result would certainly be different this time. No chance the young lad was going to win.

It didn't matter whether he was from Gaza or anywhere else, at least not to the victims or their families. Not to the young Palestinian martyr either.

All that mattered to him in the end was Allah's will and the promised dark-eyed virgins. But Allah's will was not just a question of faith, which couldn't be proved, rather a question of revenge against an Occupation which was very real. That meant a seemingly never-ending stream of young men coming forward to do Allah's bidding. However, the masterminds behind the outrage weren't really interested in the afterlife. They were wanting to make a powerful statement regarding this life.

It would resolve nothing. Of course, it wasn't aimed at resolving anything; it was meant only to keep the fight going and the occupying enemy on their toes. And it did both exceptionally well. The Israelis would now redouble their efforts to contain and punish Palestinians, and why not? Ten innocents killed and more permanently maimed. Another victory for the Palestinian extremists, but another defeat for the Palestinian people.

A café this time but it could have been a bus, a queue, a shop, anywhere. The usual mess – lots of dust, debris, the smell of burning, odd body parts here and there. It was impossible to tell which belonged to which: the teen-age Palestinian boy who had just stood outside with his oversized overcoat, the girls who were on duty to serve their customers and collect tips to boost their meagre wages, or the customers themselves who just wanted a chat with a friend or a break from the office for ten minutes or so. After the ear-shattering explosion and a blinding flash of whiteness, there was that deafening silence just for a nanosecond but which felt like an eternity, then the screaming which seemed never to stop. A familiar sequence of horror which had become part of everyday life in the city of scorpions, but which many had thought was over. After all, wasn't there a Wall now?

Two girls who had been having their frappuccinos together in the back of the café found themselves alive, just. Blood poured from their pitted faces as the broken glass had smashed into them. Sadly those faces would never be the same again. *They* would never be the same again. It was their first week after graduating from university and they had been at job interviews, friend supporting friend. Azalia and Evelina looked at each other and then at the devastating scene of mutilation and evil. They had been friends throughout their university life and each clung to the other as they staggered through what had been a place of relaxation and relationship. Now, a place of terror and torment.

No more job interviews for weeks, maybe months, maybe never. After all who wanted to employ disfigured staff? At first sight, no-one else seemed to have survived except the owner who had also been at the back of the café. As sirens wailed, the three of them stumbled out on to the street where they collapsed on the pavement with a few others, bloodied and badly injured. Passers by were cordoned off just in case and a well rehearsed paramedic system triaged them as they were being rushed to hospital.

Jerusalem. If it was once a holy city, surely it wasn't now? Didn't holiness have to do with peace, quietness and serenity; the tangible presence of something other; the place of respectful worshippers? So what was it about religion that could turn such a dream into the complete nightmare which was Jerusalem? Even Christian denominations couldn't agree how to look after their holy sites; priests seriously assaulting each other over bricks and mortar. Huxley was right. Jerusalem was the 'slaughterhouse of the religions.' What sort of nonsense was it that saw this place as the centre of the world, even the centre of the universe?

But religion had always been a very powerful motivator; it was remarkable what people would do for their religion. For centuries in this region of the world, people had been willing to slaughter each other, their animals and themselves in the cause of one religion or another. Dozens of afterlives and gods had been on offer by different priests, often in cooperation with secular leaders seeking to harness religion as a sure way of creating national fervour, gaining power and amassing conquering armies. It was, after all, an easy way to mobilise the uneducated masses to fight, so that more power, more prestige, more land, more resources might be gained.

No religion was exempt. And Jerusalem had been so fought over, the blood stank. Endless fighting down the centuries for control over a few precious square miles, and endless casualties as a result. Today there had been other casualties in Baghdad and Kabul. Previously, it had been Paris, London and any number of other cities would probably be included in that count over the next few years. But here, here in Jerusalem, human lives somehow seemed to be much more precious, at least the Israeli ones did. In the past, peace only came when the conqueror imposed it. Today, although negotiation was the accepted international way, it seemed that in this corner of the planet the conqueror still held sway. There had been any number of opportunities to make peace, but was it the Palestinian's fault of never missing an opportunity to miss an opportunity, or did the Israeli side breathe a sigh of relief that talks always came to nothing, giving them free reign to do what they wanted all along?

The morning had started so clear and promising. Early autumn was always a good season in Jerusalem still with high temperatures which required parasols outside cafés, but quickly cooled in the evening. The sun did not discriminate for it shone on the righteous and unrighteous equally. But early in the afternoon, the larger discrimination that the city now epitomised had angrily manifested itself. The peace and potential of the day had disappeared as quickly as the early morning haze, with innocent people dying and a stark reminder that the government still couldn't make Jerusalem safe.

Such political considerations mattered little to the families of the café victims. It also mattered little to the Palestinian mother of the teenager. She had no idea what he was into, much less what he had been persuaded to do. She knew in her bones that it was her Safi. She had been right to wail in her distress but now distress had turned to the ultimate anguish. A boy whom she had borne for eight months, fed from her breasts, nurtured when her husband ignored him was now dead, a terrorist. She knew that if he was ever identified, Israeli military would be calling on them and not for a cup of tea.

There was going to be deep mourning all around, as there was the last time, and the time before that, and the time before that. But not by a radical Imam in Jenin whose secret loyalty was not to Fatah or Hamas, but to Islamic Jihad and ultimately shia Iran. Safi was just one young man who had come under his spell. There were and would be others. Yes, it was more difficult to get into Israel now the Wall had been built, but there were still ways.

3

BETHLEHEM HAD SEEN this before, and this was not the first time that young Medad has been deployed on such a mission as part of his IDF squad. Just a twenty year old conscript, his call up had happened, as he knew it would, as soon as he became eighteen. Male and female, they had all gone through the best military training there was. Overtly military yes, but covertly political. Everything was political in Israel.

At the time, he hadn't known that the call up was not actually compulsory. This was not widely known but those who refused were arrested and had a mark against them for the rest of their lives in Israel. No conscientious objections tolerated here. Even if he had known, Medad wouldn't have tried to sidestep it. There was no point in making a stand, he would only lose the argument because his father, a military lifer, would have seen to that. Unlike his father, Medad was not a big man, not a natural for the army. His slight build, dark hair and alert eyes actually made him quite catch for the girls, and some of the boys! He was well aware that many a relationship started in the years of conscription; young people were just thrown together in what inevitably would become a hothouse. Few liaisons lasted the distance.

He was aware that many of his friends were dating girls in the same unit. None had any intentions of developing a long lasting relationship, rather it was a necessary distraction from the military life they had been thrust into and totally unprepared for. Just some fun. Medad thought he'd like to be a little more choosy. Maybe I don't want to play the field. Maybe I'll wait for the right one. He had to admit though, that his judgement of the 'right one' hadn't been all that good. The three girls he had dated hadn't turned out that way. But he had hormones like the rest of them, so where would the harm be?

It was when he was going through IDF training that they discovered that he was a natural gunshot. Remarkably, he had never used a gun before in his life, yet couldn't avoid being immediately classified by his trainers as a potential sniper. He quickly became one of the most accurate snipers in his unit, although he had never wanted to kill people. But no options now. In the army, his principles and opinions were as useful to him as his music. Orders were orders. He wore the uniform, so he was theirs lock, stock and barrel for a minimum of thirty-two months and he did what he was told. Now, however, he was nearing the end of his service and he didn't want anything to go wrong.

Medad had used the Bethlehem Municipality building in Manger Square as a sniper position before. He knew the layout well. The Church of the Nativity was to his left and the Mosque of Omar to his right. Opposite were various cafés and tourist shops, now shuttered up for the night and would stay that way for the duration of the curfew. Bethlehem was not really a hot bed of Palestinian trouble, but now and again frustration seemed to boil over and his unit were called in to restore order. Both the church and the mosque had been used as places of refuge in the past. The Israelis, however, didn't recognise either as such and there were bullet holes in the external walls of each to prove it.

Although Medad was twenty, service in the IDF made a person grow up fast but somehow he still thought of himself as more a teenager. However, Israeli law considered him man enough to use a IWI DAN .338 Bolt Action Sniper Rifle, a devastatingly effective weapon. In his personal unspoken opinion, it was a weapon that should have been only used by professional soldiers, not conscripts. However, his opinion was just that, his opinion.

Named after the ancient city of Dan, which was itself named after one of Jacob's sons and a tribe of the ancient Israelites, this sniper rifle had a range of twelve hundred meters so well capable for the night's mission. Most of his comrades had the M16 5.56mm automatic rifle, with the 20-round magazine. It was an American gun, but the Israelis had the latest incarnation, the M16A4. It was now equipped with a removable carrying handle and Picatinny rail for mounting optics and other ancillary devices. Israel's IDF had its share of the eight million M16s produced so far by the US military machine.

So here he was on an autumn Wednesday evening, looking down on the Square with orders to kill anyone who defied the curfew. Unless his IDF colleagues found who they were looking for, he calculated that he could be in position until the curfew ended, a long time. He pulled his coat around himself and settled down.

Most snipers had to be camouflaged as they usually operated either behind enemy lines or near the front. They had to be aware of the basics of survival such as moving tactically toward their targets. Bearing in mind that they could be outnumbered or outgunned by any adversary, they had to remain invisible as they targeted their quarry. Having accepted that he was going to be a sniper, Medad had worked hard to perfect his shooting skills using lots of different weapons, but he liked his IWI. He had also developed all the skills and instincts that allowed him to pick the right time to shoot, not too quickly, but waiting to get the best shot before the target was out of range.

However, not much of that training was appropriate tonight or any time on the West Bank. Yes, the waiting was the same, and the ability to do nothing but watch for hours and hours, then react in a split second when the opportunity presented itself. But there were no armed adversaries here with anything like an IMI or an M16 equivalent. No opposing snipers on the other side of the Square. No real opposition at all. No equivalent weapons like that anywhere on the West Bank for that matter. So he got as comfortable as he could and waited for anyone who might come into the Square.

If you had asked him, Medad didn't much like the army but the army certainly liked him because he was good at what he did, which was to kill people. Although he grew up in a settler community and was aware of the tension with their Palestinian neighbours, there was not an ounce in his body that held a grudge against anyone – well maybe his father…and perhaps his elder brother. They were both from the same mould; loud, ideologues and argumentative. Thinking back on his upbringing, he didn't know how on earth his mother had put up with it.

He was jerked back to the present… was that someone? Did he detect movement down there? Looking through the sights, he couldn't see anything. He silently chastised himself for a lapse in concentration. Part of him enjoyed these times. He was alone and he could think, not that the IDF encouraged any of it's soldier to think. But Medad did, and not just about those girls. He was dismissive of many lads in his unit because that's all they thought about, at least all they talked about, which may not have amounted to the same thing. With high levels of testosterone around in his male barracks, virtually all the talk was about women: what they had done, what they said they had done, or what they would have liked to do.

Well, perhaps he could believe some of that. Although barracks were segregated between male and female, they were all soldiers. He assumed the girls would be talking about the men in exactly the same terms, maybe slightly different in detail. But not for him the coarse language of the barrack room. Not that he was religious or gay, but his thoughts were more philosophical, more political, more independent.

He decided that he rather liked this part of Bethlehem, the town that the tourists saw. But Bethlehem was not so much a little town anymore. Rather an occupied one of about one hundred thousand inhabitants, now encompassing three refugee camps with four generations of refugees living there and divided from Israeli settlements by 'The Wall', a security barrier built by Israel that tried to keep suicide bombers out and the Palestinian population in. Initially a temporary structure, it was now said to be a cover for occupying more Palestinian land. 'Illegal', said the United Nations. 'Racial segregation' and 'Apartheid', said the Palestinians. 'Security', said the Israelis.

No deep and dreamless sleep had happened here for a good few centuries. From earliest Canaanites times, c.1350BC to its occupation by the Romans, it's conquest by the Crusaders, followed by the Ottomans, 'deep' and 'dreamless' weren't words that would immediately come to mind by any of its inhabitants. Tonight was no different. It was now the turn of Israeli teenagers armed with M16s to occupy the town, ordered to do what it took to find the Palestinian terrorists who planned and helped to execute the Jerusalem suicide bombing.

Medad had no issue with this at all. The attack had sickened him as it had done to the whole country. However, he knew that it was one thing to denounce it with words, but another to be in a place of direct retaliation with a powerful sniper's rifle. He fervently prayed that no-one would be stupid enough to venture out in this forty-eight hour period. But he would be professional and he would protect his comrades to the hilt. They were friends and after all, his name meant "friend." His namesake, he had been told by his mother, was a leader and prophet in the time of Moses, but he didn't consider himself either. Yet his mother had her hopes.

She had birthed him into a community that had a heritage to be proud of. In May 1948 residents of Kfar Etzion, a significant settlement in the Gush Etzion region, were able to hold off a large Arab army headed for Jerusalem. Unfortunately, despite surrendering to that army after three days of holding out, two hundred and forty residents of the kibbutz were massacred, another two hundred and sixty were captured, and the settlement was obliterated. A heritage which lingered long in the memory of the present-day community. This history was well taught to every child in the community. The fact that it happened to be Palestinian land wasn't, but that didn't excuse a massacre. Anyhow, in a land where memories continue to linger a long time, certain facts were somehow conveniently forgotten, by both sides.

After Israel regained control of Jerusalem and the surrounding areas in the West Bank in June 1967, a new initiative was launched to resettle the Etzion area. Several of the new residents of Kfar Etzion were descendants of the people who fought and died in 1948. It was the first settlement established in the West Bank after Israel's victory in 1967. Medad was not even born so he didn't know first hand what had happened then and whose land this actually was. It made little difference to him since it was all a long time ago and no-one was going to turn the clock back now.

As a child, he was much closer to his mother than his brother, but rather a disappointment to his father, an ex-military professional now retired and a leading figure in the community settlement. His elder brother, also a soldier, followed in his father's footsteps and probably going to be a lifer too. Not the career that Medad had envisaged for himself. He was content that his father and elder brother carried the mantle of the past, as he saw it, he would look to the future. He was Jacob to his brother's Esau. He was the lean and smooth, Yigal was the muscular and hairy.

He had been genuinely surprised, and somewhat appalled, to discover he was really good with a gun. There was no consultation as to his deployment. Nothing he could do about it. But he quite liked the reputation that snipers had and, as a man who liked just a few friends, he was quite happy to spend hours on his own.

And here he was, on his own, in Manger Square with the tools of his trade set up ready. Midnight passed. He shivered a little. Some October days were still hot, but evenings could be a little chilly, especially up on a roof. He tried to get comfortable but never relaxing his gaze on the Square.

How many people had he killed to date? Twenty. Thirty. He didn't know. He wasn't obliged to count them. Secretly, he had started a tally as soon as he had been sent into action, but that hadn't lasted. It wasn't that he didn't care. No, he thought to himself, it was because he did care. He had a job to do and he didn't want his kills permanently hanging around his neck. Besides it was all done under orders. All were legitimate. None were done in order to boast or keep his tally up with his competitors, like they did. At least he didn't think so.

Now he got to thinking, he probably could recall many of them. It had started immediately he joined his IDF group. Yes, it was that disturbance down in Hebron. Just the one that time. Then there was the time he had slotted three in short succession. That was crazy, at least the Palestinians were crazy. They just weren't rational. They were outgunned and outmanoeuvred – why did they insist on challenging us against all odds? He remembered how he had been quite frightened as his unit had come under a hail of stones. So what else could he do? He had to fire; if a stone hit you in the face, you would know it. And there had been many more after that. But he was not to blame.

He was under orders, and in the end, he knew it was all politics.

Everyone knew that snipers were a different breed to ordinary soldiers. He found that it was almost impossible to dehumanise his enemy because he usually saw his target with great clarity, sometimes observing them just for a few seconds, but occasionally for an hour or two. Even when he had little time to line up a shot, he usually took a couple of seconds to look at them. It was not something he was taught to do, in fact quite the opposite. It was just his way of respecting them. Not this time though.

It was pitch black except for a few small street lights. The night vision optics were great but he wouldn't be able to make out any facial features, just the fact of a person either being where they shouldn't be or doing what they shouldn't do. Tonight if he saw anything, it was going to be fire first and ask questions later. Yes, he thought, it might be distant but it was still very personal, even intimate. Ordinary soldiers didn't understand, how could they? But it didn't bother him at all. He was happy to be different.

His night vision eyes went to and fro, up and down the Square constantly. If he missed anyone breaking the curfew, and a member of his unit was killed as a result, that would bring disgrace on himself, his father, his brother and the whole Kfar Etzion community. There was a slight breeze, quite common at night, so he'd have to account for that in his aim. Every shadow, every possible movement was examined and only if he saw movement did he investigate through the telescopic lens ready to fire. There were a few stray dogs around and he didn't want to fire on a dog. He would never hear the end of it, for everyone in his unit would join in the joke at his expense. Since his older brother used to tease him ad nauseum, he was quite vulnerable even now. His mother would try to protect a little but it could be a double-edged sword. Mummy's little boy! His father disregarded him for the most part.

A little reddish brown gecko darted across the roof very near where Medad was couched and disappear down a hole. It was spotted with white and had supper in its mouth, a large insect. He thought geckos usually swallowed their prey whole, but maybe it was taking it to its young, though surely not in October since the reproductive cycle of the gecko would be over for the year. More than could be said for humans, he thought. He wondered what sort of life a gecko had on the roof of the Bethlehem Municipality building. Probably simpler than his, he thought pulling his attention back to covering Manger Square.

The house to house search was not happening in the Square itself but in the adjoining side streets, past the tourist shops. Manger Square was only covered because it could be the main means of escape for the terrorists they were searching for. Bethlehem was still and silent. It was now two o'clock, early morning, and the radio earpiece told him that the search was still under way. He rubbed his eyes hard to stay awake. Then from the corner of his eye, he thought he saw some movement. He recalibrated his scope, focussing the telescopic lens on the far corner... yes it was moving and too big to be an animal. Almost unconsciously he settled down his respiration and with it his heart rate in an instant. His finger slid to the trigger and even before he could engage his brain his training took over and he squeezed it.

It was done. No movement at all now. Adrenalin running high, he reported it over the radio in as calm a voice as he could manage. His young hands began to shake as they always did immediately after a kill. As he was almost always on his own, no-one saw. Killing someone always took some toll on him, at least temporarily. The enormity of what he had done hit him again for an instant, then it was gone. He knew that even if he had made a mistake, which he hadn't, there would be no repercussions. Part of him was annoyed with himself, thinking it was a weakness and part of him was glad he still valued human life.

Looking through his scope, there was no movement. He hoped to God that it was not an innocent because in his mind there was no doubt as to the success of his shot. He wasn't firing rubber bullets, or even rubber coated bullets. He'd just done his job.

4

HANI WAS A young Palestinian man who lived with his wife Ayshaa, his mother Ghalia and his baby daughter Rena, in two ground floor rooms in the old city of Bethlehem. It was a typical terraced building, four storeys high, hundreds of years old and his particular building housed twenty four people, each floor sharing a single toilet. Each residence had one bedroom, a living room with a galley kitchen to the side. The ground floor windows didn't open so during the heat of the day the door was never closed. There wasn't much to steal and besides, everyone did the same. It was a community.

Rooms were dark and low with black mildew in the corners of their ground floor indicating quite a severe damp problem. No chance their landlord would do anything and there was no law to say he should. In fact, they didn't even know who he was. His agent came round once a week for the rent and as long as they paid up they could stay. Get behind and they would be out without notice. No appeals. No tribunals.

Dust was everywhere and posed a problem for the women who tried in vain to keep the insides of their homes clean. It swirled in the breeze, in the doors and through the windows to the second, third and fourth floors. Nowhere was exempt when the wind blew, but it was worse for the bottom 'apartment' where Hani and Ayshaa lived, consequently the rent was a little lower. C'est la vie. In the evening when it was cooler and the breeze died down, husband and wife would sit on the stone threshold with the door still open to share the happenings of the day. Many of their neighbours would be doing the same, some talking, some thinking, others just sitting. But the cooler temperatures also brought out the dogs looking for food and depositing their consequential debris all around.

Although his grandparents had been refugees, his grandfather had managed to avoid being dumped in the many refugee camps around Bethlehem and had found these rooms not far from Manger Square. Unfortunately, they had both died within a few months of each other in 1987 and his father, now married to Ghalia his mother, had the place to themselves until he was born.

Squalid we might say, but significantly better than those in the refugee camps outside the town itself. There was very little furniture in any of the rooms. Hani's father had managed to get hold of a table, three chairs, an old metal double bed in the bedroom, a sofa bed in the living room and that was it.

Since then Hani and Ayshaa had not added much to the earthly possessions they had inherited. Hani's widowed mother, Ghalia slept in the bed in the only bedroom, since Hani and Ayshaa would never allow her to sleep in the communal living room. Honouring one's elders was paramount in Palestinian culture and anyway, she usually went to bed earlier than they did. So they slept on the pull-out sofabed in the living room. When the baby had arrived, Ghalia tried to insist that Hani and Ayshaa have her room with the baby, but eventually all agreed it would not work. So the baby had a basket in the corner of the living room during the night, which was then moved into the bedroom during the day. They might revisit the situation as Rena grew up.

Hani ran his father's small ironmongery shop in the back streets of Bethlehem on his own. In theory, the shop sold everything from nails and screws, to craftsman tools and household goods, the theory being that he could get permission from the Israeli authorities to import all this, which he couldn't. Much of the stock he wanted was prescribed as useful to a terrorist and, as such, there was no chance of getting it. Perhaps that's why IDF soldiers had ransacked the shop in his father's time; they had found nothing incriminating because there was nothing to find. But his father had become a permanent casualty after protesting a little too much and trying to defend his shop. No chance to say goodbye. No appeals. No tribunals. Just a funeral.

Hani, like his father, was a quiet man which was not how many saw Palestinians. They had a reputation for being emotionally volatile, but that was a misleading stereotype. Back when most of them were farmers, they were quietly content with their lot, even sometimes happy. Not so much now, especially Hani's generation who didn't know anything about agriculture, rather a lot more about protesting. Hani could certainly show emotion when something really got to him, but mostly he preferred to keep his own counsel and his mouth shut. A strong, silent type some might have said.

He never had been much of a political animal, preferring to concentrate on the business he had inherited from his father. Occasional dreams were entertained of accumulating enough money to move his shop from a back street to the main street. He was sure that was the way to increase his turnover. Location. Location. Location. But there were many like him, trying to eke out a living in the back streets which meant long hours for little return, not that there were customers all that time, but you had to be open to do business.

Sourcing supplies was difficult, finding customers who paid was difficult, keeping the protection rackets at bay was difficult. It was all difficult. He had been forced to branch out into tourist memorabilia to maintain any sort of income, and he despised himself for it. Lacking any knowledge of spreadsheets, he would use page after page of paper scoping out financial scenarios for building his business. Sometimes it felt like his whole life had been lived in this shop. He hated it, yet held it close for his father.

Apparently, so others said, he had his father's presence about him. His 6'6" height and fifteen stone weight, gave him some gravitas. He had jet black hair combed back, and could look quite menacing to anyone who didn't know him. In a fight he would certainly take no prisoners, but he hadn't had one of those since he had been set upon by three so-called friends while he was at school. But he was also smart and, unknown to him, seen as a potential leader by local Palestinian officials. He had, however, spurned all attempts to cast him in that mould, preferring at this time in his life to concentrate on being a husband, a father and a shopkeeper.

Six months ago Ayshaa, his wife, had presented him with baby Rena and this shop was all the family had to give them any sort of income so he didn't have the energy to rail at Israel. At this moment, he just wanted to live and provide for his family.

Although the shop was only fifteen minutes away from his home, on this Thursday evening it might have been fifteen miles. The curfew had been declared and he was still at the shop, stuck. He pulled out an old second-hand Nokia, the only phone he could afford. No dial tone. The Israelis had blocked all communications, so the only way of getting home was to break the curfew and run the gauntlet of Israeli snipers. In the darkness of the shop, he began to work through alternative routes in his mind.

He wondered whether his father had ever had to do the same. Which route would he have taken? There was a mass of narrow alleyways in the town and he knew them all. He sat down wondering exactly what to do. Thinking of his father was prompting further memories, of him alive and dead. He hadn't seen the killing, but had found the bloodied body two days later when that particular curfew had been lifted and his mother had sent him out to look for her husband since he hadn't come home after it had ended. No-one had told them what had happened but looking at the damage, he surmised that Israeli soldiers had thrown in a stun grenade, entered the shop, interrogated his father then hit him over the head and left him on the floor. He had bled out. It seemed to Hani that a dog would have had better treatment.

He knew a safe way he could get back home, at least he thought so. If he had been single with no wife and baby, he would have risked breaking the curfew. He was sure he could do it, but fatherhood had tempered his riskiness or was it his age? Now nearly thirty years old, he was almost an old timer. Everyone grew up quickly here, you had to. Finally he decided to stay at the shop and began to settle down for the night. The floor was hard, so he made mental note to get a mattress of some sort for the next time, because surely there would be a next time. It was nearly midnight and he was straining his ears to assess whether anything was moving outside. Nothing.

Hani was no coward, but neither was he a stooge. Yes, he was a Palestinian. Yes, he cared about his people, his nation, his country. His reaction to the assassination of his father could easily have been that of a revolutionary, a radical. If he had responded to those inclinations, his future would have been different. Very different. No Ayshaa, no Rena…and probably no Hani by now and what would that have achieved? He had seen no good results of that strategy, except the death of brave young men and the grief of older women. He had noticed that the Hamas and Islamic Jihad leaders didn't offer themselves for martyrdom. They weren't stupid. Anyway, he didn't need all those dark-eyed virgins in the afterlife… if they were really there. Ayshaa was all he wanted and he wanted her now.

They had met three years ago. So much had changed since their wedding.

He'd been forced to assume responsibility for the family long before he had anticipated, so the dream of spending much more free time with Ayshaa before they settled down and had their family was aborted. No gap year travelling round the world for them but, even within the confines of the ABC areas of the West Bank, they did have plans. What would life be without plans? They discussed possibilities, dared to think of places they could visit. They got excited about the possibilities of their time together after the wedding. None of it to be.

Ayshaa understood, but somewhere in her heart she still held the possibility of living her dream. But she never spoke of it. She was not just a lovely local girl, she was determined and intelligent with it. She was a year younger than Hani and brought up to be a wife and a mother as all good Palestinian girls were. With her dark hair, and dark eyes, she was very attractive, but no real hope of anything other than motherhood, that is until Hani had come into her life. Then she had dared to hope for something different. But that was then.

Ayshaa had to look after her mother-in-law as well. Ghalia wasn't so understanding of the Israeli security forces, with good reason, yet she didn't want to lose her son as well as her husband. She was nothing if not pragmatic. She was fifty-six going on seventy-six with no plans or dreams for herself. With a face creased with worry, she was one lady just defeated by life and exhausted. Dreams and plans were for the young; they would learn soon enough. What could she do but remember the past, and submit to the present. She saw no future, except continuous humiliation by the occupying Israelis. She recalled that in their own scriptures written hundreds of years earlier, the Jews were described as "stiff-necked", meaning stubborn and bullheaded. No change there, then.

She was grateful, however, that they weren't living in the camps. Initially these had been set up after 1948 when Palestinian land had been taken to form the new land of Israel. There had been no compensation for the Palestinian farmers who had fled to Jordan, Lebanon, Egypt, Gaza and the cities in the West Bank. Herded into tent camps initially, these farmers were used to the open air and the fields, but now they were living on top of each other with no olive groves to look after, no goats to tend, and no fields to cultivate. No shops. No schools. No hospitals. No hope. Their descendants likewise.

Ghalia was just a young girl in 1967 with no real knowledge of what was brewing. In June 1967 came the an-Naksah, the Setback. War. She just remembered that one day she was playing happily, the next, all hell seemed to have broken loose. Israeli aircraft overhead heading for Syria and Jordan. Israeli soldiers and tanks were everywhere. They came through the West Bank, through her village, through her home and never left. Occupation.

5

THAT WEDNESDAY AFTERNOON in Jerusalem would be etched on many people's lives for ever. Of course, it wasn't the first time but since the Wall went up there was no denying that the number of suicide attempts had dropped markedly. That, however, was little comfort to the mothers, fathers, sons, daughters and friends who had lost someone very precious to them. The owners of the café in this latest attack were sympathetic, but business was business. They were allowed to begin the clear up by mid afternoon Thursday. The crime scene had been released and the shopfitters would spend Thursday and Friday clearing up the premises and refitting it so trade could begun again after *Shabbat*. Insurance was a wonderful thing, if you had the right policy; even suicide attacks could be covered at a price. Because of these attacks, shopfitting had been a lucrative business for many years until the Wall had seen the number of suicide bombers fall dramatically. Quite a few firms had gone to the wall since, and there was fierce competition amongst those left. Even the larger companies were now taking people only on short term contracts.

In Bethlehem, the curfew had been in force from Wednesday midnight when that city had been identified as the place where the suicide bomber had travelled from. It was due to last until Friday midnight, but the IDF force had been withdrawn late on Friday afternoon, well before sunset ready for *Shabbat*, but nobody had bothered to tell the population of Bethlehem. As a reprisal, the Israeli military closed the main checkpoint which the men of Bethlehem used to get to their jobs in Israel for three days. Some of the construction sites in and around Jerusalem ground to a halt for lack of workers which caused them some issues, but the men of Bethlehem lost three days pay which was going to cause severe hardship. There was a lot of anger about.

Back at the IDF base, there was a full de-briefing for the IDF unit before they all disappeared to their homes, or wherever they were staying. It was the first time that Medad had a chance to hear the official result of the mission. Yes, they had arrested some men. No, they didn't know who the dead person in Manger Square was. Medad was quiet. So he was an innocent? Of course not. Why else would they be breaking the curfew? Just another dirty Arab. Someone would come along and pick them up. Medad had done his job professionally and was congratulated but he remained quiet. His friends noticed but it wasn't until the end of the briefing that they were free to talk.

Although each needed to set off to their respective families for *Shabbat*, they stayed around for an hour or so to try to persuade Medad to lighten up. They were good friends and although different points of view on the Palestinian question, would have done anything to help each other, especially in a combat situation. Military training did that. Outside of the barrack room all three were laughing and joking until they saw that Medad was not joining in as usual. Clearly he had not put the Bethlehem episode behind him, which was bad military form. You had to move on, whether victory or defeat. They urged him to do just that. If you didn't, it would gnaw away at you inside and in the end you'd have a breakdown.

Akiva suggested they get a drink before going home, just to wind down. So they went outside the camp to a local bar they had frequented previously and he went to order the drinks. A hard-line Zionist, Akiva was a tall lad with a mop of black hair which flopped over his left eye until he temporarily brushed it back, at which point it would flop back again. When he came back to his friends, they were insisting that Medad had done the right thing and Akiva added his voice to the others. His parents were zealous settlers, initially in a kibbutz, but latterly in one of the major northern settlements. They were religious fundamentalists in that they believed in a fusion of Jewish religion and nationhood. They wanted to restore not only Jewish political freedom but also an authentic Jewish religion in the light of the Torah and its commandments. Akiva, having been brought up with these views, willingly embraced them and with it, had a very negative view of the Palestinian population. He was insistent that it was the only thing Medad could have done.

"To risk the lives of the other Israeli soldiers is unthinkable. How could the life of a Palestinian be equivalent to the life of an Israeli?" The former Medad agreed with, not so sure about the latter.

"But they want to drive us into the sea and kill all of us. It would be another holocaust, and that cannot be allowed to happen. We are surrounded by enemies and sometimes we have to take pre-emptive action. It is entirely justified."

Hirsh, another friend, may not have been as blunt as Akiva in his analysis, but he concurred. Hirsh was a more stocky man than Akiva with black hair slickly combed back with gel. Heavily muscular with more than a few tattoos, Hirsh worked out every day. He was going to be a professional soldier and stay in the army after his national service was completed. He saw the military situation very clearly and leaned forward on the table towards Medad.

"Look, the initial boundaries that were agreed for the new state in 1948 were laughable. They provided no security whatsoever. Any of half a dozen enemies could have strangled us at birth with just a modicum of force. The fact that we lasted nearly twenty years with those boundaries was nothing short of miraculous."

He recounted the constant threats, particularly from Nasser's Egypt. "*The Milhemet Sheshet Ha Yamim* (Six Days War of 1967), had been coming for a long time. Just as there had been the need to take pre-emptive action then, so now." Hirsh hadn't finished.

"Besides, the IDF are the most moral forces in the world." He quoted by heart part of the shared values of the IDF:

"The IDF servicemen and women will act in a judicious and safe manner in all they do, out of recognition of the supreme value of human life. During combat they will endanger themselves and their comrades only to the extent required to carry out their mission."

and

"The soldier shall make use of his weaponry and power only for the fulfilment of the mission and solely to the extent required; he will maintain his humanity even in combat. The soldier shall not employ his weaponry and power in order to harm non-combatants or prisoners of war, and shall do all he can to avoid harming their lives, body, honour and property."

They all looked at him mouths opened. "You learned that by heart, Hirsh?" said Akiva admiringly. Hirsh would have nothing said against the IDF. They could do no wrong in his eyes.

All Israeli children learned the history of their nation, and Seth as a Christian Israeli who had arrived in Israel from the Soviet Union with his parents when he was a baby, was no different. He didn't really have the physical frame to be a soldier, but looked to be more of an academic with his steel rimmed glasses. Christian Israelis numbered only about 170,000, some 2% of the population. He was from an Orthodox background, his parents having fled because of persecution and arriving in Israel shortly after its inception. He still spoke with a slight East European accent which was no problem since there were Israelis from all over the world in the country and in the IDF. For him, his religion was an identity more cultural than religious.

He had majored in political history up until he got his call up so everyone thought he was destined to go into politics, although the fact that he was Christian might be an issue in the longer term. But he had politics in his blood and already had a job lined up after his military service was completed, as assistant to a Member of the Knesset (MK). He understood the power of rhetoric and had used it before at the debating society in high school to crushing effect. He hoped to become a fully fledged MK himself one day. He remained quiet as his friends expounded Zionist philosophy, not that he disagreed with them.

These were good friends. Some of Medad's other colleagues in the IDF group might have dismissed him as weak and a Palestinian appeaser, but he felt he could be honest with his friends. He leaned back in his chair and tried to explain his dilemma.

"Of course I understand the need for security. I even think there's a role for pre-emptive action in certain circumstances where's there's good intelligence. But this can't go on generation after generation. There has to be peace at some point. Are you saying it cannot happen until every Palestinian is killed or removed from the country? Because if so, that's stupid." Medad got passionate when talking about peace. Privately he suspected that the current military and political policies were never designed to lead to peace. That had all but been abandoned.

"So," he continued, "who is actually benefiting from keeping the current scenario in play? Surely the vast majority of ordinary people on all sides want nothing more than their children to live without the threat of war, and with a hope and a future."

He looked at his friends, "Don't they?" There was a grumble of acknowledgement all round. "Well, yes they did, but it wasn't going to happen was it? Face the facts."

So this is the future, thought Medad. A gloom settled over him. The friends were in a bar which IDF troops largely frequented, having a drink prior to going home and everyone seemed to be having a good time except him.

"Think of it this way," Seth the political historian was trying to reach his friend. He took off his glasses and began polishing them. The others looked on amused at his idiosyncrasies.

"The whole setting up of this state was botched. Britain was the country in the driving seat, but didn't seem to care for the Jewish people. Rather, they were more concerned for their place in the world and protecting their overseas colonies, their so-called empire."

Seth continued. "And wasn't it Arthur James Balfour, he of the Balfour Declaration, who said, "Nothing matters very much and few things matter at all". That tells you everything about the man. And look at the Declaration itself... a masterclass in diplomatic impreciseness and double-mindedness. He didn't quote it, but they all knew about it.

'His Majesty's government views with favour the establishment in Palestine of a national home for the Jewish people, and will use their best endeavours to facilitate the achievement of this object, it being clearly understood that nothing shall be done which may prejudice the civil and religious rights of existing non-Jewish communities in Palestine, or the rights and political status enjoyed by Jews in any other country.'

"You remember what it said? It could never be fulfilled." Seth was expounding his political thesis. "Yes, of course Zionists grabbed with both hands. It was all they had. And remember, this so-called Declaration was made in 1917. It took another thirty-one years for it to happen."

Akiva jumped in. "And it wasn't us who planned the extermination of Egypt, Jordan or Syria in 1967. It was they who planned ours. If it hadn't been for allies such as the US, we wouldn't have had an effective air force, and we would have been pushed into the sea, without a doubt. Britain wouldn't have rescued us. The lands we occupied after the Six Day War were held only to prevent another attack by those countries."

"Absolutely." agreed Seth. "Egypt and Jordan saw the writing on the wall and made peace. But Syria didn't, neither did Iran or their proxies Hezbollah and Islamic Jihad. We still have powerful enemies."

Seth looked directly at Medad, "The Palestinians have just been caught in the middle, but they have shown themselves to be duplicitous, siding with our enemies, not to mention the constant threat of rockets from Gaza." There were murmurs of assent from Akiva. This was the reality as he saw it as well.

Hirsh came back from replenishing their drinks, as Akiva was pushing the argument further. "This is why our settlement programme is so important. We must infiltrate the land so it can never ever be used against us. The world won't understand and doesn't want to understand. They wring their hands on the sidelines about attacks on Israel. They make speeches and pass resolutions, but do precisely nothing." Akiva was a hawk among hawks. In his mind there was going to be no two state solution. They should not give anything away, not ever.

"As far as I'm concerned," he shouted over the increasingly loud music, "this land is our land. We were bequeathed it by God. We lost it, but now have regained it. And we will never lose it again. We want a Jewish land for the Jews. No-one else. We will then make the wilderness and desert sing for joy, the badlands will celebrate and flower – like the crocus in spring, bursting into blossom, a symphony of song and colour." The friends, even Medad, all smiled at each other. Akiva was getting a little carried away again.

Hirsh agreed but wanted to place the military in the forefront. "We have to acknowledge that it has only been military might that has kept us alive. The only friend we have is the US. They will supply us, but even they won't put boots on the ground to support us. We can rely on only one state, our own. And you can't take chances. The first time weakness or incapacity is detected, they'll be on us like a pack of devouring wolves, and we'll be history."

"We must increasingly become self sufficient in terms of our military capability. Yes, we now have a nuclear option, but that can only be a last ditch deterrent. It will make Iran think twice before attacking us. And don't think they have stopped their nuclear programme. They haven't."

Akiva nodding added, "But the key enemy may not be Iran directly, rather their proxies, notably Hezbollah in Lebanon and Syria. We must and will do everything in our power, including military action to prevent such terrorist groups importing weaponry that certainly be used against us. If the Palestinian leadership, Hamas and Fatah, want to ally themselves with Hezbollah, they must pay the price and feel the might of the military. We cannot trust anyone. We have no alternative."

With that, the orthodox Akiva indicated that he had to go, the start of *Shabbat* was at hand. Hirsh and Seth also took the opportunity to leave and make their way to wherever they were going. Medad was left by himself. The inevitable had been delayed long enough and now a call had to be made to his mother saying he would not be home this time. More Zionist rhetoric from his father and brother was the last thing he wanted. He was nothing if not stubborn in his views and, whilst he felt misunderstood and rather alone, his desire for a peace wasn't just an intellectual stance, it somehow came from his soul. Thinking back on the conversation with his friends, he called to mind that great Jewish patriarch Job who, when he was pondering his own lonely situation, was surrounded by friends with good arguments and well meaning comments, but that somehow completely missed the point.

He looked around the bar. The music had stopped and the bar was emptying. Everyone had a place to go and he caught the bartender's eye. He too was anxious to get away. Medad now realised that he was hungry and so made his way to where he knew he could get food and subsequently made his way back to the barracks on his own. Medad called his mother on his way back with apologies, talking about the Bethlehem mission and saying he couldn't get away. He knew she would read between the lines, because his father and elder brother would be home. They had a brief comforting conversation, and he felt a little better.

6

HANI, ALONG WITH everyone else, had no idea that Israeli troops had withdrawn late that Friday afternoon although had he thought about it, he might have guessed. *Shabbat* was a family meal not just a religious one, similar to Sunday lunch in other cultures and one not many Jewish families missed. So a second night in the shop beckoned. He tried to delay going to bed so he could both to make the night shorter and to ensure he was really tired and managed to get some sleep. But it was not a good night, sleep coming only in fits and starts. Several times he awoke only to see darkness everywhere, so he would turn over and try to get back to sleep without much success. So when he woke for the umpteenth time and there was just a fraction of light breaking through the shop window, he decided he'd had enough.

He rolled over on to his knees and got to his feet. It was Saturday morning. His neck and back were aching, his mouth dry and he was hungry. He stood there for a moment listening for any sounds from the outside world. Nothing. Then the call to prayer began to sound out. *Fajr* prayer begins at *subh saadiq* (true dawn) and this would happen each day as the first of the five calls to prayer that Muslims observed each day. Prayers on Friday were done in community whereas on other days, prayers could be said individually. It didn't mean that the Imam was actually at the mosque at dawn, since it was usually all pre-recorded.

Hani reached for his Nokia. The time was four thirty, and the phone now had a dial tone which meant that the curfew was over. If Ayshaa had possessed a phone, he would have called her then and there, but she didn't. So he let himself out of the shop, re-locked it and started home. He only lived about fifteen minutes away and as he made his way through the back streets of the old city, he saw lots of other men quietly doing the same. A few nodded to him and, had he stopped, would have sought his opinion about the curfew and, of course, given him their opinions. But Hani wasn't interested in the opinions of his fellow Palestinians.

In some quarters, however, there was uproar that the men of Bethlehem could not attend Friday prayers the previous day, especially at the Omar Mosque in Manger Square, the oldest and only mosque in the old city of Bethlehem. But Hani, who would normally have gone, just wanted to get home and his route took him through the Square. Just as he came round the corner of the Omar Mosque, he saw a body in the corner up against a wall. He or she had been shot. Just once. As he drew nearer he could see the blood, now congealed, on the outer clothes and on the ground. It was a woman, an older woman. He looked around and saw a few other men some way away, but no-one near. He decided to gently turn the body over to see if he knew who she was. He recognised her immediately. It was Fadwa.

No need to check for a pulse. He had seen dead bodies before and this one was dead. She was an old lady who lived on her own just around the corner at the top of Star St. Fadwa, a widow who was almost bent double, was now suffering with dementia and probably had no idea what the time was or that there was a curfew. Her memory for times, people and places was going fast, but there were no treatments available here, no care homes where she could feel safe and secure. Difficult to live with, she had refused to leave her room where she and her husband spent their lives once their sons had grown up. Carmi, as the eldest son, would blame himself. If only he could have persuaded her to come and live with his family.

As it happened, Carmi didn't live far away. Hani stopped, called him on his phone and broke the news to him. On hearing the reaction of the household, he decided to stay with the body until Carmi and the wider family arrived. Then the wailing started. Carmi and his younger brother Helal were distraught, but for others there was palpable anger. An old lady. Shot in the dark. Doing no harm to anyone. What kind of humanity was this? She was an innocent. This must be challenged. She would be avenged.

It was almost seven o'clock by the time he eventually arrived at his own front door which was already open and meant Ayshaa was up. They hugged, knowing that each other was safe, before Hani proceeded to tell her about Fadwa; how he had found her, how she had been killed and the reaction of her family. Ayshaa's fuse had been lit and she quickly became angry and emotional. She railed against the Occupiers, the Palestinian Authority, just about anyone.

"What kind of world is this? It's murder, that's what it is. Someone has to pay. And why," she shouted, addressing her quiet husband, "why are you so… so… rational?" He might have been upset and angry if it had been the first innocent killing he knew about, but it wasn't. Not by a long way. This was life on the West Bank.

He held her close until her energy began dissipating to be replaced with tears. After a few minutes she wiped her face and began to tell him that Rena had not been well. Hani was concerned. Apparently, the baby had a slight temperature, had not been feeding as normal and she was beginning to be anxious. Perhaps the little girl instinctively knew something was not right; Daddy had not come home for two nights. Hani picked up his daughter and gave her a cuddle whispering that everything would be okay. Daddy was back.

The uproar over Friday prayers quickly merged with the anger over Fadwa's killing. Crowds quickly grew as the story got out, the women wailing and the men planning violence. They poured out of Manger Square down the steps through the Old City toward the Wall. Hani had seen this so many times before that it had become a way of life. Death had become a way of life. He was one with them. How could he not be, he was a Palestinian. His father had been gunned down by the same people who had killed Fadwa. Moreover, his business was always a step away from going bust and it was the Israelis who were directly responsible. Who else? Amid this flurry of thoughts, Hani noticed a local Fatah leader at the back of the crowd so Hani stopped to express some concerns to the man over what this might develop into.

Then an unexpected turn. "I knew your father," he said quietly. Hani was taken completely by surprise.

He continued. "I'm sorry he was killed unjustly and I know Ghalia, your mother, of course." Hani, amid all the noise and clamour, just stood there stunned. "Your father was a leader here and you also have the makings of a leader. Fatah needs men like you. In fact, your father had always talked about you in those terms."

Hani said nothing. This was a revelation. He thought he knew all about his father, his moods, his silences and his very occasional rages. The man didn't stay for an answer but melted away into the crowd, leaving Hani rooted to the spot. The son was left to re-imagine his father. Who was he really? What else did he not know? Hani began to realise that since a child he had been so taken up with his own little world that he actually knew very little about the world his father had lived in. He had never asked the questions that would have elicited the answers. Perhaps his father had been waiting for Hani to initiate such a conversation. But he hadn't, hadn't even thought of it, too taken up with his own life. The father-son conversation had never happened; all his father had done and the experiences he had been through, were lost. Now he was acutely interested and it was too late. It would all be locked up forever, with no key to access it.

He was beginning to feel a little orphaned, as if his father really hadn't belonged to him. He wasn't sure he really knew him, or them. How much did he not know? It was disturbing, almost destabilising. Is that what secrets do, he wondered. His mother must have known about Fatah. Perhaps she and Ayshaa had talked about these things, woman to woman. Now he thought about it, he suspected they had which made him him feel even more left out and alone. So Hani determined to find the right occasion to have a conversation with his mother, and discover whether there were more revelations about their life that he needed to know. He suspected that she didn't know everything about his father, for Palestinian men were quite closed when it came to sharing themselves but he was certain that she must know more than he did.

Now there were stones flying one way and rubber coated bullets coming the other way which brought him back to the present with a thump. Before long the tear gas cannisters were launched and everyone was stumbling around trying to cover their faces. Hani was no coward but he knew this could end up with the carnage of his own people. What started as the death of an old lady would most likely end up with not only the death of one old lady but goodness knows how many more young men. What was the point? More wasted lives. Where would it end? Hani suddenly wanted to get home.

That evening his little family was subdued. All knew nothing positive was going to be achieved by the rioting but equally, all understood the pent-up frustration and anger over injustice on top of injustice. Hani asked his mother, "Did you know Fadwa well?"

Ghalia responded, "We weren't close friends but we grew up together in the same neighbourhood here in Bethlehem. You played with Carmi her son quite a bit." They had eaten and, as Rena had gone to bed, it was adult time. Hani and Ayshaa kept quiet as Ghalia began to talk softly about a time when she could move freely from one place to another with her friends.

"We could get to our school without checkpoints. There was no bureaucratic red tape, no teenage soldiers with machine guns mocking Palestinian elders, humiliating them in front of their people."

She paused, as if conjuring back in her mind a specific incident. "It is all deliberate of course, designed to demoralise and de-humanise us, and it has worked well." Hani had tentatively asked a question and Ghalia, his mother, had started reminiscing. He was listening intently to gain more appreciation of his family and his father.

"I can remember our family home, my home, being bulldozed to make way for illegal Israeli homes in our garden and on our land. That was 1968 or 9, I can't remember." She began to sounding rather bitter at this point. "There was no negotiation, no conveyancing process. No payment. Nothing. My father had some money from the last olive crop he had sold and with that he took us to Bethlehem. It was a very long journey, as I remember it, but he never managed to find rooms like these, so we had to go into the camps. Most people did."

She paused again and Hani and Ayshaa just sat on the sofabed listening. Ghalia had never said these things before.

"I met your father at school. His parents had come from the Hebron area to live in the same camp. After we got married, we lived with them for a while, then with some help your father managed to open the shop. Some days I hardly saw him. He was out early and back to quickly eat before out again and I would be in bed when he came back. He worked hard and put the hours in but it was never going to be a gold mine. The income from the shop was just enough to survive but…"

She pulled herself up a bit in the only chair they had, "…but we managed better than some others who only managed with top-ups from charity hand-outs."

Hani now began to suspect where the extra money might have come from. But his mother was still talking. She was now apologising that she had none of the 'stuff' that others of her age might have had to make a house into a home, no personal valuables to pass on to her son and his wife, no knick-knacks for them to remember her by. Hani tried to say that they didn't need any 'knick knacks', they were happy to have her living with them, but Ghalia seemed to be in a world of her own now as she reminisced.

Hani now detected a softness in his mother's voice. "When I was a girl be-fore my father brought us here, we were in the country, surrounded by open spaces, trees, our friends. We had meals together in each other's houses with each family looking out for the others. All the children played together and the adults worked together. Everyone got on together."

She paused gathering her breath, "If there was a dispute, the elders sorted it out respecting each generation from the oldest to the youngest. It was ev-erything a community should be. Sure, we weren't well off materially. If there was a bad crop, we had a bad year. But we survived. Everyone pulled together. We didn't need weapons, or defensive walls. There were no enemies. We were happy. I was happy." She began to sob.

The baby woke and Ayshaa began the last feed of the day. Ghalia took her-self to her bed. To give her some space, mum, dad and baby moved outside to sit on the doorstep. It was all quiet now; everyone who could, had gone inside. Although Rena had seemed to have a problem feeding whilst the curfew was on, now she seemed content and feeding well. Maybe she instinctively knew everything was now all right although, of course, everything was far from all right.

Ayshaa had not had an easy labour. There had been no birthing pool, no candles, no epidurals, no gynaecologist consultant, no trained midwives. Just the experience of older women, but it had been enough. Her body was now beginning to be her own once more, except she was still breast feeding. Look-ing at Rena, she asked the same question she had asked many times before, not really looking for an answer because she could not see one. She just spoke into the gloom of the evening. "What do we do now?"

Ayshaa, although a product of the sustained humiliation all Palestinians had endured for decade after decade, still had a positive 'can do' attitude most of the time. For all her slightness of build, she could be a firebrand. Only occasionally, though, would she allow herself to be pessimistic. After such a moment, her eyes would flash again with an intensity of hope which, to Hani, was irrational but very attractive. The question she posed came with those eyes. They looked at Hani for an answer, saying if you don't know, maybe I do.

Hani had no answer. He was still reeling from what the Fatah leader had said. He had no answer to the family question, let alone to the Palestine question. The latter would sort out the former he was certain, but there was little hope for either. He began to recall some of the things his father had said. "Thirteen different peace plans, conferences, talks, processes, memorandi, agreements, summits. All come to nothing."

Hani thought about this, and said aloud to no-one in particular. "No. Not true. Actually, they have all resulted in more Israeli settlements, more checkpoints, more confiscated land, more elaborate laws to hem us in." He began to think it through... and somehow, we've been blamed for the failure of each of them. Are we missing something? How is it that when we do agree to something, like Oslo, it gets twisted, manipulated in the implementation?

Certainly, on occasions we have not helped ourselves. Yes we have our extremists, and yes, they give Israel the excuse to react heavily. But in many cases, the IDF or armed settlers clamp down on us first. Either demolishing homes, arresting Palestinian leaders, or a military exercise which results in the death of women and children. Then comes the predictable violent reaction from our side; then comes the blame from both Israelis and the world; then comes a derailing of whatever talks are going on; then comes a continuation of whatever policies the government had been pursuing in the first place. Then comes despair.

It was the tactic that the Serbs used in Bosnia back in the 90s. The army and the host of Serb paramilitaries would provoke a disturbance amongst the muslim population, then charge in with all guns blazing to 'defend' the local Serbs. It proved effective at delaying any intervention by both the US and

European Union, but it led to a confidence that the Serbs could do anything they liked… and they did, witness Srebrenica massacre in July 1995 with a genocide of more than eight thousand Bosnians, mainly men and boys. At least Israel hadn't done that yet and he didn't think they would.

But how does Israel get away with what other countries would certainly be sanctioned for? How can it remain immune from the widespread criticism levelled at it? Was it holocaust guilt? Was it genuine support for the only democracy in the region? Was it revulsion at the practices of some Arab dictators? Why does no-one do anything? Have the peace initiatives of the US merely been cover for the Israelis to pursue whatever policies they want?

So what's in it for the US government? Keep in step with the Jewish lobby? Yes, but surely not a sufficient reason. What about the AIPAC? (the American Israel Public Affairs Committee) They certainly seem to control much of the debate in the US ensuring that Israel get a favourable hearing. What about those Middle East policy advisers under both Democrat and Republican Presidents, weren't they overwhelmingly Jewish? And what about those Christian Zionist neo-conservative fundamentalist evangelicals? They were also part of the Lobby which supported Israel no matter what. But why?

Hani just couldn't understand it all. He sighed. It was all beyond him and he felt utterly helpless. He looked around and found himself outside on his front steps alone and it was now getting chilly with Rena's feed having been complete some time ago. He went inside to find the rest of the family sound asleep. There was nothing else to do, nothing else to say. The morning would come and life would probably happen all over again.

7

GHALIA HAD BEEN upset after her reminiscing and had gone to bed early. She was fast asleep and dreaming. At just six years old she was running, her long black hair flying out behind her. School had finished for the day and she was on her way home with her three friends running alongside her. Unusually for a Palestinian family, she was an only child but her friends were close enough almost to be her sisters. Ghalia and her friends would be in and out of each other's homes after school without mothers being too concerned. Their village in the lower Jordan Valley known as the *Ghor* was a safe area. There were no murders, no robberies, except for the very occasional Bedouin raid and children were safe from predators. It was, more importantly for her parents who owned their own land, an extremely fertile place, in fact the most productive area of the West Bank. Palestinian farmers, Ghalia's father among them, worked the land well with water supplied from the Jordan. They didn't need to push it too hard for both quantity and quality of their crops was excellent.

The Rift Valley of which the *Ghor* was a part, started much further north in Israel itself, past the Sea of Galilee and towards the Lebanese border. It went all the way south past the point where the West Bank area ended and Israel itself began. Beyond this was the harsh, rocky Judean wilderness and below that, the *Negev*. Much of this part of southern Israel was uninhabitable desert although the Dead Sea boasted valuable mineral deposits and Eilat, down on the Red Sea, offered an important holiday destination.

The coastline of the Israeli state from the Lebanese border down to Gaza consisted of a coastal plain which was also fertile agricultural land. In between these two fertile areas of the Jordan Valley and the coastal plain, were the Judean Hills in the central area mostly in the West Bank, and the Galilean Hills to the north, in Israel itself. To the east of the river Jordan were the Golan Heights of Syria in the north and the state of Jordan in the south.

It was said that it was the young who had the visions but the old who dreamed the dreams. Whether that was true or not Ghalia didn't know. She didn't think she was normally given to dreaming, but she was tonight. Her conscious had somehow stimulated her unconscious. She had no idea that, according to good authority, dreams mirror the patterns of our behaviour, reflecting who we are and what we need. So not for her the naked dream, or the one where she gets lost, nor the one where she is chased but going nowhere, although maybe she was due some of them considering her current circumstances. No, this dream was pleasant and happy. It was nostalgic and she felt uplifted. Ghalia was reliving the moments of some fifty plus years earlier.

As there was never much homework to do, she and her friends would play together in whatever backyard they happened to be in. As girls, they loved skipping and it was Ghalia who had the skipping rope and they would spend hours having fun together, laughing and giggling. Life was good. She smiled in her dream. Where are my friends now? she wondered.

She didn't know if you could ever be in charge of dreams but knew she was certainly not in charge of this one, because there was an oppressive sense of anxiety and change and she didn't like it. Mothers had began to meet their children at school and escort them home, to make sure they arrived safely. They couldn't run free anymore. The girls couldn't understand with some trying to avoid their mothers and go home with their friends as they usually did, but that didn't last. She recalled that they could only walk together as long as they were not out of sight of their mothers, who were usually some distance behind them, talking earnestly.

Ghalia tried to fight against what was happening, trying to get back to an earlier, happier time, but she found her willpower just wasn't enough. She could sense the sweat on her forehead and the back of her neck as her heart began to beat faster, adrenalin started pumping and her body began to feel her distress.

Another scene. This was better. She could now see her father hard at work in his fields. She remembered the tomatoes, cucumbers, eggplant and other vegetables he produced in the summer and the olives in the autumn, selling them both to Jenin, Nablus and other major Palestinian cities in the West Bank as well as into Israel, when he could. She remembered his strength lifting her up, and his smell when he came in from a hard day's work. Only now did she know how hard it must have been for him. Was this when Israel occupied the West Bank, or before? She couldn't remember. It was all mixed up.

She did, however, remembered the little man from the Ein Al-Beida Agricultural Union, of which her father was a member, who used to visit all the farms and collect their dues. Why was her father paying him money? Now she knew that Ein Al-Beida tried to relieve the pressure on farmers by lobbying the Israeli Civil Administration that was in charge of the Occupied Areas, but they were limited in what they could do. The bottom line was that Israel wanted the farmers to leave their land and get out.

Then in the background, she thought she could hear her father talking to her mother over the evening meal, complaining about the cost of water. Her mother was listening in silence. Yes, she knew it was at least three times more expensive for Palestinians than for the Israelis living in settlements in the Jordan Valley because Israel controlled almost all of the West Bank's water reserves, and severely restricted Palestinian access. Not only that, but Palestinian farmers were prohibited from digging new groundwater wells for agricultural purposes, without first obtaining a permit from the Israeli authorities. These permits were rarely, if ever, given and thus the Israeli army was legally able to demolishes new Palestinian cisterns and confiscate Palestinian water tanks as soon as they were discovered. Yes, this was definitely Occupation.

Another scene now. She was shouting at Israeli soldiers at a checkpoint, arguing her father's case against Israel. But they were taking no notice, it was as if she wasn't there. Ghalia felt her voice getting hoarse. She gave up, turning to some stranger next to her and started to complain to him. Did he know that almost sixty three per cent of arable agricultural land in the West Bank was located in Area C, which according to the Oslo Accords agreement was under complete Israeli military control? As soon as she said it in her dream, she wondered how she knew all this.

Also, did he know that Israel had imposed lots of barriers on Palestinian farmers? For instance, did he know certain types of fertilisers in the West Bank which the farmers had always used were now banned on security grounds? She was getting angry now. No-one was listening. Did he know that the same produce was sold at lower prices by Israeli suppliers, due to Israeli government subsidies? Did he know that Israel flooded the West Bank market with their produce, making their Palestinian goods less competitive? Why doesn't he listen? Why doesn't somebody do something, anything? Ghalia was becoming exhausted. Her body was twisting with anger in her bed.

Then someone else came into the picture. It was someone from the Palestinian Authority. Why he was there, she didn't know. He also seemed to take no notice of her. So she started shouting at him. And another thing ... why do Israelis deliberately make it hard to cross through their checkpoints? It's pure vindictiveness. Why are we forced to unload one truck on one side of the border and manually carry our produce to the other side and load on to a different truck? It takes hours and reduces the quality of the produce, and the PA is no help whatsoever.

Ghalia had never had time for them and began wondering whether that was the reason that her husband decided to get involved with Fatah, to try and change things. She remembered him saying that they never allocated more than one per cent of their budget to agriculture, but eighty-five per cent of the budget went to paying salaries at the PA's Agriculture Ministry!

She knew somehow that she was mixing up childhood memories with current affairs, but was helpless to change it. In fact, she was surprised at the vehemence that was in her, latent after all these years. She tried in her dream to get back to her childhood years before Occupation. She wanted to know more because instinctively she felt there was more to know.

It worked. She was back in her house; there was her mother and there was her school. Ghalia was happy. She loved school, and it seemed, school loved her. But now there was no school. What was happening? She was sighing in her dream because something she didn't recognise at the time seemed all too clear to her now. That time which seemed so idyllic, actually wasn't.

Deep within her, she was aware of gunfire and what she could now classify as military activity up on the hills she knew were the Golan Heights. She couldn't see anything, but she smelt the fear around her. It was 1967 and March 23rd, her birthday. Yes, she could see how happy she was, but she also saw something, what she hadn't seen then. Father and Mother were very worried. Those bangs and explosions were not close, but clearly loud enough to be heard and they were escalating day on day. In fact, as she now knew, there had been two hundred and seventy 'incidents' on that border in the first three months of the year. No wonder her parents had been tense and anxious. Men and tanks came through their village, heading up towards the Syrian border, and they weren't Palestinian. The Palestinians didn't have armies or tanks or aircraft for that matter. They had nothing.

Then sometime in April she thought, Syrian gunners fired from their Golan Heights position and hit an Israeli tractor which was farming in the demilitarised zone. She heard again the echo of this artillery fire all around the valley at the bottom of the hills where she lived, as rounds were exchanged and the fight escalated. She saw again in her dream, the waves of Israeli aircraft going against the Syrian gun positions and adjacent villages. Then she saw different planes in the sky, as the Syrians sent up their MiG jets and all-out dogfights ensued. She later learned from her father that Israel had downed six Syrian MiG 21 fighters and chased the remainder all the way back to Damascus.

Ghalia was beginning to sweat profusely. Tossing and turning, she remembered her father going out to a meeting with all the men of the village. She had no idea what was going on, except everyone was fearful and on edge, and worst of all, school was suspended. All she could do was to go out and play with her friends until her mother rang a bell, when she was instructed to come back home immediately.

What Ghalia didn't know – how could she – was that by May the main action was on Israel's southern border where President Nasser of Egypt had amassed nearly forty thousand troops and five hundred tanks on Israel's Sinai border. Her village, her parents, her friends were all threatened by this Egyptian action. As young as she was, she knew that other Arab nations cared nothing for the Palestinians. We were a nuisance to them, the gypsies of the Arab world. No-one would be thinking of us. No-one was going to look out for us. No-one even considered us.

She winced in her sleep as her adult self remembered what various Arab leaders had said over their radios. They were just playing to their own constituency and had no idea where it would all lead. Ghalia was no fan of Israel, but if these Arab states won this war, she seriously doubted they would retreat and let the Palestinians back to their farms and villages. Either way, the Palestinians were going to lose.

She recalled that there were distant relations in Jordan and vaguely remembered having met them once. She saw a building which must have been their home. Her father said the Palestinians and Jordanians were related. Yes, Jordanians were friends. We can trust them. But their June 5th attack on Tel Aviv and West Jerusalem in particular, directly caused Israel's entry into the West Bank in June 1967 and its eventual occupation. Apparently, it was not part of a premeditated Israeli plan for territorial expansion. Quite the opposite. Israel's own Defence Minister had instructed the army not to fight the Jordanians, or move into the West Bank. That position only changed as a result of Jordan's disregard for Israeli appeals to avoid hostilities, and its intensive bombardment of Israeli targets. Israel's entry into the West Bank was, at the time, an act of self-defence. They would claim that it's presence there originated as a result, not of Israeli aggression, but of Jordanian aggression. However, once in, they never left.

By June 7th it was all over. Moshe Dayan, the general with the eye patch, was generous in victory. She pictured him. To the Israelis, he was a national hero.

He announced to the world, "We have united Jerusalem, the divided capital of Israel. We have returned to the holiest of our holy places, never to part from it again. To our Arab neighbours we extend, also at this hour, our hand in peace."

Ghalia began weeping in her sleep. Words. Words. All words. They mean nothing. Another leader comes along and completely disregards the promises made by his or her predecessor. We lost everything. We can trust no-one. What did Golda Meir say years later? Shortly after coming to power, she had been asked by reporters about the Palestinian question. Her reply was, "What is a Palestinian? Such a thing does not exist."

She was spent and lapsed into a deep sleep. It was a concerned Ayshaa who had to wake her up the next morning. Most unusual.

8

MEDAD HAD SPENT Friday night at the barracks and *Shabbat* itself in and around Jerusalem. To him the Old City was a majestic place, not in any kind of religious way but just the pure history. He could feel it in the stones. Some Israelis were around but mostly tourists and pilgrims. He spent the day soaking up the place with all the nooks and crannies the tourist guides didn't know about. He had no girlfriend to visit, although there was someone he had met in the IDF that he had noticed, but girls were not on his immediate agenda. Now he needed time to think. He was feeling alone and rather schizophrenic for, as far as he knew, no-one else felt or thought the way he did. Part of him knew this could not be true, but he hadn't yet met a loyal Israeli who questioned their country's treatment of the Palestinians as he did.

He was due some leave and so he determined to seek permission the following day to take it. Maybe it would give him time to think things through. Once granted, the plan was that he would then bike back to his parent's house. He was not the 'mummy's boy' that his father and brother insisted he was, but he did value her opinions because she was much more open minded than either of them. They would have none of the qualms he had, and Medad felt that they just wouldn't understand the turmoil he was in. He acknowledged that perhaps it was because of him that there was something of a strained relationship between the men of the household. His father had been brought up in a strict Zionist household, and his brother had aped his father's views on almost everything. He was different.

There was no doubt that he took after his mother rather than his father. Perhaps that was because he was eight years younger than his brother and he had been brought up single handedly by his mother, his father being almost permanently away in the army and his brother quite independent. Even at eight years old his brother idolised his father and did everything he could to be like him, but he was a bit of a bully. The bundles the brothers used to engage in inevitably ended up with the elder using his weight and muscle to bring the younger to tears, which brought his mother into the room to protect him. They never became friends, but it was too harsh to say they grew to hate each other; they just matured into very different people, with nothing in common, except their parents.

At school, according to his teachers, Medad was intellectually way ahead of his brother, who was more interested in martial arts, especially Kapap which is the Hebrew abbreviation of *Krav Panim el Panim*, face to face combat or, battle. It was not specifically a martial art, but rather an overall training programme that included everything a commando needed; hand to hand combat, rigorous physical conditioning, firearms, explosives training, radio communications, navigation, wilderness survival training, combat first aid and foreign languages such as Arabic. What made it attractive to Yigal was that it was taught to the early commandos of the pre-state of Israel fighting force known as Hagana.

In the eyes of Medad's father and brother, these men were heroes, men to be imitated, men who conquered the land and believed God had given it to them centuries ago. As he sat on his bunk, he could hear his father's voice now in his head. "Our right to this land is inalienable. There is no debate. It is a mandate of the Torah recorded generations ago in Genesis 15:18.

On the same day the LORD *made a covenant with Abram, saying: "To your descendants I have given this land, from the river of Egypt to the great river, the River Euphrates…"*

His brother would continue the speech.

"We have been liberated from the longest occupation in history. We brought water to a thirsty country. We pump more water in a day than was consumed in all of Palestine in 1948. Thanks to us, glass and steel towers have risen from sand dunes. The forgotten and disease ridden armpit of the Ottoman Empire has become the most technologically advanced society in the Middle East. We have built a place where both Arabs and Jews enjoy a higher standard of living than anywhere else in the Middle East, except the petroleum sheikdoms. We have the highest literacy rates in the Middle East, and the lowest infant mortality."

It was almost as if they had rehearsed it. And so it would go on, the thick finger of his father now wagging in front of his nose…

"In this household," his father would pronounce, "this is what we stand for. These are our principles and we shall not depart from them."

It was useless to express the view that such Israeli geographic expansion to the Euphrates would never happen in a million years. For his father it was a tenet of faith rather than a real political or military objective. Important not to mix the two. Medad thought it was amazing what views intelligent people could zealously promote which had no basis in actuality; views which could bind people of like mind together and even sound plausible. His father might as well have been one of those American Christian Zionist preachers, holding forth on their television shows.

He knew that most Zionists had given up that literal vision since it would mean recapturing the Sinai, occupying significant parts of Jordan and half of Iraq. So they would not be giving up any of the West Bank land they had captured. Nevertheless, apparently there were those who refused to let that literal vision go, even some government ministers it was said. In their eyes, the Palestinians were no more than the Kenites, the Kenezzites, the Kadmonites, the Hittites, the Perizzites, the Amorites, the Canaanites, the Girgashites and the Jebusites. These were some of the tribes that had been dislodged centuries ago under Joshua and, as far as they were concerned, they were not coming back under any other name.

Medad recalled the times he would sit with his mother on the verandah together while his father and brother were away with the military. He could picture the scene now in his head. The severe afternoon sun would be fading and it would be pleasantly warm. They would have eaten together a simple meal of lamb stew with dill and olives followed by *halvah parfait*. She knew that he had something on his mind but would always wait for him to speak first. Mother knew her son. Then eventually, such was the tension in him that he would begin to open up and let it out. Crazy, crazy, crazy! A policy amounting to ethnic cleansing. How could intelligent people think and believe this stuff?

His mother never showed any surprise at his outbursts but continued to stay silent whilst he waxed and eventually waned. She had been raised to think and debate in an open atmosphere and so she encouraged the exploration he was undertaking. She would always end their time together by cautioning him to keep his thoughts to himself when the family was together. There are many, many different views and opinions in our country and you are perfectly entitled to have your own, she would say, but make sure you think it through and have your facts straight.

Medad would admit his struggles. "But what if I don't know what I think? What if I fundamentally differ from my father and brother?"

His mother would be quietly encouraging. "So, you have a choice between being yourself and being someone not yourself. Not a difficult decision really."

No-one else was around in the barracks, all had gone back home. Perhaps he should have gone. He wasn't a coward but he just couldn't be 'a family' at *Shabbat* in his current frame of mind. He had finished exploring the Old City once again and started to feel quite hungry, so he had stopped at the nearest open restaurant for a meal. He didn't want a three course meal, just something to staunch his hunger. His mind was still going round and round the same old arguments as he was eating not paying much attention to the place he was in. A couple of attractive girls walked in and sat down at a table. His first thought was that he needed a girlfriend. His second was what were they doing here on *Shabbat*. Did they not have a family or families? Perhaps they were thinking the same about him. He saw them glance in his direction. Maybe he should go over and say something. He could do with some company, but his mind was blank and he didn't want to make a fool of himself. He finished, paid, left the place feeling a little cowardly and headed back to his barracks.

As he lay on his bunk he began to think of his parents, why his mother had married his father, how on earth they had managed to have two completely different siblings and so on. He began to concede that her parent's generation had for the most part been brought up in much stricter circumstances, fighting for their place in the land. They probably didn't think, couldn't think of anything except success because they were the underdogs and couldn't afford to fail. Many, many people were dependent on them to preserve the fledgling state of Israel.

He understood that since the initial borders Israel had been secured by his grandparent's generation, his parent's generation had to put the country's security beyond question. This they had chosen to do by Occupation. But what was the charge for his generation? Surely now the situation had changed. Israel's existence was not in any jeopardy anymore. After all, he thought, we are the strongest military power in the region and one of the strongest in the world. What poses a real threat, though, is the health of our soul. Surely, given our history, we cannot be seen to be devoid of any sense of justice or respect for human rights. So the Palestinians are now the underdogs, not us. I suppose, it was not their fault really, they were just in the way.

"Not their fault really," Medad could hear his mother saying these words last time he went home. He had never heard his mother speak like that before. She had been speaking openly and expressing a very different opinion from his father for the first time, at least in his hearing. His heart welled up with pride towards her. All these years she had to be content to hear the hard right views of a military husband, without the freedom to express her own misgivings, and to see her eldest son take on the views of his father must have been hugely sacrificial. Lying on his bunk, Medad felt tears rising up in his eyes. All these years.

Yes, thought Medad, surely we can afford to be a little more generous in victory. We have been humiliated, trampled, hemmed in, discriminated against, persecuted for centuries in Europe. We know what that feels like, and it's not good. The last thing we should be doing is that very same thing to others. I know we have to be secure and I'm sure there's a way, but it needs a leader who can articulate a new vision and take the nation where it needs to go… and I don't know anyone who can do that. It all began to make some kind of sense in Medad's mind, but he was no politician and had no desire to go into politics. In fact, he had no idea what he would do after his stint in the IDF was completed. All he did know was that he wanted to make a difference somehow. But the task was vast and he had no experience.

He quickly surveyed the current political scene in his mind. He could not see change coming from anyone currently in public life. He wondered whether they were too scared for their careers if they tried to put forward such any peace proposals. Surely it would need a significant change in the mood of the nation for this to happen. How could this be engineered, or at least seeded? Where might that come from? Would there need to be an external ally? Did there need to be an event so transformative that the political climate changed overnight? How to get over the constant 'tit for tat' between Israelis and Palestinians which had traditionally scuppered progress?

Then he remembered the nine year old Vietnamese girl, Kim Phuc, running for her life down Route 1 near Trang Bang, naked and in flames after an aerial napalm attack, and how that had changed the status of the Vietnam war in the US. He remembered the drowning of a little three-year-old boy named Alan Kurdi on a beach near Kos, as he and his Syrian parents tried to escape from Turkey into Greece and Europe. He remembered how that had at least temporarily changed the debate in Europe over immigration from Syria. He remembered the BBC picture of whales and fish poisoned by ingesting plastic and how that had galvanised immense change in plastics use not only in UK, but around the world. Small things can trigger huge changes, he thought. But they have to go viral. How do we do that?

He did have a girlfriend of sorts but they hadn't become an 'item' yet. As he thought about her, maybe this was the time to take their fledgling relationship to the next level. Shana seemed normal; not a Zionist, not a military fanatic, not a settler, not particularly religious, just a normal person. The first date had been just a quiet drink together off base. She was vivacious and teasing, fully at ease with herself and confident in the world she knew. She came from Tel Aviv, and would probably have been labelled as a social liberal by his other friends, but to Medad she was a breath of fresh air. He had been hoping this relationship might grow a bit over the coming months but now he thought it should begin immediately.

From what he had gathered, her parents seemed to be relatively affluent; her mother a teacher at the American International School and her father a civil servant in the Criminal Department of the Attorney General's office. She confided in him her ambition to do a degree in journalism when the IDF had finished with her. He tentatively talked about his own background without talking about his opinions, but she didn't seem to be disturbed by his 'settler' background, and a second date looked promising. He would make it happen.

The end of his service in the military was beckoning and he was looking forward to leaving. There was still on-going training of course, and regular border assignments, but nothing where he had to use his gun skills for real. He was definitely in a more relaxed frame of mind and he wanted to share with Shana more of his views on the political future. He still had no real idea of what he wanted to do back in civilian life. Maybe she would have some ideas, perhaps some contacts. His leave was granted for Tuesday and Wednesday that week. They wanted to keep him available for Sunday and Monday just in case there was any further trouble in Bethlehem.

9

IT WAS LATE afternoon on Sunday and a normal working day in Hani's shop, if working was what it was called. There hadn't been a customer for days. There was no local passing traffic in the back streets where the shop was, just the odd lost tourist. Through the window he saw someone, not a customer but a Fatah official who 'knew his father'. He groaned. The little bell tinkled signifying someone was opening the door.

"I hear someone was shot during the curfew, and you were there?" The man advanced into the shop and Hani looked at him with some cynicism as he seemed a little less concerned over the death, and rather more concerned over Hani's obvious disquiet.

The man explained, "these things happen, you know. But we can't be subservient, can we? They mustn't take us for granted. We must continue to challenge them."

"Challenge them? With sticks and stones? And how did you know where my shop was?" Hani was rising to the bait, sensing that he was being tested but not caring a jot. The man said nothing but took out a pack of Marlboro and offered Hani a cigarette. Hani declined. He raised his eyebrows as if to ask, are you the only Palestinian man who doesn't smoke. Hani did but he wasn't going to accept anything from this man, yet. Hani turned away and tried to look as if he was working. He had things to do, orders to fulfil, a business to run. But his guest wasn't to be put off.

"Not many customers today," he observed. Hani looked at him and wondered how long he had been watching the shop.

"Quite a while," was the answer to Hani's unasked question. Hani was embarrassed, but wasn't going to be goaded into discussing his business, or lack of one.

"So what can I get you today? A kettle? Some hinges? Postcards?" Hani stood tall and looked him in the eye. His visitor said nothing but just smiled as he exhaled his used smoke into the shop's atmosphere and wandered up and down the single aisle looking at the half empty shelves. Hani frowned and changed the subject back to Fadwa's death.

"So where is Fatah leading us? What is the plan?" There was no answer except the shrug of the shoulders. The reply was predictable.

"We need to be patient, but we also need leaders. Perhaps a son would want to follow in his father's footsteps and make a more positive contribution to the struggle?" The man from Fatah continued walking around the shop as if looking for something that wasn't there.

"Of course, I understand if domesticity is more important than the future of the Palestinian people." He stopped and looked back at Hani purposefully. "You have your father's passion and gravitas, which is important for a leader. People will listen to you."

Hani was quiet, so the man continued to talk. "You know who the Musta'ribeen are?" Hani nodded, of course he did. Everyone did.

These were Israeli agents dressed like Palestinian protesters operating within the West Bank. They were highly trained men able to speak with Palestinian accents and expressions. In an operation, they would cover their faces with keffiyehs or balaclavas and chant against the Israeli army, sometimes even throwing stones in the direction of the soldiers. They aimed to draw in other protesters, but as they got closer and closer to the army, they would suddenly turn on the people around them, brandishing guns that were concealed under their shirts and firing into the air. Those unlucky enough to be nearest to them were wrestled to the ground so that the advancing army could take them into custody.

"Well, we believe there is a new unit now specifically deployed in the Bethlehem area. Maybe a follow on from the recent curfew." The Fatah man paused to see what impact he was having. A little, he thought, so he continued.

"These are IDF soldiers who speak Arabic as if it is their mother tongue and undergo courses to master our own dialects. They know all about our customs and religious practices and even use make-up and wigs to complete their disguise. They are very dangerous and will stop at nothing to get those they believe are our leaders, including promoting riots and stirring up our people. It may be that they even promoted the disturbance yesterday to grab specific targets."

Hani looked sceptical at that. The Fatah man ignored Hani's look and got to the punchline. "Once we identify them, we can then neutralise them. You have been here in Bethlehem for many years. You know who is who. So keep a look out for people you don't know. If these agents are infiltrating us, anyone could be grabbed and disappear for good, including you."

With those words he left. Hani walked around his shop with these words ringing in his ears and a few minutes later he closed the shop and thoughtfully made his way home. He hadn't agreed to do anything, but he knew he'd been asked and there was a price of refusing, as well as for accepting. It was rock and hard place time. As he walked through the narrow alleyways towards home he began to think harder about his father. Why had he really joined Fatah? Had he thought his son would follow in his footsteps?

He remembered his father as quite a formidable figure. Never distant, but also never intimate. That was how Palestinian men were.

"I wonder if I will ever become like my father to Ayshaa and Rena?" He thought not, hoped not. It was a struggle to remember many things about his father but he needed some clues and maybe some direction. As far as he could recall, his father wasn't a political person but he did remember many evenings when he wasn't there. Hani had just assumed he was at the shop, but maybe he wasn't.

He suddenly laughed. He remembered his tenth birthday when his father had unexpectedly given him a present he had really treasured. It was the only present he could now remember having. It had a profound impact on him and had caused him to look up to his father in a new way, almost love. And love was in short supply as he was growing up. In those days, everyone was nervous, no-one knew what was going to happen next. Fear about what the Israelis would do next was palpable everywhere. For a ten year old Hani, his little puppy became his life, his escape.

He arrived home. Ayshaa had taken Rena out for a walk in the old pram they had inherited, but his mother was there to greet him. It was just the opportunity he needed to talk about his father. He found his mother rather reluctant to talk almost as if she was breaking confidences, but conceded that there were things even she didn't find out until his death.

"There were some important men who came to the funeral and who clearly knew me, but I didn't know who they were."

"How did you know they were important?"

"They arrived in a posh car."

"Who were they?"

Ghalia paused. She was looking into the distance as if trying to remember the detail of the funeral. Hani waited for her to reply. Her wrinkled face told of a woman who had seen and experienced much in her life. Hani prompted her.

"Local officials," was all she would say. She did add that, "I suspected it was Fatah but I didn't approve of them being there and wouldn't speak to them. Fatah had so many different faces that you never quite knew who you were dealing with."

"But how did you get on together if you didn't agree with what he was doing?" His mother shrugged as if to say 'different times'. After further quiet moments, she started to reminisce.

"Your father would come home late some evenings after you had gone to bed, quite exasperated and on occasions would let slip some aspects of the heated discussions he'd been having."

She looked directly at her son, "He was always the moderate, trying to convince others that violence was playing right into the hands of the Israelis. However the operations of the Musta'ribeen made his argument difficult to accept as, no doubt, they were designed to do."

Then she her face began to harden up and Hani saw a glimpse of his mother as he remembered her years ago.

She began to speak more pointedly. "Too many people are only looking out for themselves," she complained. "Not just within Fatah, but across the Palestinian movement. And look where we are. Nowhere. They are not the ones suffering. It's women and children, the old and the sick. Yes alliances and agreements have been attempted, but there's no trust. There never has been. Of course, the Israelis love it. As long as Hamas and Fatah fight, they are happy. They keep their status quo, and we keep our status quo."

She was right, thought Hani. In the peace agreement between Hamas and

Fatah, hosted by Egypt in 2017, many good things were agreed, but Israel had insisted on the disarming of Hamas as a condition of peace talks. Of course, Israel did not intend to disarm themselves and predictably Hamas refused as well, as Israel knew they would. In one simple move, all the potential was thrown away. Deliberately.

Hani began to see that his mother hadn't lost her inward attitude. Outwardly she looked like any other Palestinian mother or grandmother. Today she was wearing a simple white head dress, not the *sha'weh* she would wear on special occasions. She also had in her wardrobe a traditional 'Queens Thob', an ancient dress made for the queens of Palestine in the Bethlehem area. The thob is the traditional dress that women wear in Palestine and different regions have their own style, colour and embroidery. The 'Queens Thob' was a dress characterized by a bow on the chest called a *talhami*. Like a bride's dress, the silk was lined with bright colours and characterised by dense embroidery on the chest. The sides were in the shape of a triangle, the sleeves wide and embroidered and the short sleeve jacket made of velvet cloth and embroidered with silk thread and reeds.

Maha Al-Sakka, a well known Palestinian cultural leader, had encouraged the nation to 'practice their heritage' so that it remained their property. "Since the first Intifada, there has not only been a struggle for our land, but a struggle of another kind, the defence of our soul, our heritage," he had said.

Ghalia took this seriously as did other Palestinian women, so they began to wear their traditional dress on all occasions, even in the demonstrations. She said it made the women feel less downtrodden and bestowed a certain dignity on them. Despite her upbringing and her negative life experiences, she was an assured lady and now looked at Hani steely eyed as if she knew the decision he was struggling with. She warned him. "Once you get involved, IF you get involved, there's no turning back. You have to be sure. You will make enemies on all sides, so the need to cultivate friends around you will be paramount to survival, let alone success. You will need to find people of like mind who will stand up with you in the struggles and not be swayed by threats. Ayshaa must also agree, otherwise you will lose her."

There were the beginning of tears in her eyes. Ghalia knew the enormous decision Hani was trying to make. For him, this conversation had begun to confirm in his mind that this was his task in life, his destiny. Yes, something needed to happen. The status quo was not an option, otherwise Rena will be having her children and grandchildren in exactly the same circumstances as Ghalia and Ayshaa. It had to change for her generation. He felt a responsibility, but he had a wife and baby. Ayshaa and Rena had not yet returned, so he took himself for a walk to help him get his thoughts together. Ayshaa was not going to be happy… and he couldn't blame her.

"Of course you must." Ayshaa was on side and, it seemed, had been waiting for this. "Your mother told me about your father before we got married. I guess she didn't want our marriage to founder when you actually got round to making this decision."

She began an emotional speech. Hani had never heard his wife speak like this before. "The Israelis need to be faced with their own lies. They lie about our flag. Yes, it has a grenade with crossed rifles superimpose on a map of Israel, because that's how we started. But we are not the same as we were. We have moderated and they have not. The Palestinian Authority flag is the one we use now. Their persistent misrepresentation of how we are now is crucifying us."

Hani listened open-mouthed. This tirade was coming from nowhere as far as he knew. But she hadn't finished.

"They want the world to see us how we were back in the 1970s, and, yes, our authorities might be inefficient and corrupt, but look at the situation we're in. We are forced to completely rely on funds from other countries, to survive even to the miserable extent we do. We have to reclaim our heritage. We have to reclaim our respect in the eyes of the world. So are you going to do this?"

Hani was taken aback. It sounded like years of pent-up indignation just gushing out. "We? Sounds like you're part of Fatah… are you?"

Ayshaa shook her head, "But I'm a Palestinian." Hani pushed her about the step he was going to take. He wanted her to be sure.

"But have you thought it through? What about Rena? What about our future?"

Ayshaa was sure. "Our life has to mean something. It's not good enough to avoid what needs to be done, if you have the opportunity to do something about it. Rena would want a hero for a father, not a shopkeeper."

The conversation ended. Both needed time to think about what had been said by each of them. Hani felt it was all moving too fast. My wife seems to have thought all this through, and I've only just started. They had their evening meal of *maqloubeh* which was a one pot rice, spice and vegetable dish. Ayshaa had cooked this dish with some chicken and some yoghurt, often though, it just had to be vegetables without the meat. Domestic chores took precedence that evening. Not much of substance was shared but quite a lot of thinking was going on.

Tomorrow, Monday, would be Fadwa's funeral and Hani began to wonder whether Mr Fatah had made sure that it would be hijacked by demonstrators. He hoped not for it would not be what Fadwa wanted, but then she didn't have any say in the matter. Funerals always became an occasion for solidarity, especially when the body had been killed by an Israeli gun. It would be a very noisy affair. Although few will have known Fadwa, Hani knew that there would be hundreds that would accompanied the coffin, held high on the shoulders of her family. The tricolour Palestinian flag would everywhere, and many of the young men would hold their arms aloft with victory fingers clearly visible.

Ghalia decided that she wanted to pay her respects and be there so, much against his better judgement, Hani said he would accompany her. Ayshaa would stay safe at home with Rena.

9

SUNDAY SAW MEDAD and his friends back at their barracks reviewing the Bethlehem mission among themselves. *Shabbat* was over and they were awaiting orders. When they received them, it was back to Bethlehem to a local funeral. Someone obviously thought it might be linked to the suicide bombing and perhaps someone on their 'terrorist' list would show themselves. They all arrived well in time with Medad taking his lone position up on someone's roof as one of the snipers whilst the rest of his unit, complete with cameras, took up their positions on the ground a little distant from the funeral procession itself. The usual was expected and by that was meant loads of demonstrators, some bricks and stones, lots of chanting and maybe a few flares all aimed at the IDF. In return the soldiers had tear gas, rubber-coated bullets and snipers if any known 'terrorists' were spotted by the film people.

Medad had no idea whose funeral it was, no idea that it was his bullet that had caused it. Probably just another unfortunate who'd given up the ghost, he thought. It was a hot day and the sweat was trickling into his eyes. Again he hoped he wouldn't have to fire. In this crowd the chances of successfully picking out the specific person who had been spotted was low. The chances of incurring collateral damage was consequentially high. Not that his superiors really cared, but he did.

He saw all the Palestinian flags and the huge mass of people. A funeral procession can never really be called good humoured, but there was no sign of violence. Apart from the slogan shouting, it was peaceful and everyone seem to be behaving. Not much longer to wait now. The body was now interred and everyone would be making their way back to their homes. Medad was breathing a sigh of relief when through his sights he thought he saw a well known local Fatah official intentionally making his way through the crowd. He watched him weave his way towards the back of the immediate entourage surrounding the coffin. That would be where family and friends would be. He stopped by the side of a young man with an older lady, and appeared to have a quick conversation. The younger man nodded. Medad was no lip reader, so although he saw lips moving, had no idea what was being said.

Then came the order directly into his ear. Describing this man perfectly, he was to take him out. He cursed loudly, steadied his rifle and sighted him. There was an immediate opportunity. He took it without hesitation. Aimed and fired. All hell broke loose. People had no idea where the shot had come from, so they fled in all directions. Thoughts of the funeral went out of all minds except the family and friends who just fell to the ground. There was nowhere else to go. The Fatah man was on the ground with the young man he had been talking to pumping his chest in vain. The dispersing crowds gave the Israelis the excuse to fire off tear gas. It was over.

Medad felt better this time not that he knew exactly why. It was not his business to determine who he killed. He just obeyed orders. Even though there were no other casualties, he tried again to see it as just his job. Nevertheless, he admitted to himself, that there remained some uneasiness deep within. These were by no means the first killings he had successfully accomplished and he often wondered how many kills would it take to completely numb himself to what he was doing. When would the anxiety go away completely? Did he want it to go away; perhaps it was a healthy response, a sign of who he really was? Did he really want to become a killing machine who felt nothing? And was it right to obey orders whatever?

Back at barracks, one of his friends approached him with congratulations for a clean hit. Medad mumbled his thanks. Seeing Medad was still in some discomfort, Akiva again tried to 'comfort' him.

"This guy was a terrorist, part of a terrorist organisation and their stated aim is to breach our security and kill our people. It's the price we have to pay to preserve our country and our way of life. We cannot wait for the moment where they find a weak spot and attack us there. Wake up, Medad."

Hirsh joined in. "If tomorrow morning one of them gets into a military base or a kibbutz and kills people there, maybe takes prisoners or hostages, that's a whole new ballgame. We can't allow that moment to come. You and our other snipers are there because we need to preserve our values. We all get sent out to do our job and you receive very accurate instructions about whom to shoot to protect us. We're grateful that you do your job well. Keep it up."

Medad acknowledged the argument, but it's all a matter of degree, he thought. Can we kill anyone with impunity? Who is making the call that someone in a funeral procession is a terrorist, and what is a terrorist?

He voiced his concerns to them all again. "I can kill anyone I'm ordered to, that's not the problem, but is it right? Moreover, is it legal? How many mistakes are we allowed to make and if I make one, is that categorised as murder or worse a war crime? We can't go on shooting people at will because that cannot lead to peace, it merely exacerbates the situation. But maybe that's what the government wants."

"Steady on," Seth could sense some conspiracy theory coming, but Medad was on a roll. "Maybe it's all part of some grand plan, after all elections are not far away. Would the order be given to kill Palestinians just to win an election? I recognise we need security, but I also recognise that we need peace just as much."

They all recognised that Medad couldn't be 'comforted' and so the conversation petered out. His friends had given up and they gradually began to move away. It was now the end of the day and Medad had his two days leave coming. The first, he had now decided, would be with Shana and the second with his mother. He just wanted to forget his 'sniping' and have a good time with Shana, who had also managed to get a few days off to go back home. It was going to be their second date. So on Monday late afternoon after completing his duty roster, his motorbike was pressed into service and headed for Tel Aviv. He reckoned Route 1 would take him thirty-five to forty minutes if he pushed it. He passed to intersection with Route 6, christened as the Yitzhak Rabin Highway, but now known as the Trans Israel Highway.

He noted that it was rarely called by it's name anymore. Rabin, it seemed, had been consigned to history. Medad liked Rabin and his policies for he believed this man alone had the right ideas. He had been re-elected as prime minister on a platform embracing the peace process. He signed several historic agreements with the Palestinian leadership as part of the Oslo Accords and had won the Nobel Peace Prize. Medad was pushing the bike hard, but thinking about Rabin. If only he hadn't been assassinated, perhaps Israel would now be in a better place.

He had been thinking so deeply that he now had no idea where he was. Had he gone through the twin tunnels or not? He didn't know, doubtless he would find out. Traffic on the road was quite heavy as it always was and he was keeping an eagle eye out for traffic cops as he weaved through the cars and trucks. It was quite hot, but the wind was full in his face, cooling him down so he was able to enjoy the ride. There was something cathartic about going faster than anyone else and beating all the traffic. He had to be careful though, Route 1 was very busy and mostly only dual carriageway.

He was now approaching the outskirts of Tel Aviv and started to wonder where he would take her? He hadn't booked anywhere, but Tel Aviv's night life was one of the best in the world, or so his research told him. There were the established spots like Kuli Alma, an underground bar on the corner of Yehuda Halevi and Allenby. It had a large outdoor area where you could start your evening, a closed room with amazing music for dancing and a third room that had live music. Good, but maybe too popular. He wanted something a little quieter.

Perhaps Sputnik, hidden down a small alley off Allenby, near the corner of Rothschild. Opened in 2016, it was a bit of a cult-status venue amongst the Tel Aviv hipster crew. Unfortunately he hadn't had time to book, and as the place got packed very quickly, with often large queues outside, he decided against. So where was it to be? He decided on The Prince, at least to start with. It was a bar located in an old building on Nachalat-Binyamin which had an excellent rooftop area with indoor and outdoor seating. Food apparently was good and drinks were reasonably priced. After that… well, it depended on how well the evening went.

He had arranged to pick Shana up at her parent's place since she was still based there whilst she was on her IDF service. He circled the area a few times on his bike to work out where the house was. He eventually found it, wishing he had a satnav on his bike rather than a bit of paper in his pocket with a goo-gle map on it. He knocked and she answered the door, her parents either out or making themselves scarce. It was a three storey house in the Neve Tsedek district. She invited him in whilst she finalised her preparations and showed him into the lounge. Not a new house, but furnished with modern chrome and glass tables and slim sofas. Some modernistic pictures on the wall, so altogether a nice suburban place. Quite different from where he came from, but interesting. It was only a few minutes before she was ready and off they roared into the centre of Tel Aviv. They were settled in comfortable chairs on the rooftop of The Prince drinking cocktails. It was already dark outside with a balmy breeze helping to cool the air. A few flies buzzed around, but none came so close as to ruin the romantic atmosphere. He was happy and after a surreptitious sideways glance, it looked as if she was happy too. She had a Noah's' Ark and he had a Polish Butterfly. There was an unspoken agreement that they wouldn't talk about IDF issues, so conversation revolved around what they would do after their military service. Shana had already committed herself to becoming a journalist, by hook or crook. He knew that. She explained that there were plenty of stories which she'd like to write but she needed some sort of qualification to be taken seriously.

But apparently there was no first degree course in journalism in Israel, and her parents couldn't afford to send her abroad, so she had settled on an Israel and Middle Eastern Studies course at the Rothberg International School, part of the Hebrew University of Jerusalem. The brochure assured candidates that it was the perfect course for a career in journalism. No guarantee of a job, of course.

After the discussions with his friends, Medad had begun to think more intentionally about his own future. He had very different views to many of his generation which made him even more determined to chart a course that enabled him to articulate his ideas to a wider public. Surely people with open minds could be persuaded to change. Journalism, however, was not on his mind. He wanted to be much closer to the seat of power and influence than that, but had not decided quite how. The cut and thrust of party political life wasn't attractive to him, but politics in one form or another was where the power lay to change things and not much more time to come to a decision. They were both out of the IDF in a few short months.

He had been looking at the International Liberal Arts programme at Tel Aviv University. It looked a good grounding for lots of careers and would be closer to Shana... except that she was now going to Jerusalem. He was still thinking about this when she looked up at him with open eyes. He looked blank.

"Perhaps some food might be a good idea?" Embarrassed, he asked whether she was happy to stay here or go on to another place. She was happy to stay so food was duly ordered and consumed with a bottle of Dalton Sauvignon Blanc Reserve. He knew how to show his girl a good time! It was a great evening, even though his bank balance was certainly emptier than when he started. But it was worth it even though he had to bike all the way back to base the same evening at a more steady pace than his journey earlier that evening. It wouldn't be a good idea to get caught after drinking his share of the wine. Now it was dark and he was thinking again. The bike was good for thinking.

Perhaps he didn't want to spend three years studying. Maybe he wanted to get straight into work, straight into the maelstrom that was public life whatever that turned out to be. The more he thought about this, the more he liked the sound of it, and the more impatient he was to get started. But how, and where?

Of course, Seth. He recalled that Seth that had an internship already lined up with a Member of the Knesset (MK) when he finished his IDF service. He didn't know who that was, but Medad guessed that Seth's views more or less lined up with Likud. Anyway, he determined to track Seth down as soon as possible, hoping that their recent conversations hadn't put an end to their friendship. Yes, definitely the way forward. He began to get excited, because that would also mean he would be in Jerusalem, as the Knesset was in Givat Ram, Western Jerusalem. Double whammy!

Seth was away until the next day, so Medad had to contain his excitement. It gave him time to calm down after that heady bike ride back to his base at Ofrit. He went over and over the plan, and it still made sense to him but it was circumspect not tell anyone, Shana or his parents, until there was a possible route in. He didn't want to appear to be over ambitious, only to fail and be labelled naïve. After all, he didn't yet have a first degree or any real experience of political life. All he had was a couple of years with the IDF and that was far from unique.

Seth was taken a little by surprise. He knew Medad's views and when Medad explained that he didn't want to work for someone who had diametrically opposite views to his own, Seth was doubtful he could help. Normally, it's who you know, or more accurately who your father knows that could get you in. Nevertheless, he would make some enquiries.

"It's not going to be easy," Seth began to explain. He had come back to Medad having made little progress.

"The thing is, MKs don't advertise internships because it's all done on a recommendation basis and there's not many MKs who share your views and they won't want anyone working for them who they might regard as an 'appeaser' or worse. Sorry."

Medad was disappointed but not surprised. "Look, I'll continue to keep my eyes and ears peeled, but there's no guarantees." Seth smiled and patted Medad on the shoulder. "I'm sure something will pop up."

Medad thanked him. Having finished with the military, he was now living at home but was desperate to get some kind of job in Jerusalem, even if it was only temporary, just to be near Shana. A couple of weeks passed with no news from Seth. He knew that he had to widen his search and so had registered at some recruitment sites. But without a first degree, the jobs on offer were menial and paid little. But he swallowed his pride and started as a waiter in a café, reliant on tips to top up a meagre wage. He enjoyed meeting different customers but it was a long day and, despite military training, he found he was now using muscles he didn't know he had!

Then out of the blue, Seth called. He had been as good as his word. "There is something called The Research and Information Centre – the RIC – next to the Knesset which provides MKs and committees with research papers and background studies relating to current debates and legislation. Basically, it's a back room job, but with access to all parts of the Knesset."

"Sounds interesting." Medad was almost ready to go for anything.

"Again, they don't advertise but my MK can get you a meeting with the Deputy Director if that works for you?" Seth was clearly unsure whether Medad would want this.

"Sure. I think that's just right for me," said Medad, hoping he sounded not overly desperate. Keeping to the true nature of intern recruitment, Seth had a word with his MK, who had a word with the Deputy Director, who called Medad in for a chat, who then found himself with an internship. It was heady stuff. One minute a waiter and the next working in the RIC with access to the Knesset.

He came out of the chat, or was it an interview, with his head in the clouds. Though nervous, he must have answered the questions well though it hadn't been that hard. His new boss was friendly and he felt he could work well here. It was who you knew, after all.

11

HANI ARRIVED HOME after the funeral with his mother later that Monday evening. Ayshaa had heard the news that there had been yet another 'little disturbance', and was anxiously waiting for her husband to return. If he felt ambivalent towards Israel before, he certainly wasn't now.

"It was a funeral." He exploded. "A funeral! We can't even lay an old woman to rest without their snipers picking out mourners and killing them. What have we come to? Why doesn't the world do something, say something? Totally unacceptable."

Hani wasn't usually angry about these episodes, more resigned. They happened too regularly to keep getting upset. He hadn't seen the point of railing against something, somebody, some force which couldn't be stopped. Yet now he had changed, was changing. He was surprising himself with his new reactions and not a little concerned. He was not used to experiencing this kind of emotion, anger that threatened to take control, if only temporarily. If he wasn't careful, he would not be any different to all those unthinking, stone-throwing youths, urged on by leaders who ought to have known better. That thought caught him and his anger began to dissipate.

Over their evening meal, he began to relate what had happened. Ghalia kept her counsel. She had been there, but Ayshaa wanted all the details. He felt the indignation and anger returning as he began to re-live the end of the funeral. The two women looked at each other. Hani was changing. He was no more a neutral observer. He had now taken sides and they knew their man had made a decision.

Later that evening, when Ghalia had retired, he shared with Ayshaa what the Fatah leader had whispered to him shortly before his untimely demise. She nodded and noted a determination in him she had rarely seen before. There wasn't much else to say. They both knew a little of what was ahead and the dangers it posed. As yet, he was unknown to the Israeli security apparatus, so he could go about his new business without being a target, and he was determined to make the most of the anonymous time he had. Ayshaa said she and Ghalia would try to keep the shop going as best they could, and look after Rena between them. He must be free.

He had to go out, but promised to get back as soon as he could. With that he kissed his wife, his daughter and his mother, left the home and disappeared into the darkness. He had a meeting to attend. As he made his way through Manger Square, down the hill and towards the edge of the town, his mind was crystal clear. He deliberately refused to allow any anger or frustration to impact him, knowing that emotions were not going to serve him amongst a group of potential hotheads. He wanted to be totally clear-headed

The Fatah meeting had already started by the time he arrived and after being frisked by the security guys, he was allowed him through. He was obviously expected. There were about a dozen men in the room, a few younger than him, but most a lot older. It was a house, at least it seemed like it. There was a kitchen, a bathroom and a sitting room where the meeting was being held, but no photographs, pictures and anything personal. Maybe the owner had died, anyway apart from the table and chairs, the place was empty. No refreshments, no tea, no hummus. It was straight down to business.

The man who seemed to be in charge immediately welcomed him and introduced him as the one who tried to save their brother who had been shot at the funeral. He neglected to say either who Hani was, or anyone else. No pleasant introductions. Tonight everyone was anonymous, probably because he was there. Trust amongst these people needed to be earned, especially with an active Musta'ribeen unit about. The discussion, which had stopped just for a second as he entered, now started up again with three or four talking at the same time. He sensed a ratcheting up of emotions as each speaker competed for the rhetoric that would convince the meeting.

Hani sat in silence, having heard it all before, thought it all before. There was nothing new, no new thinking, no new strategy. After a while when there also seemed to be no agreement, Hani was asked for his thoughts. He didn't want to speak anonymously since the chances of him getting any traction here would be nil. First, quietly talking about his father, then summarised all the arguments he had heard for more action against the Israelis. Once he had got all the heads nodding, he asked them,

"After fifty years of struggle doing the same thing, what different outcome has there been?" He left the question hanging. "We need a different outcome, not same old, same old. If we want something different, we have to do something different."

He was immediately pounced on to give his solution, so Hani allowed himself a moment to focus attention. He started to talk directly.

"There is no silver bullet, because if there was, we would have found it and used it by now. Think about it. We are, and are always likely to be outclassed militarily, so why compete and lose? If we continue in our knee-jerk responses, we get nowhere."

Hani looked around at the sceptical faces. "Let's look five years out and begin to build where we can win. For example, the Zionist lobby worldwide has had the media to itself for decades. Our message is not getting to the people who might help. We need to identify who these might be, then put in place a strategy to influence and mobilise them."

There was a shaking of the heads around the room and it was clear that they wanted to express their anger, not strategise. Hani quietly pushed a little further.

"We think that everyone in the US is against us, but many grass roots Democrats are for us. What disarms their influence are our pseudo-military activities. We get labelled as terrorists and then what might have been a positive, supportive voice is drowned out, and no-one wants to stand up for us. Many Hollywood celebrities are for us and we can use them to raise funds but we have to change our tactics on the ground. Every excuse the Israelis have to blame us has to be taken away."

Sadly, it was all falling on deaf ears. The shouting erupted again as each sought to assert his opinion that immediate retribution was needed. Suddenly amid their own angry voices, they could all hear loud voices, banging and scuffles outside. Then a shot was fired. Out the back way. Quickly. The room miraculously emptied, and they left their security guys to sort out whoever was trying to get in, or die in the process. They died. A small unit of Israeli soldiers forced their way into the now empty room. They searched the house and found nothing, since there was nothing to find. They spoke quietly into their radios and withdrew.

Hani melted away in the darkness as did the whole group, all in different directions making their way to their homes. Hani was dejected having had tried and, by his own standards, failed. They had clearly misunderstood what he was trying to say or perhaps they had deliberately sabotaged his ideas because he was an untrusted newcomer. Perhaps they thought that he was saying that they ought to roll over and accept the situation, so called 'normalisation'. Perhaps. Perhaps. What was absolutely clear to him was that any thoughts he might have had for helping to change the situation had been blown away.

But there were a lot of unanswered questions about the evening which he now began to think about. How had the Israelis known where they had been meeting? Had the place been under surveillance? Did they now have his photo on their files? Would they be looking out for him in order to take him out? Did they have a collaborator amongst them? Would they think it was him as the newcomer? Conclusion: it was a complete mess.

He had only gone about a quarter of a mile when a large explosion rocked the neighbourhood. Hani looked back to see the house where they had been meeting disappear in smoke and dust causing him to run the rest of the way home as fast as he could. He sat outside the front door on the step while he got his breath back not wanting to enter sweating and panting.

After twenty minutes or so, he opened the door and eventually crawled into bed next to Ayshaa trying not to wake her but she was still awake waiting for him to arrive back safely. He began to talk, but she cautioned him, better in the morning. He fell into a troubled sleep but she stayed awake thinking about the little he had said… with the outline of a plan developing in her mind. Come the morning, neither had slept very well but they had to wait until Ghalia had gone shopping before they could talk openly.

Hani then spent some time going through what he had heard, what he had said and what had eventually happened to break up the meeting. He felt he had failed at the first hurdle. Then Ayshaa began sharing her thoughts.

"Do you remember the Women's March in 2017 by Israeli women from north to south?" Yes, he did. "It was organised by an NGO called Women

Wage Peace, created in 2014 in the aftermath of the Gaza war." He certainly remembered the Gaza war.

"Well, there were weeks of events culminating in this north to south march of women. They were focussing on the need for a solution to end the violence rather than holding one ideological line or another. More than 30,000 women took part, throughout Israel and the West Bank. That's an awful lot of support for what we believe."

Hani remembered that Hamas boycotted it. Ayshaa confirmed it.

"Yes Hamas, through their Union of Palestinian Women's Committees issued a statement opposing the event, saying that our women were being used as props and tokenised by Anat Negev and Donna Kirshbaum, the Israeli women organising it. Typical hard line rhetoric, probably dictated by men!" Ayshaa glanced at Hani to see if there was a reaction. She hadn't meant it to sound so critical. There was none.

She continued. "They dismissed it as a part of the normalisation of the Israeli occupation of our land. Some went on to criticise the Women Wage Peace movement because they thought it failed to advocate for Palestinian equal rights, and instead had just issued a vague call for peace." Ayshaa was withering about Hamas. "Always wanting everything now. Never content to make a little ground here and there. You would almost think there were people supporting Israel amongst them, considering the way they give the Israelis every excuse to continue their policies."

She paused and tried to assess how her husband was reacting. Hani was listening hard. "You were there?" He asked. Ayshaa nodded.

"Fatah supported it. Ziad Darwish of PLO's Committee For Interaction with Israeli Society said that the women's peace march had the full support of the PLO and PA. It was the right thing to do. Mahmoud Abbas sent a letter to each of the marchers in the name of the Palestinian Authority which was very positive. Many of the Israeli participants in the march voiced a desire to have reconciliation with us and said they wanted to meet with Palestinian women. I remember one organizer saying that we all want a safe future for our children."

She paused with that far away look as if she were re-living the experience.

"We met at the Dead Sea, the lowest point on earth where they had prepared a big white Tent of Reconciliation. Everyone was dressed in white to symbolise peace and we danced together. All of us. Palestinians and Israelis. It was really genuine. There were tears, confessions, forgiveness and many friendships began."

Hani confessed that much of this he had not known.

Ayshaa had more to say. "I met an Israeli lady, Michal Froman, who told me her story. She was a religious Jewish settler who was stabbed by a Palestinian in 2016 whilst she was pregnant and she was there supporting the peace movement. I know where she lives. And do you remember a former Knesset member, Shakib Shanan, whose son was one of two border police officers killed near the Temple Mount? He spoke at the final gathering in Jerusalem's park and called leaders to sit down together. That was very moving but never going to happen, of course."

She paused again. Hani looked up. "So what is your plan?"

Ayshaa had already thought it through. "I am going to contact Ziad first to see what is happening amongst the women and if nothing, begin to resurrect it. I'm also going to see if I can contact ALLMEP (Alliance for Middle East Peace) and see if there's anything going on that I can contribute to. They're based near Hebron, I think. We women must continue to make our mark because women matter, because women are inclusive, because women gave so much trust to the current leaders on both sides and that generation of leaders have failed us."

Hani looked at his wife with new eyes. She could almost be a Islamic feminist, Hani thought. He wasn't sure what to say. Ayshaa was trying to read his mind thinking he was going to criticise.

She continued. "I know women don't have much direct political power, Dalal Salama being the sole female Fatah Central Committee member, but we have to pull what weight we can. We can have influence, not just here but in the rest of the world."

Hani reassured her. "You're absolutely right. However, my concern is what the march really highlighted. What I probably should have talked about last night. Our real and number one problem. And that is – we're divided. Unless we can find some basis to work together with Hamas, I'm not sure we'll get anywhere."

Ghalia had returned and was looking after Rena. Hani and Ayshaa were so engrossed in their discussion that they completely failed to notice her. She had been quietly listening in the background, keeping her own counsel for the moment. There were going to be many ups and downs if they were to achieve a fraction of what they were dreaming of and they were going to need a rock to turn to in those times, and she was going to have to be it.

12

CHARLES H ROWLANDS, or Chuck to his friends, was a Deputy Assistant Secretary for Near Middle Eastern Affairs (NEA) at the US State Department. At thirty, he was one of the youngest Deputy Assistant Secretaries in the organisation. His climb up the ladder was certainly due to his analytical ability as well as his gracious personality, but an African-American identity also had its advantages in certain overseas countries. Just an analyst, he liked to say, though with the ear of some very influential people. He may not have been in the position to initiate policy, but was certainly able to mould it. Married with two young daughters, life was full on in Washington and he loved it. They lived on the edge of Georgetown, quite a leap from Knoxville, Tennessee where he and his wife were born and brought up.

They had not always lived in Georgetown. When they first moved to Washington DC and Chuck first joined the State Department, they lived in one of the more seedy neighbourhoods of DC. It was all they could afford. There were plenty of those; places where law enforcement was not a priority, almost amounting to no-go areas. Gloria had insisted that they move from their rental at the first opportunity and buy a place in a better neighbourhood. Chuck needed no persuading. Schooling for his daughters was pre-eminent and he knew that the better the neighbourhood, the better the schools.

Georgetown was great for them. They mortgaged much of their income to afford it, but Chuck had reckoned his job was secure and his income could only rise. Whilst it had been hard at first, each year was getting better. Georgetown, with its cobblestone pavements, grand homes, the Chesapeake and Ohio Canal and tree-lined avenues. The girls loved the shopping on M street, although much of that was still of the window variety. Chuck and Gloria's enjoyment came from the occasional sampling of some of the top restaurants in the capital but as Chuck progressed in his career, they began to afford a lifestyle which would have been entirely foreign to them back in Knoxville.

They both came from what was called America's Bible Belt. However, Chuck was intelligent enough not to swallow the more fundamentalist beliefs of his parents or the church which he had attended, but he never quite knew where Gloria stood. In this socially conservative, evangelical part of the world, biblical prophecy was revered and interpreted literally. The establishment of the State of Israel in 1948 was seen as a fulfilment of such a prophecy. Chuck had no problem with this, after all, he was still a Bible-believing Christian. He recalled sermons on Ezekiel 36. Verse 19 said,

"And I scattered them among the heathen, and they were dispersed through the countries: according to their way and according to their doings I judged them."

Here is God's judgement on the people of Israel for their unbelief and disobedience. But verse 24 of the same chapter says,

"For I will take you from among the heathen, and gather you out of all countries, and will bring you into your own land."

Whether James Balfour, sitting in the UK Foreign Office had read or even heard of this passage is difficult to know, but when 1948 finally happened most of the Bible Belt pastors and ministers proclaimed a miraculous fulfilment of biblical prophecy. But more than that, they preached that it marked the beginning of the 'end times', when nations would converge on Israel trying to destroy it, only to bring about the Second Coming of Jesus.

Chuck was more than dubious about that, but he had no doubt that Israel needed help to survive in a hostile Middle East. Thus he had no qualms at all with traditional US policy to support Israel politically, militarily and economically. Besides it was his job to implement US policy but he did have some concerns about certain aspects of Israel's independent actions, which he did not see as in the interests of the US, or the Middle East. In his judgement, the main threat they faced was not from the Palestinians, and he wished they would concentrate on the wider region and move a little to agree a deal with the Palestinians to sort out the Occupied West Bank. He didn't think it would take much, if the Israeli government really wanted to do it. Then they could devote themselves to the real threat and maybe normalising relations with more anti-Iran Gulf States.

But at the same time, he recognised some of the issues. The Palestinians did not speak with one voice, which Israel took advantage of. Hamas, of course, was a notified terrorist organisation, but Fatah, on the other hand, was much more moderate now, although it had a terrorist past. Chuck saw it as a real shame that no matter how hard they tried, they couldn't shake off that history, especially as Israel's education system reinforced this image from kindergarten upwards. Moreover, the Palestinians had very little to negotiate with. Israel could do what they liked and did, which was a little troubling.

He was very much aware of the support Israel had in the US. Not only the Jewish lobby which was powerful in itself, but also Messianic Christians who he knew well from his upbringing. It could be a minefield. The latter thought that to support Israel no matter what, was being true to the Bible. Israel could do no wrong and shouldn't be questioned. God was at work. These pressure groups formed a powerful influence on every US administration, especially in election years. Equally as powerful as the gun lobby! And Israel knew it.

Chuck had risen through the ranks quite quickly. He was intelligent, good looking and could speak a modicum of Hebrew. By keeping his head down and not expressing his own concerns, he usually got five stars in his appraisals. As a career diplomat, he was not paid to have private views just simply flex with each Secretary of State and each President's agenda. He had served for a short time in the US embassy in Tel Aviv, in a junior capacity some years ago in the early years of his marriage. It was there he had learned enough of the language to enable him to make friends inside and outside the Embassy, amongst Israelis of all persuasions. So he knew the ground reasonably well.

But now it was Saturday morning and he was up early on his extended run. He ran every morning before returning home, showering, having breakfast with his family and still getting into the office at eight o'clock. On Saturday, however, he took an longer run when he had more time to review the week past and the week ahead. The rest of the family would be having a lie in. Gloria, his wife, worked as a researcher at a local radio station, WOL, a news/talk station on 1450 AM. The FM wavelengths had been bought out years ago by the more lucrative music stations which had hit the AM station's listening figures hard with the commensurate fall in advertising revenue. Gloria had the responsibility for recruiting interview guests for two of the daytime shows. She loved it. Chuck often reminded her that she could get more money at a music station, but she was loyal to WOL.

They had been childhood sweethearts and had married quite young with the usual reservations from both sets of parents, more from hers than his. But they were all church folk and knew each other well. Being headstrong young people, they were not going to change their plans and so parents eventually had to be realistic. They could not be stopped and so they agreed among themselves to support the newly weds as much as they could to start with. But within a short time, the young couple were self sufficient mainly due to Chuck's Tel Aviv posting. This year was their tenth anniversary and would be doing something special together, but just hadn't got around to discussing it yet. Life was hectic but good, as they just about managed each week to juggle work schedules with school runs and general family life.

For Chuck, Friday had been briefing day in the State Department. In particular, they would have separate video conferences with various Embassy staff in Jerusalem and elsewhere in the Middle East. This would occasionally include military and intelligence attaches, designated as trade personnel. Although they were under the State Department umbrella and in theory answerable to the Ambassador, practice saw a very different reporting line. Thus they might also link with Langley or the Pentagon when necessary, although cooperation between agencies and parts of government was not always as it should be.

Not a great deal of new stuff came out of these sessions. Iran still belligerent; Iraq still chaotic; Egypt still seeking Muslim Brotherhood members to arrest; Lebanon still a hotbed for all kinds of groups, usually anti Israeli; Syria still demolished and Israel still doing anything it wanted to do on the West Bank. Some slick parliamentarian manoeuvres by Likud and its coalition partners to get a vote through the Knesset. Oh, and yet another Palestinian leader had been shot by an Israeli sniper, this time at a recent funeral in Bethlehem.

Chuck had not been amused that this was offered by the Jerusalem office as a 'by the way' comment. He took over the questioning.

"Why," Chuck asked.

"Apparently he was on their list."

"What list?"

"Not entirely sure, but the Israelis have a list of known terrorists and look out for them at every disturbance."

"And was he?"

"Was he what?"

"A terrorist."

"We don't know for sure."

"Well, could you please find out?"

"We'll try," was the unenthusiastic answer. When the call was finished, he asked everyone round the table rhetorically, whether the Israelis were taking advantage of a stalemate in the peace process to take out as many Palestinian leaders as possible? He thought they all knew the answer to that. However, everyone including Israel, knew that the State Department had no real power to control or even meaningfully influence any element of Israeli policy. They had to keep doing their job, going through the motions and trying to positively engage with each Israeli government, preparing for the day when some sort of peace process would be back on the table, but many senior State Department officials had been 'let go' a few years ago and their positions had never been re-filled. They struggled to exert influence.

But it was Saturday. Gloria had plans for the day, as she did for most Saturdays. They would take a trip, eat out somewhere for lunch, get back early evening in time for a movie for the kids with pizzas. After eight o'clock in the evening when the girls were in bed, it was time for them to eat and talk. Mostly it was positive from Chuck, but Gloria had begun to detect a growing frustration in him, and wanted to draw him out. Yes, it was a good job. Great opportunity to influence policy makers, or at least there used to be. But the State Department had continued to lose a lot of the influence it had traditionally enjoyed, and it didn't look like it would ever quite get back to those days. No fault of the Secretary, it was just that the White House had centralised more and more power in itself.

Gloria listened. She was a good listener. She was anxious for Chuck and his job, not just for selfish reasons, but she would readily admit that she loved living and working where they were. The children were getting on well at school and had many friends. Life was good and she didn't want it to change. Today they had made their way over to Annapolis for what was billed as a family friendly pirate cruise on the Chesapeake. They watched their girls live life as a pirate for a few hours, searching for sunken treasure and firing water cannons. It had been a good family day out, but she had noticed that Chuck had been a little quieter than normal, a bit preoccupied.

Sunday morning came and they went to church, as they had always done. America was still a church-going country for the main, although on the East and West coasts times were achanging. The car park was almost full and there was almost a queue to get in past the 'greeters', who were handing out the week's notices at the doors. It was a large auditorium with a choir at the back of the stage dressed in white surplices each with a red top. The worship leader, a lady, was dressed all in white and was standing ready to start. At the front of the stage was a perspex lectern up front ready for the sermon and behind all of this, displayed on a large floor to ceiling curtain, was a banner with the words, "Jesus is Lord." The family found their seats near the side where they always sat and nodded to those in the congregation that they knew – mostly by sight rather than in person. The first hymn was sung together and after a little talk for the children, they would all go out for their classes and the adults would participate in hymns, prayers, the offering before settling down for the sermon.

Chuck had been relaxed up to now, but was noticeable shifting in his seat as he anticipated the sermon. He had read the notice sheet which announced that the sermon would be about Israel. His wife threw him a glance which said, "Behave."

The pastor advanced towards the lectern:

"Now, I want you to take your Bibles and turn with me to Psalm 102:13 and we begin reading in verse thirteen. This is a marvellous prophesy concerning our Lord and the land of Israel. The subject today is Israel And Bible Prophesy."

Chuck began to groan inwardly. His wife nudged him as if she had heard his groan. She knew Chuck didn't agree with the pastor's teaching on Israel. Indeed Chuck often wondered why on earth they were still coming to this church. But the pastor had started.

"People sometimes ask me why I keep going back to the land of Israel? It's because I love the land and I love the people of that land. They are God's chosen people. And this verse will help to express why we go to the nation of Israel.

Psalm 102:13.

"Thou shalt arise and have mercy upon Zion, for the time to favour her, yea, the set time is come. For thy servants take pleasure in her stones and favour the dust thereof. So the heathen shall fear the name of the Lord and all of the kings of the earth thy glory. When the Lord shall build up Zion, he shall appear in his glory."

Mark that verse. When the Lord shall build up Zion then he shall appear in his glory. That means, if we want to see when our Lord is coming in glory, we need to keep our eyes on Zion, that is, God's holy land…"

Gloria looked across at Chuck. He looked as if he had zoned out and was miles away. She nudged him again. The pastor was only into the first twenty five minutes. There was at least another twenty five to go. Chuck came to.

"… Not only are the Jews God's chosen people, they are also the people of destiny. As the Jew goes, so goes the world. If you want to know what God is up to in this world study the people of Israel, because the Jews are God's yardstick. They are God's blueprint…"

And so it went on and on. Gloria was smiling to herself. She knew exactly what Chuck was going to say as they left the church. True to her instinct, as they were leaving, Chuck expressed the thought again that they should find another church.

"I can't endure much more of that."

"But the girls have their friends there," and so the perennial good-hearted debate started again. It would happen one day, maybe.

Back at the State Department on Monday morning, Chuck tried to knuckle down to his work, but parts of that sermon kept ringing in his ears. How could intelligent people swallow that stuff? How could people be so blind as to what was really going on? He hoped none of his colleagues knew he went to that church and heard sermons like that. It was turning out to be a rather depressing day.

Following the Friday briefings, he was beginning to be concerned about what was happening in Israel and supporting the Embassy staff there. It was their role to provide the legal link between the two countries and deal with the vast range of matters that countries are involved in such as politics, economics, commerce, investment, culture, defence, development cooperation etc. But it was becoming very difficult both for them and for the State Department generally to perform their traditional role. Under a succession of Presidents, the White House had developed a direct line with the PM of Israel which often by-passed the State Department and the Embassy on the ground.

Chuck began to think seriously about making a trip to Jerusalem and his boss, the Assistant Under Secretary who hated flying himself, had no objection in principle. He discovered that there was to be a visit by a group of Senators after the recess in three months time and so he decided to wait until then and ride alongside them. Most were right wing Republicans who held very different views to his own but nevertheless, Chuck thought, I don't have to spend every minute with them.

He decided it would be diplomatic to signal the possibility of the trip well in advance to his wife so there was no surprise when it happened. One day, he thought, I must take her again and maybe leave the kids with grandparents. It would be a great holiday and she could visit all the sites she had wanted to but never had time when she was there before. She would love it.

13

ONCE UPON A time international air travel must have been delightful. Not any more. No matter how extensive the shops, how many the restaurants, how luxurious the lounges, it was airport security that was the time-wasting part of every air journey. That was partly the responsibility of the PLO for, under a young Yasser Arafat, passenger airliners were hi-jacked with regularity in the 1980s which quickly led to increased security measures at most airports, particularly for El Al. Post 9-11 and the rise of Islamic fundamentalism, those measures went into the stratosphere. Now security was a major time factor in air travel – airport arrival at least three hours before take-off for international travel. A boon for the said shops and restaurants, though.

Those who had reasonable expense accounts could mitigate the hassle by taking advantage of exclusive airline lounges, having meals in their celebrity chef restaurants and experiencing intensive spa treatments. In some cases, even security, check-in and immigration would all be handled in the lounge, so that important people didn't have disagreeable exposure to the queueing masses. US Diplomats and Senators were, after all, important people.

Chuck had been through the process more times than he cared to count, so all the pampering was a bit passé. However, he was a bit of a foodie and he was interested to know what the in-flight menu would be. As soon as the 747 had levelled out, he was presented with a menu from an immaculately turned out stewardess, who invited him to "choose from the indulgent and delicious à la carte menu designed by leading chefs from around the world." Real crockery, real cutlery, a real wine glass and real wine! He gave his order, sank back in his seat, trying to ignore the ramblings of the various Senators around him. He began to think about Israel, Palestine, Iran and the whole mess that was the Middle East.

But being the good husband he was, he spared a thought for his wife at home eating a Dominos meat feast pizza with the children, while he ate lobster tortelloni, followed by pan-fried stone bass and then a chocolate hazelnut slice. After a few glasses of an excellent deep red La Sirena Syrah 2005, from

California's Napa valley, he settled down to sleep the hours away. It would be a sixteen hour flight leaving Dulles mid afternoon and arriving in Tel Aviv about twelve hours later local time, with the American taxpayer being almost $6,000 per head lighter! He reckoned there would be plenty of time to read through his papers later.

But what a blessing to have a diplomatic entrance to a country. Minimum checks and baggage delivery which didn't depend on the efforts of underpaid, overworked baggage handlers. Then diplomatic cars which avoided the taxi queue, and every other queue which could whisk them off to their destination. Chuck was grateful. He'd slept reasonably well and was certainly fresh enough for a few welcome personal meetings at the Jerusalem embassy. Nothing of substance though, that would wait until tomorrow. But it was good to catch up with some old friends and meet some new ones whilst the Senators did their own official business amidst their own sightseeing.

One of the small inconveniences of the location change of the Embassy was that to liaise with other embassies, particularly close allies, he had to travel back to Tel Aviv. Some had consulates in Jerusalem, but most would not meet formally there, although an informal meet was usually acceptable. He didn't need to travel far to get to his own briefings the next morning, so he had arranged to have his evening meal with one of his oldest friends, an Israeli journalist who also worked freelance for a number of Israeli peace organisations.

Hagai was an interesting character, one of those rare people who seemed to get on with right and left wing equally well. Everyone knew he supported a peace process but he was well respected in this city. A tall, lanky figure, it was difficult to put an age on him; certainly over forty-five but perhaps not yet sixty. Sharp, handsome and just as independent in his personal life as his politics. There had many women, but no lasting relationship. He was a free spirit.

The American wanted to get an independent view of the current situation and he knew that Hagai wouldn't mince his words. Chuck liked Lebanese food, so he arranged to meet at the Manou ba Shouk restaurant in Ets Khaim Street. The best food in Israel! The tab was his and he wanted select the right table so he made sure he was seated well before Hagai arrived. He'd managed to catch a few hours sleep at his hotel to minimise any jet lag so he could be alert for what could be a long evening. It was now nearly nine o'clock, a respectable time for dinner in Jerusalem. His guest arrived some twenty minutes later, giving him time to enjoy a glass of Kissmeyer and re-accustom himself to the unique ambiance that was Jerusalem in the evening.

They welcomed each other warmly and once they had both ordered and caught up with family matters, Chuck asked Hagai for his assessment of the country. Hagai paused, he knew the real reason for the meet. It wasn't an issue for him so he dived straight in whilst Chuck settled back to listen.

"On the one hand," he explained, "nothing has changed. The Israelis continue to hassle and shoot Palestinians, spreading their settlements on Palestinian land. On the other, Hamas continue to refuse to recognise Israel or demilitarise. The PA in Ramallah, run by Fatah, remains caught in the middle, refusing to fire rockets, but getting nothing from Israel in return. So Hamas conclude they would get nothing from Israel by disarming, so why bother? I suspect Likud is quite happy with the status quo, certainly now the US have their embassy in Jerusalem."

He paused again and took a another sip of his Domaine du Castel 2006. Hagai was keeping an eye on his friend for any reaction. As a true diplomat, there was none visible so far. So he continued.

"That's all the visible evidence. But there are more positive things happening under the radar. Since Trump put the US embassy here and the anniversary shootings across the Gaza border, there has definitely been an upsurge in peace activism. Even opinion polls in Israel show a growing distaste for such violence. Whether it will stay until the next election is a moot point. Netanyahu has been indicted but still continues as PM. How that works, I don't know. And of course, there was that sniper shooting of an old woman a week or so ago leading to the shooting of a Fatah leader at her funeral. That was just stupid."

Chuck listened quietly. Hagai was a little emboldened since there was little comeback from Chuck. So he continued asking and answering his own questions.

"International backlash against Israeli military policies? Maybe, but probably not, time will tell. Do the PA have any sense of strategy? Are they monitoring this peace space that is beginning to open up? Not a chance. In my humble opinion it won't last long, and it's not my place to advise them. They may have their own plans, but I doubt it. They've just been opportunists so far and even then, far behind the curve. No sense of thinking ahead or building for something."

Hagai paused as the starter course was brought. He also wanted to see what reaction Chuck had. He was building up to something, but still there was no reaction.

"I need to speak frankly." Chuck looked back at him with a mouthful of *Khyar Bi Laban,* still saying nothing. Hagai now looked serious.

"The US has never thought ahead either. Let's go back to the first Intifada. By and large it was a non violent protest against illegal occupation. And I speak as an Israeli. They kept it going for a hell of a long time, longer than I thought they could. Despite peace talking in Madrid and other places, our forces unfortunately were anything but peaceful. Good cop in Madrid. Bad cop here on the ground."

Chuck was still listening, although most of this he knew.

"Then a miracle happened for Israel on Thursday January 17th 1991. The Gulf Crisis. Saddam Hussein invaded Kuwait. US and the whole world took their eyes off the ball. Did you know that, to our shame, we took advantage. We used it as an excuse to impose an almost total curfew on millions of Palestinians. Those of us who knew what was going on protested. But the government played the national security card, and got away with it. Except for a few hours here and there, it lasted for well over forty days. And then to cap it all, Saddam sent a few missiles over to Israel and the dollars and support flooded it. The government could hardly believe it. They thought they could do no wrong and proceeded to do exactly what they wanted, and the Americans would go along with it… and you did!"

Hagai's voice was breaking with emotion. Chuck sensed there was more to come and waited. Hagai wagged his finger towards Chuck.

"Here was small defenceless Kuwait, invaded and occupied by a powerful neighbour illegally. You saw the injustice and you acted to defeat the oppressor and free the oppressed." Chuck didn't need to hear any more to get the point. The parallel with Palestine was clear. If only the Palestinians had oil, he thought. Hagai finished off.

"Then when Palestinian leaders pointed out the parallels, Kuwait objected and decided to throw out four hundred thousand of innocent Palestinian families from Kuwait. You couldn't make it up. That was all down to the good old US of A."

The starters had been cleared away and the mains was now being served. Both men were silent partly to eat their food and partly to give each other a break. After a couple of mouthfuls Hagai couldn't keep quiet.

"And do you know what your own Iraq Study Group said?" Chuck didn't answer. He presumed it was a rhetorical question, so he waited for the answer. Hagai gave him the answer.

"I quote, 'The United States will never achieve its goals in the Middle East unless it deals directly with the Arab-Israeli conflict.' Unfortunately, you have now ruled yourself out as any sort of trustworthy agent in the peace process. And there is no-one else. You have been shown to have double standards, and everyone knows it."

Chuck knew it all and, feeling a little embarrassed, tried a brave attempt to defend himself and his country's policies.

"There are many good people in the State Department who want to implement the two state solution, but right now I can't see it happening. Maybe it's now in the hands of moderates on both sides right here in Israel and Palestine. But I can assure you, that there are still influential individuals who would be able to give informal support, if it was acceptable. But formally, our hands are tied. We have to follow the policies of the President."

Hagai knew all this. "I'm an Israeli. I know it's important to keep relationships with all our friends. I don't want to see us at the mercy of our enemies, or bankrupt. I want peace and security, but the past is the past. We cannot resurrect it. Whatever happens now must be with new players and new ideas, where trust can be built. The old is forever broken and cannot be fixed. From where I sit, it is the UN which needs to be endowed with more power."

Chuck was playing with his food and shaking his head. "An empowered

United Nations able to enforce its resolutions? How? Never going to happen."

Hagai jumped in waving his fork. "And do you know who is stopping that? You. The US must abandon its unilateralism, even with so called 'coalitions'. It is the US which keeps the UN weak. You fear you won't get your own way and it restricts your freedom to act where and when you want."

Chuck shook his head and wiped his mouth with his napkin. He had to respond.

"The UN is not the answer. The Security Council is totally divided, and even on the resolutions which get passed unanimously, it would need its own military, to enforce such decisions. Blue helmet troops can only be reactive peace maintainers, and often not very good at that, witness Srebrenica. Imagine such troops going into a conflict zone in which a regional power was involved, maybe one that had a nuclear programme. I'm afraid moral authority doesn't count for much when you're faced with overwhelming military force. And these so called 'coalitions', as you call them, are real. These other nations are UN members and often progressive members of the Security Council."

Hagai was not to be satisfied. "But don't you see what you've done. With your two Iraq wars and your embassy move to Jerusalem, you have driven a deep wedge between the Middle East and the West. Your ambassador has even persuaded you to delete the word 'occupation' when you talk about the West Bank. You have created new animosities, exacerbated resentment and added fears that you intend to use the peoples of the region for your own proxy reasons. Russia is in Syria, you are in Israel. Maybe not boots on the ground, but your dollars are here; your culture is here; your arms are here. Everyone else, especially the Palestinians, are collateral elements to be dominated and exploited where possible."

Hagai paused to fill his mouth with more food, but continued talking as he was eating, such was his passion.

"My friend, you must see that this is not good for Israel in the long term. You have seen yourself as the only country entitled to use force anywhere in the world. Now you have decided just to pull out everywhere leaving a vacuum which you are trying to fill with meaningless treaties. The Russians are stepping in. And China is everywhere under the radar. And where will it lead?"

Hagai could see that all these body blows were impacting Chuck. Almost apologetically, he reaffirmed his love of America. "You are a great nation. Generous and well meaning mostly. But it's all gone wrong."

Chuck was a little uncomfortable, but thanked Hagai for his honesty. He had asked for it and got it. Hagai looked at his watch. They had eaten well, but he had hardly noticed it. Time had flown. He got up to leave, thanked his American host for the evening and the chance to talk. Chuck knew much of what Hagai had said was true and the rest, if not true, was what many in the Middle East thought. And governments acted on what they thought. He wondered how his briefings tomorrow would go. How much are we living in denial? Of course there's always another side to every position, but how far are we willing to consider positions other than our own?

With these thoughts, he settled the bill and made his way to his hotel. He had been alert during the meal, his mind pushing his body on. But suddenly he felt very weary and he had organised a liaison meeting for himself and the Senators with the Israeli Foreign & Defence Committee of the Knesset tomorrow. He was not looking forward to it.

14

MEDAD HAD BEEN working at the Knesset Research and Information Centre (RIC) for over three months and was liking it. It suited his temperament much more than being a soldier. He had been thrown in at the deep end, but his self confidence was high and there was clear motivation to succeed simply because if he couldn't, his internship would be quickly terminated. And there were plenty of people who would love the opportunity to replace him. He was working hard.

Iran had never been far from the Israeli government's thinking, whether it was the arming of its proxies in Lebanon and Gaza, or the nuclear threat that the regime posed. But the US, no doubt pressed by Israel, had now begun taking unilateral sanctions against the Iranian regime ostensibly to try and bring them to the negotiating table. European governments had been less enthusiastic about these moves but it was the US that counted. The Israeli government was very satisfied. However Israeli opposition parties had tabled a debate in the Knesset no doubt hoping to embarrass the government and the RIC had to produce background papers on the issue for Members of the Knesset (MKs) prior to the debate. Medad and two other colleagues were assigned to the task.

Ostensibly it was about Iran, but it would include relations with UAE and other Gulf states who had begun to normalise their relations with Israel. It was the beginnings of an anti-Iran coalition and the price had been merely a cessation of plans to annex parts of the West Bank and the supply of military hardware. No-one else in the world had agreed that the 'Deal of the Century' was a fair settlement but again, as far as Israel was concerned it was only the US that counted. If they would continue to support their state economically and militarily that was all that mattered. Israel had got used to being rejected by the rest of the world, including the UN. It didn't bother them. Similarly, the deal's rejection by the Palestinians and the whole Arab League was also a minor issue.

Medad had access to all these documents together with virtually all that had ever been produced by the government. On the one hand it was riveting reading but on the other, some documents were beginning to be challenging for him. What the Israeli public didn't know yet but would soon enough, was that a previous Israeli Energy Minister had been actively passing secret information to Iran. Gonen Segev would be sentenced to eleven years in prison after a plea bargain process.

But there was a wider question: how much further had Iran actually penetrated the Israeli establishment? Did anyone know? Was there about to be a load of dirty washing made public which would shake his country to the core? He stopped reading. He had to. All this background information needed to be assimilated and his head was spinning. Many of his beliefs about the integrity of Israel and the Israeli government were beginning to unravel. But there was no time to indulge himself in more background. He pulled himself away from the library and joined his two colleagues for a midday meeting on the ground floor of the RIC where they would start determining how they would approach the task.

The RIC was a purpose built modern building with the atmosphere of a library, because that was essentially what it was. Established at the turn of the century, it had the task of providing MKs with reliable and objective information relevant to any kind of parliamentary activity. The group divided out the tasks amongst themselves and got to work. The project had high visibility and they all wanted to do a thorough job. Careers could be made here.

Just as he got back to his desk his mobile rang. It was Shana. Just thought I'd ring. Medad could detect some excitement in her voice.

"Sounds like you have some news." Shana couldn't hold it in any longer. "I've been accepted for my university course, so I'm coming to Jerusalem."

Medad whooped quietly. "That's great. Why don't we think about maybe going on a trip before you start? Although I've only been at RIC for a short time, I'm entitled to two weeks holiday and it has to be in the next two months. And I've quite a lot of money saved up from my time in the IDF."

Shana was well up for it and said she had money as well. "Let's meet up tonight and make some decisions. I'll book a place." Medad happily agreed.

It was with gritty determination that Medad tried to put all that out of his mind and got back to working on the task in hand. He didn't want to let the team down. They had a lot of work to do if they were going to put together a non partisan paper ready for the upcoming debate. Not easy, but then it was not likely to change Israeli government policy. Clearly Israel's Prime Minister and the US President seemed to be at one on most things including Iran, but the RIC paper needed to tread a fine line between what was clear Israeli policy backed by the US, and how the rest of the world were likely to react including a possible new American administration. Israel knew that a change in the flavour of the US Presidency, which was always a possibility every four years, might bring a change of US policy towards Israel and the Middle East. Thus it was also important to keep the Europeans on-side as far as they could.

Medad was having understandable lapses of concentration as he allowed his mind to wander, thinking about an exotic holiday with Shana. What about Thailand? Maybe Australia and then New Zealand? Or go the other way, the US would be amazing. Florida had the sun, New York the sights, Los Angeles had Disneyland, Universal Studios and Venice Beach. San Francisco had the Golden Gate bridge and Alcatraz. How much could they do in two weeks?

He was rudely interrupted by his other colleagues who explained that they had just been reassigned. As Medad had done much of the research, would he carry on taking the lead and they would be happy to help and review? This was Medad's only project, and he saw his chance to make a mark, if only he could begin to concentrate! He swiftly put aside his personal situation and began compiling a comprehensive paper which summarised all sides of the debate, the possible consequences of various actions by the main players. Iran was warning of an 'historic remorse', and declaring that they had plans to respond to any move the US might make.

Hassan Rouhani had been reported as saying: "We will not negotiate with anyone about our weapons and defences, and we will make and store as many weapons, facilities and missiles as we need."

If they sold oil to China, could they carry on? What about selling it to Venezuela? They had lots of oil but couldn't get it out of the ground with US sanctions and everyone needed petroleum. Could Iran keep developing their missile programme? What about the widespread internal unrest in the country? Could Israel influence that? Could there be widespread implications if they did? What about the impact of taking out key Iranian personnel?

The due date for submission was approaching. Finally he was satisfied with it and submitted it at noon on the day required but by the end of the day he had heard nothing. Nor the next day. Nor the one after that. His confidence was beginning to ebb away, after doing what he thought was a great job. Was this how it was going to be? Were his bosses rewriting it, or ignoring it? Was it on a shelf somewhere gathering dust? He wanted to follow it through somehow. Then right at the end of the day Sarah, his immediate boss, called him to a meeting about the paper, which meant that she must have read it and wanted to talk about it.

All she said was, "The presentation is to be at two o'clock tomorrow and it will be to the Foreign and Defence Committee together with some American guests. Please make a copy available to the meeting secretary."

Medad walked out of her office rather bewildered and should have spent the evening going over the paper in detail, but that time was spoken for. He wanted to talk to Shana about their holiday so he biked over to Tel Aviv after work where Shana was staying with her parents. Instead of going to the house Shana asked to meet at Meir Park where they could walk and talk. Meir Park was situated in the centre of Tel Aviv and a great place to walk. It was named after Tel Aviv's first major, Meir Dizengoff, and was now home to the Tel Aviv Municipal LGBT Community Centre.

It was a lovely evening. Medad, feeling more secure in this relationship, took Shana's hand as they wandered round the lake but he wasn't going to push too hard, too fast. He was encouraged that she seemed as keen as him to take this trip, however, no final decision was taken, except the US seemed to be a good option. Not long now and she would be in Jerusalem on her course. Hallelujah!

Medad was up early next day and headed straight for the office where he spent all morning re-reading and inwardly digesting his report. He bounced a few questions and possible answers off those of his colleagues who had time to indulge him and at fifteen minutes before two o'clock, he gathered up his papers and began to make his way to Sarah's office. On arrival, she beckoned him to follow her. They went across to a Knesset Committee room and entered quietly. It didn't take long for him to realise that the American guests were US Senators and there was a black guy taking a lead in the questioning.

Discussion was well underway on the topic of so-called Palestinian terrorists and was there a 'shoot to kill' policy or not. And if so, who had authorised it. Medad and his boss, sat quietly on chairs at the back of the room, listening and trying to feel the atmosphere of the debate. It seemed to Medad as some sort of liaison session with the Americans. When the role of IDF snipers began to be discussed, he edged forward unconsciously, pricking up his ears, but keeping his mouth firmly shut. One or two of the Americans didn't seem happy with what they were hearing, the Israeli contingent, however, didn't seem particularly perturbed, probably understanding that their PM and the American President's relationship was much more important than any diplomatic exchange.

"Of course we don't target indiscriminately."

"Yes, there is full accountability."

"Our snipers are fully under control of senior officers."

"No, we don't target members of the press, Palestinian or otherwise."

"Yes, we do exercise considerable moral and ethical judgement."

"No, live rounds are only fired when our soldiers or the border is at risk."

Medad almost began to shake his head, when he quickly remembered where he was. He wished what the MKs were saying was correct, but he had himself seen things through the sights of his rifle, which he would carry with him for a long time to come. Unarmed people that he had been ordered to shoot, for example. He knew of snipers who had passed through the IDF before him, who were seriously disillusioned, some who suffered PTSD and some had taken refuge in alcohol and drugs; others had broken cover and written to newspapers, started blogs and joined peace organisations.

The Chair finally called a halt to that discussion and announced the meeting would move on to the Iran situation. He beckoned Medad forward. He looked at Sarah aghast as if to say, "me?" She motioned him to step forward to the front.

The Chair was already introducing him. "Our analyst will now summarise his paper on Iran in five minutes and then answer your questions."

It was clear that they all had a copy of his paper and had certainly read the summary if not most of the rest. Medad was listened to attentively by the Americans and, it seemed, courteously by his own side. The two hours of questioning and debate that followed was intense on all sides.

Finally he was released and walked back to his office exhausted. Some of his colleagues who had contributed to the paper were still at their desks. He gave them a quick thumbs-up before disappearing to a local bar for a drink. After the first drink, he decided it had gone pretty well and was silently congratulating himself, when he was joined at the bar by the black guy.

"Hi, I'm Chuck Rowlands."

15

AYSHAA HAD BEEN thinking about a trip to Dura, south-west of Hebron, for some time. This was where the office of ALLMEP was or used to be since there was also a Jerusalem address. Unfortunately, Ayshaa did not have a permit to go to Jerusalem and without such, would not be able to get through the military checkpoints. Jerusalem had a separate status and was outside the Oslo ABC land classification system. Every Palestinian who wanted to get into Jerusalem had to have a separate pass, which she would not get, so Dura it had to be. But there was no point in just setting out and hoping someone might be there. They might be travelling, in conferences or now completely based in Jerusalem. She had no way of knowing. Hani had an old Nokia which wasn't a smart phone and they didn't have a computer.

She knew she could start the conversation with the Women's March for Peace and her part in it, but then she would have to move quickly on and make her pitch. It had to be a professional approach from an organisation but she wasn't part of one. So she made one up. It was to be called BWP – Bethlehem Women for Peace. She explained the purpose to a few of her friends over a group lunch of hummus and bread whilst Rena was sleeping. To Ayshaa's surprise, they immediately got it and signed up.

One of them, Ethar, had done a basic IT course run by a community project for women, and had managed to get an old laptop from them. She offered to set up a few web pages and to make it look professional. Ayshaa suggested that Ethar checked out the ALLMEP site and make the web pages as complementary as possible without directly copying them. It would allow Ayshaa to talk about some of her ideas for positive action amongst the women of Bethlehem and about the possibility of BWP joining their organisation. Another friend, Israa, said she'd like to spread the word and recruit other women to the cause. Somebody else said they'd do the same. There was not a little excitement generated.

Ayshaa arrived back home late afternoon still quite excited. After making the evening meal and putting Rena to bed, she began to share what had happened that day with Hani. Ghalia was out visiting a friend, so they were on their own. She didn't want to blurt it all out to Hani, who she knew would not appreciate such an approach, so she had gathered her thoughts together, toned down some of the excitement and tried to be relatively objective in her explanations.

Hani listened carefully to everything she was saying, thinking about both short and long term implications. He had been surprised at Ayshaa's response to the Fatah approach a while ago. Now he was surprised again at the level of her strategic thinking. Once again he was looking at her through new eyes. He wanted to support her but he had concerns about her safety, her travelling, the baby, the household etc. etc. He didn't want to be the typical Palestinian man who insisted on keeping his wife at home, but on the other hand…

There was no doubting, he was impressed, even a little awed. "You will need your own phone and I think I can get my hands on another Nokia which will be good enough to make phone calls." Now unconsciously he began to put his hands through his hair and think ahead.

"You will also need funds. Are you going to ask people for a membership fee? I suppose it can't be much because your friends won't have much but will it be enough to cover the cost of travel and do what needs to be done? What about a bank account? You will need to select a few friends to be a committee and be accountable for money spent."

The questions and comments kept pouring out as he thought through what Ayshaa was trying to set up. He assured her that he would back her all the way.

"Are you going to try to get some of the more wealthy women in the main town involved? Who might do that? What about opposition? Where might that come from?"

Ayshaa listened patiently to this stream of thought which she knew would happen. She understood he needed to have some ownership of it and think it all through. There was no way she could do this if he was not fully behind it. When Hani had exhausted his questions, she acknowledged that she needed his help and no, she hadn't yet thought through all the implications.

She persuaded Hani that until there was some positive connection with

ALLMEP, further planning would be a waste of time. The immediate task was to phone them and see if she could visit in Dura. It would be a three and a half hour journey on three separate buses, the 231, 380 and 254, then a four mile walk at the other end. She had done her research. Ayshaa secretly hoped for a lift from the final bus stop to her destination, but was prepared to walk. In fact, if it came to it, she was prepared to walk the whole twenty-two miles. Hani was concerned at the distance and any military activity there might be along the way, but there was no stopping his wife now. Once she had her Nokia, she would make the call.

True to his word Hani procured another phone from Ramallah. This one was a Samsung smart phone for his use only, so he gave his Nokia to his wife after deleting all his contacts and messages. No sooner did Ayshaa have the phone than she started making good use of it. She rang ALLMEP, but no answer so left a message outlining who she was, what organisation she was from and saying she would call again in a day or so, hoping it sounded professional. The temptation to call back in an hour was real but knew that would be too pushy. It was a waiting game until either a return call or try again the following day. In the meantime, she got on with being a mother, wife and daughter-in-law but her head was buzzing with ideas and schemes.

She had to have some proposal to offer which would contribute to the objectives of the ALLMEP organisation, so she spent some time on Ethar's laptop reviewing their website. It was clear that this organisation had lots of experience in social change, education and activism. This was good, just what she wanted. Also, they were committed to building strong people-to-people Israeli-Palestinian relations, but as Ayshaa read further her heart began to sink. These were highly educated people with extensive international contacts. Their directors had been invited by multiple organisations to speak on a number of issues related to the Israeli-Palestinian conflict, and she was just a Palestinian housewife. Yes, she was reasonably intelligent but no formal qualifications, no car, no contacts, no standing. Her self confidence was taking a knock. What did she think she could possibly do?

The only element of the website that lifted her slightly was their focus on grass-roots Palestinian initiatives on women's empowerment. That was exactly what she wanted to focus on. She wanted to empower herself and the women of Bethlehem, especially those in the refugee camps surrounding the old city. The laptop was put away and she began to think of how the women in her circle could be empowered. As she talked with Ethar, her vision began to take shape.

Then one of those moments of connection happened which gave Ayshaa a real break. Ethar started looking for a magazine that she had been given. "Look, here it is. This is exactly what I think you're talking about," and she tossed it over to Ayshaa. It was from an organisation called the Bethlehem Christian Institute, or BCI which startled Ayshaa somewhat.

"But this is Christian! We can't use this. We're Muslims. How on earth did you get this? Does your husband know? They're only interested in converting us. They don't want to help Muslims!" Ayshaa sounded so aggressive that Ethar was taken back. She gulped as the tears began to form and Ayshaa immediately apologised and put her arms around Ethar. It took a few minutes for Ethar to calm down. She asked Ayshaa to have a look at the magazine before she made a final judgement. "If you don't want to pursue it, that's fine. It's your call."

Ayshaa stayed a little longer, being profoundly sorry for her reaction and wanting to make sure Ethar was recovered. She didn't want to lose her friend, so took the magazine home, promising to read it through before coming to a conclusion, but not sure whether sharing it with Hani would be a good idea. He might react even more strenuously and she might not be able to deal with that. As she thought about her own reaction, she felt even more ashamed of her behaviour.

She and Hani were in this together which meant that nothing should be hidden, but she determined that she would read this magazine first. If it was a non-starter, she would take it back and not mention it to her husband. If, on the other hand, there was something to learn, then she would alert him to the potential problem and then present it positively, hoping that he wouldn't have the same reaction as she. Laying in bed awake that night thinking about it all, she began to realise that this project was becoming all-consuming; Rena was taking a back seat in her thoughts and she hadn't really spoken with Ghalia for a few days. She sighed. *How on earth am I going to keep the right balance here?*

First thing after Hani had gone to the shop, Ayshaa sat down with Ghalia and tentatively shared some of the ideas that the group had talked about the previous day. She had decided not to mention either Hani's concerns or the BCI magazine to her until she had thoroughly vetted it herself. She wanted to hear a general reaction to her ideas before asking her mother-in-law if she could help with Rena from time to time. She needn't have worried. Ghalia was ahead of her. Her response was overwhelmingly positive, and yes, she could take more responsibility for the household, and for Rena, on days when Ayshaa was away. She just had to ask. Ghalia couldn't possibly have heard Hani's concerns but she knew her son and reassured Ayshaa that he would be positive, but that he would take a day or two to think it all through.

Ghalia graciously offered to take Rena out with her for a hour or two that morning giving Ayshaa some much needed free time. She settled down on the sofabed and read the magazine to find out a little more about BCI and its aims. It said that the aim of the magazine was to give women some ways that would contribute in moving toward a future with some positivity. *So far, so good,* Ayshaa thought.

She read on. *The vision to provide a voice to the voiceless in a male-dominant society.* It was started by a lady called Mariam to build up self-worth and enable Palestinian women to understand that they could be agents of change in their community. All of this sounded fine, but there were Christian bits, quotes from the Bible, that Ayshaa was very uncomfortable with. *It still sounds as if they wanted to convert us,* she ruminated. *Perhaps I need to meet this Mariam to see if there is any common ground. A meeting with her would add one to my number of contacts and would be a dry run for the main meeting down in Dura.*

She was now ready to talk to Hani.

16

WHILST AYSHAA WAS exploring her ideas, Hani was having clandestine meetings with one Fatah party official in particular. He seemed to appear out of nowhere at the shop, then disappear again. He was wanting to know what Hani's intentions were after the disastrous end to his first meeting. For his part, Hani was thinking hard because this was a big decision and he did not feel his local Fatah group were very responsive to his thoughts and ideas; in fact, he was concerned they might see him as the betrayer of the group.

The fact that his father had gone this route and had been well respected encouraged him, but there were a myriad of other considerations. For one, Israeli snipers tended to take a dim view of Fatah leaders and seemed to be able to take them out at will. He had a wife, a mother and a daughter to think about. Another key concern was finance – his finance. If he was going to do what Fatah were asking, he would need to give up the shop, so where was his income coming from? His ironmongery business was worthless. No big bucks from any sale.

He was assured that the group would trust him and there were funds that could pay him, even more than he was earning from his business. Hani looked doubtful. But on second thoughts, perhaps he should go with it, he could still keep the shop. He wouldn't need it to live off but that was not the point. The shop provided an explanation for his income and finding products gave him the excuse to travel throughout the West Bank. He could keep whatever incremental income he got from Fatah to maintain the rent and the appearance of employment and maybe use it as an office in the future.

It was explained to him that what he had said at the aborted Fatah meeting some weeks ago in Bethlehem had been heard in Ramallah, reported to higher levels and received favourably. He was invited to Ramallah to meet with officials who would make him an offer. He remembered his mother's words that there would be a price to pay whether you accepted or rejected these advances. Was he now too far in to walk away? Was he willing to pay the price of becoming a part of the Fatah machine, and what was the price anyway?

He didn't know, but both he and Ayshaa were now on an inexorable path, sometimes together, sometimes on their own, but pursuing the same goal. He shivered inside. Life was going to change radically.

Fatah, formerly the Palestinian National Liberation Movement, was a Palestinian nationalist political party and the largest faction of the multi-party Palestine Liberation Organization. Thus the President of the Palestinian Authority, Mahmoud Abbas, was a member of Fatah. It's two most important decision-making bodies were the Central Committee and the Revolutionary Council. The Central Committee was mainly an executive body, while the Revolutionary Council was the legislative body. Elections were held for both organisations, but it was a typically Middle Eastern political organisation in that the important things were agreed and implemented outside these formal arenas. Power was informal.

So the die was cast and Hani, instead of staying at the shop, put up the 'Closed' sign, got into the man's car and was driven to Ramallah, at least that's where his driver said they were going. There was no conversation on the journey, leaving Hani to wonder what on earth he was doing. The desert tarmacadam road ahead rippled in the heat of the day. As he looked out of the window en route, he found himself musing about the blanched landscape, the occasional Bedouin encampment and then in stark contrast brand new Israeli settlements being built in the scrub. Yes, he thought, they are making the desert bloom, but using our water.

"Water is life," he remembered someone saying, "Control one and you control the other." He couldn't disagree. Looking at the newly built Israeli houses, he saw that they were very western with gardens, grass and proper roads for their cars. By contrast, the few Palestinian villages they passed looking as if they belonged in a century earlier with no signs of life, no land to farm, no olive groves to tend. How did we get to this? He didn't begrudge people decent houses, but what he couldn't understand was the total obsession of the conquerors to persecute and humiliate the conquered.

The car swerved around a pothole. They were on Palestinian roads, not Israeli ones. Clinton and his (literal) road map! As they neared Ramallah, the road began to get better. Funny that. The car weaved through the city with something of an arrogance. After all, this vehicle was on PA business. Cynically, he wondered why there were no outriders. Even amongst the have-nots, there were still haves. Hani had never been to Ramallah and was open-mouthed at the new civic buildings which housed the Palestinian 'government'. Where has all this money come from and what on earth are people doing in those buildings?

The car was pulling up in front of a large modern building. Hani got out and followed his driver into the atrium. He felt like a rural peasant being taken into a modern city. His driver seemed to be, well, much more than a driver. People nodded respectfully whilst he just ignored them and made his way unopposed by security to the lift. Hani had never been in a lift before, and was desperately trying to look as if this was just normal for him. Of course, he did this sort of thing every day. The lift stopped at the third floor and they got out. Hani was shown to a row of chairs and left there.

He began to think of Ayshaa and her determination to do something for her community. Perhaps he should have discussed his decision to go to Ramallah but, he convinced himself, it wasn't yet a done deal. No point really. They had already agreed the direction of travel ahead for both of them and this meeting might not be what he was looking for. In reality though, his mind had been made up if the deal matched what had been floated back in his shop. There were key questions to be asked. He had to know what was on the table.

Hani was called into a room and invited to sit. It was none other than his driver behind the large desk. Hani stopped in his tracks. "Apologies. As you see, I'm not just a driver. I needed to get to know you."

Hani drew in his breath, wondering who on earth he had been speaking to these past weeks. He moved forward to sit in front of the desk as directed. Hani looked round, "You have a slightly better office than I do," he noted. Without responding, the PA official made his offer.

"We would like you to take charge of the Bethlehem zone. It was what your father did, until his untimely death."

No small talk then. Hani was a little surprised and it occurred to him that they probably knew a lot more about him than he had realised. He quickly recovered himself.

"What will that involve?"

"Well, we have many party members in that zone who can be your arms and legs among the people, but they will need guidance from time to time, especially if the Israelis decide to invade." Hani pushed his interviewer. "What kind of guidance are you talking about?"

"Leadership," the reply came back. Not much of a conversation here, thought Hani. But the official continued.

"Policy is made here in Ramallah, and although many think our actions are sporadic and uncoordinated, that really isn't the case. The job is to implement policy in your zone."

Hani had his list of questions which he methodically worked through. He was patiently listened to and each question answered, though not always as fully as he would have liked. But he felt there was a limit as to how far he could push. He detected some sort of parallel agenda underlying everything he was told which troubled him a little. He guessed that would become clear as he went on. So when he had exhausted his questions, he said yes he would.

"Excellent," was the reply.

The official was not one to waste words, but Hani admitted to himself, seemed to know what he was doing.

"We would also be grateful if you would come to the meetings here in Ramallah with other zone leaders to be part of the team." It wasn't a question or a request.

Of course Hani was willing to do that. Transport might be a problem he thought. But even as he thought it, the man said, "Arrangements will be made to pick you up." Hani realised that Fatah was not such a chaotic organisation as it seemed on the outside.

He was asked for his bank details and for his signature on an employment form. Goodness knows what he was actually signing, but no time to read it. If it was good enough for his father, it was good enough for him. The anonymous man was speaking again. He wanted Hani to know the fig leaf of democracy that existed.

"Obviously we have democratically elected people who help to make and agree policy. We just implement it. Now, there will be another meeting in

Bethlehem soon which I will organise to introduce you. You will recognise many from the last meeting. After that you will be responsible and your first task will be to find out how the Israelis knew of the last meeting and ensure that the leak is fixed."

They were both on their feet by now with little chance to ask further questions as he was shown to the door. His final words to Hani were that he was well thought of, and not to 'muck it up'.

Hani came out into bright sunshine relieved that it was over but still feeling way out of his depth. However, the decision had been made. It would be what it would be. He had to give it a go. Looking at his watch, there was some time before his lift back to Bethlehem, so he walked around Ramallah for an hour or so. He saw that all the nice new buildings had been funded by sympathetic overseas governments. There was a full gamut of ministries housed in the various buildings and wondered again what on earth went on inside since they really didn't have a country to govern. Arafat's tomb and the exhibition building behind it was next on his mini tour and he wondered what the great man would make of his legacy. Yes, he had made many mistakes. But it was not his fault that Rabin had been murdered and that Israel had jumped at the chance to ignore everything that had been agreed at Oslo.

The Americans were so foolish, he thought. Either Clinton really wanted to help but had no idea what was happening on the ground, or he couldn't care less as long as he got the votes he needed at home. So all the Israelis had to do was stall until another President came to power, then carry on with their plans as if nothing had been agreed. Easy. Yes, we Palestinians were stupid to react to Rabin's assassination with lots of terrorist attacks on Israel, but we all knew what Israel would do. In the light of that, there was no holding some of the radical factions back. But who's to say that talking would have done any better?

The principles of Oslo were sound. Arafat had actually done a good job. Obviously too good for some in Israel; resolving differences with words, not violence; two states for two peoples; negotiating a complete end of conflict. Yes, that was what Hani had hoped for, but now that was all gone. Well, perhaps not all gone, there had been some lasting gains. Not many it's true, but there had been some Israeli withdrawals and agreed areas of Palestinian self-rule. And there had been a long period of security cooperation and relative quiet.

He knew, though, that many thought that this was giving the Israelis too much. All the drawing of maps and borders was just cementing the status quo. It was a way Israel could bank all their gains until the next time they wanted more land. There was never any investment in peace itself, certainly as long as the Israeli military could do virtually what they liked, anywhere they liked, in the name of so called 'security'.

Leaders signed documents but that did nothing to build trust and partnership among their peoples. No wonder Hamas refused to be a part of it. But he, Hani, was now a part of the organisation which could not accept the Hamas strategy. It wasn't a strategy for peace, that was for sure. It was just a circle of violence which kept up the pretence of fighting the Zionist state, a fight they could never win.

Hani made his way back to where he would meet his ride home. As he was driven back, he pushed the past to the back of his mind and concentrated on the future. The immediate future would be to talk to Ayshaa and the next to attend the Bethlehem meeting which was in a week's time. Beyond that, he didn't know. Thinking about the men at the Bethlehem meeting he had briefly attended, he hoped they could be persuaded to think non-emotionally, otherwise he was not going to enjoy it. He hadn't led a group of men before; in fact he hadn't led any group before. He wasn't really a loner, but much of what he had done had been on his own, more out of necessity than choice. His father had been a self-made man and had preferred to get on with things himself, so father and son hadn't really worked together. He was going to have to learn it all as he went along. He hoped he wouldn't make many mistakes and 'muck it up'!

Ayshaa was home, giving Rena her food. His baby was now on solids, if you can call hummus a solid! But she chewed contently on pieces of bread. When Hani walked it, she immediately began to gurgle and smile. Hani smiled back and gave her a kiss on her forehead, then greeted Ayshaa. She looked anxious and a little tired. "We thought we would surprise you and come over to the shop today, but you weren't there?"

"Ah!" Hani almost automatically made a dismissive wave, then immediately regretted it. Why hadn't he been open with Ayshaa? *We were only at the beginning of this new life and already we're falling down.* He recovered.

"I have some news, good news. Let's talk as soon as Rena is in bed." Ayshaa didn't look at him. She nodded her head.

"Yes, well I have some news as well."

Hani looked at her and, perhaps for the first time, realised that this had actually already developed into a partnership of equals and those Palestinian male instincts and reactions had to be tamed otherwise their marriage wouldn't last. He disappeared into the bathroom ostensibly to wash, but also to gather himself together and break the competitive spirit that was rising up in him. He had to get a grip.

"I have an apology to make to you as well," It was Ayshaa taking the initiative and wanting to clear the decks. Hani looked up surprised. Rena was asleep in the corner and Ghalia was still out. Ayshaa went on to talk about the BCI leaflet, her immediate reaction and, now she had read it, what she was now going to do. It was an apology of sorts, but mostly a statement of action with no seeking of permission.

Hani noted it showing that he was not altogether happy with the way things were going, launching into some quite aggressive questions about how Ayshaa saw the link with BCI developing. Ayshaa tried to ignore the tone in Hani's voice and took the opportunity to explain about all she was thinking. When she was finished, Hani didn't comment, rather he told her about his meetings with Fatah officials at the shop and then the trip to Ramallah. She also asked questions about how Fatah saw the future; some Hani was able to answer, some not.

A quietness developed as each was absorbing what was happening to them. This was definitely not the normal Palestinian cultural pattern, and not how either of them were raised. Neither of them had any model for this. If their work took so much of their commitment that it weakened their relationship...

Later, as each lay in bed, thinking in the dark, both were privately wondering how this was going to work out. It could go either way.

17

CHUCK HAD COME straight over to Medad at the bar, held out his hand and introduced himself. An open-mouthed Medad shook it. The American settled himself on the next bar stool.

"What are you drinking? A beer? I'll have the same." He called to the barman, "and another one for my friend here."

It was just five o'clock and the bar had only just opened, so they had the place to themselves, but not for long because it was the usual watering hole for people who worked in the Knesset and the immediate governmental surroundings. Not, however, for MKs, for they had their own place. Popular not just because of its location, but because of the ambience. It had old stone walls and lots of old timbers giving it a log cabin look. There were tables opposite them and some sofas in one of the corners with candles liberally spread around. Wifi connection came as standard.

Chuck was looking around, giving Medad time to get himself together. "So how did you think it went?" Medad avoided his gaze and eventually gave a tentative reply.

"I think it was OK. What did you think?" Chuck didn't answer the question immediately while he took a pull on his beer. "I know you wrote the paper, but why do you think they asked you to present it?"

Medad wasn't expecting that question. He had assumed that his paper was a good one and merited being presented. Sensing there was another agenda going on, he stammered out some oblique answer which said nothing. He was waiting for the answer to come from the American. It wasn't long in coming.

"It was a good paper and you presented it well and answered all the questions we threw at you very competently. In fact, I was impressed which I think, was the object of the exercise." Medad's mind was racing. What was this guy saying? Was it a good paper or not? Had he been used? Was this Mr Rowlands trying to mess with him? Was he a friend or an enemy? And why was he here talking to me?

Medad now turned his face towards the American and suggested he ought to be a little more transparent and say what was on his mind. Chuck realised that Medad was relatively new to this kind of work and decided to comply. He paused.

"I meant what I said about the paper and your presentation. You may have a great career ahead of you." Medad latched on to the word, 'may'. Chuck chuckled.

"The big picture is this. Your government wants to keep us, the American government, on side and happy. They don't really mind what is said as long as we continue the support we give. But we are very well aware that Israel will do precisely what it wants to do. We know that not everything it says for our consumption is exactly what their policy is, or what will actually happen. You fulfilled your role perfectly, whether you were aware of it or not."

Medad was thinking fast. He was beginning to see the games that were being played. Chuck slapped him on the back and suggested they change the subject. Medad agreed and offered that he and Shana were thinking of coming to the US for a trip shortly.

Chuck was delighted. "Where are you thinking of going? It's a big place." Medad explained that they had not yet decided. So Chuck immediately jumped in and made them an offer.

"Hey, why don't you fly to Washington first. I'll meet you and you can stay with us for a couple of days, then fly off west, south, north, wherever." Suddenly the Stars and Stripes began to play out and Chuck took a call on his mobile.

"Your boss is on her way. I'll make myself scarce. Here's my card. Call me when you have some dates,"

And with that, he disappeared. Medad started wondering what he should say to his boss. He decided to play it cool and let her make the running. Sarah came through the door in her light blue trouser suit looking every inch the woman in charge. No need to scan the bar to find Medad. He was the only one there.

She walked over. "Not drowning your sorrows surely?" Medad shook his head. "I think they call it baptism by fire. Not a bad way to see what people are made of."

Medad looked at her. "And did I drown?"

Sarah laughed. "Not at all. Your paper was excellent as was your presentation. Our American friends were very happy."

Medad paused. "And was that the object of the exercise?" Sarah looked straight at Medad. "Of course. It's a game we play. They know it. We know it. It's called diplomacy. Wasn't it Oliver Herford who said that diplomacy is lying in state. Of course we don't lie; they want to know that their voice is being heard, and we give them that assurance."

Medad smiled trying to convey that, of course he knew this all along. He knew that Sarah must have taken a risk in projecting him forward, but it had clearly paid off and her happiness probably meant that her bosses were pleased how it had all worked out. So if she was happy, then he was happy. She patted him on the back, said she would see him tomorrow and disappeared.

It was now half past five, so he finished his second beer. He still reckoned he was perfectly able to ride his Kawasaki KLE, so he began to make his way over to Shana's place. He loved the power of this bike; only 500cc but with real acceleration and, more importantly to him, it could take a passenger. As he weaved his way through the streets to the student quarters again on the bike, he began to think about his future and how this current project might move him forward.

Then his mind turned to Shana. Because of his work and her moving from Tel Aviv to Jerusalem, the opportunity to take the trip before she started her studies had vanished. She lived at the Scopus Student Village complex at Rothberg with hundreds of other students. All had a single bedroom with air-conditioning and seemingly all mod cons. Although small, it was adequate for her. It had a bed, desk, chair, closet and free wi-fi, with shared kitchen and bathroom facilities. Since she had started her university course in Jerusalem, they tried to meet at least a couple of evenings for a meal at one of the student cafeterias. There were quite a few of these around the student blocks and Medad met her at the current favourite for the evening. It wasn't exactly fine dining, but it was affordable for both of them.

Medad had been living at home since leaving the IDF and commuting into Jerusalem. Shana had been in her University halls of residence only for a few weeks and he had visited her room only once thinking that maybe he could stay over some nights instead of biking back home. But her room was too small, perhaps it would suffice for the odd night here and there but no more, almost certainly a design necessity imposed on the architect by the university authorities. As an intern he wasn't earning enough to finance a place of his own and, although he had funds from his time in the IDF, he wanted to save as much of that as possible for their trip. The calculation was that before his bank balance was down to zero, he would have been promoted and have a decent salary which would allow him to live in or near Jerusalem. At least, that's what he had told his parents. His mother was particularly happy to still have him at home, even if it was only for a few hours each day. What Medad hadn't shared with them was his thought that maybe in Shana's second year, she could move out of Scopus and they could share a place.

They were in her room, he lounging on the bed, full of confidence and excitement. She was sitting on her chair at her desk finishing off some writing. He began to energetically outline his day to Shana; the presentation, the American, the feedback from Sarah and his thoughts of the future. He wasn't looking at his girlfriend but looking at the ceiling and re-living his experiences as he retold them. Shana turned round to listen but as he went on and on, her gracious listening turned to annoyance as he seemed totally taken up with himself and not at all interested in her day. She had been saving up lots to say about her course and in particular the module she was studying currently – The Emergence of the Modern State of Israel. When Medad had finally finished, she immediately began talking about Zionism, where it had come from and how it had influenced her country. The course traced the emergence of Zionism and the Israeli state from the late nineteenth century until today by looking at some of the foundational movements and moments in Israeli history. As with most Israelis, she wanted to understand why Zionists were so passionate about their land.

She had now turned her chair towards him and in lecture mode explained, "I can understand how this became such a strong element in our culture, after all, we have probably the most comprehensive written history of any people, and for centuries our land was consistently denied us. I know that some Jews never wanted to come back to this land. But until we retook the land, there was never a choice. Now there is."

Medad had been listening hard. Thoughts of his day had evaporated. He looked at her slightly alarmed. "Are you becoming a Zionist?" Shana shrugged. "Maybe. I don't know. I'm just learning." She turned back to her desk.

Medad was becoming concerned and expressed the hope the course was going to be objective rather than propagandist. Shana detected his disapproval and became a little more strident. "I think I know the difference between academic papers and propaganda."

Medad hurriedly tried to backtrack and calm troubled waters. "So what do you cover on the course?" Shana, still not giving ground, passed him a copy of the course outline to read.

Themes you'll explore include expressions of alienation and discrimination, the perceived ethnic gap, and schisms in Israeli society, including Jewish-Arab tensions. You will learn about the broad range of influences that have shaped Israeli society and politics: European, Ottoman, Middle Eastern, Jewish, and Palestinian.'

Medad tried to contribute rather than criticise. "I suppose one of the tensions we have at the moment which is shaping us is the tragic loss that many Israeli and Palestinian families have suffered. And neither side seems to recognise the pain of the other. Each side continues to believe the propaganda fed to them which demonises the other."

Medad was trying, but Shana wasn't interpreting his efforts in a positive light at all. She was upset and as he continued to dig himself into a hole, she began to get angry. But oblivious to her feelings, he ploughed on.

"I think any reconciliation is going to be really difficult to achieve, until most people meet a real person on the other side and understands them. There is a public brainwashing going on that has to stop, otherwise any attempt at peace will collapse. It just doesn't allow the prejudice on the ground to change."

Shana was listening in stony silence, but when she did speak, the gap in perception between them was all too apparent. "You're beginning to sound like a Palestinian, and I'm not sure Israelis have been brainwashed, or Palestinians for that matter. Attitudes reflect exactly what is happening on the ground. It is an historic gap between two peoples which will probably never be resolved. It is what it is."

Medad continued to push his argument further. He had now sat up on the bed facing her. "But don't you think that most Israeli and Palestinian families just want to live in peace, provide food on the table and see a safe future for their children?"

He continued. "If I remember correctly, opinion polls at the time of Oslo supported the two state solution. However, most doubted it would ever happen because each side believed they could never trust the other side. Our government in particular, was guilty of portraying the other side in caricature mode. 'Palestinians are all terrorists' was the insidious message. But they weren't and aren't."

Shana was shaking her head. "I thought you worked for the government. How can you be so critical of your own people?" She was staking out her independent thinking and certainly not wishing to budge just to please her boyfriend.

Medad was finally getting the message that he had to be a little more careful with his words. He realised that he was already pushing his own views too fast and too far for Shana, which wasn't a recipe for the future he had mapped out. He wanted a good relationship with her and after all, she was at university to explore all ideas. Medad admitted to himself that she was entitled to her views so he needed to stay cool. He tried to change the subject to the US trip, without letting on that Chuck Rowlands had invited them to Washington. At this moment, that might push her over the top. Nope, she didn't want to talk about it.

Silence had descended and there seemed little reason to prolong the discussion, if discussion it was. So he excused himself and made a quick exit hoping time would heal things, but he wasn't sure.

18

MARIAM HAD SHORT jet black curly hair, a winsome smile and, it transpired, three teenage children. With her family, her work with Palestinian women and a counsellor for BCI, she had her hands full but looked totally in command to Ayshaa. Although clearly well educated, she was open and welcoming which is what Ayshaa needed.

Ghalia was looking after Rena for the morning while Ayshaa got ready and went to her meeting. She had left home as well dressed as her wardrobe would allow. Her mother-in-law knew how important this was to Ayshaa, although she had her doubts about her working with a Christian Institute. It would not be what she would have done... but times were changing. Her time was nearly over and it was the young who needed to tread their own paths, and make their own mistakes.

Reminiscing was for the old and she could certainly do it with the rest of them. Ghalia firmly believed that it was vital to remember the past for memory was a great weapon. That's why all Palestinians continued to remember Nakba Day. This collective memory was an active process which Israel could never defeat. This was one area which Israel could never control although they certainly tried with the Nakba law which came into existence in March 2011. It authorised the Israeli Finance Ministry to carry out financial measures against any institution that commemorated Nakba Day.

The Jews themselves had maintained their collective memory for centuries and was probably the main thing that held them together throughout the centuries of persecution and oppression which they experienced across Europe. In Ghalia's opinion, the Palestinians must do the same, not just to learn from mistakes, but to build on what had gone before. Foundations couldn't be rebuilt by every generation, otherwise nothing would ever get finished. She felt her generation had laid the best foundations they could, given the circumstances they found themselves in. Of course there had been mistakes, every generation makes those. But what sort of building could Hani and Ayshaa's generation build? She didn't know.

Ghalia had determined that she would take Rena with her to one of her friends that morning. She didn't have that many friends left and those she did have, she wanted to keep. She anticipated that Ayshaa would be gone most of the morning and she wanted to set out early in the cool because she knew that she would have to return in the heat of the day. At last Ayshaa was ready to leave and Ghalia said she looked great. She wanted to build the confidence of the daughter-in-law because she could see how nervous she was.

The Palestinian housewife arrived in the BCI reception area a little before the agreed meeting time. It gave her an opportunity to assess the organisation; apparently a lot can be deduced from the reception area of an organisation. The receptionist was pleasant and offered her a drink while she waited. Ayshaa passed on the drink, preferring to wander around the spacious area, looking at the pictures of staff and the layout of the property along with the plans for a new extension. It seemed to her that BCI had a lot of money. She wondered where it came from. Overseas probably, she thought.

Mariam didn't keep her waiting long in reception, and soon they were both in an office upstairs sipping mint tea. "So what do you think of BCI, and please call me Mariam." Ayshaa was a bit nervous and Mariam was putting her at ease.

"It's much bigger than I thought, but then again, being a Muslim, I never really thought about it." Mariam picked up on the deliberate religious reference that Ayshaa had made.

"We work with anyone, Muslim, Christian, even Jewish. Yes, we are Christian, but our goal is to serve all the communities we operate in. Bethlehem is quite a mixed religious city and the last thing we want is for it to divide on religious lines. We are all Palestinians and we work together."

Ayshaa thought this was a positive start and as she looked at Mariam, Ayshaa outlined her organisation such as it was, explaining about the Women's March, how that had impacted her and what she wanted to achieve. It was quite a speech from someone who had never been in this situation before.

Mariam looked back at Ayshaa. "And you have done all this yourself?" Ayshaa nodded. "You are truly a leader in your community and to be congratulated. I would very much like to work with you, if that were possible?"

"I must ask one question first." Ayshaa was feeling a little uncomfortable. "Are you doing your women's work just to try and convert them from Islam to Christianity? Because if so, I cannot work with you. You must understand that this is critical."

Mariam took her time to answer. "I don't want to give you pat answers, so let me explain our vision, then you may decide whether you can work with us. Yes BCI is unashamedly Christian as you are unashamedly Muslim. Our students are from the Christian community who want to be trained to serve and encourage others. We are open about our faith, just as you are. If we are asked questions, we will answer them, but the Women's work is for all Palestinians and is separate from the Institute. I want to give every Palestinian women increased self worth and a positive identity."

Ayshaa liked most of what she heard and told Mariam so. "If we do work together, there will be many who will be suspicious of you. If any get the slightest impression that you are out to convert us, everything will collapse and we will have to press ahead on our own. Our husbands will see to that."

Mariam nodded. Ayshaa continued. "I think the next step will be for you to come and meet my team, if you can. They need to be in agreement before we can discuss any projects and move forward." Mariam nodded again. Ayshaa, now brimming with confidence, asked Mariam to call her with some possible dates and gave her mobile number.

With that, the meeting was over. Mariam came down to reception with Ayshaa and they rather awkwardly shook hands. They weren't at the hugs stage, yet. Ayshaa started walking back home thinking about what she had learnt and wondering whether such a partnership would ever work. She didn't want BWP to be strangled at birth by a needless religious upset.

When she got back, Ghalia and Rena were still out so she phoned Ethar and Israa. Ethar, who had given the magazine to Ayshaa, was relieved but didn't quite sound herself. Ayshaa made a note to call her back when she had spoken to Israa. When Israa answered the phone her voice was wobbly and sounded as if she was crying. Ayshaa was alarmed and said she'd be over immediately. She dropped everything and ran over to Israa's house, a good twenty minutes away. When she came through the door, she saw Israa with swollen lips, a bruised face and walking with a decided limp. "My God! What happened?"

Israa sat down and tried to explain between sobs. "Well, Adawi went to work as usual. He works in Jerusalem, you know." She paused and collected herself together. "Apparently the Israeli girl with the M16 at the checkpoint refused him entry."

Ayshaa knew what that meant. Israa continued, "He had the permit and has had no problem up to now, although some of his friends had been refused on previous occasions. He lost a day's pay, which we desperately need for food. He was embarrassed, ashamed and humiliated."

She paused between sobs. "He had the permit," she repeated, "I don't understand. But she wouldn't let him through and there's no appeal, you just have to accept it. It seems so random and spiteful. Maybe it's meant to be. Anyway, he was very angry, both against Israel and against women. When he got back I just happened to be in the wrong place at the wrong time."

At this Israa burst into tears. Ayshaa put her arms around her to comfort her. There was not much to say. It happened a lot to Palestinian women...and girls. It was a patriarchal society from top to bottom. The men had the power and some of them abused it. There was no law against it; a man could do what he liked in his own home.

Ayshaa gently asked Israa, "has Adawi done this before?"

"On occasions, yes."

"Have the children seen it?"

"Not directly, but it is sometimes difficult to hide the bruises."

Ayshaa thought. This is what Bethlehem Women for Peace must start addressing. Even as she thought this, she wondered about Hani and his reaction at the BCI magazine. Would he ever abuse her? She thought not. Did his father ever attack Ghalia? She didn't know. Maybe she would share Israa's story with Ghalia and see where it led. Her mother-in-law might even want to join BWP.

As Israa calmed down, Ayshaa decided to tell her about the meeting with Mariam at BCI, if only to take her mind off the beating. Israa seemed glad to set her mind to something different. She was not unintelligent, but she hadn't got any formal qualifications from school. She had been married quite young and she was quick to see the future possibilities that Ayshaa was talking about, but was understandably concerned about what Adawi would think, if he knew. Ayshaa was expecting this because Ethar had expressed the same reservation, so they all agreed to keep it to themselves until something was agreed. After all, it might not happen.

Just as Ayshaa was about to go, Israa let something slip. "You know about Ethar, don't you? Or rather Abdullah, her ten year-old?"

Ayshaa blinked. "No. I don't think so, I've only just spoken to her."

"Well, he's in an Israeli prison."

Ayshaa couldn't contain herself and shouted. "What!" She calmed down enough to ask. "Why, I don't understand."

Israa then told the story: he was with a group of older boys who had been throwing stones at the checkpoint after one of their fathers had been refused entry through the border. They had all run away and had thought they had escaped. But they must have had cameras and Abdullah was identified and taken away.

Ayshaa was reeling. This morning she had been talking to Mariam about the problems with women generally and, within a few hours, she found out that her closest friends had huge problems themselves that she had known nothing about.

Israa was still explaining. "There is a place where Ethar did get some help. It's called Ghu-sin Zay-tun, here in Bethlehem. It means Olive Branch. It would be worth you talking to Ethar about it."

"Yes, yes, I will." Ayshaa was furiously thinking. How much of this is going on of which I know nothing? As she made her way back home, her determination grew to do something about this. It wasn't just a community project anymore, it was about helping her friends and their friends and their friends. It had just got personal.

Ghalia was glad to see her back. Rena was playing up and the grandmother had no energy left. Ayshaa expressed her gratefulness to her mother-in-law who, in turn, wished that she had the energy to do more. Ayshaa recognised the tiredness in her voice and apologised for being away so long. She then took the opportunity to explain why she had been late and started telling her Israa's story. Ghalia had settled into the chair and was listening intently.

She closed her eyes and sighed. "Domestic violence is all around. It's all behind closed doors and it's no use asking, everyone will deny it. You just have to wait until the women open up. Of course, it might be too late then, but that's the way it is."

Ghalia's voice trailed off as she began thinking of past friends who had experienced the same kind of mistreatment. "It's a curse," she said, coming back to the present.

Ayshaa decided to bring Ghalia into the inner circle. "I want to do something about it. Have you heard of Bethlehem Christian Institute?"

Ghalia looked up quickly. "Yes, but they are Christian." Ayshaa showed Ghalia the magazine that had started it all off. "Please tell me what you think."

With that Ayshaa started preparing the evening meal. The conversation was over, but seeds had been planted. She would see how they grew before going any further. The next day Ayshaa had determined to talk to Ethar about Abdullah. She took Rena with her to give Ghalia a break. It was a good visit with Ethar opening up immediately. Her immediate shock and tears had now subsided and she told of how Abdullah had been arrested at night.

"Israeli troops banged on our door in the early hours yesterday and forcibly removed him. We had no idea where they were taking him or why. His hands were tied with plastic ties and he was blindfolded."

She broke down. "He's only ten," she wailed. "We don't know what's happened to him." For the second time in two days Ayshaa was putting her arms around a friend due to the Occupation. It took a good ten minutes for Ethar to regain some sort of equilibrium and to dry her eyes. Ayshaa had gone into her kitchen and fetched a drink. Ethar continued her story.

"But I found some things out about where he was when someone suggested I contact Ghu-sin Zay-tun. They made some enquiries for me and discovered that he was charged, found guilty and imprisoned. It was a military court so neither parents nor lawyers allowed, even if we could afford one. He was then promptly put in prison. We don't know for how long or for what he was charged. It may not happen often here in Bethlehem but they say that many children are subjected to interrogations, often accompanied by physical abuse."

Ethar broke down again. Ayshaa just held her and waited. "They said he may have signed a confession, but it would have been in Hebrew, so he would have no idea what he would have signed. The people at Ghu-sin Zay-tun said that detention of a minor inside Israel is in contravention of Article 76 of the Fourth Geneva Convention, but what good is that to me?"

Ayshaa asked about Ghu-sin Zay-tun. "Who are they and what do they do?" Ethar confessed that she had not heard of them before and suggested that Ayshaa might want to meet them.

"I saw a lady called Lara who was very nice. You know," said Ethar brightening up, "they might be another contact that might be useful for BWP." Ayshaa promised to follow this up.

Life is getting hectic, she thought, and I haven't even started yet. At this rate, I'll never get to Dura. No-one has called me back; maybe I don't need them to be involved right now.

19

HANI WASN'T LOOKING forward to his Bethlehem mens meeting, but it was tonight. So rather reluctantly after his evening meal, he set off. He had been told to be at another 'secret' location early. If he was going to lead this group, he knew he had to put his stamp on it immediately, there would be no second chances. Two men were outside the house, presumably security. He had a quick word and they were obviously expecting him which was encouraging. He expressed his sympathy for the guards who had been killed at the last meeting and asked if they knew them. They did.

"I'll see what can be done for their wives and families." Hani didn't know what Fatah's policy was but thought he could get something to cement his leadership.

The men nodded. "It's a chance we take. We know the risks." Hani shook their hands and said he would find out where the leak came from and fix it. The men obviously thought the extra money was worth it, though he guessed the wives and children might not agree.

"Any idea how the Israelis knew about their meeting?" They shrugged. They weren't regulars, yet. Hani was irked that it didn't seem to bother them.

He looked them over and, not seeing any bulges in their coats or anything in their hands, asked,

"How can you defend yourselves and us?"

The men offered their hands with a knife in each. Not much good against munitions, thought Hani. They're just look-outs really and, in fact, if they're standing outside this house, it's just telling the Israelis where we are. It was so obvious to him; he was angry that two men had been killed needlessly. Maybe there hadn't been a leak from the men, but perhaps just an Israeli drone taking pictures. Things needed to change.

"You might get a friend or two to keep a watch out further up and down this road to act as lookouts. Might save your lives." They said it was a good idea and promptly asked, "What about money for them?"

Hani said, "Up to you. You have the security money to share, so it all depends if you feel lucky!" He felt pleased that he had the opportunity to demonstrate leadership and exercise his authority at this early stage although the men looked rather disappointed.

Hani went on into the house. He didn't know whose it was, maybe no-one's, for again it looked quite empty. He got the chairs arranged how he wanted, and he didn't have to wait very long before men began to arrive. These were not people voted in, they were merely appointed as Hani himself was. The meeting hadn't yet started, but the shouting certainly had, so he made a mental note to get some women nominated by whoever did the nominations, because he felt they would listen more and shout less.

Hani had brought a hammer from his shop. He banged it on the table next to him with a crash. The table cracked, but he got silence and their attention.

"The first order of business is to discover who leaked the venue of our last meeting, and I will have only one person speaking at a time and I will indicate who will speak. Anyone disregarding this will leave the meeting."

They all looked at each other wondering if anyone was going to call him out. No-one did. After that the meeting went well, but no-one had any ideas about the leak, if there had been one. At the end of the meeting, as everyone was leaving Hani drew Fayad aside, as the oldest member. When they had the room to themselves, he offered Fayad his respect as if he were his father. This was important since the Palestinians have great respect for their elders. He then broached the subject of the leak. Fayad was non-committal, but indicated that he might be able to make some progress. That's how it was left until the next meeting in a month's time, unless there was an urgent necessity.

As he made his way home, Hani was generally happy but concerned about security. Lots of subjects discussed. Deliberately, he hadn't made his position clear on anything, just allowed everyone to speak in turn. He kept his own counsel for the most part. It seemed to be appreciated, and as a first meeting in charge, he hadn't made any enemies, at least none that he knew about yet. He had the contact details of each member and planned to have a series of get-to know-you sessions with each over the next month. He anticipated that they would all be in touch with each other anyway. He planned to say as little as possible, asking questions that drew the other out, so he could understand each person's position on the key issues.

It was two days later that a visitor arrived at the shop and asked when it was going to close. It was his erstwhile driver and interviewer. Hani was firm but respectful and greeted the boss, ignoring the question.

"So when are you going to close the shop?" The question came again.

"When I don't have time to open it," was Hani's reply. "Until then it will be my office." The man from Ramallah shrugged as he settled down on the single plastic chair that was in the shop. He wanted to discuss the meeting and any progress he should know about it. As Hani started to explain, some of his guest's reactions told him that details of the meeting and how he had handled it was already known. His conversation with Fayad and his planned individual meetings with other members was clearly not known but was received positively. Hani made a mental note; he needed to find out who the plant was in the group, and until he knew who was who, he would need to watch his step.

Hani hadn't had much time to talk to Ayshaa in the last few days. It was all getting very busy and missing each other was not to his liking. This evening, he had asked Ayshaa to put some time aside to catch up. In particular, he wanted to know what she intended to do with BCI, since he thought if she went ahead, it might have an adverse effect on his leadership of the group. The men, all Muslims, might not like the association with a Christian Institute.

When finally they got some time to themselves, both were a little hesitant after their last conversation. Hani was sat on the chair with a drink and she perched on the sofabed. Hani felt he needed to take the lead and clear the air.

"I think we have to be more open and honest if we're both going get through all this. We haven't really started on this journey yet and already barriers are going up between us which I don't want to happen. Can't we just share what we're thinking and doing with each other?"

Ayshaa tucked her feet under her body in a defensive posture. She didn't know how Hani was going to be, whether considerate and thoughtful or masculine and bossy. So she started hesitantly.

"I feel the same way you do, but sometimes there are ideas, thoughts which are kind of confidential with the people each of us is working with. I'm sure you have some things on the go with the men which would be inappropriate to share with me."

Hani looked a little sheepish. "I suppose so. But if there's anything which will affect the other, then we ought to share that."

Ayshaa agreed. Knowing that there was one particular issue that concerned her husband, she spoke up. "So I suppose you want to know about BCI?"

Hani nodded. "If you start working with them in your work amongst the women, the men will definitely know, because their women will have to tell them."

Ayshaa countered. "Well, we haven't decided. If we do, it will be because they are the best people to partner with to achieve what we want to achieve and, in any case, we won't do it officially with BCI, but just use one of their team." She pulled her feet out from underneath her and continued with a bit more confidence.

"I think you would need to tell the men first and encourage them to support BWP which is only going to help their wives and families. Then make it very clear that religion is not part of our programme and that we must all work with everyone, Muslim or Christian. We are all Palestinians and we are all under Occupation."

Hani thought about it. "I'm not sure that will work, but let's wait until you decide you're going to use them." He thought this might be the right time to broach the subject of women and the 'mens' meeting.

"Actually, I was thinking that I want some women in amongst the team anyway. Fatah have set a 20% participation for women in political positions, so I don't see why the Bethlehem branch should be any different. It will be a hard sell and it's not the first thing I want to do. It will have to wait until the right time, which is not now."

Hani was thinking fast now. "Actually, it might be a good move to have you come to a meeting soon to outline what you have in mind for BWP. You'll have to prepare well though." Ayshaa, taken a bit by surprise, just nodded and they left that subject there for the moment.

She started talking about Ghu-sin Zay-tun, what they did for Israa and that she was going to check them out whether they would be partners with BWP. Without waiting for Hani to comment on that she went straight on to ask Hani about the men's meeting. Hani outlined it as honestly as he could and said,

"My first task is to find out if there was a leak and if so where it came from. It cost the lives of the two security guards and I need to do it before the next meeting. That would be stabilising both for the group and my leadership."

The discussion went on for quite a while, covering quite a lot of subjects including what the future might hold. Few decisions were taken but both felt a little better. When they finally got to bed, it was almost as colleagues rather than as man and wife. Ayshaa on the inside of the sofabed went straight to sleep. Hani, on the other hand was on the outside of the sofabed thinking hard; perhaps that's how it has to be… perhaps that's the cost…perhaps… thoughts soon merged into a dark dream about the killing of the Fatah official at the funeral and him pumping his chest.

The next morning while at the shop, he had a call from Kamel. "I have fixed it." Hani was still thinking over last nights conversation with Ayshaa. "Fixed what?"

"The leak." said Kamel. Hani was now fully alert. He knew what that meant and he wanted to know every detail. "Tell me." Kamel was never one for much conversation. "No need. I have fixed it." Kamel was also a man of secrecy but Hani was insistent.

"Ramallah will need to know and I need to know." Hani waited for the detail. There was a pause on the line, then the explanation.

"One of the men has a boy in prison in Israel. He was interrogated and admitted that he followed his father a few times when the father disappeared from the house in the evening, just to see where he went. We can't blame him or the father."

Hani was relieved and angry; relieved that it wasn't more serious and angry that the Israelis would torture a boy which had caused the lives of both their security men. Kamel continued. "Did you know every year between 500-700 Palestinian children, some as young as 12, are detained and prosecuted in the Israeli military court system."

Hani didn't know. "Also," continued Kamel, "the father wants to know if you want him to step down." Hani asked who it was. "Zeyad," came the reply.

He was quite an influential member and Hani saw an opportunity. "I want to meet him." He also asked Kamel whether any other men had boys in prison. He said no. The meeting was arranged for later that day, so Hani closed the shop early. He didn't want to be late home every night.

On his way he noticed that IDF forces were still active in and around Bethlehem. He saw a group of six heavily armed soldiers challenging an elderly woman who was selling chocolates to those going to the mosque. As they pushed her, several men tried to come to her rescue, but were driven off by the soldiers as they sought to arrest the woman. For a moment it all looked very ugly and the soldiers began to brandish their weaponry. Eventually they got their way and the woman was marched off, with locals looking on despondently.

Hani scowled. He was desperate to get involved and try to rescue the woman but knew he had to remain anonymous. There were bigger things at stake, he couldn't afford to be arrested. And yet, what's bigger than defending an old lady against abuse? His conscience was severely bothering him. He tried to defend his own actions with that game-changing word 'strategic'. No, he couldn't afford to get involved in a single tactical incident when the strategic was at stake. As he strode on his conscience wouldn't allow him any peace, but he forced his mind to overrule it.

He also knew that this kind of behaviour was usually a ploy by the IDF to provoke a more serious incident giving them the reason they needed to call in reinforcements and really get stuck into the the Palestinian population. He didn't know if this was the result of orders from further up the chain of command or whether groups of IDF troops were just doing their own thing... for fun. Sadly, it was not unusual behaviour and seemed to happen all over the Occupied Territories, part of the attempt to demoralise the population and get them to leave.

With many misgivings, Hani skirted the trouble, trying to avoid being recognised by any of the locals and carried on to meet his man. Zeyad was understandably downcast, nervous and seemingly unable to meet Hani's eyes. He was expecting a real bollocking, but instead Hani put him at ease and reassured him that no-one else need know. He would inform Ramallah and the Bethlehem group that the problem was fixed – no names needed. Bethlehem's Fatah leader didn't even have to ask for loyalty, the man was so grateful. He also explained that he might know someone who might be able to help his son, thinking of Israa's story with Ghu-sin Zay-tun, and said he would be back in touch. Here was also an opportunity to get Ayshaa's BWP known to the group and maybe pave the way for a few women to get appointed. He made a mental note to talk to Ramallah next time he was there, or maybe the 'driver' who called at the shop.

On his way back home he passed a play area bought and kitted out by some European government. He couldn't see which. Five boys were playing football and one of them seemed quite good to Hani. He wondered what chance the boy would get to hone his skills and play for the national football team of Palestine. It was true that in the past few years, the Palestinian team had witnessed remarkable development thanks to coaches Jamal Mahmoud and Abdel Nasser Barakat. Still not winning many matches though.

He remembered the tragic story of Mahmoud Salah, a 15-year-old Palestinian boy, full of life and playing football with his friends in al-Khader town in Bethlehem. The ball had crossed the wire near an Israeli military checkpoint and the youngster had gone to retrieve it. They had opened fire on him and a bullet had ripped through his left leg. He was arrested by Israeli forces and was moved to a hospital for treatment. After a three-day coma, Salah woke up to find his left leg amputated. No more football.

It was these needless incidents that helped to drive Hani on. He made a detour via Manger Square because that's where the nearest cash machine was. He didn't want cash, but thought he would check whether Ramallah had put anything into his account. As he stood there waiting for two American tourists to finish talking and draw out their cash, he recalled the assault on Manger Square in 2002. They said you could still see bullet holes around the entrance to the Church of the Nativity. He was much younger then, but he remembered Israeli warplanes, tanks and infantry launching a huge attack on Bethlehem. His father had been incandescent. Maybe that was what triggered his involvement with Fatah. Of course, Israel's prime minister then had been

Ariel Sharon and Hani didn't think Israel could get away with that now, but you never knew.

They had all been woken up in the early hours as Israeli helicopter gunships fired missiles into targets around Manger Square and the Church of the Nativity. Over the next few days, there had been the continual low rumble of tanks and armoured personnel carriers fanning out around the town from Beit Jala, and from the direction of Rachel's Tomb, close to the Jerusalem city limits. Then came the bulldozers, which were lined in rows blocking the main entrance to Bethlehem. He remembered they hadn't any water or electricity for days and his father could not get to the shop – not that there would be any customers. Apparently, a nun had been shot and several other innocents who were trying to protect their premises and belongings.

He continued to wait in line until finally the American tourists had done their talking and got their shekels. Hani got a mini print out of his bank statement and saw, with astonishment, how much they had put in. It was a lot more than he had been expecting. He began to feel he'd been bought, and Fatah would be expecting a significant return on their money.

20

CHUCK ROWLANDS GOT back to the US both concerned and comforted; concerned because he knew the Israeli game that was being played and could do nothing about it, and comforted because in Medad he thought he might have found a rising star with whom he could work and whom he could influence. Not immediately he knew, but seeds had to be sown and he felt he had planted some good ones.

He reported back to his bosses on both counts. The State Department was nothing if not pragmatic. They were diplomats, after all. They knew the game. His report to them was comprehensive and he was upfront with them about Medad, but neglected to mention the possibility of him and his fiancée (or was it just his girlfriend? He couldn't remember.) coming over to the US for a trip at his invitation. He did however, mention it in passing to his wife, who was just glad to have him back, as were the kids who gave him a smothering welcome. He was a lucky man to be so secure in his relationships at home.

Medad, on the other hand, wasn't as secure as he had thought he was. The assumption that Shana would share his points of view and not have differing, conflicting opinions had proved to be seriously misplaced. Thinking about that now he was slightly ashamed, but also a little disturbed at the thought of lots of arguments with her about Zionism, Palestinians, peace and all the things he had already worked out in his mind. Was that male chauvinism on his part? He considered it. Well, if we're going to live together, go on trips together, then there had to be a level of agreement, didn't there? Exactly what level that was eluded him for the moment, but perhaps it would all sort itself out or perhaps not.

He was day dreaming in the office about the Shana situation when his desk phone rang and Sarah, his boss, asked him to come through. She asked him to take a seat which was a first and he began to wonder if this was it; his internship about to come to a shuddering halt and he was going to be out on his ear. How humiliating. What would his parents say? He wouldn't tell them. What would he say to Shana? He'd have to tell her. More humiliation. He would just have to try and get another internship. Couldn't be that hard. He now knew quite a few people. Yes, he'd be fine.

Sarah was speaking and he had missed what she was saying. He apologised. She was asking how would he like to take a job with the civil service.

"It would be a proper job, not an internship. Specifically, in the Political Affairs Directorate within the Foreign Ministry. The Head of Political Affairs reports directly to the Director General but also has access to the Minister, so it would be quite influential."

Medad's mind was racing. Sarah was looking at him rather confused. "Apparently you made quite an impression the other day and they would like to you to be transferred. You'd be working for the Head of the Middle East and Peace Process Division."

Medad was reduced to stuttering. Sarah was looking at him, her eyebrows raised. "You're not interested?"

Quickly recovering, Medad stammered out, "No. No. I am. It's just a surprise, that's all." Medad had researched the Ministry of Foreign Affairs early on in his search for an internship. He knew it was one of the most important ministries in the Israeli government, implementing Israel's foreign policy, and promoting economic, cultural, and scientific relations with other countries. He knew there were normally intelligence and psychological exams that had to be passed, like the Psychotechni Exam. He asked Sarah about these. She suggested he make an appointment to talk with Dan at the Ministry, who would be his boss.

The interview or was it a meeting, was to be later that same day so no time to prepare. He just had to go as he was and be as he was. Dan turned out to be a 39 year old, who Medad recognised from the session with the Americans. He was a slim man already losing his hair, but instead of having a 'comb-over' had shaved it all off. His dark eyes were sizing up Medad.

"You did a good job with the Americans. I think we were all impressed. You have good analytical skills."

Medad nodded, not really knowing what to say. Dan continued, "normally, the process to be accepted to a job in government can take several months. Also *protexia* (having connections/ knowing the right people) is the key to being considered for the majority of positions." Medad was nodding again. He knew all this.

"But often, as you may know, many of our positions are filled before they are officially announced or posted publicly (*Michraz Tafur*). This could be one of those occasions. I have a position and you have already proved your calibre."

Dan looked at Medad a little closer now, "I understand you were also an IDF sniper and quite a good one, so they tell me?" Medad was still nodding unable to say much.

The boss got up and moved around his desk, "so, you will be working in the Palestinian Affairs Department, and I need to know today if you will take the position."

Medad thought that it was time to speak and that decisiveness was the most important quality to exhibit at this moment and said, "Yes, with pleasure."

Dan came over to him with congratulations, offered a handshake and said that all details would be emailed over to him with a starting date in three days time, after *Shabbat*. And that was it. Medad left the office in rather a daze, but felt he should go straight back to the RIC to let Sarah know what he was going to do. She wasn't there, so he left her a resignation message thanking her for his time there. He then collected his personal bits from his desk and said goodbye to his colleagues, who shook his hand seemingly already in the know. His parents, even his brother seemed pleased when he phoned home.

Shana, however, seemed off hand and not at all interested. I've blown it, Medad thought, but he was completely at a loss to know what to do or say to improve the relationship. It seemed that she was so totally immersed in her course and absorbing the history of the nation of Israel that he had become a side-show. He felt bereft and lonely again. A trip to the US together seemed scuppered let alone the prospect of living together somehow in Jerusalem. He decided to let things lie for a bit and see if she would call him. In the meantime he had a new job to get to grips with, and he didn't want to fail at that. He thought he had finally found his niche.

So had Shana. She was learning things she had never known, or if she had known, had not taken any notice of. Of course she knew about the biblical origins, but her family had never been religious and so she hadn't really been interested. Neither had the centuries of humiliation in various European countries attracted her attention. There was just one man whose politics had caught her attention and she was now fascinated by his ideas.

Theodor Herzl. Born May 2, 1860 in Budapest, it was he who founded what became known as political Zionism, a movement to establish a Jewish homeland. Shana had not heard of him before. Apparently, he wrote a pamphlet called '*The Jewish State*', and had organised a world congress of Zionists to meet in Basel, Switzerland in 1897 which failed to get much international support. He then became first president of the World Zionist Organisation, again which she had never heard of, but died more than forty years before the establishment of the State of Israel.

Shana began to realise for the first time that this was her history. Some of these facts she remembered from school days, but they had not meant much to her then. Her family never spoke of such things and, she suspected, would not approve of her interest. Nevertheless, she was at university and she could do as she liked. No-one, not even Medad, was going to interfere. This is what she had come to university for, even if he hadn't bothered.

Now Chaim Weizmann was a name she had heard of and it was he, she recalled, who started the influx of Jews to Palestine, which at the time was ruled by the Ottomans. World War 1 changed everything and Britain became the major player to do business with. The Zionists had persuaded James Balfour to issue his famous (or infamous) declaration but Britain, in an effort to summon all forces to defeat Germany, had typically made conflicting wartime promises to the Arabs and the French who had interests in Lebanon and Egypt. All very messy.

She was in her room, at her desk, with only her desk light on. She looked at her watch and saw she had been reading solidly for three hours and it was now ten o'clock. She sat back in her chair and thought about it all. To her mind, it was all amazing, almost like the Wild West in America. Exciting. Exhilarating. She felt part of it, made herself a drink and decided to do another couple of hours reading.

While the Jewish Haganah were trying to bring in Jews into Palestine by any means they could under the noses of the British, local Arab leaders who were violently opposed any Jewish state also objected and began creating serious disorder culminating in the Arab Revolt of 1936-39. The British navy had a blockade in the Eastern Mediterranean attempting to stop Jews from entering Palestine. It seemed the British were being squeezed by both sides by the Jews and the Arabs. Those Jews they captured were taken to camps in Cyprus but many were not detected and got through the blockade.

Shana was silently cheering. It was a game of cat and mouse which she knew they would win. Many Haganah leaders became senior political leaders later: Yigal Allon, Moshe Dayan, Yitzhak Rabin, Menachem Begin and Yitzhak Shamir. Amazing men. Shana was in awe. She had not realised how difficult it had been to establish the State of Israel and wondered how many of her generation really appreciated this.

But Shana was nothing if not a feminist, so where were the women in all this? Were there any? She researched and found Rosa Welt-Straus, a trade unionist, who was appointed as leader of the first women's union in 1919. And of course, Israel was the third country in the world to be led by a women prime minister, Golda Meir, but that was back in 1969. So where were other women? It was now approaching midnight and her yawning persuaded her to stop and get to bed. She was feeling satisfied somehow. It was right. They needed a country, and now they had one, and she was glad.

Shana was beginning to discover her interests and passions, and maybe the subject of her thesis which she was going to do later in her course. The next morning she was happy and went off to lectures as normal. As she walked to the main teaching area, she saw other girls arm in arm with their boyfriends and began to think of Medad. She certainly liked him; not sure if she loved him and not sure if Medad really loved her, but they could be good friends. Would it progress from there? Might depend on how much they had in common by the end of the year.

As far as she was concerned, the jury was still out!

21

GHALIA KNEW THAT Christian communities suffered just as much as Muslim communities on the West Bank. But she was a traditional Palestinian lady and a Muslim. Whilst there were far fewer Christians than Muslims on the West Bank, they all had a common problem, Israel. It was true that the men mostly kept themselves to themselves within a Muslim context, the women... well, they tended to be little freer if the men were not involved. She did know some Christian women neighbours but they were acquaintances rather than friends. She also knew many, who had been part of the Christian community, but had left the country because they had family elsewhere and could. She couldn't. There was no sense of blame; who would want to stay under Occupation if they could get out?

Israel treated both Christian and Muslim Palestinians the same. Back in 2015 the Israeli High Court reversed a previous decision to halt work on one section of the Wall which would have separated the mostly Christian-populated Beit Jala and the Cremisan Valley near Bethlehem. It would have also separated the Cremisan monastery from its sister convent and school. Ghalia remembered that immediately the ruling had been changed, Israeli forces hastily uprooted dozens of olive trees belonging to the Christian Palestinians. Their land had been completely levelled with no consultation as part of plans to resume the construction of the Wall close to the illegal Israeli Har Gilo settlement.

Palestinian Muslims had fared no better, even before 1948. Ghalia recalled her grandfather talking about life under the Ottomans. With wealthy Arab landlords living in Egypt, and Bedouin tribes raiding whenever they could, Palestinian life could involve suffering even then, before Zionism impacted them. They were always the tail and never the head. If Ghalia had no respect for Israel, she certainly had no respect for the other Arab nations. It seemed to her that their lack of aid to the Palestinians was a deliberate ploy to keep a running sore for the Israelis and a stick to beat the UN with.

She looked at this magazine from BCI again not knowing quite what to make of it, but she needed to think about it before Ayshaa got home that evening. It was certainly well produced and was full of nice words, but her instincts were that it was better to work within your own religious community. Trust was the key to working together, and it would take a lot for trust between Muslims and Christians to be developed. On the other hand, she mused, there wasn't much trust even between some Muslims. Perhaps the future was to work across community lines and maybe they would all be stronger if they did. She didn't think that the Imams would like it, but then they didn't help much either. It all came down to personal relationships, she concluded. If trust could be built between individuals, that could then multiply and infect a community. But what took years to build, could come crashing down in an instant. She had seen that before.

Ayshaa arrived breathless and apologetic. Ghalia had been looking after Rena for most for the day. Although she didn't complain, her grand-daughter was certainly glad to see her mother. Rena was beginning to toddle around the rooms they rented, though not allowed outside just yet. That meant she was staying up a little longer and had fewer sleeps. More child-adult time required and less adult-adult time therefore. After all, thought Ayshaa, she must be my top priority. We're doing this for her and her generation. It would be tragic if in doing this we were to gain political and community breakthroughs, only to lose the child we were doing it for.

Whilst Rena was playing with some toys culled from a local charity, Ayshaa asked Ghalia what she thought of the BCI magazine. She hesitated trying to think of the right words and avoid an emotional response, but voicing the issues as she saw them.

Ayshaa noticed her reluctance and so decided to jump in and see how Ghalia responded. "They are doing the same work that we want to do and as long as there's no hidden agenda to try to convert us, I think we could begin to explore some things." There, she had said it.

Ghalia said she understood, but warned that Muslim-Christian relation-ships were always on the edge. She reminded Ayshaa that the percentage of Christians in the West Bank and Gaza was only about 2% it was said. In Beth-lehem, she conceded, because of its special place in the Christian narrative, the percentage was over 40%, so it might be easier here than elsewhere.

She sighed. "I can remember my parents saying that in our villages Christian and Muslim worked side by side before 1948. Most of those villages, over five hundred, have now been flattened. But it is true that Palestinian Christians have been an integral part of the Arab Palestinian culture and civilization."

Ayshaa was encouraged to continue building her case. She knew that in the current Palestinian Legislative Council in Ramallah, Palestinian Christians held more or less 8% of the seats, far more than their percentage of the overall population.

Ghalia confirmed this. "Of course," she said, "Some Muslims objected and saw that as undemocratic, but were never able to change it. Then there were the Samaritans who numbered only about three hundred and twenty persons, but had one seat on the Council which also caused some resentment. But Christian holidays such as Christmas and Easter were still widely observed throughout Palestine, and people from both religions visited each other during religious festivals. In Jerusalem, schools run by Christian churches have a majority Muslim student population. They don't try to convert them."

Ayshaa decided to keep quiet and let Ghalia say all she wanted to say. So she continued in the same vein.

"Some of the Christian women I know are very embarrassed by the fact that many of their fellow Christians in Europe and North America are taught to have an unquestioning support for Israel. Mostly evangelicals and fundamentalists, it's true. They have ignored the impact that the Occupation has had on our people."

She now looked directly at Ayshaa. "I understand from the BCI magazine that they are evangelicals?"

Ayshaa admitted it and said she was not wholly comfortable, but she would have to have assurances on that score. Ghalia cautioned her to go step by step, but also conceded that there were as many Christian Palestinian women who needed help as their Muslim neighbours, and there were lots of both in Bethlehem.

Rena had finished playing and was tugging at Ayshaa's clothes. Food was needed and Ayshaa disappeared to the other end of the living room where the kitchen was to prepare the evening meal, but continued to think. Hani arrived home shortly afterwards and privately showed Ayshaa the mini bank statement with the Fatah payment in it. She gasped. She had never seen such an amount in their account. What does it mean?

Hani responded, "I might have sold my soul. Remember what mother said about it being a one-way journey, or something like that. I have to make it work, because there's no going back now."

Later that evening, when Rena had been put to bed and Ghalia had also retired, Ayshaa talked to him about the Christian-Muslim issue which she had been discussing with his mother. Hani told her of examples of good co-existence between the two communities that he knew, even in Gaza.

"Apparently, there was a school in Gaza part funded by the Catholics which had more than twelve hundred students, a thousand of which were Muslim. The priest there, I think a Father Emanuel, says he wasn't preaching Christianity as such but rather spreading the light of knowledge in Palestine. Not entirely sure what that means. Anyway, he says he is first an Arab, then a Palestinian, and then a Christian."

Ayshaa was looking rather perplexed, "No, I'm not sure either." Hani thought some more. "I think I also heard my father say once that on one Christmas Eve several Hamas officials dressed up as Santa Claus and distributed presents to Christian children in Bethlehem!"

Ayshaa stared at him. "I have never heard that before. It sounds like a fairy tale." But Ghalia had come into the living area for some water from the kitchen, and had having heard Hani, confirmed it.

"Yes, that was in 2003. There was a lot of tolerance and respect between the two communities then. Maybe still is. Back even further in 1990, Hamas issued Declaration number 67, cancelling a general strike which coincided with the religious Christmas holidays, but that was a long time ago, and I'm not sure that would happen today. But they have always demonstrated respect for Christmas religious festivities, as long as it was under the umbrella of Islam."

Ghalia disappeared, leaving Hani and Ayshaa to continue discussing what each were doing next. Hani had his second meeting with the men shortly, at which he was going to challenge them about the 20% women quota and to kick that off, to invite Ayshaa to talk to them. The question at issue was, should she talk about the possible 'Christian' dimension?

Ayshaa wanted to be upfront, "Why avoid the subject?"

Hani was a bit defensive, "I'm not avoiding it, I just want to lay more groundwork, otherwise if I get an absolute NO, it will be impossible to change." He was already seeing each of the men separately prior to the meeting, and thought that there were one or two who were not loyal members of the team. Whether either or both of them were reporting to Ramallah, he didn't know. In his mind, once he had seen them all he would have a better idea of how to play it.

Ayshaa said she was going to see Lara at Ghu-sin Zay-tun. Although Christian, they did not sound evangelical and that might play better with the Muslim community. Hani nodded thinking that might be a better option. He had been quite impressed with what he had heard so far. The next day she was there and her first question was exactly that.

Lara laughed. "No. In fact, our own religious beliefs never get in the way of our work with the community." She began to explain in some detail what they were about.

"You know that in English, *Ghu-sin Zay-tun* means 'Olive Branch', and developing peaceful relationships is the essence of our mission. We help resolve disputes within the Palestinian community using the traditional Arab form of mediation, known as *sulha*.

Ayshaa interrupted the flow. "You also have access into the Israeli military?" Lara looked at Ayshaa.

"Ah. You know Ethar. Yes, sometimes our director, my husband, can use some influence with one Israeli commander to fix a problem, but it's not often. Shall I continue?"

"Sorry. Ethar is one of my leaders, so I wanted to thank you for what you're doing." Lara was nodding. Then she sighed, "I know the strain that this puts on our community in general and each mother in particular. You see, there are both psychological and physiological consequences of the long-term conflict we are all experiencing, and this is magnified for women because in our culture women feel themselves powerless."

Ayshaa was the one now nodding in agreement. "So," continued Lara, "We have specific programmes that empower women, but also children, youth and men, if we can interest them. And," she laughed, "nowhere will you see a Bible or a priest. We want to be, and are, an integral part of the whole Bethlehem community."

Ayshaa briefly explained what BWP was and what they wanted to achieve. Lara listened carefully. "I love your ideas and the work you want to do. If you're happy, I'd like you to meet my husband Omari. I'll just see if he can do that now."

Lara was out of the room for no more than two minutes when she came back with a big grin on her face. "Yes, let's move to Omari's office." They moved just a few doors down a wide corridor. Omari got up to meet Ayshaa. He was a not a tall man, but had broad shoulders, thinning hairline and a big Palestinian smile. It was not a grand office by any means, just a desk, some cabinets and in the corner a settee and two easy chairs. Omari invited Ayshaa to sit and offered her a drink. Coffee, tea? Ayshaa, a little overawed, settled on black tea. While Omari himself went over to a little kitchen area and poured the drinks, Lara explained she had to be somewhere else. They shook hands. "I've a feeling we'll meet again," were her words as she left.

"Forgive me," started Omari, "Lara has told me all about you and the vision you have in two minutes." He laughed. "She's a bit of a whirlwind. But from what I hear it sounds as if your aims are very similar to our own and maybe you have more links with those who need help than we do. How can we work together?"

Ayshaa had not been expecting such an immediate offer, but she instantly liked Omari and felt she could trust him. She invited him to tell her why he had started Ghu-sin Zay-tun.

"Well, as I'm sure you already know, the closure of Jerusalem and restrictions on movement in the West Bank and Gaza, has created enormous hardships in Palestinian society. Unemployment is high, but obviously varies depending on the severity of the closure. But with Israeli confiscation of Palestinian land to build settlements and construction of the Wall, we have less and less land on which to live and work."

"Are you saying that it's just land poverty that is the problem?" Ayshaa wanted some clarification.

"Not just, but it's one of the roots of our issue. It's just as much a dependency issue. More and more of our people lack the means to meet even the basic needs of their families. Combine that with a very patriarchal culture and such a complicated situation feeds a cycle of violence at every level of society. As a result, we face a growing demand for the work of conflict transformation, mediation and reconciliation. We do this amongst our own people, but we are also trained for wider service, if the doors open."

Ayshaa asked what these might be. Omari explained, "If the time ever came to talk meaningfully with the Israelis, then Palestinians will need experts in such fields as human rights, democracy, negotiation, and cultural dialogue. Ghu-sin Zay-tun may be able to make a contribution."

Ayshaa took a moment to digest this. While she was doing so, Omari said, "I think I've heard of your husband, Hani."

22

OMARI WAS A Palestinian who had not been confined to Palestine, or the Middle East for that matter. He had travelled the world. As well as gaining degrees and doctorates in a number of American universities in politics and international law, he had developed a lecturing circuit explaining the Palestinian situation to hundreds of people in the US and Europe who had grown up believing that the word 'Palestinian' was synonymous with the word 'terrorist'. But he had been born and brought up in Bethlehem, which was now his home and his base.

Wherever he went, his consistent argument had never been totally anti-Israel and pro-Palestinian. He always stated his belief that Israel had a right to exist, and there was room for both nations to co-exist.

"The problem is not with Israel's right to exist, rather with successive Israeli government policies that had deliberately aimed to build a Jewish state just for Jews. My contention is that the fathers of Israel never intended to build a multi racial, multi religious liberal democracy, and that their successors have continued these policies to include the West Bank, which has been detrimental to both nations."

It was a matter of fact, Omari would contend, that although thousands of Palestinians fled the incoming militant Zionists in 1948 into Jordan, Syria and Lebanon, subsequent Israeli policies had tried, but completely failed to rid the land of the indigenous population, just as Australia and New Zealand failed.

"But," he would point out, "those countries and others, have had to come to terms with the discrimination of the past and repented of what previous generations had done. Even South Africa, although never trying to rid the land of the black population, had eventually to come to terms with the racial and doctrinal discrimination against its indigenous peoples. Through Nelson Mandela and the Peace and Reconciliation process, black, white and coloured in that country now had equal rights in law, and at least a chance of personal freedom though clearly there was a long way to go."

Omari fervently believed that the same process would have to happen one day with the indigenous Palestinian population. History had shown, he would argue, that such indigenous peoples could not be kept corralled and deprived for ever. The system created to maintain such an unjust status quo would inevitably breakdown, whether internally or through external pressure. He declared it was morally wrong and could not last. At this point Omari would have his mostly liberal audience with him.

"I would be the first to admit that the Palestinian leadership cannot escape criticism. It began by embracing violence which perhaps was understandable since the land was taken from them by violence, but still not acceptable."

"And," he would admit, "Yasser Arafat, the PLO leader, had led his militants to war not just on Israel, but on the global community through the violent hi-jacking of passenger aircraft in international airspace."

He would pause to see conservative members of his audience nodding their heads at this point, but he had a big BUT coming.

"What perhaps is not so well known is that in earlier times Israeli activists weren't too bothered about committing terrorist acts themselves. For instance, on July 22, 1946, a bomb planted by the extremist Irgun killed ninety-one people, including twenty-eight British subjects. So whose side are you on? The cliché that 'one man's terrorist is another man's freedom fighter' is true for each of us, because we all take sides. So who is the terrorist and who is the freedom fighter?" Omari knew that posing the Palestinian issue in these terms would not necessarily help to change perceptions. Most people lived within their own political and social bubble. They only mixed with like minded people tending to reinforce the truths of their own bubble. For such, debate merely concreted existing views and expanded the clear water between them and those who held opposing views. What Omari was at pains to point out to liberal and conservative alike were the historical precedents.

"Many historical examples have shown that violence does seem to have achieved initial results, for example in South Africa and Zimbabwe. But the peoples of these nations have never inherited what was promised and never experienced the peace and prosperity they were entitled to expect from their leaders."

His conclusion: "The fruit of violence is never a sustainable peace." At this point, the radical section of each side of his audience would shake their heads. They both interpreted his path of non-violence as a weak position which only maintained a status quo. He would put his hands up at this point to quell any disquiet.

"I will freely admit that as far as the Palestinian position is concerned, that there is not much to show for all the non violent words spoken. But Hamas, Islamic Jihad, al-Aqsa Martyrs' Brigade and other smaller splinter groups have not much to show either, even though these were severally supported by Iran, and formerly Syria. They have never possessed the military capability to seriously trouble an Israeli state equipped and funded by the US. All their violence has done is to maintain a state of unrest where the ordinary Palestinian family is the loser."

At this point, Omari would begin to explain how the real issue for Israel was not the Palestinians at all. Of course they wanted land and more Palestinian land but it was Iran, now that Syria had imploded, that was the real enemy. It made sense for them to make a good settlement with the PA on the West Bank. This would have the advantage of putting a carrot in front of Hamas if they wanted a similar deal, exposing the most marginal terrorist groups and concentrating their limited resources where the risk was greatest.

The Palestinian academic never tired of arguing his case and it seemed that such an environment suited the young Omari. He was intelligent, handsome and charismatic and it was at Princeton when, in his early thirties that he met a young Israeli also studying for his doctorate. Daniel was a few years younger, but oddly they got on really well. Maybe that was because Omari was Christian rather than Muslim. They debated, argued, played sport, dated girls, shared all the pursuits that single young men at university engaged in. It was a wonderful time for them both possibly, Omari would say, the best time of his life to date. On coming to the end of their time together, each knew they were destined for different things. They left the best of friends without ever promising to look each other up in the future. Something told them that others would make that impossible, as both wanted to go back to their roots.

Daniel would go back to Israel, while Omari would develop his lecture tour in the US and eventually to Europe for another five years. After a long time away from home, Omari decided to return to Bethlehem, get married much to his mother's delight, and see how he could best help his own people. It was the construction of the Wall that spurred him on to set up some kind of community peace organisation to try and do what he could to bring people together, whether Muslim, Christian or Jewish.

He had a lawyer's qualification and a keen mind to go with it. So, once registered, a whole raft of legal and other work was open to him. He planned to travel abroad and reconnect with the lecture tour cities to raise money for his charity at least once a year. Thus Ghu-sin Zay-tun was born. He felt that the Arabic language was the right language to use, since all Palestinians used it and they would all know that the olive branch was a symbol of peace. It was a good start and he was able to use the financial gifts that were coming in to support himself as he developed the vision and defined exactly what was needed and what he could do.

He was happy to allow it to grow slowly so that the right staff could be hired and that a solid and sustainable reputation could be built. He quickly found that there was a mountain of work that he could do both dealing with inter-Palestinian disputes and also Israeli-Palestinian issues. Decades of repression had become the incubator of all sorts of ills, especially in the refugee camps. People whose ancestors were farmers, now living on top of each other, dependent on other people for their sustenance and permits to find work. It spawned domestic violence, child cruelty, poverty and depression.

He, himself, was fortunate to have been born and brought up in the main city in a relatively prosperous home. His father was a lawyer, which is probably where Omari's inspiration came from. His mother never needed to go out to work, but she helped in the accounts department at Bethlehem University. Not surprisingly, he had been well educated and had lacked nothing. He never had any trouble in obtaining permits and seemed to be able to fly out and back whenever he wanted provided it was approved, of course. He was lucky.

Now to give something back, at least at community level. Politics was certainly a possibility, but he really didn't want to get into politics. He'd rather leave that to others and support those he could identify with. Palestinian politics, as he explained in his lectures, was a rather murky business. He felt cleaner outside it all.

After Ayshaa had left their meeting, Omari began to think about them. They were an interesting couple. Hani was clearly involved at some level with Palestinian politics and his wife in community work. Omari considered this a great combination, which led him to wonder whether his wife, Lara, might want to go into local politics one day. She was certainly capable and would provide a way for the ethos of Ghu-sin Zay-tun to begin to influence local policies. Omari started looking for an opportunity to raise the subject with her.

A number of cases had already been taken on by Ghu-sin Zay-tun which needed the weight of Bethlehem's municipal council behind them. He began to share the details of them one evening over their meal. They had been married for a few years now and children had not come along, so Lara had thrown herself into Ghu-sin Zay-tun where there was no shortage of work to do. But she was already beginning to think of a more independent career. In the end, it was she who asked Omari whether it would compromise his charity work if she stood for election.

Omari had never considered any downside to Lara being involved in Bethlehem politics, and said he would be delighted to support her if that was what she chose to do. Funny how these things turn out, he thought. He was sure it would take more than one attempt, especially as she was a woman trying to enter a man's world, or what had been a man's world. At this point, he wasn't aware of the PA's edict that there should be a certain number of seats allocated for women. So surprisingly for both of them, Lara got elected. She was now a councillor and was looking forward to making something good happen, particularly for the women of Bethlehem.

Omari cautioned her not to expect breakthroughs too early. Politics was the art of the possible, not necessarily the art of what was required. She also needed to keep her eye on what to do to ensure re-election. Omari thought that it was more likely that she would have the support and base to achieve more in her second term rather than as a newcomer. But at least a new journey had started.

23

HANI'S SECOND MEETING with the men was just about to start. The security men were still at the door. Hani shook his head and he ordered them to go further up and down the road keeping in touch by phone. They each had their own mobile with which they could call Hani and each other if there was any semblance of a threat.

Once the meeting started, Hani dealt with the leak quickly and moved on without leaving opportunity for comment or questions. He had met with almost all the men separately in the last few weeks, and felt he had a good grasp of where each of them were on the important issues. Apart from the two men who he wanted to watch carefully, he thought he had a loyal team. His strategy would be to try using the loyal ones to keep the independent ones in order.

The room was the same one they had used last time, although Hani had given some thought to moving the meeting about, say having two or three places and not notifying which place they would use until an hour or so before the meeting. But he had not come to a decision and it would involve finding another two other empty houses. Not easy when living accommodation was so difficult to get. This place was still as empty as before which tended to heighten the noise level when they all tried to speak at the same time.

Ramallah seemed happy with the resolution of the leak and told him to keep his team clean. At this meeting he set about outlining how he saw their task. It was twofold: firstly to keep ears and eyes on Israel and any troop movements, any house demolitions and any kidnappings. Ramallah wanted to know about everything, and he wanted to know before Ramallah told him. He organised his men, most of whom had jobs of one sort or another, so that the main areas were covered. Those who had permits to work in Jerusalem were tasked with listening to as much Israeli gossip as possible. He would then decide whether any further action was merited.

Secondly it was to help strengthen their own community. "We can't do it all ourselves but we need to be able to oversee what goes on from a distance. I'm proposing that we pick one or two community action groups and support their work. To this end, he had already asked someone to review what was going on in the area and come to the next meeting with a recommendation."

He paused to see the reaction. There was none except for his two dissenters. They objected. "No-one outside the group should be able to meet with us, otherwise another leak might occur."

Hani, expecting the objection, immediately overruled it saying, "I've thought about that and will take sole responsibility and, by the way, I've already agreed it with Ramallah." There was no agreement with anyone in Ramallah but it did serve to silence them, at least temporarily. At the end of the meeting, he took aside Kamel and Zeyad who he felt he could trust and asked them to keep in with the two rebels and to let him know of any trouble was brewing. He knew he was taking a risk, but he saw it as a calculated one.

When he got back home, Ayshaa could see that he was fairly happy with how the meeting had gone. He outlined the plan for the next meeting. She would come with him but not come in until all the men were seated. He asked her to talk about Ghu-sin Zay-tun and not mention BCI. In the meantime could she find a way to chat to the wives of all his team except the two rebels? If they bought into her vision, then there was a probability that the men would too.

It was exactly what Ayshaa had in mind. She would go with Ethar. It would take her mind off the continued detention of Abdullah. The next morning just after Hani had left the home, she called Ethar on her Nokia and an excited voice replied. "We've got him back. He's here. I can't believe it."

Ayshaa was delighted. "I'm coming round right now." Sure enough, there was one happy family. Everyone was smiling and laughing, although Abdullah was looking a bit sheepish. Ayshaa shared in her friend's excitement and happiness before asking the question she was desperate to ask. "How? Did they just release him? Did someone intervene?"

Ethar explained. "It was Ghu-sin Zay-tun. They did something. I don't know what... and I don't really care. My little boy is home."

Ayshaa could see the opportunity, but she waited until Ethar had calmed down. She didn't want to appear to use this event for her own ends. She wasn't... not really. Eventually, Ayshaa told Ethar what Hani had arranged, and how she had thought of talking at the men's meeting about Ghu-sin Zay-tun as a partner.

Ethar could see the way it was going. "I don't want to get involved. I don't want any names. I don't want to know who these people are. In fact, I don't want anyone at all to know what happened to Abdullah. I want him to get back to a normal life with his friends as if nothing had happened."

Ayshaa said, as a mother, she understood but pointed out that although the refugee camp where Ethar lived was large, it was a close community and word would spread easily. It was news. Ethar seemed to understand but said nothing. Ayshaa decided not to push her, but wait until just before the men's meeting, then ask again. It was too good an opportunity to miss. Ayshaa began to realise how much of a politician she was becoming.

She related this back to Hani who also saw the opportunity and encouraged her to talk to Ghu-sin Zay-tun to get more information and perhaps finalise the partnership with BWP. Through the efforts of Israa, Ethar and herself over the past few weeks, they had more than a hundred women now signed up, with more to follow as Ayshaa began to contact the wives of Hani's men. Although they weren't actually doing anything yet, this was a platform to talk more positively with Ghu-sin Zay-tun.

Ayshaa called Lara to thank her and Omari. Lara was certainly glad that Abdullah had been freed, but wouldn't say what role they had played, except that it hadn't been easy. Ayshaa moved on to talk about the progress BWP had made and to explore what activities they might do together. They agreed to hold a series of meetings of not more than twenty women per meeting, to find out what issues the women faced and what help they would like. A plan would then be drawn up and it was at this point that Lara stopped. She looked at Ayshaa questioningly.

"Sorry but I have to mention the subject of funding. We are a charity which relies on funding from others. We can give our expertise but our time is limited. If we expand our programmes with BWP, we will almost certainly require some extra funding."

Ayshaa started looking rather glum. Hani had mentioned this right at the beginning and she had tried to avoid the issue. "I don't think most can afford much."

"I agree it mustn't be much per person, but it would add up and ensure that those who came were fully committed. My personal time is also limited since I am now a Bethlehem councillor."

Ayshaa thought about it and agreed. Privately, she wondered whether Hani could get some funds from Ramallah and so, on her way home, she decided to ask Hani if he could get quite a large sum for BWP, since he seemed to be in favour at the moment. She also had an idea to print a free newspaper of sorts. Not a major one with lots of pages, but a free paper, tabloid size with maybe eight sides. She had no idea who would edit it or how she would get it printed. Those details could come later. No point in thinking about that until she had the money. But if Fatah saw the opportunity for a paper in Bethlehem which carried their point of view, it might be the start of something bigger.

Hani thought about it. "That might be possible, but I don't think they would give it to BWP. They would probably see it as money for us."

He paused. "You know, now I think about it, I think there's a PA news-paper of sorts in the Nazareth area aimed at tourists as well as locals. It's a precedent, and Bethlehem has a better tourist record so maybe something on those lines might be possible." It was left there.

Over the next week or so, Ayshaa had to rely on Ghalia more than she would have liked to look after Rena, as she tracked down and approached the wives of Hani's men's group. Most were supportive, if a little sceptical; a few not interested, but no-one outrightly hostile. Ayshaa was satisfied, but wondered what conversations would be had with the husbands after her visits. Well, that was Hani's problem, and she was sure he could deal with that.

Hani seemed to be spending less time at the shop and more time in Ra-mallah at meetings which he rather enjoyed. It was much more satisfying that waiting in the shop for the odd customer, then sending them away with the words, 'sorry I don't have that in at the moment.' Unbeknown to him, he was being groomed for bigger things. He was seen as a fresh face, charismatic yet approachable, with the wisdom of someone much older. He was on the 'up'. There was no problem in principle with additional funds either for women's mentoring (as long as their husbands agreed!), or a paper, however, a formal proposal had to be prepared and signed off.

Back in Bethlehem, Hani was on home turf. He was getting more secure in Ramallah and beginning to understand how things worked there, but this was his base, his community, his people. He was growing in stature and finding himself more comfortable in his skin. Both Ghalia and Ayshaa saw it. Even Rena seemed a little more awed when her daddy arrived home. He was determined, however, to keep his feet on the ground, no matter what the future held… and he knew there were certain to be some serious downs to come at some point. Although he wouldn't call himself a politician, he clearly was and he was learning the game fast. He had to.

It all made Ayshaa think harder about ensuring the family kept together. She would talk to Ghalia at length about how she managed to do it with her husband, Hani's father. It wasn't quite the same situation, but often it was down to the women to keep a stable home for the men. That's how Palestinians lived. But she definitely didn't want to give up what she had started, so she had to find a way through.

Ghalia's advice was simple. "Try to enter his world as much as possible, but also keep pulling him into your world. Keep both worlds colliding and impacting each other. After all, you're working for the same end, aren't you."

So, it all came down to listening and talking. The pressure they were living under came to the fore one evening when Ghalia suddenly collapsed. They immediately called a local ambulance which thankfully did come quite quickly, but paramedics diagnosed a heart attack and said she needed to go to an East Jerusalem hospital in the Israeli sector which specialised in heart surgery. Hani's heart sank. He knew the process. He knew of people who had died waiting to get the transfer from the West Bank to Jerusalem. It was a long and tough procedure. It meant that firstly, they needed to contact the hospital before they set off, then to send copies of Ghalia's medical records. After medical permission, they needed financial permission i.e. to show they had the money to cover the treatment costs.

Once that was done they knew that no vehicle, even an ambulance, with Palestinian green and white plates was allowed to cross from the West Bank into Israel. They needed an ambulance with yellow Israeli plates. That meant they required a 'back-to-back' ambulance transfer on the border. To do that, security permission from the Israeli Military District Coordinating Office (DCO) had to be sought. They had to call the DCO and give them their name and ID so that a security check could be done. Permission might be given or refused. The whole process could take anything from hours to days. The specifics of the case, emergency or not, was not considered. It depended solely on how the Israeli military assessed the patient's security risk and, it seemed, their mood on the day.

Ghalia would need to be looked after by Ayshaa full time until all permissions came through. Finally, after two days, security permission from the DCO came through and Hani called for a Palestinian ambulance in which they travelled to one of the main Jerusalem checkpoints. When they arrived, they had to wait until permission from Israeli soldiers was given so they could enter the changing area. The soldiers checked Ghalia's ID, the number of the ambulance, the ambulance staff's IDs and finally with the DCO. Hani was refused permission to go any further. He waited until he saw the ambulance move to the designated area.

The Palestinian ambulance parked a little way from the Israeli ambulance and Ghalia was transferred from one ambulance to the other. There were soldiers, security personnel and other assorted people all around the checkpoint watching what was going on. No privacy for an old lady. Just as the transfer was about to start, it began to rain quite heavily. Hani could see the paramedics arguing with the soldiers about an umbrella to cover their patient. Permission was refused. He began to get seriously worked up. The paramedics couldn't wait, so Ghalia was transferred in the rain. The ambulance then left for the hospital blue lights flashing.

As he saw the ambulance disappearing in the distance, Hani was clenching his fists and shaking with rage at the disrespect and inhumanity of it all. But he knew it was of no consequence to the soldiers and protesting would achieve nothing except to get him arrested with photographs and fingerprints taken. Not a good idea. He managed to contain himself and just stood there watching, even after the ambulance had disappeared. Then he set off on the long journey home. He was not a happy man.

24

MEDAD WAS NOT a happy man either. He had arranged with Shana to go down to his home for the weekend but, at the last minute, she had texted him to say that one of her friends had invited her to stay for the weekend in a relatively new Israeli settlement on the West Bank. She had not said to Medad whether her friend was male or female which left Medad wondering whether this had been done deliberately. This news gave Medad further cause for concern about Shana's thinking both about him, and about Zionism. Maybe she didn't want to meet his family just yet. Maybe he didn't want to meet hers. All he could do was text her back and wish her a good weekend.

The settlement she was heading for was part of the Gush Etzion cluster of settlements, south of Bethlehem in the Judaean mountains, which now amounted to over 70,000 people, all on land captured after the Six Days War. What Shana hadn't picked up was that this was where Medad came from, albeit a different settlement than the one she was going to. She was travelling to Gevaot, which had not long been recognised by the Israeli government. Settlers had just started appropriating this land in 2014, the first required step but there had been a delay in recognising Gevaot due to the lack of defined boundaries. It was on the frontier and Shana was excited to see what life was like here.

What she saw, she liked. The views and natural surroundings were enthralling. The air was clean with very little pollution and crime rates were very low compared with the rest of Israel. People seemed really kind and she could see that they made a real effort to get along with each other. A real community, which tended to be a little more patriotic than in the metropolitan areas that she was familiar with. Shana could tell that Shira was really proud of her home. There were some local industries and places of employment, but most commuted elsewhere to work. The settlers were all Jewish so there were no real minority areas such as in her home city of Tel Aviv. But they weren't Hareidi, the ultra-orthodox Jews, although Shira said that they made up a significant section of settlers on the West Bank. Usually, they lived in their own cities, had very large families with synagogues on each street. Shana thought they sounded interesting, yet really strange.

They were in the garden sipping drinks, Shira talking about college. But Shana wanted to carry on the conversation with Shira about the Hareidi as she seemed to know a lot about them.

"Well, their cities are really well run and frequently win prizes for aesthetics and civic management. Bus services are good and frequent which is important for those of us who can't yet drive but want to get out and go places, and the prices of most things are lower." Shira admitted, "sometimes we go to the nearest Hareidi city and do our shopping there. The streets are wide and there are numerous parks and playgrounds for children."

Shana thought she might like to live in such a place. "Sounds idyllic." Shira cautioned her. "There is no secular schooling. It's all religious and you have to learn the Torah off by heart. Not for me. But they aren't the only religious ones. Then you have the National Religious people. They comprise about 35 to 40% of the settlers. These are the ones you see with the knitted yarmulkes, and the slogans about Love for their Fellow Jew."

Shana raised her eyebrows.

"Yes, they actually exist. Their settlements are also well-run with many of the houses above average. Unlike the Hareidi, they are more tolerant with religious observance varying from one place to another, but a growing proportion of their youth are much less religious than their parents which they worry about."

Shana acknowledged that her knowledge of settlements and settlers was growing from a very low base. She was intrigued as to why people would want to settle in such odd places so Shira suggested they take a walk around the neighbourhood.

On the way she explained, "Not everyone is a religious settler. There are also many secular settlers like us. We have no particular religious beliefs, but we want to help ensure the existence and survival of the State of Israel. As there is an on-going housing need because of continued immigration, all available land for building is to be used. The military are tasked with protecting us, and as soon as the camp is set up, the utility companies have to provide water and electricity to us. So, why not move here? Nothing to lose."

They stopped at the edge of the settlement. As she looked out over the valley, Shana saw a village on its own, quite different to the settlement.

She asked Shira what that village was called. "That's the Palestinian village of Nahalin. They're Muslim and you can see their mosque on the far side. It's now surrounded by all the Gush Etzion settlements. It used to be a bee-keeping centre and maybe still is, I don't know."

Shana was still asking her questions. "And what are those black bins in the tops of the houses?

Shira explained, "They don't have their own water supplies now. We limit the water so there's enough for the settlements. When it does come on, they have pumps usually by the front door which they turn on and fill up their tanks. The white tanks which we have, are not reserve tanks but solar panels to pre heat our water."

Shana was beginning to feel a little uncomfortable. She changed the direction of the conversation. "And what is that place on the hilltop over there." She pointed in another direction to what looked like a farm.

Shira said, "That's a place known as Dahers' Vineyard. It is now run as an educational and environmental farm called the Tent of Nations."

Shana was intrigued. "Are they Israeli?"

Shira said, "No they aren't Israelis but Christian Palestinians, Lutheran I think. We'd like them to move, but they won't. Palestinians have an irrational emotional link to their land."

Shana was looking at the surrounding land, trying to comprehend what was happening here. "So you have Muslim and Christian Palestinians in this place. Do they live peacefully together?"

"Sure," responded Shira, "but its extremely frustrating. We can do so much better than they with the land, but they won't budge. Christians or Muslims, it makes no difference. They're all Palestinians."

Shana was now holding some binoculars. "I can see the road that goes to the farm and it is blocked."

Shira confirmed. "Yes, some of the settlers wanted to put some pressure on the Nasser family who own the farm to sell to us so they tipped a load of rubble on the road leading to the house. It hasn't worked so far. They have another way out, but it's a longer journey for them."

There was a cloud of dust which Shana could see on the road past the farm access. It was a coach. Shira took the binoculars to have a look. "It's another load of tourists visiting them. They have a lot of international visitors who come to help with their harvests. Hundreds, I believe; Swedish, Dutch, English, American, all sorts."

The coach pulled up next to the rubble that was blocking the farm road. About thirty people got out, climbed over the blockage and made their way up to the farm. Shana made a mental note to look up their website to see what was really going on there. While she was thinking this, Shira was saying, "Some of the settlers even went so far as to dig up olive trees belonging to the Palestinians, but they still wouldn't sell."

Shana was a bit shocked. "Isn't that illegal?"

Shira explained that they were on the front line here, not quite the Wild West, but not far off. Here the conversation stopped and they went back to the house for their evening meal. Over the meal, there was a conversation about house demolitions. Shana kept her mouth shut. She had asked enough questions for one day, feeling that Shira might be seeing her in a different light and she didn't want to lose her friend. Then her father started talking about a demolition that was due the next day. After the meal when both girls were on their own together, Shira asked if Shana wanted to observe it. She explained that they usually happened very early in the morning. The occupiers were given notice by the military that they had to be out by a certain time, then the bulldozers would move in covered by soldiers.

Shana hesitated, but said she would like to. So they agreed to get up early and go to a high spot above Nahalin, where it was to happen. At 6am, they got to the spot with binoculars, and found that they were almost too late. Lots of military, two giant Caterpillar bulldozers and a Palestinian family wailing outside. Shana counted father, mother and five children, ranging from about twelve down to a baby no more than six months. The father was pleading with soldiers to no avail. They were laughing.

The noise had brought out lots of other villagers who also remonstrated with the soldiers. A few youths threw some stones and then ran away. Shana could see the tangled mess of steel rods and concrete which had been the house, and lots of the family's possessions scattered about. There was a smashed fridge on its own away from the wreckage, which must have been thrown clear. Children's toys, books, cushions, chairs and various bits of kitchen equipment were being retrieved by the family now the bulldozers had done their job. Their friends tried to help, but mostly it was in vain. The mother was inconsolable and was being comforted by the other women of the village.

Shana said she had seen enough. For the rest of that day, she was quiet. She didn't want to go out. She just wanted the time to pass quickly so she could get back to her room on campus. Shira, though, seemed to take it all in her stride.

"It was necessary," she said. "If an order had been given, then it was right. They must have done something wrong."

Shana didn't argue. That weekend, she had seen stuff with her eyes that she never knew about. She could hardly believe it and she definitely didn't like it. Was this Zionism? Was this happening everywhere on the West Bank? Why had no-one told her? She suddenly felt very naïve. How many others in Israel knew about this? Were they turning a blind eye, content to live in their own bubble? Was this what Medad had been saying, and she hadn't believed him? She could feel her face reddening with embarrassment as she thought of the conversation she would have to have with him in a few days.

Medad was pleased to get the text asking to meet up. *Perhaps she hasn't dumped me after all, but I'll play it cool.* But before he could ask about the weekend, Shana said she wanted to apologise for her attitude and Zionist arguments. She then outlined what she had heard and seen. Medad was quiet. He had never seen a house demolition either. He knew they happened, but hearing the details from Shana made him sit up. He knew facts and figures, but had never experienced the inhumanity, the emotion of it. He confessed that he knew that there were over forty-eight thousand Palestinian structures which had been demolished, with hundreds made homeless. He was ashamed of the military, in which he had served, but he knew how easy it was to get hardened to the everyday brutality of being in the IDF.

25

CHUCK HAD FINISHED lunch and was back sitting at his desk when his desk phone rang. Someone from the CIA was wanting to meet up that day. He took a minute to look in his diary although he already knew he had no other meetings that day. There was no reason not to and, as he suspecting it was about who should be 'running' Medad, he updated his diary and headed over to Langley. It was only fourteen kilometers away and as long as he went now, he could do it easily. Coming back wouldn't be the same in the middle of Washington's rush hour.

Reviewing the situation with Medad, he recognised that he couldn't fight the CIA if they really wanted to take over. But he wanted to be in the loop and hoped to use his personal relationship with Medad to accomplish what he wanted. After an hour long discussion, it was agreed that for the time being, Chuck would be the main contact but that their own operative in Jerusalem would also make contact. It was not difficult to see that 'the time being' was not going to be very long.

He heard that Medad was no longer an intern, but had been recruited to be an analyst for Palestinian Affairs. From Chuck's point of view this was excellent news and he decided to call Medad to congratulate him as a way of cementing the relationship. He wanted Medad to see him as influential in his career development. In Chuck's mind, Medad was his and he was going to try and keep it that way. The discussion also forced him to admit that he was hosting Medad and Shana at his home as part of their US holiday.

Medad's mobile rang. The number wasn't in his contact list so he hesitated before answering. He was surprised and quite pleased to hear from Chuck. "I hear congratulations are in order. Couldn't happen to a better man." Chuck was laying on the charm.

Medad was surprised again. "Is nothing secret in the world? Did you have anything to do with it?"

Chuck declined to answer directly and tried to laugh knowingly. He didn't want to lie. He hadn't, but he didn't want Medad to know that. "When are you coming over to the US? My wife is really looking forward to meeting both of you." He sounded really friendly, and Medad was also happy to be friendly because he saw opportunity for himself in the relationship.

Medad explained that he and Shana were meeting tonight over dinner to agree dates. "By the way," Chuck hesitated, "I need to clear up the nature of the relationship between you two. Is Shana your girlfriend, fiancée or what? We Americans liked to get these things straight."

Medad mulled it over for a second before giving the 'girlfriend' answer. At least for the moment, he added. It gave him an idea which had been in the back of his mind for a while, though at one stage he had thought it was impossible, but now... Perhaps they were too young, perhaps not. Anyway, he would be ready but when the time was right.

"Well, text me dates when you have them. Looking forward to chatting with you." With that Chuck was gone.

The dinner date went well. The food was good, the music smooth and the atmosphere all he had wanted. They had agreed dates and Medad had talked about Chuck and how he had invited them to stay over in Washington DC. She seemed delighted, and since her return from her 'settlement' weekend, she was anxious to get the relationship back on an even keel again. Having done a little shopping on the way he was ready, but something held him back. At the end of the evening, he gave her a lingering kiss, as if to make up for what he hadn't done. And they went their separate ways as just good friends.

Shana made her way back to her college room a little depressed. Her instincts were strongly indicating that Medad was going to propose, but he hadn't. She wondered whether that was because of her weekend away, which she was now bitterly regretting. She was still not entirely sure if she loved him, but at the same time she couldn't envisage life without him. Maybe that was sufficient, or was it? Medad for his part, was severely punishing himself for his cowardice. Why had he held back? He didn't know. He was prepared. He had the ring. Well, what was done, was done.

The next day Medad was reading restricted background papers in the office about Israel and the Palestinian Authority not lodged in the RIC library.

He was now part of the executive branch of government and not in an advisory position anymore. The first set of papers was about the Palestinian Authority. The PA did suffer from some unique disadvantages in as much as it was not a state, and had no control over the territory it supposedly governed. In fact, as Medad knew, the Israeli military was the ultimate authority in the West Bank, together with the Civil Administration. But he had no sympathy for the PA: the rule of law was weak, the so-called parliament never met to pass laws, there was excessive executive interference, the justice system lacked independence and government jobs were awarded on the basis of cronyism rather than merit. But who was he to complain? Medad liked to think he got his job on merit even if there was no 'fair competition' or transparency. More to the point, he thought, was the fact that senior and influential Palestinians were granted tax and customs exemptions without any legal basis. Apparently, Medad read, the amount of wasted funds was enormous. The investigative report he was reading documented eight cases concerning influential officials, where the amount wasted reached $357,600 which could have gone to alleviate the suffering of their people.

There was an Arab based group called The Coalition for Accountability and Integrity, which conducted such reviews on many states in the Middle East. It was required reading. Its report on the PA was damning. It was the amount spent on the so-called security services that Medad found incredible, especially since they were not really in charge of security anyway. The review found that the total annual amount for salaries for the ranks of Major General, Brigadier General, Colonel, and Lieutenant Colonel, in 2016, reached the amount of 238.7 million NIS per year, equivalent to the annual salary of 13,000 soldiers.

Public funds were allocated to non-existent entities, such as Palestinian Airlines. Apparently, they have hundreds of staff and a Board of Directors, but no planes and no airport! Then there was the infamous case of the Presidential Palace. This giant edifice, 50,000 sq ft for the Palace itself, plus another 40,000 sq ft in other buildings, cost the 'bankrupt' Palestinian Authority, $17.5 million. Medad recalled the public uproar about it which forced Mahmoud Abbas to convert it into a public library. Medad laughed out loud as he read this. His colleagues looked up and he explained. They all knew about it. It was a joke!

But as Medad delved further, it transpired that the PA and its leadership weren't the only ones to be found to be corrupt. It was in Israel too, and at the heart of public life. The mayor of the city of Hadera, Zvi Gendelman was accused of fraud, breach of trust, and obstruction for allegedly providing favours to a local contractor, Sammy Levy, in exchange for support in a municipal election in the city. Then there was the case of the Interior Minister, Aryeh Deri who was forced to resign from the government after police said they were recommending indictments against him on a slew of corruption charges, including alleged crimes committed while in office. Even Benjamin Netanyahu had been investigated by the Tax & Finance Department for accepting benefits in exchange for advancing certain businessmen's interests. He had been charged and currently was hiding from the law in office.

Then, the biggest of them all – Netanyahu's former lawyer no less, David Shimron, together with five other high profile figures, was indicted on bribery charges in what has been called one of the largest graft schemes in the country's history. It was a case of suspected bribery involving the purchase of military submarines worth hundreds of millions of dollars. Some of this he knew from the media, but here it was in unbelievable detail. Medad couldn't stop himself reading. It was known as Case 3000, and although there was no evidence that Netanyahu was directly involved, nevertheless he was questioned by police over suspicions revolving around Israel's acquisition of submarines manufactured by the German industrial giant Thyssenkrupp. The key figure was Miki Ganor, a former agent for the German shipbuilder and a suspect, who in July 2017, signed an agreement to cooperate with the investigation. The sums involved were so astounding that investigators were initially loath to believe the state witness who supplied them.

Medad sat back in his seat. Press speculation had not been far from the mark, but on reading the detail he felt personally humiliated. These men had let down Israel. How could they laugh about the Palestinian Authority when this was happening in their own back yard? Israel could not accuse the PA of corruption when it was also tainted. He looked round. Everyone was working on their screens. He guessed they already knew. He didn't bother to share it. No joke now!

His own screen now buzzed. He had mail! Dan, his boss, was outlining a prospective meeting with officials of the PA. These happened from time to time with Ministers and it was their job, as civil servants, to prepare papers and also have preparatory meetings with officials. Before he resigned over Gaza policy, Avigdor Liberman, the former Defence Minister, had met with the PA's intelligence chief, and with senior Fatah officials who coordinated relations between Israel and the PA. The meeting was also attended by a Major General who was the Coordinator of Government Activities in the Territories (COGAT). Now a new round of meetings was to be held to discuss the possible lifting of restrictions on the part of Israel in Area A. This is an area designated to be under full civil and security control of the PA.

That was some time ago and nothing had happened since Liberman's resignation. The PA officials' demand was that the IDF stop entering Area A, and also wanted to negotiate economic agreements between Israel and the Palestinian Authority which would allow the PA to develop Area C and allow investments there. Medad was asked to prepare a paper outlining the pros and cons of a number of possible stances Israel might take, including Liberman's hard line position.

Medad was clear where his own personal opinions lay, but had to rigorously examine each option with a risk analysis. Nevertheless, he found it nigh impossible not to signal his own preferences even if vaguely. It made him wonder how influential officials could be if a Minister wanted to listen. The truth was, however, that Ministers themselves had lots of preconceptions and prejudices. They mostly demanded, even bullied officials into doing what they wanted, and to 'skew' papers their way for political purposes. For example, it was amazing the number of times 'security' issues were raised, usually with Gaza, when an election loomed. But it was also in Hamas' own interest to keep a hard-line government in Jerusalem to keep the faithful true to the cause. Making peace did not seem to be anyone's ambition.

He worked hard over the next few weeks without knowing exactly when, or if, a meeting was to take place. He put draft after draft before Dan, and had discussion after discussion with him over the options chosen and their consequences. Finally a paper was approved and passed upwards, before being sent on to the Minister without major changes. Medad breathed a sigh of relief and thought that if the Minister accepted the document, it might signal some change in policy. Before that could happen though, it might have to be submitted to Cabinet for approval. Maybe that was why no date had been set. The PA were not going away so the issues and timing were solely for the Israeli government to discuss and agree. Now that Likud and Netanyahu were still in power, any talks were likely to be cosmetic at best.

Medad shared his fledgling hope and obvious concerns for any meeting with Shana, although none of the detail. She was in full support for whatever his paper said. It seemed they were really back on track together with Shana a lot more interested than she let on. She could see journalistic opportunities everywhere, but now wasn't the time to debate Medad's views. She wanted to support him and hopefully be positioned to help if possible.

They had booked their American trip and although Medad had reserved his holiday with Human Resources, he was sincerely hoping it didn't clash with the big meeting with the Palestinian Authority, if it ever happened.

26

WITHOUT GHALIA, AYSHAA was severely limited in what she could do. There were no nurseries available, and even if there were they would have taken a large chunk of the monies that Fatah were paying Hani which were now all going to pay for Ghalia's hospital treatment. So she had time on her hands and, as a stay-at-home mum for much of each day, she thought it could be valuable thinking time, if she didn't go mad first.

It was no exaggeration that Omari had surprised and shocked her. How did he know of her husband? Hani had never indicated that he knew Omari. Maybe he didn't, but somehow she was impressed and perhaps that was the point. Clearly Ghu-sin Zay-tun was well connected, which made her feel a little more confident about teaming up with them... and going public with it.

Hani got in very late that night after seeing Ghalia across the border. He had walked all the way back through the maze of narrow unlit streets. It had been raining and although it hadn't lasted very long, by the time he got home he was soaked to the skin. He didn't want use his Fatah connection to get a car but wanted to be independent of them for as long as possible and allow them into his life only as far as was necessary. He also wanted to use his walking time to think. Somehow walking in the rain helped him ponder the decisions he was making and where he was going. But thoughts of his mother continually interrupted his deliberations. He didn't dismiss them for he was, wanted to be, a good son.

No specific epiphany had been experienced by the time he had arrived home. After pulling his wet clothes off, he crept silently into their sofabed hoping not to wake his wife. It was unheard of for Hani to sleep in, but the next morning he did much to Ayshaa's frustration, for she wanted to talk to him about Omari. He took his time washing and trimming his stubble at the kitchen sink. This was his time and, although it was in the open sitting room, he kept the illusion that he was in his private area insisting that no-one was allowed to talk to him. Seeing some overall greyness in his hair in the blotched mirror, he had to admit to his mirror image that he was running on near empty. Too much going on. Too much demanded of him.

But Ayshaa was impatient. She was wanting to go out but needed to talk to him first. He sighed. Eventually he turned round and she asked the Omari question, but he was completely unable to help. He had no idea how Ghu-sin Zay-tun would have heard of him. It was only later that day he remembered Zeyad. That must be it. Zeyad, or maybe Kamel, must have told Ghu-sin Zay-tun about him. Now Hani thought about it, he wasn't at all happy with that. It was vital that he remain anonymous not just for his own life, but for the PA group in Bethlehem.

Whilst Hani sought out Zeyad and Kamel, Ayshaa was preparing for her meeting with the men. It was to be in a few days and she needed someone to look after Rena. Israa offered if Ayshaa could deliver Rena to her house on her way to the meeting, so one small problem solved. The larger problem was to anticipate the objections and questions that a group of quite aggressive men might make. She worked hard on this and bounced her thoughts off her friends and co-founders of BWP, until they all thought she was as prepared as she could be.

Ayshaa not only wanted to talk about what they, as women, wanted to do, but she also wanted to be able to say... "and this is what we are currently doing." She would have Zeyad on her side as he knew Ghu-sin Zay-tun was working to get his son out of an Israeli prison, although without any concrete results as yet, although they had received a message from their son in prison through Ghu-sin Zay-tun, for which they were grateful. But apart from Zeyad, she had little idea of the rest.

So she arranged for Lara to come to Israa's house to meet the team, and as many of the wives of the men who wanted to come. Nearly all of them came, having heard Israa's story. This would be their first meeting of twenty. Lara outlined who she was.

"*As-salamu alaykum*. My name is Lara and work with Ghu-sin Zay-tun. I think all of you have heard of what happened to Israa and her family." Heads were nodding around the room.

"Well, I'm really glad we were able to help in this case. As you know, getting anything from the Israelis is difficult but this time we had *tharwat jayida*, good fortune. It doesn't happen every time."

Lara was trying not to raise hopes that Ghu-sin Zay-tun had some 'silver bullet' to solve all their problems with the Occupying Power. She hurried on for she really wanted to talk about the women's empowerment programme and what kind of opportunities they could provide for the women of Bethlehem in conjunction with BWP. Twenty minutes later when she asked if anyone wanted to come to these meetings, many nodded enthusiastically but others tentatively, as if thinking about their husbands.

One older woman spoke up, her voice trembling a little, "and what happens if our husbands find out and we are beaten?" There was a murmur of emotion rippling around the room. They all recognised what this meant. Ayshaa spoke up, "Many of your men are on the Fatah committee for Bethlehem. My husband wants to talk about this at their next meeting. We won't meet together until after that."

Overall Ayshaa thought it was a good start. The women all wanted to feel safe and empowered, not be so dominated by husbands, sons or anyone else but they were also submissive and scared. Lara cautioned Ayshaa to make sure that the women had their husband's approval otherwise word would spread and the whole venture would be scuppered.

"I suppose," said Ayshaa thoughtfully, "I could always arrange a much more informal session over tea for those who felt they couldn't come to a formal session. Maybe I could do this via the children who have had traumatic experiences with soldiers."

Many of the women, not just Israa, recognised that their children had suffered trauma and were continuing to do so, but were not equipped to do anything about it. The result was that their disaffected young people turned to more violent means of protesting, rather than the non-violent options that Ghu-sin Zay-tun embraced. They all saw that the best way to support the people of Bethlehem and Palestinians in general was to try to create a healthy society. They themselves were not able to end the racism, daily indignities and poverty that characterised their lives, but they could begin to change mindsets and perhaps channel the reactions of their children more positively. At least they could try.

Hani, in the meantime, had tracked down his man and found it was indeed Zeyad who had mentioned him. Although Zeyad insisted it had been in a very positive light, Hani patiently explained to him how important it was that his name be kept out of the public consciousness because the Israeli military had eyes and ears everywhere. Hani made a mental note to reinforce this to the men at the next meeting.

Both Hani and Ayshaa were on edge the whole day before the evening meeting with the men. As it turned out, the meeting was very positive, apart from the two rebels who sniped continuously at Ayshaa. This she turned to her advantage by citing it as an example of what she was fighting against. She knew from Hani that this would happen and that she would not win them over. So the strategy was to isolate them and portray their views, rather than them personally, as anti-women and indeed anti-Fatah. Ayshaa felt she had a carte blanche to go full steam ahead. She had now put out of her mind the original trip to contact ALLMEP. She had too much to do here.

Hani was positive as well and felt his authority was now secured. He could now travel up to Ramallah with a new confidence and new ideas to slide into his meetings. Whilst he was there this time, he learned about a prospective meeting between the Israeli government and the Palestinian Authority. No-one knew when it might happen, and although the PA was always willing to meet as it gave them a chance to list their issues and maybe obtain some concessions, whether it happened or not was always up to Israel. This meant that they only called meetings when they wanted something so rarely did both sides come away from such encounters with any wins. Hani, knowing that he would never be asked to be part of the meeting, expressed the desire to input ideas, if that was appropriate.

As a reflection of his rising stardom, Hani returned to Bethlehem with a state of the art laptop, complete with a USB modem allowing him internet access wherever he was, all paid for by the Palestinian Authority. They wanted him to be contactable not just by email, but by Zoom. Since he was still a little uncertain about the organisations that Ayshaa was working with he was, with a little training, able to research BCI and Ghu-sin Zay-tun for himself on the internet. He had never wanted to meet the leaders of these two organisations, but rather to understand more about them so he could protect himself from any possible backlash.

Then he got the email. It was his first one. It was from Ramallah and it informed him that he was to be part of a group set up to prepare for the meeting with Israel, if and when it should happen. Would he ensure he was in Ramallah in a week's time for the first session. Hani read it through a number of times, trying to understand not only the message, but any underlying meaning. Having shared this with Ayshaa, they both decided that he must spend the week putting together his views with cogent arguments, and evidence where necessary. He decided that not only did he need Ayshaa's input, but also that of some of his men.

Zeyad and Kamel were obvious choices, but he didn't want just 'yes-men' contributions, but views from more independent, yet loyal minds. He would ask Kamel, being the elder statesman of the group, for three or four suggestions for other men he should involve, out of which he would choose two. Fahed and Omar were chosen and, after swearing them to secrecy with unspecified serious consequences for any leaks, he outlined the opportunity they had. Initially, Hani allowed them to list all the complaints against Israel they could think of just to get it all out. They all got very animated, as he knew they would, so when they began to repeat themselves, Hani stepped in and set out specific headings which would enable them to organise their thoughts.

When they had finished, Hani had a comprehensive list of issues. He explained that they would not all even be mentioned, but some would and maybe they would get some movement on a few. The men looked discouraged. Hani encouraged them to imagine if they made a little progress at every meeting, what that would look like in five years time. They had to play the long game. To push his point home, he asked them to think where the Palestinians might be now if that approach had been started thirty years ago, instead of always asking for the everything and getting nothing.

When Hani got back to his shop/office, he took the issues generated and began to put potential solutions against them. He didn't want the meeting with the Israelis just to be a complaining session which it could easily degenerate into. It put them in the role of a child moaning at a parent. This was how things had always been done, but that was not how he wanted the Palestinians to be positioned. He wanted to begin to suggest solutions which would cost Israel very little, but which would mean a lot to Palestinians, either in terms of human morale or economic benefit.

His phone buzzed. It was a text from the hospital notifying him that Ghalia was ready to be discharged. Her diagnosis had been unstable angina so fortunately, there had been no need for surgery which was a blessing, financial as well as personal. She had, however, been put on a regime of medication. Hani thought that drugs were generally available in Bethlehem, if you had the money to buy them although he knew that government or charitable institutions would be cheaper than private pharmacies, who tended to charge much higher prices. These institutions were generally Palestinian NGOs financed by external benefactors. But even the cheaper prices were way beyond the reach of a large proportion of the population. He researched availability via his new laptop, and was astonished to learn that, according to a recent PCBS household expenditure survey, drugs represented around 50% of a Palestinian household's expenditure on health.

The message also informed him that his mother would be dropped off at the checkpoint six o'clock that evening by an ambulance. His bank account had been accordingly debited. It had all been cleared with the military, so she could just walk through, which didn't leave him much time and since he didn't have a car, he hired a taxi to bring her back home. The Fatah money was certainly coming in useful. However, he considered the 'just walking through' as rather optimistic.

Although it took some time, the documentation supplied by the hospital seemed to do the trick with the military, and by half past six she came through on the Bethlehem side alone with her little bag looking rather bewildered and dazed. Hani quickly spotted her, escorted her to the taxi, and they were on their way home.

27

MEDAD AND SHANA were on their way to Tel Aviv airport. Shana had arranged with her parents for them to overnight at her home ready for an early start. In the four bedroom house there was a room prepared for each of them, mother and father making Medad feel very welcome. It was up early and out of the house before anyone else was awake for the short run to the terminal via a taxi. Not for them the luxury of diplomatic travel, so they found themselves queuing up for the routine security questions that everyone went through leaving Israel.

"Where do you live?" "What do you do?" "Where are you going?" Girls with IDF uniforms were conducting the interviews. It was quite perfunctory as they had Israeli passports. They knew this would happen and they submitted to the examination graciously. Eventually all but one queue was behind them. Check in done, suitcases dispatched and hand luggage invisibly searched by the security machine; they had been passed safe to fly. A visit to a couple of duty free shops to buy some little presents for Chuck's two girls and they joined the other four hundred odd passengers for the final queue to board the 747. They had both consumed a coffee and pastry whilst they had gone through the various airport processes, confident that shortly they would be getting a more substantial breakfast on the aircraft.

No delays. As soon as everyone had been seated, they heard the front door closing and the aircraft slowly being shunted backwards by the low profile pushback tractor. The aircraft's APU (Auxiliary Power Unit) was still powering all the services on the aircraft and Medad now noticed the sound of each of the jumbo's four engines being powered up in turn. Once the tractor had disengaged, he felt the plane moving forward towards the runway slowly. He turned to Shana, smiled and held her hand. They were on their way. It seemed only a few minutes later that the noise of the engines increased and they felt the power of the Rolls Royce engines push them back into their seats. They were speeding down the runway, ready to fly.

It was a long flight to Washington DC. Medad filled the time by watching movies that he had never seen before, and there were many of those since there were no cinemas in the conservative settlement where he came from. Shana, on the other hand, had been brought up in liberal Tel Aviv which was rife with cinemas. The Lev Dizengoff in the centre of the city was open seven days a week with six screens. It showed many top box-office films and she had seen most of the current ones so, in between meals and sleeping, she immersed herself in her Kindle.

Although the plane touched down slightly early at Dulles, they arrived at a time when the President and Congress were at loggerheads over the new budget which meant that the federal government had run out of money and public employees such as immigration officials were not getting paid. Unions had only agreed a minimum level of personnel at airports, so there were queues all the way from the plane's exit door to the two immigration desks that were operating for all landings. Medad texted Chuck when they were out of the plane to explain their delay. Chuck already knew it would be a couple of hours at best and commiserated.

When they got through the bureaucracy, Chuck was there to meet them, to apologise and make them feel welcome. Rush hour in DC like most large cities wasn't an hour and even at eight o'clock in the evening there was still plenty of traffic, but they made it to the house in Georgetown without too much delay. It was by no means at the top end of the range in this neighbourhood which apparently could sell for over $12m. However it had four bedrooms and plenty of living space on the ground floor. Nicely decorated but definitely still unashamedly a kids house. No space to park any cars except on the road where the curb was reserved for residents. The trees lining the street gave the area a relaxed look and the two Israelis certainly felt welcome.

Gloria greeted them and while Chuck took the two main bags upstairs, she introduced the and the children explaining that they had helped her prepare a simple meal. It was now nine o'clock in the evening and from experience, Chuck knew that they needed to retire for the night. Shana still didn't really know who Chuck was, except he was a friend that Medad had met in his intern days. No doubt she would find out more soon. Gloria showed each of them to their separate bedrooms and wished them a good nights sleep.

The family stayed downstairs while each of their guests used the family bathroom and retired to their own bedroom. Shana slept well, but Medad had a fitful night even though very tired which he put it down to over-thinking what Chuck wanted from the relationship. So next morning, over a breakfast of cereal and eggs, Medad was still yawning. By this time, the children had already left for school leaving Chuck to announce that he and Gloria had taken the day off work and were going to take them sightseeing around Washington.

It was a bit of a whistle-stop tour in Chuck's Buick GMC, a huge car which, according to Medad, only lacked bullet proofing, oh and a mini bar. They passed the White House, the Capital Building, the Washington Monument, Lincoln Memorial and the Smithsonian before Chuck parked the car and they took a walk. Medad found himself together with Chuck, with Shana and Gloria some way distant laughing together.

Chuck made his move. He remarked, "I notice that you haven't told Shana who I am," He quickly added, "I understand of course, but I have a request to make."

Medad said nothing. Chuck explained his role at the State Department and how they wanted to steer Israel to a more conciliatory relationship with the Palestinians. "I think that you want the same thing and perhaps we could help each other. I recognise that you are on the side of peace, and thought that it might be possible for us to work a little more closely together for the peace effort."

He further implied that he might be able to provide information which would help Medad make his arguments more effective, if and when he was in a position to influence the right politicians. Medad was not naïve enough now to miss the agenda... or the opportunity. He liked Chuck and definitely wanted to play a peace role in his country. They walked on a little way further in silence. Chuck didn't speak, neither did Medad who was thinking hard. Chuck was a rising star and it might be good to have a closer relationship, both personally and professionally.

Finally he spoke, "How it might work?"

Chuck didn't answer immediately, but then said, "Perhaps we could agree in principle now, and speak more when your holiday is over and you've had time to be sure." It was agreed. Chuck offered his hand, and Medad shook it. The women walking behind saw the handshake.

Chuck and Gloria had arranged for a babysitter that evening so they could take Medad and Shana out to experience Washington's evening atmosphere. They ended up in a very classy restaurant, Bistro Bis on Capital Hill, where Chuck had booked a table. His guests were provided with a menu without prices, so they could choose their meal without any guilt. In fact Chuck was the only one to have a menu with the financial facts. The couples got on really well without talking politics at all – somewhat of a miracle, thought Shana.

It was about halfway through the meal that a loud voice behind Medad and Shana exclaimed 'Chuck!' An older, well dressed man came up to the table with a greeting. He looked super smooth and confident as if he dined here every night of the week. Chuck stood to his feet and introduced his friend first to his wife, then to Medad and Shana. Medad also stood up and shook him by the hand. The interloper explained he was just someone from the office and apologised for interrupting their meal. "Delighted to meet anyone from Israel." And with that, he disappeared into another room in the restaurant.

Chuck apologised to Medad and Shana and explained that coming here they were bound to meet some government people. This was one of the restaurant that was frequented by many politicos. At this, he quickly glanced around the room and pointed out several senators, some journalists he knew and other senior officials in various parts of governments. The price of dining at a good restaurant, he explained. Still no name was forthcoming. The rest of the meal was uninterrupted and very enjoyable.

The following day after breakfast, Gloria wished them a great holiday and disappeared off to work. Chuck then drove Medad and Shana to the airport for their flight to Los Angeles, and the start of their west coast seven day tour. After waving them off, Chuck made a quick call on his mobile to Langley and spoke with someone for a few minutes before getting into his car and driving to his office at the State Department.

Although Larry was based in Jerusalem, he had been asked to come over to Washington purely to bump into Medad at Bistro Bis. He was not on anyone's payroll as such, but was paid to complete certain tasks given to him by his masters at Langley. They had determined that it was he who would be handling Medad in Israel. It was his responsibility, therefore, to 'secure' him. He put down his phone after the call with Chuck and thought for a second. The young Medad had looked very comfortable in the restaurant. Perhaps he was already on side. He hadn't been expecting such an easy conquest. Then again Chuck was not a professional in his game, so he had no certainty that what Chuck thought he had secured, was actually secure.

Once Medad returned from his trip to Washington, Larry had only twenty-four hours to make it definite before his target flew out of the US. Yes, he could do it in Jerusalem but he wanted Medad to think he was based in the US. So the question playing in his mind was, should he make another meet with Medad before he left, but this time without Chuck and have the detailed discussion with Medad himself now to 'secure' him? Larry knew that Chuck wanted to close the deal himself, and after all he was the one Medad trusted. The fact that he was not a pro might actually be an advantage, but it was his role on the line and he needed to be there, somehow.

He called Chuck and said that he wanted to be somewhere around when they had their final conversation, just in case he was needed. Chuck was reluctant, thinking he might screw the whole thing up. It was agreed that Chuck would close the deal with Medad, but if Medad was having second thoughts, then Chuck would introduce him again, then bow out of the conversation. Before the call ended, Chuck gave a last piece of advice to Larry, advising him not to offer any financial incentive. Medad was a man of principle and wanted to help his country, not think he was betraying it for personal gain.

Oblivious to all the inter-agency rivalry that Washington and its hinterland were renowned for, Medad and Shana flew to Los Angeles to spend a hectic few days at Venice Beach, Universal Studios and walking along the Hollywood Walk of Fame. They were holding hands, recalling names on the pavement they knew and wondering who the others were. Next day, a quick hop to San Diego to visit the zoo, then a longer drive inland to Phoenix in their hire car and up to Flagstaff and the Grand Canyon with Shana's hand on Medad's knee.

They decided to take the Bright Angel Trail. They were young and Medad had something in mind. At the end of the Trail was Plateau Point where they could gaze over the cliff edge at the surging Colorado river hundreds of feet below them. Shana had been thinking it would happen at some point, but was taken completely by surprised when Medad quickly when down on one knee and popped the question. Completely unconscious of other trekkers nearby who subtly moved away to give them a little space, they immersed themselves in each other for an hour before deciding to make a start back.

With that adrenalin running, the long journey back to the top didn't seem that difficult, although Shana admitted the last uphill mile and a half was rather strenuous even though Medad had taken her backpack on his front as well carrying his own on his back. But they made it! Gloria had waxed lyrical about Grand Canyon and urged them to fit it into their schedule, but even her ambitious description didn't do it justice. It was breathtaking and they were very happy.

Medad had been hesitant about talking to Shana about his business relationship with Chuck, but now he knew he had to. Picking the right moment was crucial, he thought, and it unexpectedly came over their evening meal, because it was Shana who brought the subject up.

"I like Chuck and Gloria," she started, "and I know you met Chuck when you were at the RIC, but that's quite a way from holidaying over here and being invited to stay at their house… and what was the handshake all about?"

Medad was wondering where, how to start. His prepared intro didn't fit the conversation now and he desperately didn't want this to be an issue between them.

"Well," he started, just as the main course was brought to the table. A moment to think. He quickly decided to go through it all chronologically. Ten minutes later Shana had nearly finished her fish and Medad hardly started his .beef.

"I've not committed to do anything yet," he paused.

Shana reached out her hand and put it over his. "I think you're right. If it helps establish a peace process fine. If not, you can withdraw, right?"

"Absolutely," said Medad. "I haven't told Dan yet and I don't think I will, at least not yet."

Medad lay wide awake long after Shana had gone to sleep wondering what on earth he was doing. He knew what his father and brother would think of it all but, more importantly, he wondered what his mother would think. The next thing he knew Shana was shaking him awake so, he concluded, he must have slept a bit, although it didn't feel like that.

Today it was a drive from Flagstaff to Las Vegas, just to see the night lights; they had no intention of going into any casinos. Then through Death Valley heading for San Francisco. A day admiring the Golden Gate Bridge amidst the mist from the Alcatraz vantage point and the final day back at the airport queuing for their return flight to Washington. The whirlwind tour was nearly over.

So when Medad and Shana arrived back in Washington, it was as fiancés. They seemed very happy to Chuck, although he was still not sure if Medad had talked to Shana about him or what he had proposed, nor was he sure if he should mention it in front of both of them. He decided in the end that Shana was Medad's responsibility and if he agreed to the proposal, Chuck would not mention it. If, however, Medad was reluctant to agree, then he would raise the issue of Shana as he had nothing to lose, and he really didn't want to expose the young Israeli to Larry at this point. There would be plenty of time for that in Jerusalem. He thought he could appeal to Shana explaining that this might secure a safer future for their children. Gloria, who had no inkling of Chuck's business dealings, was just delighted with their romantic news and opened a bottle champagne to celebrate.

Larry also had his own plans. He needed to have a relationship with Medad and not leave it to Chuck alone and so he planned to gatecrash the final meeting anyway. The meet was set up at a Washington Wizards basketball game that evening. They were playing Miami Heat. It was the first professional basketball game Medad and Shana had been to and they were looking forward to it. Before the game started, Chuck and Medad went to buy hot dogs and drinks which was the opportunity for Chuck to cover some of the detail.

Medad, being a cautious type, suggested a 'see how it goes' basis. Chuck agreed that was the best approach and he guided Medad back to the seat before Larry found where they were. Shortly after, Chuck received the call he was expecting, and a not-very-happy Larry asked what was going on. Chuck excused himself for a moment.

"Work," he sighed. "I won't be long, I hope." He then tried to reassure Larry that the deal was on and there was no need for him to meet Medad right now. In fact, it would be counter productive. Best if Larry was the one to take the first of the promised documents to Medad when he was back home. He could then wine and dine him and establish his own relationship. Larry grunted that his bosses were not going to be pleased that he'd been cut out here in the US. Chuck ended the call and went back to his guests and the basketball game.

The next morning saw Medad and Shana safely on a United flight to Ben Gurion Airport, Chuck in his office at the State Department writing his report, and Larry meeting with his boss at Langley to determine their next move.

Shana went straight home from the airport as it was still college vacation for another three days, and he went back to his office telling great stories of how wonderful the US was, and how everyone should go there at least once. Truth to tell, nothing was going on in the department and it was all a little boring. No sign of any meeting with the Palestinians, and anyway the papers were all ready. They would have to be updated, but no need to do that until a date was finalised, otherwise they'd be doing it every week.

A week or so later Medad was sitting at his desk and his mobile went. It was an unknown contact but Medad answered it. Larry, the guy who had bumped into them at Bistro Bis was in town and wanted to meet up. Unfortunately Chuck wasn't over at the moment, but he hoped he would do. Lunch was arranged at Primitivo, not far from the Knesset. Larry didn't seem as friendly as Chuck. He was older, more businesslike, more confident in his abilities, even a little bit arrogant. Medad carried on munching his mains, whilst Larry was outlining a far wider relationship than Chuck had talked about.

"You see," explained Larry, "the relationship which we have with Israel is extensive. We can offer you certain information that may come our way, but we will need something in return."

Medad kept his eyes down on his meal and refused to show interest or disinterest in what Larry was saying. The American seemed oblivious to the reception Medad was giving him.

"All those fighter jets have got to mean something, haven't they?" Medad treated the question as a rhetorical one and said nothing.

"In short, we would like a two way arrangement whereby each of us provides something of value to the other. What d'ya say?"

Medad finished eating just as Larry stopped talking and started on his. Medad felt he had grown up in the last month or so and begun to understand what politics and business relationships were about. He was not to be browbeaten, so he excused himself, went to the cloakroom, took out his phone and made a call, while Larry carried on eating. Chuck answered his phone at the other end. Medad explained where he was, what he had just heard, and that he felt let down. He closed the call before Chuck could respond, went back to the table, thanked Larry for the lunch and left the restaurant. If his mouth hadn't been full of a philly cheese steak sandwich, Larry would have let out a loud expletive.

Shana was now back at her halls and later that evening at their usual meet, Medad explained to her what had happened. She squeezed his hand and affirmed he had done the right thing. Do you think Chuck will call you later?

28

WITH HIS MOTHER safely at home, Hani's mind was back on business, but Ayshaa's had to be on Ghalia. Why was it always the women who had to pick up the pieces? She knew her mother-in-law was going to need proper recuperation which didn't mean looking after Rena everyday, or any day. So either Ayshaa was going to have to limit her activities or find someone to look after her daughter. As far as the former was concerned, BWP was going very well, but she had put the idea of a newspaper to one side for the moment. There were now four ladies groups up and running and each had agreed to a small donation to the charity. As to the latter, she had no idea.

It was time for Ghalia's pill – only one, but four times a day. Ayshaa offered it with some water whilst her mother-in-law swallowed it screwing up her eyes, her body shuddering. She was not used to pills and, if the truth were known, didn't trust them. Each time she declared to whoever was listening that she was fine and didn't need them. But she took them to please her daughter-in-law and off she went to lie down, leaving Ayshaa to do some housework.

It was a disappointment to Ayshaa that no-one from the main city had responded to her invitation to join BWP, but only those from the refugee camps. Palestinians from the main city were under exactly the same restrictions as those in the refugee camps, with the women still struggling with the same male dominated home life. However, they were usually better off, some owning or renting property, some having their own businesses, others enjoying reasonably good jobs. That meant they could contribute more to the costs of the women's programme if they got involved.

When Lara had met the BWP team she had explained to Ayshaa in a quiet word afterwards that four groups was her maximum for the moment. Her own workload was now full and she couldn't commit to any more groups although she thought there was still a latent demand out there. They could both see the positive results of the programme already as nearly all the participants had benefited. Their demeanour was different, their heads were held higher and they were more positive in themselves, even though nothing had actually changed in their home environments.

Ayshaa had been thinking that she would like to be trained to do what Lara did, and lead a group, especially if Lara's time was going to be limited. But with Ghalia's condition, that didn't seem a possibility, at least in the short term. So her mind turned back to BCI. Lara had said that she knew of them but Ghu-sin Zay-tun and BCI had never worked together as far as she knew. Now Rena was crying, wanting food. Her thinking time came to a hasty conclusion.

"So this is how it's going to be for a while," Ayshaa was speaking out loud to herself. She was frustrated but determined to keep to some sort of routine for Rena's sake. It didn't even cross her mind to ask Hani to help with this. It was not what Palestinian men did, and even Hani would have had an identity struggle with that responsibility.

Hani was at the shop. His struggle at the moment was keeping Fatah and the PA at arms length. It was becoming more and more difficult for he now really needed the monthly income they gave him and found himself more and more at their disposal. He didn't altogether regret it and, at times, he found himself enjoying the cut and thrust of his new responsibility and the new relationships he was having to navigate. At the back of his mind he had the shop so that he could always go back to it, but now he wasn't sure if he ever wanted to go back. In fact, looking into himself, he discovered that there was more to him than being a shopkeeper. As Ayshaa had said, Rena didn't want a shopkeeper for a father, but someone who could change the destiny of his people.

Woah! He came out of the daydream quickly. "I'd better keep my feet on the ground and keep myself in check. Stop fantasising about destinies!" He knew he had an important document to put together, so he quickly corralled his mind back to the job in hand. There was nothing new in the issues his men had raised but what he now needed to do was to set out a series of demands…no, not demands, a series of… yes, opportunities. He wanted to develop a range of Palestinian responses for each issue ranging from the ideal, which Israel would never agree to, to the minimum which the Palestinians would not accept… unless they had to.

They would start with the ideal and negotiate their way down the list hoping they could settle as near the top as possible. To do that, he also had to set out benefits to Israel for each level of concession. This was a lot of work, and he needed other brains to go over this before he submitted it. Who had the mental capacity and, more to the point, who could he trust? None of his men were capable of thinking at this level, so he had resolved to ask Ayshaa. She had previously given some real help both in original ideas and in sparking his own thoughts, but he also needed a man's perspective.

He yawned and suddenly felt really tired, and it wasn't for lack of sleep but simply the energy being expended on the project. He'd have to do a better job at pacing himself otherwise a breakdown would be beckoning. Enough for one day, but still immersed in the project as he walked home thinking about what benefits he could conjure up for Israel. He was almost home when he remembered he had to pick more medication for his mother. He was annoyed with himself and his stride increased as he tried to minimise the extra time this was going to take. Back to Manger Square for cash, on to the pharmacy, then home.

Ghalia was definitely weaker than she had been before the heart problem. Fear was in her eyes, a dread that she wouldn't fully recover and get back the energy she used to have. He did his best to allay those fears but not very successfully, and was well aware that Ayshaa was having take all the carer responsibility pulling back on her own work. He was thankful to her for that, so all he could do was to trust that the medication would do its magic and that, given time, his mother would recover.

After their evening meal when Ghalia had retired, he began to share in detail with Ayshaa what he was trying to do. She was happy to give her input but her time and energy was now severely limited. She agreed that it also needed a man's viewpoint, especially as it was men he was trying to persuade. Out of the blue she thought of Omari, the founder and director at Ghu-sin Zaytun but hesitated to suggest him, fearing a Christian-Muslim debate might be kicked-off. However, she did make a mental note to try and arrange for both men to meet. But where, and how?

Some days passed and Ayshaa was no nearer discovering how to get these two men together. She had found out that Omari was happy to meet, it was Hani who was the issue. She finally arranged for Omari to visit Ethar and her husband. They wanted to thank Ghu-sin Zay-tun for bringing back Abdul-lah, and Hani agreed to see them as well. It was done, well nearly. Omari was primed, so it was just up to her husband. She hoped that they wouldn't just be men, but that they would talk!

It was Omari who made the first move towards Hani when he arrived. The two men shook hands and gave each other a traditional Arabic Palestinian greeting, '*As-salam alaykum*', meaning 'Peace be with you'. Conversation was a little stilted to begin with and mostly revolved around the freeing of Abdul-lah. Ayshaa occasionally glanced at them as they all drank their arabic coffee and was relieved to see them still talking at least. The tension gradually eased as Omari answered Hani's questions about how Ghu-sin Zay-tun operated and what expertise they had. Hani's shoulders, which had been tight, began to relax as refilled his coffee and helped himself to some falafel. He began to see why Ayshaa had aligned herself with Ghu-sin Zay-tun. He had to admit to being impressed, but still a little suspicious. They were fellow Palestinians no doubt, but he was Muslim and Omari was Christian.

The gathering came to an end and each made their way home. Ayshaa pushed Rena in her pushchair with Hani, deep in thought, walking alongside her. We're almost a normal family, Ayshaa thought as they made their way through the streets. As they approached the shop, Hani kissed Ayshaa good-bye and made his way inside, whilst Ayshaa carried on towards home to check on her mother-in-law. Ghalia was making some progress, although Ayshaa was still a little concerned over her shortness of breath and unwillingness to stray far from the rooms. Like Hani, she hoped that time and her medication would allow a full recovery, although that had yet to start manifesting.

Hani was seated at his desk and started to work on his document. He was beginning to run out of ideas and wondered if he had bitten off more than he could chew. The concept of producing these 'opportunities' for Israel for each of the issues he wanted to raise was no doubt a good one. It was good preparation for any negotiation, and the Palestinians didn't have much to bar-gain with. He recalled when Ariel Sharon was Israeli premier, their withdrawal from Gaza wasn't a negotiated move, rather a unilateral move even though it forced many settlers to abandon their homes and move back into Israel. Perhaps that's how it's going to be.

He was deep in thought, and not a little frustrated with himself, when his phone vibrated signalling an incoming call. The number was not in his contact list, so he didn't recognise it although he saw that it was a Bethlehem number. He let it ring out to see if the caller would identify himself and perhaps leave a message. It was from Omari saying how he enjoyed the conversation they had this morning and, whilst he didn't know exactly what Hani did (Hani had been quite coy about revealing much about himself), if it helped the Palestinian cause, he would be happy to help in any way possible.

Ummmm. I wonder if I should. Could be risky, especially if certain people found out that our negotiation position had been shared with not only a non Fatah person but a Christian, albeit a recognised community leader. The coincidence of the call and his struggle to find a suitable person to share his thoughts with, was quite telling with him. He didn't believe in fate, or that Allah would intervene in his life, but there was something pulling him towards making a return call and suggesting a further meeting. Yes, he would but he wouldn't talk about the document yet, rather test out the man and see if the relationship was going to be a real one. He was really testing out his own instincts.

Now his laptop was buzzing and he was invited to his first zoom call. It was the PA Security Chief wanting to talk about his preparedness for any Israeli-Palestinian meeting. Hani had never met him face to face, just seen him in meetings. To say he was surprised was an understatement. Hani confessed that he was preparing a document with the main Palestinians issues and possible solutions against each one. There was a pause, and both men stared at each other for a few seconds. The security chief then muttered something about Hani's reputation, which Hani didn't quite hear. "I'd like to see it in a week's time please." It wasn't a request and Hani didn't take it as such. The call was ended before Hani had the chance to say anything more. Now I have no choice. He returned Omari's call, apologising for not picking up, and said he'd be delighted to meet up again.

29

MEDAD DETERMINED THAT he would not call Chuck first. It was Chuck's move and his explanation for Larry's behaviour had better be good. The following day early afternoon Israeli time, which probably meant that it was quite early US time, Chuck called from home. After an apology for Larry's behaviour, he confirmed that, yes, Larry was CIA which means he knows a lot that's going on in the wider Middle East which might well impact Israel.

"He has access to some information that I don't and which he should have given you at your lunch. He has passed it to me in the hope that I can get it to you. Unfortunately it can't be done over the phone or in an email or letter. So it means me trying to get across to you, unless…you would agree to give Larry a second chance?"

Medad hesitated and said, "I'm not sure. We really didn't get on."

Chuck was quiet for a moment and then said, "In the service of our countries, it would be nice if we had the luxury of liking everyone we dealt with. It doesn't happen. He has something which you need to see."

Now Medad was quiet and of course, Chuck was right. What if Larry was Larry? Did it really matter?

While Medad was thinking, Chuck said, "Think about it, but not too long because the information is current… and Larry will be back over to Israel in a week's time." Chuck was still pushing the myth that Larry was based in the US. Medad promised he would consider it. He had no idea what this information was or whether it was going to be useful to him or not. He decided he wanted some cover internally, so after a meeting with his boss about an entirely different subject, he casually asked,

"I guess the US provides us with lots of useful information, how do they do that and who might receive it?" Dan in a similar casual tone answered, "Sure. US input comes into the government in a variety of ways: the military, the Foreign office, directly to the PM's office and probably into Mossad. There might be more that I am not aware of."

Dan was answering whilst doing something else and not really paying full attention. Medad's next question was,

"And how useful is that information to our department?" Dan stopped moving papers on his desk and looked at Medad, who began to think he had overplayed his hand.

"If it's relevant, it's passed on." Medad muttered his thanks and, as he left the office, Dan's eyes followed him.

The following day Medad had decided not to go ahead with Larry, if that was his real name, which Medad was beginning to doubt. After his meeting with Dan, he was beginning to feel a little exposed, and also realised that both incoming and outgoing calls could be traced if sometime in the future the authorities wanted to investigate. He was sure that whatever information they had wasn't worth his career, and that there were other ways the US could get Israel's attention. It felt like a weight had been lifted off his shoulders. He felt normal again. Until...

It was Friday, the first day of the Israeli weekend and he had arrived at the agreed coffee shop and was waiting for Shana on one of the outside tables. It wasn't busy and while he was waiting he decided to make a quick call to his mother.

"I'll be coming home for *Shabbat* this evening, if that's ok?"

His mother was delighted. He was concentrating on the conversation when, out of the corner of his eye, he thought he saw someone looking suspiciously like Larry passing behind him. He silently cursed himself for being paranoid and then cursed Larry, until an envelope 'accidentally' dropped on the outside table he was sitting at. He quickly looked up and saw whoever it was disappearing round the corner at speed. He was so startled that he stopped talking to his mother and stared at the corner of the café.

"Hello Medad, are you still there?"

Medad jerked back to the conversation. "Sorry, Shana's just arrived. See you later."

Shana hadn't arrived, but he couldn't say someone looking like a CIA man called Larry had just put an envelope of his table and promptly disappeared. There are certain things you don't tell your mother. He ended the call glued to his seat.

He stared at the envelope on the other side of the table and, making no move to touch it, screwed his neck around to see the writing on it without moving from his seat. God, it had his name on it. He suddenly looked around to see if he was being watched, spied on. It all looked normal. Nobody suspicious that he could tell, but then a professional wouldn't look suspicious. He looked again at the envelope as if somehow it was poisonous or about to incinerate the immediate surroundings. It was left untouched as Medad thought through the implications. He was now pretty sure it was Larry.

Just then Shana actually arrived and joined him at the table apologising that she was late. Medad got up to get the coffees leaving the envelope on the table. While the barista was making the lattes he saw Shana pick up the envelope and look at it. He wanted to shout out to leave it alone, but embarrassment stopped him. Medad came back with not only the coffees but two pastries and Shana immediately asked him about the envelope. Whilst she sipped her latte, he explained what had happened and admitted that he didn't know whether to take it or not.

She was concerned. With a mouthful of pastry she said, "This surely means they, or someone, is following you or they knew you would be here waiting for me." Shana was beginning to feel very uncomfortable and started looking over her shoulder at other people on the terrace. Medad was sure someone would be watching to see if he took it and if not, to quickly scoop it up before it fell into other hands.

"We could leave it here, go inside the café and see who comes along to pick it up." Medad was working through the scenarios. "Or I could take it back with me and open it tomorrow in the presence of Dan, my boss. Or I could open it now and then decide whether to tell Dan."

Another ghastly thought occurred. He quickly told Shana about his conversation with Dan the previous day. "So," he mused, "What if it isn't Larry or the Americans. What if it's my own people testing me out? And what if they're filming this?"

Shana brought him down to earth. "What would you do if you didn't know Chuck or Larry or any of it, and someone dropped an envelope with your name on it in front of you?" She looked at him.

"I guess I would open it."

"So let's do that."

His hands were actually shaking when he started to open the envelope. Medad was quietly admitting to himself that he was not made for this cloak and dagger stuff. He was a straight man in more senses than one. Shana was now peering over his shoulder. If anyone was filming this, Medad thought, it didn't look like any of the spy novels he had read. Then again, he hadn't read that many. The message was typed and curiously short. It related to the Knesset elections which were due in six months time, and talked of secret meetings to provoke a crisis in Gaza, allowing the government to go in 'all guns blazing', playing the security card as a way of ensuring their re-election. That was it.

They looked at each other. There were no names, no meeting dates, no details of what was planned. Nothing of any substance. Shana was first to say what they were both thinking. "That doesn't mean it is true. It's been a suspicion of the peace groups for years."

Medad was wondering, "What if this is just the teaser and whoever had dropped the envelope has all the explosive details. Because if they do, and it is verifiable, it would be just that, explosive!"

Shana was following his logic, "That would place corruption at the very heart of our democracy. But why you? Why not a journalist? There are many creditable journalists working for serious papers who would be in a much better position than you to investigate, verify and publish."

Medad finished his coffee, "That's obviously not what they want. They don't want to bring down the government, but they do want to prevent an onslaught on Gaza. That must be it."

Shana was thinking hard. "This message is designed to draw you in. You can't do anything with this as it is. Anyone you show it to, whether government official or journalist will dismiss it unless there is more information. So the question is, are you going to be drawn in or not? And if you are drawn in and they give you more information, will it be credible enough or will they want to keep drawing you in so there's no turning back. What is it they think you could do with the information that they can't do themselves?"

The rest of the day was ruined. They spent the whole of it debating the issue backwards and forwards. Meanwhile, Medad had the envelope with its contents burning in his pocket and by the end of the day, they were no further forward. They said goodbye to each other and went their separate ways. Medad spent the night tossing and turning without getting much sleep at all but by the morning something had clicked in his brain. He had come to a decision. It was so obvious, he wondered why it hadn't happened yesterday.

He would show the message to Dan first thing on Sunday. That would cover him internally both ways – whether it was the CIA or his own side. In his heart of hearts he didn't think that Dan will have had time to set the meet up within two days, so he was pretty sure it was the CIA man. He would be careful not to mention Larry, and only if pushed would he reference Chuck, and only from the session at the RIC. Not straightforward, but the best he could do.

Dan stared at the envelope and the message. "Tell me again how you got this," was his repeated question.

Medad patiently explained it all again. "We were just having a coffee. It was supposed to be just a normal weekend day with my fiancée. I was sitting, waiting for her. I was on my phone, someone swept past dropped the envelope on my table and disappeared."

"Oh. Congratulations, by the way."

"Thanks."

"And you have no idea who it was?"

"No, but he clearly knew who I was, and my position in this Department."

Dan rocked back in his chair, trying to think through all the issues from his perspective. After going over it for a third time and asking whether this was anything to do with his questions about the US a few days go, Medad said he didn't think so, and was dismissed.

As he looked back through the glass of Dan's office, he could see that his boss hadn't moved at all. He saw him eventually pick up his phone and Medad knew he no longer had any control over what was about to happen.

The next few days were so normal as to be boring. No word from Larry. No word from Dan. No word from Chuck. He hoped he hadn't lost a friend because he really liked Chuck. But Larry was not supposed to in Israel until next week? Maybe Chuck himself had been under pressure from the CIA to do what he had done. His mind started to turn over the message again. It could be true. If Dan or someone from his own side didn't follow through with him at some point, he might give Chuck a ring. Surely it was too important to allow the government to try to suppress it. He knew the correlation of 'security' concerns with upcoming elections, but had always believed the government when they said that it was Hamas trying to interfere in Israel's elections. However, if something did get out, he knew he would be in the firing line.

A week went past and nothing. He was not sleeping, not concentrating and not making any sense. Shana began to get worried and so she advised him to try to square the circle by calling Chuck. Whatever he had to say might relieve the stress that Medad was putting himself under. It couldn't get much worse. When Medad finally agreed to it, he was almost ready to do anything. Shana gave him a burner phone that he could use so the call could not be traced back to him unless someone was actively listening but he had to take a chance. This was assuming that Chuck would pick up on a number he didn't recognise. If not, he could always leave a cryptic message so he would know it was Medad.

Chuck did indeed pick up. "I thought it might be you. How are you?" He sounded unconcerned, almost innocent of everything that was going on.

Medad envied his control, his laid back American attitude. Leaving normal pleasantries aside, Medad jumped in. "Is the message real? Do you have names, places? Do you have recorded conversations? Who has fed you this information?"

Chuck listened and recognised the stress that the younger man was under. He also brushed aside small talk and answered. "Yes. Yes, places. Just transcripts. Can't reveal any names."

Medad was trembling and walking around in circles in Wohl Rose Park as he attempted to grasp what he was being told. He found himself asking what was he supposed to do with this?Chuck didn't answer directly, but just said, "Hold it together a little longer." Then hung up.

30

IT WAS AN unlikely scene. A Christian and a Muslim working together to bring about a better peace for their nation and Israel. Hani had weighed it all up yet again on his way to Ghu-sin Zay-tun. Was he doing the right thing? Was Omari trustworthy? If there was a leak from somewhere, how vulnerable was he? He decided yet again that he had no other choice. He had outlined the task to Omari over the phone and Omari had indicated he would be delighted to help. There was a back door to his building which Hani could use if he felt it was necessary and Omari had cleared a room in their building ready for work.

Both of them sat around a table with snacks and coffee working on Hani's document. They kept all details in paper on the table although Omari thought a whiteboard would help them to see things more clearly. In the end he bowed to Hani's security fears. Neither of them knew whether their work would ever see the light of day, but they both thought it had the potential to be a key document in a succession of Palestinian-Israeli talks, so it was worth giving it their best shot.

They worked solidly for the whole week that the Chief had allowed, before they were both satisfied that they had covered as much ground as possible. Each evening all papers would be gathered up and Hani watched Omari put them in his safe. Hani had wanted to keep them himself, but Omari persuaded him that if he got mugged on his way back home, it would be the end not just of the talks but for him. It was a measure of how much Hani had come to like, trust and respect the Christian Palestinian that he agreed. To have a man of Omari's intellect and standing in his corner was reassuring for he anticipated a bumpy journey ahead in Ramallah if he was going to change attitudes.

Hani emailed his document to the Security Chief and to his 'driver', and waited. It was a few days later when a car pulled up outside his shop and the man from Ramallah announced they were going to back to his office, together. For a moment Hani looked alarmed. He had heard stories before of people simply disappearing. Perhaps his document had threatened someone's position?

"Perhaps," his driver smiled, "I ought to introduce myself properly. Jamal Youssef Rajoub. I shall be chairing the coming talks between Israel and the PA."

Hani looked at him. Jamal was a heavily built man who clearly liked his food, and one of the perks of Ramallah and an expense account was access to lots of calorie-laden food. To say Hani was taken aback was an understatement. He stared open-mouthed before muttering something that sounded like, Oh! Yes, it looked as if the man could throw his weight around, for sure. However, his smile seemed genuine and having recruited Hani in the first place, the Palestinian from Bethlehem felt he had to trust him… at least for the time being.

"What about the Chief of Security. He was the first to ask me for the document. Isn't he going to be the chairman?" Hani was oblivious to the slight he had given to his boss.

"You think he would make a better chairman?" Hani quickly realised his mistake, but Jamal patted him on the back. They both got into the black Mercedes which seem to accommodate Jamal's frame quite easily. As the car wound its way to Ramallah, Jamal commented,

"I heard what you said at the first Bethlehem meeting you attended. I must say I liked it, but you must be aware that not everyone in Ramallah did. There are factions within factions there, and one has to tread very carefully."

He went on, "Although you only emailed your document to me and the Chief, he copied a number of other people and," he paused to get the right words, "it has caused quite a stir and, as usual, there are people for and against. I have to say that I have come under some pressure not to include you on the team to meet the Israelis… if we ever get to meet them. But I wanted you and you clearly have another sponsor somewhere high up in the PA. Don't take it for granted, however. Such support can evaporate as quickly as it emerged".

He paused to let Hani gain some appreciation of the situation and let this information sink in. Jamal continued. "I needed to get to know you better, hence the driving."

Hani thought that for the second time in as many days, he had got himself an ally. But he was increasingly on his guard, not necessarily taking words spoken as the complete picture of actions that might be taken. In any event, he was determined that neither Omari nor Jamal were ever to know that the other existed. It was the only way he thought he could try and maintain some control. It transpired that the session in Ramallah was for the whole of the negotiating team to meet each other, and to try and agree their positions. Jamal explained to Hani,

"At this first meeting our aim should be to keep our powder dry and let others do the talking. There is never a lack of people wanting to let off steam and talk passionately about their demands and what the PA should and should not do. From this, we should be able to understand where each person is coming from, who might be on side, and who will never come round to our perspective."

Hani nodded. This was something he was used to. Hani had already picked up the word that tied them both together, except he didn't really know Jamal's position or where his red lines were. 'Our' aim; 'our' perspective!

He felt simultaneously affirmed and unnerved. The increasing comfort he had felt around Ramallah was vanishing quickly as a feeling of complete dependence on a man he didn't know engulfed him. He could be thrown to the wolves at any moment of Jamal's choosing so it was important not to let any sign of weakness show that could spell personal disaster. No choice now, though. He was beginning to get used to being in situations where he seemingly had no choices. He pulled himself together. Of course he had choices. Well, at least one choice; he could walk away. But not yet.

True to form, the meeting was awash with passion. Jamal chaired the session with minimal intervention, content for all attendees to speak if they wanted to, and most wanted to, even if it was at the same time as everyone else. Hani, who was not sitting next to Jamal for good reason, said nothing. As the newcomer, he was content to be ignored and just observe each man around the table. It was soon obvious that he wasn't the only one keeping quiet and observing the debate. He discovered later that the Chief of Security had sent his Deputy, Abd Alraheem, to keep an eye on things and report back. The Chief was clearly displeased that he had not been given the chairman's role and he was not about to let anything slip through his fingers.

Also, it appeared that no-one on this team had been given his hard-worked document, although he knew the Security Chief already had a copy. He made a mental note to inform Jamal if he didn't already know. At first he was a little annoyed after all that work, but quickly realised that it was all about timing. If the attendees had been given access to it for this meeting, it would have been quickly savaged and they would not have been able to table it again. In fact, Hani began to realise that it might be a good idea never to table the whole document in the talks with the Israelis, but use it as their hidden script as issues came up. For the moment though, this was a home fixture to be successfully concluded before the away leg. Lose here, and they would surely lose there.

The meeting came to an end after two hours when Jamal banged on the table. "Thank you brothers. I think we all agree on the key demands we need to put to the Israelis." There was no debrief with Jamal, who promptly disappeared and another man approached Hani with orders to drive him back to Bethlehem.

He needed to stop at the CDS pharmacy in Ramallah on the way home, so he could get more medication for Ghalia. Since he would be coming to Ramallah quite regularly, he had decided to give it a 'once-over' to see if this was a better facility than Bethlehem. He guessed it was likely to be better stocked given all the important PA people in Ramallah. His local pharmacy was often out of stock, the building was old and it was without air conditioning. So he found himself examining this building just to see if drugs here were likely to be well kept. It was a two-floor building with two cold rooms for drugs that needed refrigeration, and what looked like quite a lot of stock which Hani could see from the reception area. The building seemed to be well protected against birds and rodents, but there was neither air conditioning nor heating, and ventilation didn't seem to be adequate either. He noticed an alarm system and wondered whether it had ever worked. Much of this type of infrastructure on the West Bank looked good but, in his experience, rarely worked. He noticed that none of the personnel seem to wear uniforms and that they seem to be understaffed which meant that he had to queue for about thirty minutes while the medication he needed was prepared.

But then they were on their way. There was little conversation in the car as neither man knew the other, which made trust difficult. In this environment, trust seemed to be in very short supply and completely dependent on the nature of a personal relationship. Although he hadn't really done anything all day except listen and queue, Hani felt quite exhausted. The driver dropped him off at the shop and he made his way home. He still didn't want Ramallah to know where he lived, although he suspected someone knew. Ayshaa was giving Rena her food, Ghalia was resting and so Hani collapsed into a chair. Over their own meal later, they briefed each other on the events of the day, then decided no more business. For the rest of the evening, they would be just a normal Palestinian married couple, except that they weren't.

The next morning Hani, refreshed and energetic, called Omari. He valued Omari's friendship and wanted to keep him abreast of what was happening, which was not a lot! He explained about the meeting and his own strategy of keeping quiet and seeing where trouble might lie. Omari thanked him and affirmed that such an approach would have been exactly what he would have done.

He paused before he said, "tread carefully my friend. In my opinion, our document is the best basis for moving the Palestinian cause forward that there has been for many years. I have been privileged to gain your trust and help. Please be assured that I want to do all I can to ensure it is not sidelined or dismissed."

Hani was not quite sure what he meant, but he went on to explain that his wife Lara was now a Bethlehem councillor and knew those who represented Bethlehem in Ramallah at the Palestinian National Council. She might be able to obliquely find out who was lining up with who. Hani was dubious; the possibility of drawing in another person, even Omari's wife made him nervous. Omari picked up his reluctance and encouraged Hani to think it over. Nothing would be done without his say so. Just as the conversation was ending, Omari dropped another bombshell. Apparently, he had some old contacts within Israel, specifically a friend which he had made whilst in the US. He thought the person he had in mind had gone into the Israeli civil service. He would have to check but if so, there might be an opportunity to link with like-minded people, in confidence, to see what was being prepared from the other side and who was making the running.

There was a lot less reluctance at this suggestion. Hani made only one provision, that his name should not be mentioned. Omari agreed. Later that day, after some research, Omari made his call. Dan picked up the phone and Omari introduced himself and waited.

31

MEDAD KEPT HIS burner phone on, hoping that he might use it for one last conversation before disposing of it. He was still awaiting a call from Chuck and had not decided how to deal with whatever information was given to him. It all depended.

At last his phone buzzed. Chuck was on his way with a cryptic message. "Phones are not safe, neither are emails or any form of paper. I'll find you."

Hardly a conversation, but then if you thought some entity might have computers word-searching phone conversations, then the less words said the better. Perhaps Chuck had even scripted his message to ensure there were no 'pick-up' words. Medad didn't know. What he did know was that he didn't want to play this game. Some of the angst he felt was relieved by the fact that he had let Dan know what was going on – well, some part of what was going on.

Unknown to Medad, Dan was also having his day disrupted. A voice from the past on the phone which he had never expected to hear again. "It's not Daniel anymore, just Dan."

"Coffee?"

"Yes I can manage a coffee somewhere."

"Jerusalem?"

"Yes that would be easiest."

"Near the Ministry?"

"Absolutely not." Dan suggested a place in the old city near the tourists sites: Timol Shilshom located on Yoel Salomon St. It was a quiet place where 'people came to get a great cup of coffee, to read, and maybe have lunch'. Omari suggested eleven o'clock, which suggested to Dan that if the coffee went well, there was the opportunity to stay on for lunch. Dan was a little suspicious, but also intrigued and wondered what his erstwhile friend was up to.

Both arrived at virtually the same time, almost bumping into one another. There was a tenuous shaking of hands and greetings in English as they made their way to a table. They gave their orders and looked at each other. Both had aged a little, Dan losing more hair than Omari, but the latter rather weightier than when they were both in the US. Both allowed themselves the luxury of, 'do you remember when… and whatever happened to so and so, just for a few minutes. Dan admitted to being married with two children, a boy and girl and Omari just admitted to being married. Children had not happened for them, at least yet. It seemed to bring a little friendship back between them outside the political divide.

This initial conversation moved on to exchange biographical details about what had happened since they last met in the US. It wasn't just small talk, because both were interested in how their respective careers had developed. Omari clearly knew where Dan was and expressed his congratulations. Dan, for his part, expressed his surprise that a lawyer of Omari's talent would have gone into charity work. Omari explained that he didn't quite see it like that, which led him on to the delicate subject he wanted to raise.

Dan listened carefully as Omari outlined what he had come to say.

"A little while ago I was contacted through Ghu-sin Zay-tun to help put together some thoughts on the Palestinian approach to any peace process." He paused to see Dan's reaction. It seemed as thought his erstwhile friend was listening hard.

"Now I confess that there are many different factions within the Palestinian Authority, as probably there are in and around the Israeli government. Each faction represents a view on Israel, but more importantly, they represent power points and power people within the Palestinian Movement. I couldn't bet on which will gain the ascendency in any Palestinian-Israeli talks, but I have complete confidence, in fact I know that there is a strong peace faction who want to move forward without the usual impossible demands and passionate hype which the PA is known for." Omari paused again, took another sip of coffee and waited for a reaction from Dan. Both men were quiet, sipping their coffee. Dan eventually broke the silence.

"This all sounds interesting. Of course, I don't speak for the government, I'm just a civil servant." Omari noted Dan's reluctance to add anything to the conversation, but he was encouraged that nothing negative had been expressed. He felt he had sown seeds and that further pushing would only damage his cause so he began to talk more about Ghu-sin Zay-tun, and what it was doing. Dan seemed grateful not to be pressed further and genuinely interested in the work that Omari had founded.

Lunch didn't happen and both men were soon on their way. Omari had given Dan his card with the implicit message that it was Dan's turn to call if he wanted to talk further. A further handshake, a vague promise to keep in touch, and that was it. As Omari made his way back to Bethlehem, he was satisfied that Dan had agreed to meet, but anxious that the seeds may have been sown on stony ground. Should he have said more, pushed a little bit more? Time would tell. He hadn't promised Hani any immediate results, and so far there were none.

For Dan's part, he went back to his office deep in thought. First he had Medad with his letter, and now Omari with his PA contacts. What to make of it all? Surely they must be linked in some way. He knew that the government he worked for was not in favour of giving the Palestinians any more ground, rather it favoured literally taking more away and giving it to settlers! He also knew where his Minister stood on the peace issue and he didn't think his own opinion counted for much. Dan would always say he was a mere implementer of government policy, but of course that was never the case, for top civil servants everywhere had a great deal of influence and leverage if they wanted to use it. So what was he going to do?

As with all such bureaucrats the world over, the answer was do nothing and wait. Although he had been seen to lift his phone after his meeting with Medad, that was just window dressing. He wasn't going to call anyone, certainly not his boss, until things were a lot clearer. At the moment there were just a few jigsaw pieces which neither fitted together nor made any sense in his mind. He didn't have the answers to the questions that he knew his boss would ask. That would not be good for him. It would place him on the back foot and definitely not the way to keep his career going upwards. But he was beginning to be suspicious of Medad.

For his part, Medad had decided to avoid Dan for a while if he could. He didn't want to be pushed for further details, because he had no further details to disclose until Chuck showed up. And there he wasn't! It was Larry, just casually leaning against a bench as Medad took his usual lunchtime route. Medad made to keep walking thinking that Larry must have been following him for a day or so to know his normal routine. Larry caught up with him.

"Look, I would like to apologise if I inadvertently offended you last time. I really hope we can put that behind us because there's a lot at stake here."

Medad stopped and faced him up. "Where's Chuck?"

"Ah, you know, a black man in Jerusalem, a bit conspicuous if he wanted to be invisible." He began to walk alongside Medad still talking. "I'm sure you know that most governments in the world had divergent groups within them, some for and some against Israeli policies towards the Palestinians. Yes?" Larry was still a bit patronising.

"Well, the US government is no different and maybe worse than most. Although the President has one line, many in the plethora of other agencies have other lines. I want to promote the cause of negotiation and peace, but I have to go outside normal lines of communication to pursue that and have a bit more freedom than Chuck."

Medad still walking at his usual pace wasn't saying anything. "You know, we're taking one hell of a risk trying to pass information to you, maybe more than you are." That didn't rate with Medad at all who grimaced but said nothing and increased his pace walking through Sacher Park. Larry kept pace but stopped his not very persuasive pitch and surreptitiously passed Medad a memory stick. "It's all there. I have to go."

And with that, he veered away without saying anything about what it was, how the Americans had come by it or how Medad should use the information. Medad continued his lunchtime walk, heart beating a little faster, lungs breathing a little shorter and brain working a little harder than normal. God, this is crazy!

He decided that he shouldn't use either his work PC or his own laptop to open the stick. So it would have to be an internet café, but not just yet. If he was being monitored, and he hadn't spotted Larry in the previous days, he thought he'd leave it a day or two and just follow his routine until he felt safe enough to get to one. He had thought about passing it to Shana and getting her to download the data, but dismissed it. It was not right to reduce the risk to himself by increasing the risk to her, but he would tell her what had happened. He wanted to keep her with him on this, but he also valued her judgement.

"Bloody Larry," was her response. But she suggested they do a touristy walk along the Via Dolorosa on Friday, and he drop into the Ali Baba internet café while she browsed in another shop. They could then meet again for lunch somewhere and continue their Friday day out. This they did. Medad scoured the documents on the stick for some time. He didn't have a photographic memory, but it was good enough to understand what they said. If it was true, it was all there. Names, dates, conversation transcripts.

He was beyond taking everything a face value anymore, so he began to run through possible scenarios in his mind. Was this just normal government security preparation prior to an election, or was it a cabal of extreme right wingers intent on forcing the government to use war in Gaza as an election tool? And did that matter anyway? Also, how on earth did the CIA get such data… unless they got it from someone on the inside of government or the cabal, who had their own agenda… and why give it to him? What was he supposed to do with it?

He pocketed the stick, wiped out recent history on the PC he had used as best he could, and set off to re-join Shana. They talked in low tones over lunch, Shana trying and failing to prevent Medad seeing conspiracies everywhere. As they walked back to her pad they were still hotly debating the issue. As a journalist-in-the-making, Shana was in no doubt what a scoop this might be for her and might well enable her either to get a top investigative job, or go freelance. Medad was aghast at what Shana was proposing.

"No, no, no. This is far more important than a media scoop." He suddenly realised what he had said and how it had sounded. "Sorry, what I meant to say was this moment is not right time for a media release, although I do think it might come to that. I certainly recognise the power of what such a scoop could be, both to the government and to you. It would be a great opportunity…" He tailed off as Shana looked at him with disbelief. He decided to stop digging.

Then the thought crystallised; had they come to him specifically because of Shana and her ability to get the story in the media? It seemed highly unlikely, he concluded. He didn't want to verbalise this without appearing to start off another disagreement.

"I think the next step is to keep Dan in the loop and report back to him. Of course, that doesn't rule out you leaking it later." He hoped that this would ameliorate Shana to some extent. Shana didn't want to challenge Medad any further and offered to make a copy allowing Medad to give the original stick to Dan which he did the next day.

Medad tried to have the 'why me?' look on his face as he entered Dan's office. His boss was immediately alert when he went in. Medad explained that a stranger had handed him the memory stick while he was walking in Sacher Park, then disappeared. He clearly knew my lunchtime routine and could have been watching me for a few days. Asked whether he had viewed the contents, Medad said he had. He had privately concluded that it was the only way he could keep some control. Dan nodded and inclined his head to the door. Medad took the hint.

32

AYSHAA WAS BEGINNING to feel a little left out. Hani seemed to be where the action was and she was almost back to being a stay-at-home mom, and it was certainly not what she had envisaged for herself. Her husband seemed to be home less and less and, when he was, he was too tired to manage more than a two second cuddle in bed before turning over and snoring. She was beginning to wonder.

Ghalia was making very slow progress. Whether she would ever be back to her old self was rather doubtful which made Ayshaa worry a little, both for Ghalia herself and for what life might be like for both of them if she needed long term daily care. The young mother was all too aware of the shortcomings of the Palestinian health system. The expenditure per head for the Palestinians was about $250, whereas in Israel it was $2000, with average life expectancy being ten years higher in Israel than in the Occupied Territories. Infant mortality in Israel was 3.7 deaths per thousand, whereas in the West Bank it was 19 which was a statistic that said everything to Ayshaa, as she remembered her own experience giving birth to Rena.

But now that was a distant memory. She had recovered and Rena, no longer a baby, was now able to toddle around their rooms with lightening speed. Everything near the floor had to be moved out of the way, otherwise it would get the full Rena treatment. Ayshaa was experiencing what many modern mothers feel: the baby, toddler, was the light of her life and a part of her was enjoying this part of Rena's growing up, but sometimes it was downright boring. It didn't exercise her brain very much so, in her mind, she was hatching all sorts of plans and schemes probably never destined to see the light of day. However, she was able to attend some of the classes that Lara was leading but unable to commit the time to train properly, though having watched Lara, she reckoned she could do it.

After some thought, she decided to start a class specifically for mums and toddlers. This meant she could take Rena along to play with all the other babies or toddlers. The word was getting around and there was no shortage of mums wanting to do something, anything to have adult conversations, new relationships and if it was teaching them something, so much the better. There were still a number of women who had expressed interest, but had been stopped by their menfolk, either because the meetings contained a mix of Muslim and Christian, or they didn't want their wives learning anything which might loosen their own authority and power.

Then out of the blue, a pleasant surprise. A call from Mariam at BCI took Ayshaa by surprise. Mariam had been hearing some good things about BWP and wanted to catch up so Ayshaa invited her to the next mums and toddler meeting. Although she didn't have a toddler, Ayshaa thought it would be acceptable to the other women, if she introduced her appropriately. Mariam was impressed with the group and how Ayshaa was leading it, especially as she had no formal training. Ayshaa explained that she had been working with Lara from Ghu-sin Zay-tun, but unfortunately, Lara was now fully committed and well, needs must. In turn, Mariam explained that she had a day free in her week and would be delighted to give that day to BWP. Possibly she could do both a morning and an afternoon group if that worked for the women, or if not that then some one-on-one mentoring for Ayshaa.

Ayshaa thought for a minute, "Delighted to have you but as long as you are willing to come under the BWP umbrella and BCI was not mentioned, at least to begin with." Mariam was willing. Ayshaa didn't mention it to Hani as he seemed too busy with Omari and Fatah, although in retrospect she dearly wished that she had. Things went well, at least for the first few meetings that Mariam did on her own. But then came trouble with a capital T.

One morning at a meeting which Miriam was leading, there were about fifteen women gathered in Amira's house. Mariam was talking about how to defuse a potentially violent situation and they were about to do a role-play. There was much laughter as they tried to imitate their own husbands in being verbally aggressive.

Suddenly a group of Palestinian men burst into the home where the women were gathered. Amid screams, two of them each dragged a woman out of the house, presumably their wives. The other three set about ransacking the place and shouting "Death to Christians", and *"Allah u Akbar."* The women were pushed to the ground as the men went crazy. As soon as they could, the remaining women crawled out of the door and scattered, except for the women whose house it was, and Mariam. Fortunately, this was not a baby/toddler session, so it was only the women who had scrapes and bruises as they struggled to get away. At first, Mariam tried to protest and defend the women, but she was hit over the head and fell to the floor, moaning. It was bedlam. The sound of crashing, shouting and crying resounded throughout the immediate neighbourhood, but no-one came to help. It was as if people knew exactly what was happening.

Ayshaa hadn't been there when it happened, but one of the women called her after escaping from the house and, leaving Rena with Ghalia, she raced to the house to see for herself what had happened. She wanted to comfort the woman whose home had been damaged and just as importantly, help to clean it up before the man of the house got home. She arrived at the door and rushed straight in.

"Oh my God!" She looked at the scene of destruction. Then she immediately turned to the Amira and Mariam, "Are you all right?"

Mariam was already comforting the lady of the house, and applying a wet bandage to her head which was bleeding. Mariam herself was shaken and bruised but otherwise able to function. It was clear that someone had uncovered the BCI connection and Mariam was not safe, nor were any other women who were associated with her. Ayshaa immediately called Hani to say what had happened. He was silent for a moment and Ayshaa thought he was going to say, "I told you so," but instead he listened carefully and said, "Ask around to see if anyone had seen anything out of the ordinary on their way to the session."

Ayshaa promised to ask. It transpired that one of the ladies had seen a number of black cars with tinted windows around but Ayshaa knew that there were wealthy men who drove around in big Mercedes all the time. When she told Hani, he wasn't so dismissive. He asked his wife to find the names of the two women who were dragged off and any other names that the women were prepared to give up, then call the PCP (Palestinian Civil Police) if only to log the incident.

The service from the PCP was variable at best, but this was not always the fault of the individual officers. They were under-staffed and under-equipped, a direct result of being under-funded. With only about 3% female officers, their male colleagues could be a little authoritarian in their approach, so the most common complaint people had about them concerned the abuse of power but also nepotism and bribery. These were all linked since these public sector jobs were highly sought after as they guaranteed a job for life, and a uniform! Because the intake was rather haphazard and training wasn't as thorough as it should have been, the level of service they gave was not the best.

However, most said that they did a reasonable job, after all the PCP was all they had. So the complaint was called in and logged, but no-one was staying around waiting for any officers to arrive. It might be tomorrow, maybe the next day, or maybe a couple of weeks later. Ayshaa's faith was in Hani to sort it out because she appreciated that unless the community knew that the perpetrators were punished, she could say goodbye to her work. Hani began using his contacts to identify possible owners of Mercedes limousines. There weren't that many.

The three women cleaned the house up as best they could and suggested that when the husband got home, his wife should avoid going into specific detail about what happened, except that some men had disrupted their women's group. Ayshaa gave her Hani's mobile number if her husband wanted to get in touch. In the meantime, Hani had found out that the two men who had taken their wives were his two dissenters, so he was a little annoyed that Ayshaa had accepted their wives into her group without telling him, but maybe she didn't know.

Hani knew that it was bound to be a problem when these men found out their wives were attending BWP since they had voted against her at the last local Fatah meeting. So now Hani had another problem. The men regarded their wives as their property and because Hani had no jurisdiction over that, there was little that he could do. He did wonder, however, whether it was a deliberate ploy to target him and his leadership. But all he could do for the moment, was to hope the PCP would file charges, then maybe he could finally move against them.

For the other three men, it was a different matter. Their wives were not there, so they had no personal interest. They could be charged with criminal damage, if the PCP could find out who they were, but no-one recognised them and the dissenters were not giving anything away. It was just a matter of time, Hani told Ayshaa, they would be identified at some point, then dealt with. In the meantime, it was clear to Hani that Mariam had to stay away. Ayshaa was already repentant. It was a puzzle, though, how news had got out that Mariam was from BCI since Ayshaa had been really cautious about Mariam's background, and there had never been any real animosity between the Muslim and Christian communities before, especially in Bethlehem. So where had this anti-Christian stuff come from?

In the succeeding days, Ayshaa made a point of visiting both local Imams to see if they knew about the incident and, more importantly, knew the perpetrators. There were only two mosques in Bethlehem, both were Sunni: the Al-Hamadiyya Mosque in the west of Bethlehem which served the majority of the town, and the Mosque of Omar in the Old City on the west side of Manger Square. This particular mosque had an interesting history, in that it was founded by Caliph Omar, who having conquered Jerusalem, had travelled to Bethlehem in 637 CE to issue a law that would guarantee respect for the shrine and safety for Christians and their clergy. It would indeed be a major turnaround if now that mosque was fermenting anti-Christian sentiment. As it was their local mosque, Ayshaa was sure this was not the case. She knew the Imam and thought there was a possibility that he might have heard or seen something which would have led to the incident. Maybe he knew the men behind it?

The Imam had heard about the incident, as had most people. "I'm glad to see you and that you are unhurt."

Ayshaa didn't bother him with the fact that she wasn't there herself. He continued, "I'm also glad to have the opportunity to reassure you that I had no knowledge of the men, nor do I approve of what they had said or done."

As if to demonstrate this, he reminded Ayshaa, "I'm sure you know that in the past, before the advent of light bulbs, it was common for Muslims and Christians in Bethlehem to offer olive oil to light up the surroundings of the mosque together, as evidence of religious coexistence in the city. I would like it to stay that way." There was nothing much useful from the other Imam either.

Sunni Imams, contrary to some perceptions, do not themselves lead the mosque. They are part of the leadership team and it is the team who choose the Imam. His role is to lead Islamic worship services. In fact, the word 'Imam' itself means 'to stand in front of' in Arabic, referring to the fact that the Imam stands in front of the worshippers during prayer. They might also fulfil pastoral roles, like counselling, advice and visiting the sick, as well as being recognised as religious scholars. Preaching or Da'wah would also be part of their role within the prayer service, Da'wah being equivalent to the Christian word 'mission' and generally means calling people towards Allah and His instructions. Ayshaa found both Imams very supportive of what BWP were doing, but disappointed that neither knew the men concerned. However, they both cautioned her to use Muslim group leaders for her work. Well, they would, she thought.

Hani had immediately instructed his loyal men to compile a list of those who owned black Mercedes limousines. As he perused the list, he didn't see any obvious connections, although it was certainly helpful to him to have such a list. It was beginning to look as if these men came from outside the city, and if so, he didn't rate the chances of the PCP finding them. It was down to him to see if his two dissenters would talk, at least to find out what it was all about.

Neither Hani nor Ayshaa wanted to spark off an inter-Palestinian conflict between the Muslim and Christian communities, but both had different reasons; Ayshaa was solely concerned with BWP, whereas Hani was totally focussed on the talks. This sort of division would certainly serve to complicate that process, as the Israelis had a tendency to exaggerate such issues to deflect attention from giving way on anything in negotiations. This could play right into their hands, and Hani knew it. Jamal would definitely be unhappy and certain factions in Ramallah would not be slow in taking any advantage they could.

So the incident was played down as more of a domestic issue. Nevertheless, Ayshaa's concern about Hani's focus was growing.

33

DAN WAS SITTING at his desk, partly working and partly wondering. It was now a month since he had met with Omari and just less than that when Medad had dropped the memory stick on his desk. There had been no news on any Israeli-Palestinian talks and thus, as Dan saw it, no need to do anything. He had read all the documents on the stick and had admitted to himself that if it were made public at the wrong time, it could cause the government some serious anxiety, if not bring it down.

He judged that Medad held similar views to his own, not that he would admit that to his junior. However, he was keenly aware that his minister was Likud and therefore didn't. In fact, the PM had probably given him the Palestinian portfolio precisely because of his hard line views, so Dan had to tread carefully. As he thought about the dynamite he now possessed, he found himself increasingly thinking about how he might circumvent government policy and push it towards a more peaceful and cooperative path with the Palestinians. The part of him that was the civil servant felt guilty at this, but the part that was a father and husband felt rather exhilarated.

His regular meetings with his Minister were always diaried, but a call from his office one Friday morning was not one of his scheduled sessions. Dan's first thought was that somehow, someone had told him about the memory stick and he was to be carpeted. He felt weak at the knees, but pulled himself together and made his way to the minister's office. He was kept waiting for some time – standard power play – but finally he was ushered in and it all became clear.

"Talks are to begin shortly. Are you ready?"

Dan answered with a confident, "Yes".

The minister looked him in the eye and said, "I've been reading a document prepared by one of your staff, a Medad somebody?"

Without waiting for a reply, he then proceeded to muse that he had met a Medad once when he was visiting an IDF group. "A sniper, I think."

Dan was happy to confirm that this was indeed the same person. The minister nodded, "I think it's a decent document as a starter. Your department will lead, but we don't want to give anything away do we?"

Dan was forced to agree. With a brusque, 'excellent', and 'be ready', the meeting was over. As soon as Dan got back to the office, he called Medad in and told him the news. "It's going to be you and me to lead. Of course, there will be others from the Defence ministry so we have to try and get them on our side if we are going to make progress our way."

Medad was noting the 'we' and the 'ours', but was also thinking fast. "But it is the Defence ministry that is involved in the... er ... documents!" Medad's alarm showed in his face.

But Dan was well aware of the issue, and responded by declaring that it was crystal clear where they would be coming from.

He gave Medad instructions. "Find out who in that ministry leaked the documents. They might be on 'our' side and thus would be the only hope we have of vital insider information to help us prepare."

Medad wandered back to his desk in a daze for, after waiting in vain for weeks, now it was all go. The only thought in his head was to contact Chuck for the whistle blower's name, but maybe that's what 'they' were hoping for. Maybe 'they' could trace a call. Maybe 'they' would charge him as a traitor. They. They. But he had to trust someone. There was no other option, he would have to call Chuck. It would probably be Larry who turned up, but now he couldn't care. He just needed a name. He still had his burner phone, although he knew he should have disposed of it weeks ago. He thought, one more time.

There was no answer, so he left a message simply asking for a name. No small talk, in fact no other words at all. Chuck would understand, so nothing else to do except wait. Back in the office after his call, he dug out his preparatory document and began to try and refresh his memory, but despite his best efforts he wasn't taking much in. He couldn't wait until the time to leave the office when he could share it all with Shana. He needed to talk with someone, and she was the only one he really trusted.

She was cool about it. "I'm sure Chuck will get back to you, after all, that's why he gave you the information in the first place. But whether he does or not, there's no point in stopping now. You've got to run with what you've got. It's all or nothing time."

Shana, although still studying, was also looking ahead to her journalistic career and, it seemed to Medad, wasn't feeling the same stress that he was. Although she knew she couldn't use the information in the documents yet, her journalistic instincts were tugging at her. What a scoop it would be.

She tentatively asked, "what are you and your boss going to do with documents? And can we trust Dan?" Medad confessed that he did not know, but he was beginning to think that Dan could be an ally.

"If I can't trust him, then the government will already know about my involvement in something not to their liking and be taking steps to neutralise me… and you. Shin Bet certainly wouldn't leave any stone unturned but nothing has happened so far…" Medad was beginning to believe that Dan hadn't told anyone. But, because he couldn't be certain of anything, he suggested that maybe Shana should take some precautions to shield herself if the proverbial hit the fan.

She looked at him, "Like what? We're in it together and it's for the best cause, peace." It was Shana who, at the moment, seemed the stronger of the two.

"I don't know but these are uncharted waters. Anything could happen." She invited him stay over hoping that might calm him down and bring him some peace. He didn't need a second invitation, not that either of them slept much even after some robust exercise. Medad ended up on the floor next to the bed and predictably, was exceedingly stiff the next morning.

Dan, on the other hand, had been busy. He also had read the negotiating document through again, together with all the documents on the stick which Medad had supplied. Armed with a refreshed knowledge of the information he had been given, he procrastinated for a whole day before finally deciding to call Omari.

It was the beginning of *Shabbat*. Dan's family weren't particularly religious but they celebrated the Friday evening meal for the children's benefit. Although there was a plethora of things that observant Jews will not do on *Shabbat*, such as driving, working, or even turning on a light switch, there are a host of things they will do in order to 'make the *Shabbat* a delight'. Dan's family didn't go in for the three *Shabbat* meals. Once the Friday evening meal was over, the following day was a day to do whatever you wanted. That Saturday morning proved an ideal time for him to slip away from his family and meet the Palestinian.

He had decided to travel to Bethlehem since Omari had come to Jerusalem last time. By this he was signalling that he was serious. He booked a lunch table at the Al Karawan Restaurant near Rachel's tomb. The cuisine was Mediterranean and had great reviews, not that the food was his focus. What was important, was the conversation. Dan arrived a little early and sat at the table with his drink, getting used to the place and its customers. Omari arrived on time and this time Dan stood and embraced his old friend and Omari responded, a little surprised but saying nothing. He didn't want to embarrass his host.

Dan invited Omari to order and when they had sent the waiter away, they got down to it. There was no further need for small talk. Dan explained what had happened at his end with no holds barred, just without names. He gave an outline of the contents of the memory stick, again no names. After about ten minutes of explanation, Dan sat back and said that, of course, he would now have to kill Omari! They both laughed. The food was arriving, so further conversation was stopped for a few minutes, giving both men time to assess where they were.

Omari was first to start. "I must say that I was rather taken aback at the start by the openness that you showed." He smiled, "and I would like to try and reciprocate."

Again without names, Omari went through who his contact was and something of what they had done together. No specifics, but he explained,

"Our sole aim has been to try to build a lasting peace which would respect the two nations." Dan was listening. Omari went on, "Just as there are groups in Israel who want a hard line to be maintained, there are also factions within the PA that wanted to scupper any agreement because it would halt their gravy train. We can't guarantee anything."

Dan hesitated before he made his next point. "I would like to find a way of keeping channels open, but there can be no official meetings between an Israeli civil servant and a Palestinian official or any Palestinian come to that. It would be too dangerous, for both parties. But maybe such people could meet occasionally as friends. But no documents, nothing written down."

It was agreed that each might obtain a separate mobile exclusively for use between the two of them and install WhatsApp to send an occasional message, since it was an encrypted service. Dan didn't want to mention that he knew Mossad had ways of getting in through the WhatsApp back door if they wanted to. But if it ever got to that stage, it was probably all over anyway.

Omari left first, making his way back home and ten minutes later Dan emerged, making his way back to Jerusalem. Both men were deep in thought, wondering where this was going to lead them. Neither was naïve enough to know there weren't great personal risks along this path, and both were wondering how much to tell their respective spouses. For his part, Dan decided to say nothing for the moment, but Omari decided to say much more to Lara, who already knew about Hani.

He also decided to speak to Hani about how they might meet together more discreetly so as to protect themselves. This had to be done face to face, and definitely shouldn't be done either at Hani's shop or at his office. Oddly they decided to meet in a public space at the WalledOff Hotel in Caritas St, right next to the infamous Wall which Israel had built.

The Wall itself, some eight hundred kilometres long and growing, was supposed to be a military structure built by the Israeli government to enforce a higher level of security. But it also happened to enclose specified parts of Palestinian land and annex them, principally for settlers. As the WalledOff said in its literature, 'depending on who you talk to it's either a vital security measure or an instrument of apartheid.' There was no doubt that its route was highly controversial and illegal according to the UN. Also of no doubt, was that it continued to have a dramatic impact on the daily lives of many people. On the Israeli side, the severe concrete Wall was ameliorated by brightly coloured domestic mosaic tiles, whereas on the Palestinian side, the Wall was full of slogans and graffiti, much of which was amazingly humorous, considering what the structure stood for.

There was an Israeli watchtower right opposite to the entrance to the hotel to add piquancy to their discussion. The downstairs of the WalledOff boasted a piano bar which served food and drink from mid morning and also had a gallery and museum with exhibits ranging from a waxwork of Balfour to maps showing where Israelis had stolen Palestinian water. It was the idea of Banksy, the British graffiti artist who had provided the initial funded and was a great tourist attraction. It was just five hundred meters from the checkpoint to Jerusalem and a mile from the centre of Bethlehem,

Omari brought Hani up to date with both his conversations with Daniel, or Dan as he now wished to be called. Both agreed that as the date for talks was getting closer, although no actual date had been set as yet, they had to take steps to protect their relationship and conversations. They also thought that WhatsApp was a good way to communicate and that the Museum in the Hotel was a good place to meet since it had many nooks and crannies, and was usually occupied by tourists.

Omari's mobile buzzed. It was a WhatsApp message from Dan.

34

ANGRA MAINYU'S BUSINESS card implied that he was a low level Iranian trade diplomat in Beirut, but there was virtually nothing truthful about any of those words. He was not a diplomat, he had nothing to do with trade in the conventional sense, and definitely not low level. But he was Iranian. In reality, he was a member of the feared VAJA, the Ministry of Intelligence of the Islamic Republic of Iran and a part of the Quds Force – a unit of the Revolutionary Guards which had carte blanche to carry out 'intelligence black ops' anywhere in the world.

The Quds Force directly financed and supported proxies in many foreign countries, best known were Hezbollah in Lebanon, Hamas and Islamic Jihad in Gaza. Quds reported directly to the Supreme Leader, Ayatollah Khamenei and so by-passed any political or diplomatic considerations. Department Five was the one which dealt exclusively with Israel and was Angra Mainyu's total responsibility. He had a reputation amongst some akin to the meaning of his name, which was 'source of evil'.

Iran and Lebanon had a long relationship, mainly through the Lebanese Shiite community, the largest of Lebanon's eighteen recognised sects. Many Lebanese clerics came from Iran, trained under Iranians or had strong Iranian connections. The first leader to mobilize Lebanon's Shiite community was one, Musa al-Sadr, an Iranian-born cleric from a prominent family of Lebanese theologians. In 1974, he founded the Movement of the Disinherited to aid Lebanon's Shiites. It then formed an armed wing called Amal during Lebanon's civil war, which remains one of Lebanon's two major Shiite parties.

It was Iran who built on this Lebanese Shiite base to nurture the birth of Hezbollah in 1982, and it was Iran's operational and financial support which shaped Hezbollah into a powerful militia against Israel. Their strategic successes against Israel over a number of years forced the Israelis to withdraw from Lebanon altogether and abandon their proxy, the South Lebanon Army, which was almost totally routed by Hezbollah.

Iran continued to be a pivotal player in Levantine politics and through its proxies had a wider appeal with so-called 'rejectionist' factions in Syria and militant Palestinian groups opposed to any peace with Israel. But it was in Lebanon where it cultivated its base. Its advocacy of Shiite rights, its social services, political patronage and its resistance against Israel, created a political base of some strength. In this way, Hezbollah's ties to Iran served to upset Lebanon's fragile political balance and heightened sectarian tensions. Lebanon, in part due to Iranian influence, was fast becoming a failed state.

None of this was news to Angra Mainyu. He wasn't so concerned about the past as the future. He had a job to do and was going to do it, whatever the cost. He hadn't been responsible for the former Israeli Energy Minister who agreed to spy for Iran, but he quietly laughed at the ease at which Iran was able to infiltrate its enemies and its friends, Iraq and Syria. Which reminded him; he hadn't heard back from his Palestinian mole within the PA. He would have to order him to slip over the border into Lebanon again for a meeting. There was no way Angra Mainyu was going to chance the border. He was much too valuable.

He had been working on one of the top PA security personnel for three years. This man was now deputy to the Chief of Security, partly due to intelligence fed to him by Angra Mainyu which had impressed the Chief. The Deputy had succumbed to the lure of money but once hooked, had been filmed and recorded by Hezbollah so that he could never extricate himself from the relationship. He was theirs unlike the Chief, who had never shown any interest in extra income probably because he was skimming enough from the PA as it was. But Abd Alraheem had been different. At any time they wanted, the Iranians could expose him, anonymously, of course, but not yet while there was important work to do.

There were rumours that an Israeli-Palestinian summit was about to happen, and Iran thought they should be represented somehow at the table. It was their right. After all, they had funded the militants from the beginning. It was straightforward, but not easy for Abd Alraheem to cross the border. There had been many meetings with Angra Mainyu and Hezbollah in Lebanon, so he knew where and when to cross. But although he had done it many times, it was always a risky business and in recent weeks there had seemed to be a measurable increase in Israeli military presence on the Blue Line.

This was the line published by the UN in 2000, for the purposes of determining whether Israel had fully withdrawn from Lebanon. Since then Israel had constructed a northern concrete Wall – eleven kilometres of it – along the Blue Line designed to protect local Israeli communities from attacks and infiltrations by Hezbollah. Operation Northern Shield, as it was called, had unearthed a number of tunnels dug by Hezbollah under the Wall, and cleared them. These had presented different problems for the insurgent tunnel diggers than the Hamas tunnels further south. The terrain in the north was hard and rocky unlike the soft sandy soil of the south which demanded different techniques.

As far as Israel knew, they had blown up all the Hezbollah tunnels. Fortunately for Hezbollah, one had been missed. It was one of the original test tunnels which had not been used during the war and had never been upgraded for military use. But it could and was used for kidnappings as well as allowing limited movement from Israel to Lebanon and vice versa. Abd Alraheem had used this route before. He didn't like it, but there was no alternative. It was small and he was not.

Once arrived, he waited at his safe place for any Israeli patrols to pass and, when clear, he quickly made his way to the mouth of the tunnel almost wholly hidden by the scrub. He took some deep breaths and began the journey. It would take him thirty minutes to bear crawl most of the way with the occasional belly crawl where the rock hadn't been fully been excavated. It was as difficult as he had expected, and he hated it. But he loved the monies that went into his bank account every month. His was not a principled arrangement but a simple way to monetise his hard-worked for position.

The meeting with the Iranian was a twenty minute car ride from there and as usual, there was a car waiting for him to emerge, grunting, sweating and shaking dirt from his hair and clothes. No expense spared for the traitor! The Hezbollah driver grinned at the state of the man, then turned his head away lest the Palestinian should see. Angra Mainyu, in the meantime, had been waiting patiently in a local farmer's house, sipping arabic coffee and enjoying some kibbeh, courtesy of the farmer's wife. Abd Alraheem arrived, still recovering from his ordeal and still a bit dishevelled; it was the signal for the farmer and his wife to make themselves scarce. The Palestinian was not invited to sit or share in the kibbeh, but he was offered a coffee.

Angra Mainyu didn't waste his precious time but jumped straight in without even looking at the still standing visitor. "When is the summit?"

Abd Alraheem, nervous in front of his real boss, shuffled forward a little. "The Israelis have not given dates yet, but our intelligence suggests it will be soon." He looked hopeful that this explanation would accepted.

"Who is chairing the Palestinian side?"

"Jamal."

"Why not the Chief?"

"The President is playing games." In a bid to gain some credit with his master, he offered, "But I am on the working group preparing our negotiating stance."

Angra Mainyu snorted. "Negotiation! Israel does not negotiate, they tell you what they are going to do. That was how it was in southern Gaza and that is how it will be on the West Bank."

Abd Alraheem was at pains to point out that this time it would be different. A proper negotiation document had been prepared, different from anything they had done before. Angra Mainyu sneered. "And who prepared that... you?"

"No not me. It was the guy in charge of Bethlehem, name of Hani." Angra Mainyu finished his kibbeh and was wiping his mouth.

"I'd like to see it." Abd Alraheem quietly cursed himself for mentioning the document. "Even I don't have a copy, only the President, the Chief and Jamal."

The Iranian slowly looked up from the table and stared directly at the Palestinian. "I think I said I want to see it." The Palestinian flinched and bowed. "Of course. It is your right. I think I know how I can do it."

Angra Mainyu didn't bother to respond. He put his coat on and departed without another word, leaving Abd Alraheem in the room alone. Determined to show the locals that he was a senior person and worthy of respect, he sat down in Angra Mainyu's seat, called for the farmer's wife and demanded another coffee. Twenty minutes later he signalled that he was ready to go back to the tunnel.

Meanwhile, Angra Mainyu was on his way back to Beirut thinking that he badly needed that document and if Abd Alraheem was not going to come through with it, he would need a Plan B. Although he could neutralise the Deputy Chief at a time of his choosing, the Deputy was still useful, if he obtained the document. If not…

The next day he met with leaders of Hezbollah, which was no longer just a terrorist group on the edge of the political system, but now a recognised political party in Lebanon. Although their base was always the Shiite areas of the Biqa Valley, southern Lebanon, and southern Beirut, they had formed an alliance with similar pro Syrian parties back in 2005 to form the March 8 bloc. This now had a dominant position in Lebanon politics and despite recent waves of unrest, would remain unchanged even if the figureheads did change.

Hezbollah was vehemently anti-Israeli and therefore was intensely interested in any developments which might impact the status quo. Their objective was to keep the Palestinians in play as a thorn in the side of the occupying force and therefore, did not want any agreement between the two. Fatah and the Palestinian Authority were seen by them as selling out the Arab cause and cosying up to Israel both for personal gain and international recognition, neither of which had any attraction for Hezbollah. They could not, would not recognise Israel or give up the fight to eliminate them from the land. If some kind of summit was now due between the sides aimed at negotiating better relations between the Palestinians and Israel, they needed to somehow scupper any chances of success.

Angra Mainyu neglected to tell them about the document, partly because he didn't have to and partly because it would be his failure if he was unable to obtain it. The report to his masters in Tehran was similarly edited. Although he had grown up in the politics of Tehran and the Revolutionary Guard, he was never sure of where the solid ground was. Not many people were. It was like constantly shifting sand; one minute you were the darling of the Ayatollahs and the next you were out of favour and watching your step, otherwise that could be the end.

Ayatollah Ali Khamenei had been in power since 1989 and was the Supreme Leader. The country had a Guardian Council whose role it was to approve or veto legislative bills from the Islamic Consultative Assembly, which was the Parliament. It also had the power to approve or forbid candidates seeking office to the Presidency and the Parliament. Six of the twelve members of the Council were Islamic *faqihs*, experts in Islamic Law, and were directly selected by the Supreme Leader. The other six were jurists nominated by the Head of the Judicial System, also appointed by the Supreme Leader.

In addition, Ali Khamenei controlled the armed forces, judicial system, state television and other key governmental organisations. His authority extended to issuing decrees and making final decisions on the economy, environment, foreign policy, education, and even the planning of population growth. His power was absolute.

Hence Angra Mainyu was taking a profound risk. If the regime heard about the document from any other source he would have some serious explaining to do, and he knew they had tentacles everywhere. However, he had a narrative which he hoped would hold up under scrutiny. But the prize for getting the document, when no-one knew of its existence, would be immense. He was excited but he had to think of a Plan B and, at the moment, he didn't have one. It was true that he did have other lower level contacts in the PA, but to bring them on stream so quickly, and for such an important task, would entail a major exposure risk. Was it worth it?

35

AYSHAA WAS MORE than a little frustrated. The PCP showed no signs of identifying the other three culprits who had caused so much damage to Mariam's BWP meeting, let alone capturing them. What was worse, Hani was warned off taking any action against his two dissenters. Links with the Palestinian Security apparatus were being employed to shield them. Hani had suspected it; now it was fact. He had to assume that everything he and Ayshaa were doing in Bethlehem was being reported back to the Chief or his deputy. That changed things only a little.

Gradually the women's work got going again with Lara and Ayshaa re-taking the lead. They had to limit themselves to a manageable workload, but were always on the lookout for future leadership potential. The link with BCI had stalled and whilst Ayshaa still valued Mariam's friendship, they could not even be seen together, let alone working together. It was disappointing, but perhaps only for a season.

Everything, it seemed, was revolving around the proposed Israeli-Palestinian meeting and Ayshaa was wondering whether the Palestinian side were building up expectations too high and were going to be disappointed. It was like uppers and downers; the higher the high, the lower the low. And with volatile Palestinian emotions, violence could well erupt if hopes were dashed. She had seen it before and concluded it was just part of the Israeli strategy to crush and depress the Palestinian population. If it resulted in a few demos and stone throwing, great! That gave them the excuse to deploy tear gas, bullets and make more arrests.

She knew the men loved politics, Hani being no exception. Yes it was serious, but it was also a game to them; who could outwit the other side and get personal advancement. Sometimes, admittedly, a deadly game but therein was the challenge. Surely it needed more women to get involved in the political process, but what chance was there of that? Even in liberal western democracies, the percentage of women in front line politics was low.

Ayshaa was trying to give some serious thought to the issue whilst at the some time feeding Rena, listening to her mother-in-law and surveying all the yet to do housework. Life was regressing. She had briefly thought about getting pregnant again. Briefly. At least Hani had agreed to contraception, unlike many of her friends and neighbours. Whilst she loved Rena dearly, she was desperate for her daughter to get to a more independent stage and liberate her mother. Another baby would relegate her to the home for years.

With Rena now in bed and Ghalia also turned in for the night, she was for another few hours, as free as she'd be until morning. Hani not yet returned. In fact, sometimes he didn't return at all if he had meetings in Ramallah. She thought she knew her man, but doubts were beginning to creep in. The fact that the men who had disrupted her meeting had not been identified and by now were unlikely to be so, had led to immense frustration. It wasn't his fault but he was the only one she could rail against.

She had picked a fight with her husband, Hani responded and a full blown row had ensued. She demanded to know why he wasn't backing her up. He replied that he was and that she should calm down. That inevitably escalated the row further. The result: he left to spend the night at the shop and she slept alone. Ayshaa was not backing down. There was still the steely determination within her to do whatever it took to succeed, Hani or not. Breakfast came and went. No Hani. He didn't come back that day. She assumed he had gone to Ramallah, so she spent the day thinking and planning what she might do in the future.

Politics was not really that attractive to her, but there was no doubt it was where the power lay to make changes, and change was what mattered to her. Perhaps, she thought, I'm dismissing it because of male domination. They have certainly fashioned it to their way of working. But what if women could re-fashion the system? Could it happen? Would it work? Would it be better? She thought she knew the answer to that.

A patriarchal society and an authoritarian regime were sure ways to keep the status quo and, although there were elections, such plebiscites never had been the touchstone of democracy. They could be delayed, fixed, even by-passed. The Arab world in particular was expert in these things, Russia very good and Africa wasn't bad at it either. China didn't even bother with the pretence. Ayshaa knew all the arguments against women being involved: women don't want to stand for election; women are not interested in politics; women are not educated enough, and so it went on. Yes, female candidates did face numerous challenges to gain voter support, particularly male voter support, but the real issue lay at the top levels of power where electoral outcomes were manufactured, even manipulated, by the ruling elites to ensure their survival while maintaining the façade of fair and free elections.

Ayshaa knew that in Palestine as in some other Muslim countries, quotas had been introduced to encourage women into parliaments. But more often than not, when women had been elected, they found themselves so outmanoeuvred by men who knew the complexity of parliamentary rules and procedures backwards, that they became marginalised in the institution and many gave up. The led to a lack of confidence amongst prospective candidates and indeed voters who wanted their vote to count. Women, it transpired, needed a coherent party system whereby they could be supported in their first years and if this couldn't be done, all the effort expended to procure women candidates in the first place would come to nothing.

It was clear to Ayshaa that without women who could flourish in such systems, no reforms aimed at making life better for women e.g. policies concerning education, health etc., were going to be enacted. She knew from personal experience that women across the Middle East continued to face numerous daily challenges that had remained unaddressed for decades; soaring rates of domestic violence, honour crimes, antiquated personal status laws, and unequal wages. She was equally sure the men were not about to embark on change any time soon.

But she could see that the mood was changing, even in Muslim countries. Women now allowed to drive a car in Saudi! Unthinkable only a few years ago. Yes, still a long way to go and maybe just tokenism, but it signalled a change for the better. Ayshaa wanted to push at a door that was beginning to open for her generation, which had been totally denied for her mother-in-law's generation. In urban areas particularly there was an undeniable shift beginning. Even in some conservative Muslim countries, women could now be seen as community organizers, voter-recruiters with some actually becoming elected politicians and the odd leader here and there. Ayshaa classed herself as just a community organiser so far, but her path was set out, if she wanted to take it.

Tunisia was a great example. As far back as in 2011 there were forty-nine women elected to parliament out of a total of two hundred and seventeen members, forty-two of them were part of a party called Ennahda. It was well-organised and had a widespread grassroots structure, thanks in part to women's organising and mobilising efforts in support of the party. They had mobilised and politicised so many women that when the time came to implement a gender parity quota, it had no problems recruiting qualified women from within the party structure.

Well, thought Ayshaa, she had a solid community base in Bethlehem and she knew that Lara had followed a similar route to become a Bethlehem councillor. A conversation with Lara was next on her political agenda when they next met. It wasn't urgent, and in the meantime she could broaden her community engagement as much as possible as a first step. Having come to a decision, she decided it was time for bed.

For the first time in years, at least as far back as she could remember, she had a vivid dream. She knew that supposedly she always had dreams, but this morning she knew she had dreamt and could even remember bits of it. She was not just a councillor, she was the leader of Bethlehem's council. It could only happen in that very strange world that is dreamland for that position was traditionally reserved solely for the Christian community. She was standing up in the forum and passionately making her case for a new by-law to ensure gender parity in every part of Bethlehem life; political, economic, social and legal. The annoying thing was that she couldn't remember the outcome. She recalled seeing men looking at her strangely and the few women members standing up and cheering, something councillors would never do. But there was a sense of emptiness which suggested to her that her motion had been defeated. She felt spent, having given her all and not having anything to show for it.

The following morning she found herself going over it, as far as she could remember. Perhaps it was an omen not to go into politics, or maybe the contrary. She was a little confused but determined to keep it on the back burner.

Palestinians were not a superstitious people by and large, but Ayshaa thought dreams meant something and she would watch for further signs.

Hani was a considerate man, at least he thought so, but Ayshaa knew that he was not a feminist. He was a male Palestinian and while he wanted more women involved in community action, she knew he wasn't sure about women in political leadership. He had been brought up as part of a male dominated society and his religion endorsed that, not that he was overly religious. Once he had seemed to support her but now he had grown distant and she was not sure how much they were agreed on anything anymore.

Corruption was one of the issues they had agreed about. It was at the heart of so much that was wrong about Palestinian and Middle-Eastern affairs. It was why Hani had never used his position to move from their little home to something more substantial. In his eyes, that would be corrupt. That decision served to embarrass those Fatah people who had used their positions to move upmarket, so it hadn't endeared Hani to any of those. Nevertheless, Hani had certain principles and would abide by them no matter what. He was stubborn in that way and Ayshaa admired him for this, but he was definitely becoming a different man than the one she had married.

She forced herself to stop thinking and heaved herself out of bed, washed and started the chores. Rena needed to be up and have breakfast. It was amazing she wasn't awake already. Ghalia needed help with her medication. And the place was a tip. Hani would be back at some point, so she had to make an effort, she didn't want any criticism from him about the state of the home. She wondered whether Lara had experienced the same conflict; the brain hatching up all sorts of dreams and plans whilst the body still having to cope with household duties because the man of the house was free to come and go at whim.

She hadn't been resentful at first because when she got married to Hani, this is what she had expected. It was what her mother did, what her grandmother did, and probably her mother before that. But now? She thought there had been an agreement that there would be an equality between them, but it only seem to go one way… his way. If she had been more educated, perhaps her indignation at domestic confinement might have been greater from the beginning. But this morning was a mums and toddler's session which Lara was taking, so she looked forward to that and focus her mind on BWP. She could take Rena and, having seen that Ghalia was up and moving, she set off. It was an enjoyable morning with some private time afterwards for both of them to discuss women's issues in general and what could be done to improve their lives.

Lara confessed, "You know, being a councillor is rather frustrating. Words are the only weapons available and they don't seem to get very far. Palestinian men don't seem to realise that their women often became the 'shock absorbers' in the conflict."

Ayshaa concurred, "Yes, I know families in Bethlehem who are hesitant to let their women leave the house alone, due to the deliberate targeting of women and girls by Israeli forces. Many of them are often unable to reach work with the consequential financial impact that has. Also, I've heard anecdotally that girls are missing more days at school than boys."

Lara replied, "It wouldn't surprise me. I think all this is triggering a reproduction of patriarchy in our community and at the moment, there's no-one taking action to break it."

They were both expressing concern that those men who were in a position to make a difference, didn't want to do anything except moan and demonstrate. They would point out that there was a Ministry of Women's Affairs (MOWA) in Ramallah, with a mission to promote and the empower Palestinian women.

But Ayshaa was critical of those in Ramallah. "I don't know who those women are, but whoever they are, they have become isolated from their grass roots communities. They seem to be more interested in entrenching their position with the men who wield power rather than seeking to identify with women on the ground."

Lara said she had tried to engage with them but not a great deal of success. "I think, like the men, they see the Occupation as the central factor in the position of women and instead of seeking ways that might already exist to advance women's rights on the West Bank, they are waiting for national rights to be sorted first. It's a mistake."

There was general agreement about the size of the task. Lara, as a politician, felt she had her finger on the pulse of the key women issues of her nation, but how translate that into actionable policies. As she and Ayshaa talked more, Lara highlighted an Al Jazeera item that had reported a rise in recent years in Palestinian 'honour killings', murders carried out by family members against their own women who were accused of 'immoral sexual conduct' or of carrying on a friendship with someone not approved by the family i.e. the man of the household. Ayshaa sighed. She knew about other issues that she wanted changed such as girls under the age of 18 who wanted to file charges of rape had to be accompanied by a man. Yes, there was a lot to do.

It seemed an impossible task to change a culture under Occupation. Ayshaa and Lara both went quiet...thinking.

36

THE DATE FOR the summit had been set. Hani and Jamal had only three weeks to put final preparations together. Much of that time would be arguing internally about how they would conduct business from their side. Hani never liked to use the word 'negotiation', although that's what his mind was fixed upon. He preferred to use the word 'discussions', for if the Israelis heard the word 'negotiations' he felt they were likely to pull up the drawbridge and merely dictate. They didn't see any equality between themselves and the Palestinian Authority. Hani wanted the Israelis to think they were open discussions, and in that way draw them into compromises. He thought it was their only play.

Jamal, absently running his hand over his ample mid-section, began to express some concerns about the two members of the team who were part of the Palestinian Security Services. "I've spoken privately to the others and I'm certain that they will take their lead from me but the Chief is adopting a hard line which, I think, emanates from his Deputy."

Hani expressed some at this concern since the Palestinians were in no position to take a hard line on anything... unless someone wanted the summit to fail. Of course, in any new world order there were no guarantees that any current beneficiaries in Ramallah would remain in their posts. Jamal was sure that many of them were quite happy with the status quo. In fact he had seriously thought about it himself although he wouldn't reveal that to Hani.

As a senior Palestinian official of some years, he had enjoyed relatively good relations with the Chief up to now, even though he knew the man had been appointed to his role because he was a close friend of the President rather than because of his security expertise. But their relationship was being strained because he had been overlooked for the chairmanship of the talks. So Jamal decided it was no use having a formal meeting with the him to persuade him to corral his representatives because that might further intensify his antagonism, and his Deputy, Abd Alraheem, would inevitably be there. So he set about trying to influence him in more indirect ways, one of those being through the President with whom he could meet without the Chief or his Deputy to discuss the Palestinian stance on each issue.

The strategy was having little success for while the President was supportive of the general direction, he declined to interfere with the Chief on internal security matters. Jamal was at the point of reluctantly accepting that there would be a split Palestinian position and that he would have to use his chairmanship as a way of controlling the sessions. He didn't want to take things to a vote for fear that the Security apparatus would be, quietly but effectively, wielded against other members to make them compliant. He knew some of them would inevitably capitulate. It was a dangerous situation for it wouldn't take much for his side to then splinter in front of the Israeli delegation; then he would really be in trouble.

Up to this point, Hani had not disclosed any of the information to Jamal that Omari had passed on to him. Although it was highly compromising for the Israeli side, Hani was finding it difficult to see how he could use it. A controlled release was his aim, ensuring it was published to maximum effect and not thrown away. He admitted to himself that it showed a lack of trust in his boss, but he could see no other alternative. The only way he could envisage it working to full effect was if a third party leaked it at a critical point in the discussions, with a view to throwing the Israelis off balance. Whether it would have that effect was anyone's guess. It might just work to close down any future meetings, and that was definitely not what he wanted.

Hani returned to the 'hotel' he was staying in, vexed and weary. Not much thought had been given to Ayshaa, her work or their family. Home seemed a world away and as he was sitting alone in his room with a bed, small desk and a 15" television at the Hommus Hostel on Raffaele Ciriello Street, he began to feel depressed. No doubt Jamal was in a four star hotel enjoying a four course meal and a swim in the heated pool, he thought, and he was slumming it in a two star hostel. As these thoughts were allowed to go round in his head, he felt he deserved better. After all, he had produced the critical document.

Such notions are difficult to dismiss when you're away from home support. Personal demons can alight on your shoulder, whisper in your ear and grind you down. In Ramallah, they must have had plenty of practice for he couldn't shake this one off. There was no television back home so he switched on hoping it might provide a suitable diversion but after an hour he concluded that regardless of the dozens of channels on offer, all were totally unwatchable.

He decided a walk would clear his head. He exited the hostel and began to head towards the centre of Ramallah. If he had met a woman at this point he might have taken the opportunity for a distraction. He was sure there were places here – lots of men with money away from their families. Yes, it was naïve to think it didn't happen. How would that work for him? He began to fictionalise some tempting situations before pulling himself together and looking around. He had been walking for about thirty minutes and didn't recognise any of the buildings. He suddenly had an anxiety attack which he had never experienced before. He knew every inch of Bethlehem and was confident in his home town but not here. Here he was an outsider.

Now his confidence was being shaken. Quickly he began to retrace his steps anxious to find landmarks he might recognise. He eventually found his way back chastising himself for his momentary weakness. However, the panicky experience of not knowing exactly where he was had no doubt unsettled Hani, and his normal self assurance was fast seeping away. It caused him to question the basis of his self-confidence, if this was all it took to shock him. As he walked through the door of the hostel a distraction presented itself, and he suddenly felt he deserved it. They went up to his room and thirty shekels later he fell asleep only to wake at three o'clock in the morning and rue what he had done. He didn't get back to sleep.

To take his mind off his foolishness and Ayshaa, he got up and tried to concentrate on the talks once more. He would fill his mind with the issues and opportunities of the next few weeks; guilty thoughts had to be marshalled and dispatched. Easier said than done, however. He demanded that his mind come into line with his will. This was his mission. This was everything he was, but thoughts of Ayshaa were never far away. He desperately needed understanding from her not confrontation, and some real rest and recuperation when he went back. Whether he got it or not was in the lap of the gods. Perhaps he didn't deserve it now.

He laid his papers out on the little desk and he fully intended to work through them, but it wasn't long before he laid his head down and drifted into unconsciousness.

In Jerusalem, Medad was still waiting for some response from Chuck. The clock was ticking and he was getting impatient. He felt the tension mounting within himself. He needed to keep cool. Somebody would surely be in touch soon. But what if Chuck was on holiday... what if he was away from his phone for a couple of weeks... what if he had no more information and thus no need to reply... there were plenty of what ifs? For the ultra cool sniper, Medad was learning a lot about himself; he didn't like having to depend on others whom he could not control. As a sniper, everything was in his control. There were no dependencies.

And there he was... again. Lounging up against a tree in the same park, looking as if he didn't have a care in the world and nothing mattered. Larry. As before, he sidled up to Medad as he was walking by and slid a memory stick into the Israeli's pocket.

"It won't self-destruct, but destroy it anyway," he whispered. Then he was gone. Medad's heart was pounding as he struggled to carry on walking as if nothing had happened. Maybe I'm getting better at this, he thought or perhaps not. He had deliberately decided on an early lunch break today because he was feeling claustrophobic in the office, definitely more psychological than real. So Larry must have either had eyes on the entrance to his building and quickly moved to the park, or he had been there for a while on the off chance Medad might come out at lunchtime, which he didn't everyday. What on earth would have happened if he hadn't come out at lunchtime for days?

Medad carried on walking, heading for a sandwich bar. After grabbing something to eat and consuming it on his way back to the office, he made a decision. He would not take the stick directly to Dan, rather he would keep it in his pocket, wait for Shana and do what they did last time. The afternoon went really slowly and while he was desperate to see what was on the stick, he didn't want to rush out of the office and draw attention to himself. At the end of the day, he took his time, lazily sorted out his desk and casually walked out towards the campus where Shana was based.

Shana was enjoying her college times, even her brief flirtation with Zionism. As she surveyed the journalistic scene though, she was dismayed. Every year dozens of students were leaving her university alone to look for journalist jobs. Demand for jobs hugely outstripped the supply with everyone targeting the same newspapers and on line publishers. Just as with Medad, it seemed to be who you knew rather than your ability that counted. So, the story that Medad was involved with grew ever larger in her mind. This was her way in. She just needed everyone to hurry and make their minds up about what should happen, then she would write the story. She allowed herself the same daydream a number of times, where she was the freelance correspondent to whom all whistle blowers would go to release their stories. She would be famous. Everyone would want her.

Well, she reasoned, there was nothing wrong in dreaming. Where would we be without dreams? What would have happened to the US black population if Martin Luther King hadn't had a dream? Yes, she would go on dreaming, but in the meantime she would need a place to live at the end of her course unless she wanted to go back to her parents' house in Tel Aviv, which she didn't. Her future was with Medad, and on the phone he sounded quite excited.

"Larry was in the park at lunchtime and gave me a stick."

"Have you looked at it?"

"No. I thought we'd do what we did last time."

"Do you want to go now?" It was now six o'clock in the evening and Shana thought the internet café might be full.

"Yes. Can you get there in twenty minutes?"

"Sure. See you." Shana experienced a shudder of excitement. Surely now they would soon know the name of the whistle blower in the Defence Ministry.

They arrived at the internet café within a few minutes of each other and together looked at what was on the stick, but it wasn't altogether what they were looking for. True there was another document, but when opened, it proved to be unreadable. Looked like Arabic. They looked at each other. This was hugely disappointing. Medad looked lost. What was he going to tell Dan? He had no other leads. His mind was in a daze. Surely there had to be something else hidden here. Medad tried everything he knew to see what else was on the stick. But it was actually just one document in Arabic. What was this all about? Were they playing games with him? And how did the Americans, the State Department, the CIA, whoever, get hold of an Arabic document? Neither Medad nor Shana could fathom what it was about but evidently it was important since Medad had been instructed to destroy it.

Medad was thinking aloud, "If we tried to get it translated, that would mean involving another person in the secret; another uncontrollable element. I don't think so."

Shana understood but said, "We can't possibly learn enough Arabic in time to do it themselves but I know some friends who do and could possibly be sworn to secrecy."

Medad said a loud NO. They quickly looked around to see if anyone had noticed what they were saying. Thankfully no-one had.

Then Medad had a brainwave. "Aren't there on line translation apps available on the internet?" Shana nodded.

He started typing. There were lots of companies specialising in this type of work, but that was not what Medad was looking for. However confidential the site claimed to be, it was not confidential enough for him. But Google Translate looked promising. He wanted this translation untouched by human hand, or rather, unseen by human eye.

He knew that Google had algorithms that could track what he had asked for and offer him more of the same, but he thought it might just apply to that café's PC, and not his personal domain. What he couldn't guarantee was that some other algorithm wouldn't flag up the search to some agency like Mossad or the CIA, who would then see the contents. Actually, he thought, maybe that's what the CIA were actually doing. Maybe they were monitoring translation services to see if Medad was using the information. He pulled himself together. He had no choice. He looked at Shana and they both nodded to each other. "Let's do it."

They knew these automatic translation facilities weren't always word perfect, but that was fine. Word for word accuracy was not required, he just needed to get the general gist. There had to be something really important in there for it to be passed to him. He highlighted the text in the document and submitted it. The resultant document was immediately saved on the same stick. They didn't even look at it. The browsing history was wiped off the internet machine although Medad wasn't that convinced that it couldn't be recovered if someone really wanted. But someone had to know that the document existed to want to try and recover it, and currently he, Shana and the Americans were the only ones who knew about it.

Another thought struck him. Had the Americans also given this to another party? What if someone thought Medad was unreliable and had also leaked it to someone else? He had no way of knowing and reluctantly decided that he would have to trust they were on the level. But the truth was that he trusted no-one, except Shana.

There were, of course, no answers to his questions. All he could do was to follow the path others had set him on and hope he could maintain control as far as possible. Shana was first to leave in the direction of her campus and Medad, about five minutes later, on his bike with the stick safely in his pocket. Lots of thoughts as he raced home. His family had a desktop which they all used at one time or another, so he determined that he would use that to read the document. It would have to go to Dan the next day and he might not be best pleased at his internet café excursion with such sensitive information. But it was the only way he could keep the control he needed. He was sure he had done the right thing. As he neared his settlement, he realised that he could remember virtually nothing about the journey he had just done. He shuddered. He wouldn't tell his mother.

She gave him a strong hug and a warm welcome and he suddenly realised that when he was away, she probably lived most of her life on her own. Although his father had retired from the army and was part of the leadership of the settlement they were in, he got the impression that he still seemed to spend most of his time away from the home. As he hugged his mother back he began to feel guilty about wanting to live with Shana in Jerusalem. Surely his mother didn't deserve that.

As he moved into the house, he discovered that his elder brother had come home for a few days, so the evening was going to be hard work. Medad had to discipline himself not to get into an argument about Zionism, the land, the terrorists, the peaceniks etc. etc. It is true to say, he failed miserably and his mother took herself off to bed early. So it was quite late when his brother also retired which gave Medad the opportunity to access the family desktop and read the document. When he did so, he got the shock of his life.

He sat there staring at the screen.

37

HANI AND OMARI were at the WalledOff talking about the factions in Ramallah, Hani doing most of the talking and Omari the listening. The tourists had departed and they had the piano bar almost to themselves, not to Hani's liking who preferred to hide in amongst lots of people. There was a lovely smell of coffee and something citrus which he couldn't quite place. It had become their regular meeting spot and it suited both of them.

Omari could picture exactly what Hani was describing in Ramallah for he knew very well his countrymen's proclivity for passionate disagreement. It was a cultural trait for sure, but definitely exacerbated by the degrading Occupation they had been in for fifty plus years. The only story most outsiders ever heard about Palestine was one related to that conflict. The character of the Palestinian to the outside world was either a furious young man with a keffiyeh wrapped around his head slinging stones at Israeli soldiers, or a woman in her hijab wailing in front of her destroyed home. It was the Palestinian as militant or victim.

While caricatures must have some degree of truth to be recognisable, the full truth is always different. But if the representation is repeated often enough, it can easily become the full truth and almost impossible to change. Omari had often wondered how to change the image. He thought it would take a mammoth public relations campaign, but maybe then only change if there was some agreement with Israel.

He was sympathising with Hani who was expressing some cynicism about his fellow Palestinians in 'government'.

"It's probably the same the world over. Our job must be just to do the best we can. In my judgement, we have done the best work that has ever been done in this area on the Palestinian side. If there was ever a time to make progress it is now."

Hani was more downbeat, thinking about the rabble that was the team tasked with conducting the discussions.

Omari encouraged him, "Leadership is the key and with someone strong at the helm, the rabble will toe the line eventually. It's not wholly on your shoulders"

Suddenly Omari's mobile buzzed. It wasn't his personal phone, so he knew it was Dan and he saw a WhatsApp message. Unwilling to disclose his Israeli contact to Hani, he put the phone away and apologised for the interruption. After a few minutes, he excused himself and went to the men's room. He looked at the message from Dan.

Earlier that morning, Dan had been in his office going through ministry papers as usual. Nothing new was happening. The papers for the summit were done. Nobody had anything to add it seemed, although Dan knew that anyone who took exception to something he had put forward, wouldn't raise their issues until the last minute, exerting maximum pressure to elicit a change. Medad had been keeping an eye on Dan through the glass, wondering when the right moment would be to drop his latest bombshell. This was the moment. He headed for his boss's office, walked in and shut the door.

Unusual, but Dan didn't object. He immediately stopped what he was doing and asked Medad for the name. He paused before explaining, "I don't have a name as yet, but I do have something else."

He passed the stick over to Dan confirming that, yes, he had looked at it. Dan inserted the stick into his desktop and began to scrutinise the contents. Just two files, two documents, the same size. He raised his eyebrows, looked at Medad and opened the first one.

"Arabic! What the hell!" Medad explained that the second document was a rough English translation of the first, neglecting to reveal his internet café excursion. This time, instead of nodding towards the door, he motioned Medad to sit down. Progress, thought Medad.

Dan started to read the English document. He hadn't got far when he raised his eyes and looked at Medad,

"Is this saying what I think it's saying?" Medad nodded. An expletive from Dan. "So the Iranians have a mole inside the Palestinian Authority? Thinking about it, that's not particularly news, except we have what are supposed to be bilateral talks coming up."

Medad nodded again. Dan's voice was rising, "How the hell did you get hold of this?" Medad said he thought it was an American. Dan's eyebrows raised again and his voice went up several notches higher. "They also have a mole inside the PA as well? So everyone has a mole inside there except us... well, that's probably not really true!"

He hadn't meant to say that out loud. He nodded Medad towards the door. "And I still need a name", was his parting shout.

Dan began thinking, wondering whether he should speak to his Minister, and if so, exactly what he should tell him. If he did, it would be a gift to Likud and would certainly serve to harden the stance of the whole right wing coalition. If he didn't, and it all came to light, he could probably be successfully prosecuted for any number of crimes. Mind you, he thought, I could be arrested for not revealing this information sooner. They might even charge me with collaborating with an enemy state, even if that state was the great US of A. So more of the same just makes the prosecutor's life that bit easier.

He concluded that, apart from his own career and personal future, it would serve only to stymie the talks before they had even started, and he didn't want that. God, he wished now he hadn't opened that stick on his desktop. But no turning back, he had to press on. What was to be his next step? Probably a message to Omari. It would be good that his contacts knew this, because it was going to be up to the Palestinian side to sort it and expose the man. If the Israelis did it, the whole Palestinian side might walk away in solidarity which would be a gift to his hard-liners.

So Omari picked up the WhatsApp message from Dan at the Walled Off and read and re-read the message sitting on the can. He got up abruptly, fearing he had been in there too long and his friend would be wondering where he was. Hani was looking curiously at him as Omari walked back towards the table. Some sort of explanation was in order, so he told Hani what his Israeli contact had messaged him. An Iranian mole inside the PA linked to the security services.

To Omari's surprise, Hani didn't show much of a reaction. He just nodded and muttered to himself, "that explains a lot." When Hani understood that there was a document in Arabic that laid it all out, he insisted on having it as the only way to convince his side. It was over to Omari to try and get it. They both got up together to leave.

As Hani made his way back to the shop, he texted Jamal to see if he could meet, either at the shop or in Ramallah. The shop, and he could be there in a couple of hours. True to his word, two hours later a car pulled up outside and Jamal got out. He came into the shop and for the first time really looked around. He hadn't really looked in detail at the little ironmongery shop before. As he surveyed the scene, he saw more empty shelves than stocked ones, and those that were stocked only had merchandise on the edge of the shelf. Jamal looked up enquiringly at the shopkeeper. Hani muttered something about stock meant capital being tied up.

"How on earth did you make a living out of this?" Jamal wasn't putting Hani down but genuinely couldn't see how anyone could make any money from such a shop.

Hani replied, "We got by." Jamal was of the opinion, and expressed the view, that Fatah had come to his rescue just in time. Hani didn't answer, but instead changed the subject to the matter in hand.

"I have a source," he said slowly, "which I cannot reveal, but who says there is a document giving incontrovertible evidence that there is an Iranian mole in the PA Security set up."

Jamal tried to sound sceptical, "That's just tittle tattle," but his eyes gave him away. They were looking at Hani with some intensity. Hani could see that he believed it all. Lots of questions from Jamal and just a few answers from Hani meant they needed to get the document. The most crucial of those questions was regarding reliability of the document.

Hani gave him a sideways look. "We both know this is true. It all makes perfect sense."

"What about the reliability of your source?"

"Total", was the word Hani used. No, he couldn't say anything more to Jamal about the source… plausible deniability.

*

It was the next day that Dan and Omari met in Bethlehem and a memory stick was passed between them. Even though they went for a cursory walk, the conversation was rather succinct. After a few minutes Dan went back through the checkpoint to his car and on to his office, whereas Omari walked back to the WalledOff having WhatsApp'd Hani to meet him there. He mused on how easy it was for an Israeli to come through the checkpoint to Bethlehem, compared with how difficult it often was for Palestinians to go the other way. As he walked, he could see the looming Wall with its watchtowers. He smiled as he saw again the words scrawled on the sides of the Wall: 'make hummus not walls', and 'Mr Netanyahu, tear down this wall!'

Hani was already wandering through the exhibition area. He was watching a video called, "5 Broken Cameras", a deeply personal, first-hand account of non-violent resistance in Bil'in, a West Bank village threatened by encroaching Israeli settlements shot almost entirely by Palestinian farmer Emad Burnat, who had camera after camera snatched or broken by IDF soldiers. It was remarkable if disturbing footage now uploaded onto YouTube.

Hani saw Omari moving round the exhibition, but made no attempt to greet him. Omari surreptitiously passed by Hani and the stick was duly slipped into his pocket. Without a word, Omari left and walked back to his office deep in thought. It's all getting very murky. He found himself conflicted: on the one hand, he really couldn't afford for all this to impact his charity, but on the other, he would never forgive himself if this attempt to help his country failed for lack of support. As he was walking, he decided to go home rather than back to the office. He'd had enough for one day.

Hani, however, went back to the shop and downloaded the file on his laptop, before messaging his boss to say he had it. Jamal didn't want it emailed to him, rather he would come by the following morning, first thing. Hani now had to go home and face Ayshaa. He took his laptop home to make this document the main topic of the evening. While it would deflect attention away from him, he also genuinely wanted to see what Ayshaa thought of it. It would be the first time he had spent an evening with his wife since his hostel night. He steeled himself as he came through the door. He had no intention of confessing.

After the rest of the family had retired, he loaded the document and passed the laptop over to her. "Can you let me know what you think?" he asked.

She looked surprised to be asked, but started to go through the document with an increasing disbelief. "How can you negotiate with the Israelis if you know there's a mole at the heart of the Palestinian Authority." Her venom at her own government surprised Hani, and he looked embarrassed as if it was all his fault, being a Fatah 'employee'.

His wife moved quickly to reassure him that she was not aiming her vitriol at him. He had been pacing the small room whilst she read and now sat down rather heavily admitting that he had suspected the person in question, but now there was nowhere he could hide. He will get what's coming to him... soon.

As promised, early the next morning Jamal came to collect the stick, but he didn't stay and hardly said anything. He had more important things on his mind. So both sides now knew who the mole was inside the PA. The information was highly significant but both sides were working hard to understand how such information could be used to advance their own cause. Jamal and Hani came to the reluctant conclusion that whilst it was good to be fore-warned, they needed other evidence to convince the Chief. For the moment, it was a waiting game.

Jamal still knew nothing of the Israeli Security documents, but was rather concentrating on working out the best way to neutralise Abd Alraheem. He decided to put one of his own men to shadow the Deputy and monitor his movements.

Meanwhile, Medad was still pursuing Chuck's messaging service for the name of the Israeli Defence whistle blower. He assumed the same route would be followed as last time. So he religiously went out at lunchtime everyday through the park to see if Larry was there. He never showed. There was no more he could do and the talks were now only two weeks away.

38

SHANA WAS IN full journalist mode, thinking about all the inside information she could obtain, the stories she might write, and she still hadn't left University! She had decided she could do both at the same time if she could get the scoops her husband could supply, and it was a big IF because currently Medad was insistent that she couldn't break either story that Larry had supplied. Shana understood his position but it was her personal opinion, and she expressed it forcibly, that leaking it to the media was the only way those stories would achieve anything.

Knowing she had these stories in her back pocket, was the stimulus she needed to start her freelance career right away. She saw no reason to join the queue of prospective graduates flooding the journalist market. Why not seek out stories and begin writing now? She was sure she could still get her university work done and get the grades she might need. If editors were any good, surely that was the way to impress.

She thought about the settlement she had visited in Gush Etzion, and the idea of Zionism. What made these people tick? Why start with a tent on a hillside, almost always on Palestinian land, and hope to make a new settlement? It seemed to be straight out of the Old Testament, conquering the Amorites, the Jebusites, and the rest of the 'ites, and perhaps it was. She allowed her mind to wander – she was still in touch with Shira on social media, so she already had an immediate contact, although Shira might not like the angle she would take. But why not write under a pseudonym for specific stories? Anyway, she thought, tuck that one away for future use. Not everyone wanted to hear an exposé of the Israeli settlement movement.

Shana determined to make a list of all likely media organisations, not only Israeli or Middle Eastern, but European and North American so that she could target stories to particular news/magazine/digital organisations. Hours spent in the university library enabled her to categorise what kind of stories and slant each publication seem to prefer. Although it was painstaking work, she was happy that she was beginning to lay a foundation for future success.

Whilst undertaking this research, she uncovered another related story. It was the increasing influence of the Ultra Orthodox Jews that caught her eye. She had learned a little about them while visiting Gush Etzion. She knew that they were evangelistic, in the sense that they wanted to extend their influence throughout the country, but she had not appreciated how much of that was already happening. She had believed that Israel was a secular state, yet different people were warning that these rabbis were intent on imposing their strict religious views on everyone, women being a particular target. There were significant efforts by Jewish religious extremists to try to impose gender separation in public, in elections, on buses, and in the street, all in the name of a morality that was supposedly agreeable to God. Shana didn't ride on buses very frequently but apparently informal gender segregation had already begun on buses a few years earlier. She could hardly believe it.

At first only one bus line was 'kosher,' but soon the men were sitting in the front and the women in the back on more than 60 bus routes. It had been reported that there was an instance on bus number 497 from Beit Shemesh to Bnei Brak where a women had been asked to move to the back of the bus in accordance with ultra-orthodox customs, and no-one on the bus defended the woman's right to sit where she wanted. The bus company refused to act and the government did nothing, both afraid of the religious right.

Shana was horrified. It was almost like segregation in the US had been. Now her attention had been drawn to this issue, she began to notice other things. For example, it looked like women had disappeared from advertising posters in Jerusalem. She remembered at the university there had been separate hours for men and women at the swimming pool, not that she ever went. Swimming was not her thing. On the basis of these observations, she began to do some specific in-depth research.

She and Medad had previously talked about getting married, although neither was in a rush. They were told that when they did want to tie the knot, they would have to go to a rabbi. Although a supposedly secular society, there was no civil marriage in Israel. And if you wanted or needed to get divorced, again rabbis were the only place to go. It was they who decided if you could or couldn't. She and Medad had briefly looked at trying to bypass the religious element, for neither was particularly religious. It was Medad who found out that under a law passed in 2013, Jewish couples who held a ceremony in Israel not approved by the rabbis, risked a two-year jail term as did those officiating.

Shana believed if she pulled all this together, there was a definite story here. After all, it was almost Islamic! There might not be a market for such a story in Israel, but there certainly would be outside. A new rush of excitement went through her body as she felt she had an immediate route into what she wanted to do, so with even more investigative fervour she ploughed on. She found out that burial societies forbid women from giving eulogies. This had always been so in Jerusalem, Beit Shemesh, and Bnei Brak which are Israel's ultra-orthodox strongholds, but it was becoming more widespread in places where secular Israelis lived.

Another disturbing fact regarding children. Road safety had always been part of a child's education, but now, Shana found out, as part of these lessons, all Israeli children were having to learn and say the Traveller's Prayer. Also known as the Wayfarer's Prayer or *Tefilat Haderech* in Hebrew, this is a prayer that Orthodox Jews would recite at the beginning of a journey. The prayer asks God to deliver the traveller safely, to protect them from any dangers or perils they may encounter along the way, and to return them in peace.

This is the prayer:

May it be Your will, Lord, our God and the God of our ancestors, that You lead us toward peace, guide our footsteps toward peace, and make us reach our desired destination for life, gladness, and peace.

May You rescue us from the hand of every foe, ambush along the way, and from all manner of punishments that assemble to come to earth. May You send blessing in our handiwork, and grant us grace, kindness, and mercy in Your eyes and in the eyes of all who see us.

May You hear the sound of our humble request because You are God Who hears prayer requests. Blessed are You, Lord, Who hears prayer.

Shana's immediate thought was that it was a very nice prayer. What was wrong with that? She began to interview local parents and discovered the real issue was the religious inculcation of the nation's children without their parents permission.

Then she came across a rumour, though not substantiated, that rabbis now had an official position within every kindergarten. She already knew from her visit to Gush Etzion, that ultra-orthodox schoolchildren didn't learn either Maths nor English, but just learned to recite the Torah, which was a concern. But if that was with the permission of the parents and it clearly was, then who could object? It would be when this was spread out to secular schools that it could become a problem. Shana began to see the shape of her article. This, it seemed, could be a deliberate long term strategy to undermine the secular state of Israel and turn it into a theocracy.

When she asked Medad about some of the things she was discovering, he reminded her, "Do you remember our military unit had a rabbi attached to it?"

Shana remembered, "Yes I do remember, although I never really understood his role." Medad concurred, "I'm not really sure either except that he said prayers before we went out and sometimes when we got back. Some of the guys were clearly religious, but most took no real notice, just let it happen."

Shana started thinking about rabbis in the military. "So the whole military has an underpinning of religion?"

Medad tried to give her some balance. "Yes, but every military force throughout the world, as far as I know, has chaplains or padres. It's no big deal. I guess it gives some peace and reassurance that they are doing the right thing."

Shana mulled this over. She knew she tended to overplay her arguments occasionally, especially when she smelt something rotten. She gave in on the military, but continued her research and a few hours later came up with a news report.

"Listen to this. An infrastructure minister wants to place power plants under the supervision of rabbis so that even electricity will be in compliance with religious purity laws."

Medad had to agree this was nonsense, but he encouraged her to lift her eyes up from the instances she had found and see the bigger picture.

"Are these isolated instances or is there a pattern? It's important to ask what it all means and careful to be as independent as possible seeking merely to ask questions, seek interviews and just report what she found, and not to go on a crusade."

Shana tried to take this advice to heart and began to step back. What was really happening? Was it really threatening, or was it simply people with a point of view, expressing it and lobbying for it, in good old fashioned democratic style? Good questions. She could even include these questions in her piece.

She came across an article by Israel Rafalovich, which itemised some of these concerns and began to pull these threads together. His thesis was that ultra-orthodox radicals were increasingly occupying key positions, thereby imposing their stamp on the secular majority. He claimed that Israeli's secular democrats were growing increasingly worried that Israel's future might resemble Saudi Arabia more than Europe. One of his conclusions was that Israel's shift toward orthodoxy was not merely a religious one. Since the vast majority of Orthodox Jews were also against any agreement with the Palestinians, the chances of reaching a peace deal was rapidly diminishing. Bingo.

Now she began to see the link between the secret document about the plans of the Israeli Security forces and the Ultra Orthodox. This was more than a religious quest. This was the undermining of democracy itself and the introduction of permanent Palestinian apartheid. She spoke with Medad about it and he promised to give it some thought and be on the lookout for any confirmation that the religious were involved.

But Shana was already convinced, her passionate investigative instincts on full throttle. If that were to be the case, the ultimate source of authority would no longer be the state and its institutions. It would be the ultra-orthodox, who wanted its holy men, holy scriptures, rituals, and prayers to be pre-eminent.

Almost sounds like Iran, she thought.

39

HANI AND JAMAL were in conference together. Jamal was feeling confident as he outlined his plan to neutralise Abd Alraheem. Hani less so. He warned that there was as yet no real acceptable evidence of Abd Alraheem's treachery, and what's more, he might not be the only Iranian/Hezbollah mole. They both wanted to agree a plan to keep him in check since the summit was nearly upon them. All they had to do was to hold their own side together and keep tabs on the other side. Easier said than done. But so far, the monitoring of Abd Alraheem had not shown up anything out of the ordinary.

The Deputy himself was still trying to get hold of Hani's document, but was finding it rather difficult. The direct approach to the Chief had failed. Only on 'a need to know' basis. Abd Alraheem snorted. He was the guy on the negotiating team and his boss wouldn't give him the key document that was going to be followed in the meetings – the sooner he got sacked the better. He, Abd Alraheem, would do a much better job. At least he had a track record in security, whereas the Chief's track record was his friendship with the President. He, Abd Alraheem, would bide his time… and then strike like a horned viper!

He was under severe pressure to provide his paymasters with the document and was beginning to get desperate. Perhaps an indirect approach was what was needed; someone in the Chief's office who could be persuaded to get access to the safe where all important documents were kept. He was sure it would be there. There were a number of possibles, and he began to look up each of them on his security database and from there to their relatives. Anyone with any sort of vulnerability would be interesting to him. He wasn't bothered.

"Yes!" He shouted out loud in his office, thrusting both arms aloft. She would be ideal. Her husband worked for Security, but quite low down in the pecking order which meant he could be quite clever here. This could be both carrot and stick. She was a trusted aide, who the Chief clearly took a fancy to. Although he didn't know if the relationship had gone further, for his purpose he didn't need to know. It just needed the suggestion to her husband that it might have. Of course, if she obliged him in his request, that needn't happen and her husband would be promoted, at least temporarily.

Late one evening, Jamal got a call from one of his men. Abd Alraheem had left the office in his car, but was not going home following his usual route but rather following a direction north past Nazareth, towards the Lebanese border. He had a briefcase and a sidearm. What did Jamal want done?

He thought quickly. "Have you got your camera with you?"

"Yes."

Jamal issued his instructions. "Take pictures of his car at key stages along the journey as you follow him, and particularly as he crosses the border. Find a good place to wait and watch for his return and take more pictures. Then follow him back. I'll send some back up just in case he stays overnight. He'll text you to find out where you are."

They needn't have worried about any overnight watch, the Deputy only disappeared for a couple of hours. Once he had dropped out of sight, the tracker followed the trail from his half hidden car to the entrance of the tunnel, then hid himself. As the traitor emerged from the dirt of the tunnel and walked back to his car, he was photographed again. He was looking very pleased with himself and, seemingly oblivious to any possible surveillance, was not taking appropriate precautions. His completely inadequate glance around confirmed his impression that the place was still deserted. Not only had he been clocked but the tunnel had now been discovered.

He was cock-a-hoop thinking about how his prestige and effectiveness had gone up in the eyes of the Iranian. He was safe. He had delivered what was wanted. Yes, he had taken tremendous risks with his own position but he was secure. Now all he had to do was to reassure the woman and promote the man. It didn't need to be permanent. In fact, nothing around Ramallah was permanent, he thought, except the Chief and the President both of whom seem to go for decades denying others their rightful promotion.

Angra Mainyu was indeed pleased. He sat in the farmhouse kitchen again eating and drinking courtesy of his hosts. Always look confident and assured, was his mantra. At last he had the document to send on to his masters. He wondered whether it was worth all the trouble, so he took his time staying at the farmhouse for an hour or two while he read the document with growing admiration.

"Somebody knows what they are doing", he murmured to himself. "This Hani character could be a real threat." He put the document into his own briefcase, threw Abd Alraheem's away and ordered his driver to take him back to Beirut.

Before he went into his embassy the next day, he went to The Print Shop Sarl, operated by Kompass. It was on the ground floor of the Blue Building in Omar Ben Abdelaziz street, Hamra sector. He knew the manager and could copy a document himself on an old fashioned Xerox machine which didn't scan the document, but used the original selenium drum process to produce copies. He didn't want anyone looking at the document and was taking no chances of anyone retrieving a digital copy. Attention to detail. Take no chances. More mantras. Then a quick call from the embassy on a secure line to his boss, and a flight to Tehran with the original document, a copy being in a locker at the airport. He would not pick this up directly on his return, but would wait a few days before doing so... just in case.

The reconnaissance of Abd Alraheem had been completely successful and Jamal was now looking at the pictures with date and time on them. Perfect. His plan was still intact. In fact, he now had incontrovertible evidence of his treason, with no need to commit further resources delving into the man's finances which, he was sure, would reveal amounts of money which he could not legitimately explain.

His attention now focussed on the missing briefcase. If there had been nothing in it, then he would have left it in his car. So what in particular did he pass this time, to whom and how long had this been going on? Jamal suspected Hezbollah, although he had no evidence yet. Doubtless, whatever it was would end up in Tehran. He decided to pull the surveillance on him for the moment so not to spook his target. He would wait and see what happened.

*

Medad was getting impatient with Chuck and the Americans in general. He had no idea what was going on across the other side of the world but it wasn't helpful. In fact, it wasn't Chuck holding things up because he wasn't actually privy to the name of the Israeli Defence Department whistle blower. He had been pulled into a CIA operation just because it became known to them that Chuck had developed a good relationship with this rising star in the Israeli government. However, he was banned from contacting Medad directly for the moment, assuming merely a postbox function. Meanwhile an argument was raging inside the CIA between two factions, some who argued for the leaking of the name, and others who didn't want to blow the cover of a significant intelligence source.

Larry was not a decision-maker. He was simply one of their covert field operatives resident in Israel. The debate was well above his pay grade. In fact, he had never been on any pay grade. Larry, aka Jim Ryland, did not even have diplomatic cover. He had lived in Israel for decades, was married to an Israeli woman, had three children, a dog and ran a small, but flourishing plastics business just outside Jerusalem. It gave the US complete deniability and gave him a rather lucrative additional income which was paid into a US account in his home town of Greenwich, Connecticut where he and his family returned two or even three times a year. There he had a large house, car, boat, every-thing the family might need for a great holiday, all funded by the generous US taxpayer.

He had no idea what was on any of the memory sticks he had passed on over the years, and neither did he want to know. He was his own man, which sometimes led him to be a little over confident, some might say arrogant. He had experienced a little wrap over the knuckles for the first meeting he had with Medad, but these things happened from time to time. He wasn't worried.

Chuck, on the other hand, was worried. It was all above his pay grade as well, but his CIA contact had been told his opinion in no uncertain terms. Something had to be said to Medad, otherwise they would lose that relation-ship for good and Chuck was firmly on the side of releasing the name. The decision was taken, however, to deny Medad the name. They knew the talks were imminent, which was why they had given him the information in the first place, but they could not, would not risk further exposure of their mole. Medad and the Israeli negotiation team would have to manage without, at least for the moment.

It was decided that Chuck should text a cryptic WhatsApp message to Medad simply saying 'Not possible'. There was no point in using Larry. It also had the benefit of keeping the Chuck-Medad relationship alive, as best they could. Medad was hugely relieved to see the WhatsApp come through on his burner phone, but equally disappointed and discouraged to read it. Dan was not going to like it. Medad felt responsible, almost as if he personally was withholding the name, but he was also angry. Angry to be dragged into something and then left high and dry; angry to be used as a pawn in someone else's game; angry that this risked all he had done for the peace process. Predictably, Dan didn't like it, didn't like it at all. He demanded to know who these Americans were. Medad continued to feign ignorance. What else could he do?

At that moment, it looked as if Dan was going to cut him loose from the delegation but he restrained himself. Medad left his office downcast, hopeful he might still be involved. It was true that Dan was seriously thinking about it. He suspected that young Medad was not telling the whole truth and that undermined trust in his protégée. But it was too late to change personnel now and if he sacked Medad, it would call into question his own judgement. Besides, Medad had done all the ground work. It would be risky to leave him out, and who knew, there might be other information coming his way.

Dan had his suspicions about where all this incriminating data was coming from, but he desperately needed to verify it before he could use it. There was no way he was using such dynamite without knowing where it came from. There was an outside possibility that it was a setup but he didn't think it was, which was why he had given it to Omari. He calculated that the best option was to surreptitiously release it, then any blowback wouldn't come back on him. He knew that if it was traced back to him or anyone in his department, it could spell complete disaster.

The time for analysing was over. The preliminary talks were about to start.

40

AYSHAA AND HANI were not talking. Ghalia looked worried and even Rena seemed to be catching on to the silences and occasional harsh words between her parents. Ayshaa was sitting on the steps outside the front door, Ghalia and Rena having gone to bed. She thought back. She had been proud of her Hani, who had come from nothing to be a major player in the Palestinian hierarchy. But now it seemed to be the only thing he thought about and lived for. He never asked about what she was doing and, in her eyes, her work was just as important as his. Perhaps it was inevitable that this should have happened.

She had many friends so she didn't feel lonely, although there was a deep regret that things had turned out as they had. Yes, she knew that her work could have become all-consuming, but she had kept the balance between work and family, whereas Hani hadn't. He seemed to have reverted to the standard Palestinian male. For her part, she would not become the standard Palestinian female, but continue with her work as well as looking after Rena and her mother-in-law. The sun had now disappeared behind the tall buildings that surrounded her and the temperature was dropping. She went inside. It didn't seem that her husband was coming back tonight either.

Hani was at the shop tinkering with his stock and wondering whether to go home or not. He was not happy with himself, but what could he do? He also was thinking back over the past few years. "How did I get here?" The truth was that he was not a major player in the PA for apart from Jamal, he was nothing. He still considered himself an outsider, and was seen as such by many who had been around Ramallah for years. The city was very suspicious of newcomers. The in-crowd didn't like outsiders because in their eyes it meant more competition for the available money. Hani knew it was essential to be always watching his back. Every time he went there he felt the jealousy of this city, which had become the de facto capital of Palestine,.

It wasn't their choice of capital, of course. Although the Israelis occupied East Jerusalem, and had done since the 1967 war, Palestinians continued to live there and hoped that one day that city would be their capital. The move of the US embassy to Jerusalem was a slap in the face, as was the Trump administration's cancelling of aid to them. Hani would be the first to admit that much of the foreign aid was wasted. He could be scathing about the nepotism, corruption and wasteful, egotistical building projects that had consumed funds that could have been better spent on the ordinary people. Nevertheless, as long as Israel held the keys to the Palestinian economy, they needed financial help.

So Ramallah was the administrative capital of Palestine, whilst East Jerusalem was their designated capital. For Israel, Tel Aviv still had many trappings of a capital except that the Israeli parliament was in Jerusalem. Only a very few countries recognised Jerusalem as the capital of Israel, Russia being one of them but confining their recognition to West Jerusalem. They had recognised the East as the capital of the future Palestinian state. The US had not offered the same political compromise.

Although Jamal worked in and around Ramallah, his family had lived in East Jerusalem for generations. Currently, his wife and four children still resided in their house. He was rarely there though, because if he went in and out too regularly, it would be deemed that his 'centre of life' was outside Jerusalem, his ID would then be revoked and he would never get in again. Fortunately, because of his job, he was able to support his family with funds which they could draw upon. But it was by no means a normal family situation. If asked, he would probably have said that there were no normal family situations anywhere in Occupied Territory.

Hani had no idea about Jamal's family until it cropped in conversation as they reviewed their proposed discussion with the Israelis about East Jerusalem. Obviously, his personal status and that of his family were crucial to him, but Hani cautioned him to not let his personal situation affect the discussions. Perhaps it would be better if he, Hani, led this agenda item... if they ever got to it. Jamal was one of 420,000 Palestinians who had 'permanent residency' ID cards for East Jerusalem. Because that part of the city had been ruled by Jordan prior to 1967, he also carried a temporary Jordanian passport. It didn't, however, have the national identification number of a full Jordanian citizen, which meant if he ever wanted to work in Jordan, he would need a work permit, which in turn meant he had no access to any Jordanian governmental services or benefits. In fact, the passport was completely useless.

He, his family and all Palestinians living in East Jerusalem were actually stateless. They were not citizens of Israel, nor were they citizens of Jordan or indeed, Palestine. They lived in legal limbo. Israel treated them as foreign immigrants, who lived there as a favour granted to them by the state and not by right, despite having been born there. They had to fulfil a certain set of requirements to maintain their 'centre of life' status and lived in constant fear of having their residency status revoked. This is what Jamal wanted to change. He felt it was an essential first step to later discussions about East Jerusalem as the capital in more than name.

Even for those who were born there, such as Jamal's children, if they could not prove that their 'centre of life' was in Jerusalem and that they had lived there continuously, they could lose their right to live in the city of their birth. He wanted legal assurances for all Palestinians who had residency, but may have lived outside the boundaries of Jerusalem for any period of time, whether in a foreign country or even in the West Bank, to have their right to go back and live there if they chose to. But that was going to be a tough ask. Israel wanted to empty East Jerusalem of Palestinians, not let more in.

Hani attempted to move on to other issues, but Jamal was fixated on this one for understandable reasons. He railed at the unfairness of it all and the helplessness he felt for his family.

"You know," he complained, "we must submit a host of documents including title deeds, rent contracts and salary slips etc. to 'prove' our right to live in the place where we were born!"

Hani sympathised, but Jamal was on a roll, "And any Jew around the world has the right to move and live in East Jerusalem if they so desire, no questions asked but not us."

It was true that settlements here had been encouraged and, it was reported, about two hundred thousand Israeli citizens now lived in East Jerusalem settlements under army and police protection, with the largest single settlement complex housing forty-four thousand Israelis. Those who emigrated to Israel did so under Israel's Law of Return and also gained automatic Israeli citizenship. The Palestinians, the indigenous population, had no such right of return.

"Isn't it transparent to the whole world that Israel wants to clear East Jerusalem of non Jews, and populate the whole city with Jewish Israelis?" Jamal was still going strong.

"And since 1967, Israel has revoked the status of fourteen thousand Palestinians. This isn't Palestinian propaganda, it has been authenticated by B'Tselem, an Israeli human rights group."

Hani was quiet, thinking there was probably more to come. Better let it all out now rather than in the talks.

"My own family home is in the middle of several fortified Israeli settlements, designed and built to infringe on our freedom of movement, privacy and security. It's all contrived to force us to move."

There was a gritty determination that Hani detected in his boss. "But we are not going anywhere. They will have to drive us out with bulldozers."

Hani tried to break Jamal's momentum. He began to talk through options for East Jerusalem that he had outlined in his document. Israeli leaders in the past had been poised to accept a deal that would have given Palestinians oversight, but not full control, of the Old City's Muslim Quarter and parts of its Armenian Quarter, leaving the Christian and Jewish Quarters under Israeli control. The problem area was the thirty-five acres known to Muslims as the *Haram al-Sharif* (Holy Sanctuary) and to Jews as the Temple Mount.

The deal his document proposed was that the Palestinians have at least temporary oversight of the site that holds the golden Dome of the Rock and al Aqsa Mosque, and Israel control of the Western Wall and the plaza in front of it. As a back up, there could be an independent force to oversee the entire Old City and adjacent holy sites, including portions of the Mount of Olives that overlook the old city. Not ideal but it would, according to Hani, be a step in the right direction and could be revisited down the road.

But Jamal was in no mood to look at any of this dispassionately. Hani gave up. He couldn't go through all the other issues like this. They had yet to talk about borders, who controlled what in the ABC areas, refugees, prisoners, security and a host of smaller issues. Hani was beginning to despair of making any progress. He was an outsider trying to show he had empathy with all his colleagues, but also attempting to keep them rational, objective and persuasive. Ranting would play right into the hands of the Israelis. It was now four o'clock in the afternoon and they decided to give up for the day. The next day were the prelims, but only about formats, ordering of the agenda, who sits where, and other ways of playing the diplomatic game. They still had time to go through the main issues, he thought.

Dan and Medad similarly were going through their documentation. Unlike Hani and Jamal, they had no immediate way of controlling their Security and Defence colleagues on the Israeli delegation. It was extremely unnerving to go into talks when you knew that you're own side was divided. Because of this Dan decided to try and meet the other representatives one by one to try and work out their attitudes to the various issues.

His Minister was the head of the Israeli Ministerial delegation rather than the Security or Defence Minister, which was a blessing in that it meant that Dan would be the Chair of the working group, with the Minister coming in at the end to agree or disagree. Obviously he would keep the Minister informed as they went along. This gave him the cover he needed to have individual meetings and have access to whatever papers had prepared for the negotiations by those individuals. If such documents weren't disclosed, Dan could disallow them. In contrast to Jamal's tactics with Hani's paper, Medad's document had already been carefully circulated so enabling Dan to judge where individuals were in relation to that.

Although the relevant Ministers were hard-liners, not all their civil servants personally reflected those views and in fact, at least one of the Ministers seemed to be less hard line in private than he was in public. Nevertheless, collective cabinet responsibility meant that all had to hold to the agreed government line. Dan felt he could manage the working group he had been given, it would be when the Ministers came in that problems might begin. He and Medad would have to play it by ear. They had to be imaginative and creative not only with words, but ideas to achieve the breakthroughs they sought.

On the day of the preliminary talks both delegations arrived with their

Ministers in Ramallah to a certain degree of pomp and ceremony. The media required this and the Palestinians particularly, had to show their statecraft such as it was. Ministers stayed for the photos and then left as quickly as they could in their BMW's and Mercedes. This was the first time that delegates had met each other. And so the shopkeeper met the sniper.

41

JAMAL SHOULDN'T HAVE pulled surveillance on Abd Alraheem. When reviewing it all later with Hani, he admitted that it had been a serious lapse in judgement. He had thought that the photos about his incursion into Lebanon to meet with Hezbollah had given up all the information on the Deputy that he needed and had been confident that the man was completely at his mercy. What he had not done was consider the wider implication of the visit and any potential ramifications. Jamal didn't know, for example, that Angra Mainyu had given Abd Alraheem a specific task to fulfil on the West Bank.

The largest mosque in Jenin was the Fatima Khatun Mosque, otherwise known as the Great Mosque of Jenin. It was next to the Fatima Khatun Girls School, but it wasn't to this mosque that Abd Alraheem was headed. He had set off from his office in Ramallah at about six o'clock in the evening, stopping only at a police barracks ostensibly to see a colleague. He left his station wagon at the back of the building and went in through a side door intending for anyone on surveillance to note that he could only have been in the barracks for a short time. But there was no-one was on active surveillance. After about twenty minutes he exited the building, climbed back into his car and drove off.

He took a rather circuitous route out on Altira Street, 'wiping his backside' as best he could, and up the 450 through Halamish and Kedumim. The sixty seven miles to Jenin would take about two hours he estimated, which meant it would be quite dark when he arrived. Although he had never been to this address before, he had been given precise directions and he was confident of arriving on time.

This was a much smaller mosque on the outskirts of Jenin better known for its more radical leadership, and this is where Abd Alraheem was headed. The Ministry of Religious Endowments and Affairs as part of the Palestinian Authority, had the power to forbid preachers which contradicted the PA line and they had intervened at this mosque on more than one occasion. But not being allowed to preach on Friday mornings, didn't stop a radical message still being propounded to groups of impressionable young men on midweek evenings.

Ahmed al-Fahd, the Imam, was in the Shi'a tradition. Unlike Sunni Imams in Bethlehem, Shi'a Imams are regarded as men of God par excellence having all the attributes usually reserved for God alone. It is believed that these Imams are chosen by God and are free from committing any sin, *ismah*. Such leaders expect to be followed without question which bequeathed considerable power especially over the young. Ahmed al-Fahd had already been alerted that someone from the PA Security Services would be calling as a friend on a certain day, at a specific time.

It was exactly ten o'clock when Abd Alraheem arrived at the house of the Imam in his station wagon. They had never met before and were unlikely to meet again, but Abd Alraheem was welcomed into the home as an honoured guest and offered traditional Palestinian hospitality. The dwelling was quite old and not in a good state of repair, at least it seemed so to the Palestinian security man. The room into which he was shown could have been no larger than Abd Alraheem's kitchen. The floor was carpeted and there were three small alcoves with old tiles over the top of each. The Deputy sat on the carpet against one wall whilst the Imam sat against an opposite wall. Few words were exchanged. Hospitality was received with grateful thanks and once consumed, Abd Alraheem got back into his car and headed back to Ramallah.

While he was being honoured in the house of the Imam, three young men who were Ahmed al-Fahd's protégées, were unloading the contents of the station wagon, specifically, semi-automatics, pistols, ammunition, plastic explosives and wire cutters courtesy of the Palestinian police back in Ramallah, but without their knowledge. They carefully carried their booty from the car into a garage at the side of the Imam's house and closed the double doors. Cut-to-size timber boards covering a hole in the floor were removed and stacked carefully against the garage wall.

It was a mechanics pit which didn't look as if it had been used in decades. The young men were using a simple kerosene lamp to light up the garage and, in this light, the hole looked like a grave with old timbers shoring up the sides and a hard sandy bottom still stained with oil. The flickering light gave the garage an erie feel. The one who had drawn the short straw was lowered into the pit while the others handed the stolen goods down to be safely stored.

Suddenly there was a sound outside and they all froze. They listened intently for what seemed like an eternity, but no-one came knocking at the garage door so they quickly finished up. The timbers were replaced over the pit and the young men disappeared separately to their own homes hoping that their haul was safe at least for the moment. Ahmed al-Fahd had insisted that the cache had to be moved to another location within forty-eight hours. He had to be clean. And so it was, that the protagonists came back the following night to move the haul to another secret location.

An Israeli settlement had been founded west of Ya'bad town, near Jenin a matter of months previously. It had started as an expansion of an illegal outpost, established on private Palestinian land. A single colonist settled there first claiming to be a shepherd, but soon the army installed mobile homes, brought more colonists, and started preparing for roads and linking the land to mains water and electricity. Tareq al-Amarna, the head of the Palestinian Thaher al-Abed Village Council, had declared the incident to be very serious and had condemned it in the strongest terms, stopping just short of calling for reprisals.

Now a fence was in the process of being erected around the settlement which had grown to over one hundred people and was still expanding. It was a clear provocation to the Palestinian families who owned the land. The old men sat in the square of the Palestinian village and moaned but a few of the young men from the mosque decided they wanted to do something about it. They shared their thoughts with the Imam at one midweek meeting who did little to dissuade them. He could do nothing directly to help of course, but indirectly he might be able to procure some supplies. As it happened, friendly Imams in Lebanon were able to pass on the request and it didn't take long for Angra Mainyu to hear about the situation and decide that the project fitted well with his strategy of pitting Palestinian against Israeli. His PA sleeper in Ramallah was ordered to supply the requested items from PA police stocks.

As far as Angra Mainyu was concerned, it didn't matter what the plan was, or whether it was successful. All he wanted was conflict and the deeper the better. The Imam also had his own agenda; if some young men died as martyrs as they attempted to strike at the Jewish invaders, then that would be a win for them – paradise, and a win for him – satisfaction. What was there not to like!

Abd Alraheem had been totally confident of the secrecy of his movements that night. After all, he was a trained security man unlike his boss, the Chief. He knew all about anti-surveillance strategies and had employed them extensively on the way out of Ramallah, to the barracks and until he was on the road to Jenin. He was sure he was clean. Unfortunately for him, his car had been seen suspiciously parked at the back of the police barracks, and being loaded with 'supplies'. The registration of the car was noted and passed to Ramallah. The PA bureaucracy would normally have never flagged this up to anyone. It would have been the subject of a minor report which would have been written out and filed.

But coincidentally, Jamal had previously alerted some trusted security officials of his interest in the Deputy because of the Lebanon trips. A report of a car at the police barracks in Ramallah would never have normally got to Jamal for his attention, except that one bright young man working at the barracks recognised the car registration as belonging to Abd Alraheem. While he was still inside the building, the young man in question was ordered by Jamal to quietly ascertain the car's destination. After a cautious drive following Abd Alraheem, the young man reported back as he was approaching Jenin. The Deputy's car was followed through the city to the outskirts and its journey's end.

Once Jamal heard the final destination and the nature of the 'supplies', he knew that meant trouble. There could only be one reason. Someone or some group was planning a hit on an Israeli target of some kind. Jamal told the young man to stay put. He had no idea it was a settler community, there were so many it was hard to keep track of them. Not only would an attack on an Israeli target ruin the chances of them coming to the talks, it was also just plain stupid. It would be met with an overwhelming response from the Israeli military in which many innocent Palestinian people in the village and maybe in the city of Jenin would die. Whilst he understood the extreme frustration of the Palestinian population, especially the young men, he could not allow any violent incursion to happen. There was a bigger picture to consider.

Jamal needed to intervene. First he needed to know who was involved. To this end, he sent two trackers, *ayin* as the Israelis would call them, to rendezvous with the young man and observe the mosque for any suspicious movements in or out, twenty-four hours a day until they discovered who was involved. The how and the when would, he hoped, quickly follow. The men took eight hour shifts. During busy times at the mosque, each of the three took turns to stretch their legs and walk around the mosque mingling with other worshippers in order to identify any rear exits. Having determined that the front was the only entrance and exit, they retired back to their room to watch and wait.

After a couple of days of this, the men began to get restless and moan to each other about the fruitlessness of it all. Although they were holed up in a friendly house part way down the road from the mosque, the room they occupied had just a single bed, two chairs and not much else. They had access to a toilet and washbasin shared between them and the fifteen other occupiers of the three storey building. A slightly opened window didn't stop the room getting stuffy and the air stale and dank. Untold plastic bottles and food containers spread everywhere didn't help.

Finally after four days, they spotted a group of four young men entering the mosque at about eight o'clock on Wednesday evening. A debate then ensued as to whether these might be the conspirators or not and who should leave the room to check them out. A quick call to Jamal prompted them into action. The two trackers left the house, stationing themselves at each end of the street. No matter which way the group went when they came out, they would be covered. About two hours later the group left together, clearly unaware that they were being watched, and went back the way they had come talking excitedly. Both trackers followed a little distance away, knowing that if they split up, they could each only follow one.

*

In Ramallah, Jamal's file on Abd Alraheem was now ready to use when the situation called for it and the Deputy was oblivious to the fact that evidence of his treachery was piling up. He completely believed he could justify that he had no links to events in Jenin, and anything happening there was nothing to do with him. However, he did keep his ear to the ground expecting some news to break about an attack on Israel of some sort.

He was not disappointed.

42

NATAN BERKOWICZ WAS personal aide to the Israeli Defence Minister and a senior civil servant. He was an old hand in the department and had served a succession of Defence Ministers of differing coalitions, but mostly with a Likud majority since that party had been in power for quite some time. The secret of his longevity was not just his experience, but his skill at getting things done. He was almost an invisible man, one that no-one outside the Department particularly noticed and therefore someone that didn't pose any threat. Well dressed in grey, with the occasional splash of black, he seemed to merge into any background. Quietly spoken in his public role, but in private rather an odious man.

He was no fitness fanatic, but kept himself in shape through a combination of walking his Canaan dog, Babka and a disciplined intake of calories. A Canaan was the national dog of Israel and, if known, gave a clue as to the political leanings of the man. He had shunned marriage and children to single-mindedly pursue his right wing agenda, for the future of his country. If he wanted sex, he knew he could get it whenever. As one who lived alone, the dog was a close second in his life to his job. She was clever, confident and territorial, and since this was his third Canaan, he knew that unless she had early training, she would end up 'owning' her master.

Natan would never allow that to happen. He was the boss and imperceptibly he 'trained' his bosses with the same diligence as his dog. But he knew the score, his job description was only to advise, propose and suggest. For a civil servant though, he wielded a lot of power. Everyone knew what Natan said was what the Defence Minister said, and the Prime Minister and Defence Minister were tied at the hip.

Likud was a right wing party that had never been able to form an outright majority in the Knesset, but had managed to build successful coalitions with five other smaller parties: Kulanu, Bayit Yehudi, Shas, United Torah Judaism, and Yisrael Beytenu in order to retain power. In Israeli political life outright majorities were rare, the skill lay in being able to persuade smaller right wing parties to compromise on their demands if they wanted to keep centre-left parties in the cold. Likud was certainly good at that.

Natan was supposed to be a neutral civil servant, but everyone has their own opinion. It was Natan's opinion that even Likud was not right wing enough, which was why he had been gently suggesting to his Minister that meeting with Major General Hersch might be in his interests. He had been privately meeting with the General's aide for some time, a friend he had known since university years ago, a fact not generally known either in the civil service or in political circles. It was not particularly a secret, but both men saw no need to go out of their way to make it known. It was not relevant to anyone else.

Those two, alongside ten others, comprised a small group of influential men (no women) who wanted to see a permanent majority right wing government in Israel, at least until the Palestinian 'threat' had been solved. They did not make public pronouncements, seek or give media interviews, write articles, books, blogs or indulge in any other form of mass communication. They felt their agenda could best be served by staying in the shadows and influencing politicians and opinion formers from within.

Not for them the activities of The Public Forum, a right wing group which had released a video slamming an organisation called the New Israel Fund. This fictional video was set in the Israel of 2048 and presented an imaginary scenario in which the name of the country was changed from Israel to "Israstine," the prime minister was leftist MK Ahmad Tibi (Joint List), the president was MK Zahava Galon (Meretz) and the Bible was outlawed. The film also featured a high school named after Yasser Arafat, with a sign saying it was founded by the New Israel Fund. However much they approved the content, this was not their style.

Natan couldn't quite recall when he first heard the news of a potential meeting with the Palestinian Authority but it caught his attention immediately. He knew there were 'peace doves' around in government and the civil service, and the thought that they might have manoeuvred a negotiation session where concessions might be offered was startling news, one which was abhorrent to him. Through the usual channels, he arranged a hurried meeting of the twelve in an upper room of the exclusive Boutique Alegra Hotel, a little out of the city centre in Ein Kerem village. Each of the group arrived separately and at well timed intervals so as to avoid garnering attention. The room had also been booked under a third party name, all designed to provide complete anonymity.

Natan was in the chair, as he had called the meeting. He outlined the rumours of a Palestinian meeting and, although such a meeting had not yet been diaried, it was of sufficient interest to spark quite a profound discussion among the gathered. A number of actions were agreed, one of which was to arrange a meeting as soon as possible between the Defence Minister and Major General Hersch known to be sympathetic to their cause, after suitably briefing both men. The meeting broke up in the same way in which it had convened. There had been no food, no drink, no credit card, no footprint.

Over the next few days, Natan began dropping seeds of a meeting with Hersch into the mind of his Minister trusting that, with a little watering and sunlight, those seeds would germinate as they usually did. It was day four when Natan felt he could wait no longer and moved into harvest mode. He was in the Minister's substantial office going through the usual routine at the beginning of the day. He was standing whilst the Minister sat behind his desk. He then more formally proposed to diary a preliminary meeting with Major General Hersch to gather first hand what the army's position on any proposed talks with the PA. The Minister didn't look up from his paperwork and said nothing. After about ten seconds, which felt to Natan like ten minutes, of standing in front of the large imposing desk, the civil servant began to feel a little uncomfortable and rather exposed. He then broke one of his golden rules, which was 'when there's silence, don't rush to fill the gap.' He was so taken aback that he blurted out, "Of course, it's entirely up to you Minister."

His Minister looked up, "Yes it is, isn't it." For the first time in this relationship, Natan was feeling at a loss. His attempt at manipulation had not worked, at least it wasn't having the impact he was used to having and had hoped for. While he was getting used to a failure, an unusual experience for him, the Minister had passed on to other areas and the meeting with the General became a closed subject unless the Minister chose to open it. The civil servant retreated without his usual swagger and with the Minister lifting his eyes to follow his exit from the office with the hint of a smile.

Natan got back to his office, sat down to collect himself and rehearse what had just happened. He wasn't going back to the eleven to admit defeat. He had never done that ever, and he wasn't going to start now. He had time, well at least a few days, to concoct and implement a plan B. The matter, however, was taken out of his hands entirely. Two days later he was still trying to come up with a workable plan B when he was called into the Minister's office to be informed that, following an invitation direct from the General, a private meeting had been arranged and he was to attend. Natan was astounded and muttered a relieved, "Yes, Minister," and a quiet, "I should have thought of that." It transpired that the General was more than willing to oblige when his own aide outlined a scenario where serious concessions were going to be given to the Palestinians to assuage world opinion. Something had to be done, and the General was the man to do it.

The meeting was to be at the General's office and only the General, the Minister and their two aides were to be present. Natan expressed concern that such a location was not secure enough, but his Minister waived him away. "Nonsense!"

43

BACK IN RAMALLAH, it didn't take long for most of the prelims to be agreed. If the truth be known, the Israelis didn't think they would be there that long and so weren't bothered, and the Palestinians were so delighted to have the talks at all that they probably would have agreed to any requests that the Israelis demanded. The decisions at this stage were all about venue, seating, hours spent actually discussing and negotiating and time with their own sides. There were other less important areas left to secretarial staff.

It was decided that the real negotiations would start in one week which gave Hani and Jamal time to thrash out crucial bargaining points on the remaining issues. Jamal seemed to have recovered his cool and was happy to begin reviewing the border issue. Most maps outside Israel still had the Green Line marking out the 1948 West Bank border with Israel. However, that historical line was not going to be the start point of discussions from Israel's point of view. The intervening decades had confined the Green Line to the history books and Hani was glad to hear that Jamal wasn't insisting on starting there. If he had tried to, the talks would have stalled immediately.

Israel would start with lines which reflected the 'facts on the ground'. That meant not only recognising Israeli settlements, but the most compelling fact on the ground – the four hundred and thirty mile network of concrete walls and electronic fencing that the Israelis had built in the West Bank. Rather than following the internationally recognised Green Line, this 'separation barrier' carved out deep chunks of Palestinian territory enveloping sprawling Jewish settlements such as Ariel and Maale Adumim. These were still growing and Israel planned to take a lot more of the West Bank land for such settlements.

Jamal was not ready to recognise such settlements and Hani agreed. Although there was an implicit understanding that Israel would offer the Palestinians a comparable amount of land in exchange, that had never been defined or agreed. Both Jamal and Hani recognised that this would be an almost impossible negotiation to have. For Israel to change their border would require them to make painful and divisive decisions to evict thousands of hard-line

Jewish settlers from deep inside the West Bank. This would not be an election winning strategy since every Israeli government was a coalition with the votes of the settlers and the religious right being crucial.

Hani wanted to push hard on this issue initially, knowing the Israelis would resist. His last play would be to try and agree a narrow strip of land through southern Israel between the West Bank and Gaza which the PA would control. They would assert that this would enable them to better control Hamas and maybe get Gaza back under Fatah control. Of course, the opposite was also possible but that would be left unsaid, not necessarily unnoticed.

If that wasn't successful this time, and it was unlikely to be, it would be a marker for the next round of discussions. The strategy this time would be to follow up this Israeli refusal with more palatable issues where the Israelis might feel they could give ground. That was the way to make small incremental gains. Each would be seen by their constituents as making progress – the Palestinians for achieving some concessions and the Israelis for being flexible and listening to global opinion.

Next was the refugee issue. More than four and a half million Palestinian refugees were living in political limbo. They were in refugee camps within the West Bank, in Lebanon, Jordan, and around the world. Many were descendants of those who fled their homes during the formation of the modern-day Israel. Successive Israeli governments had totally opposed allowing them to return to their lands which were now occupied and farmed by Israeli settlers. It would also be a migration that would threaten the country's status as a majority Jewish nation. Such a right of return could not be agreed without the inclusion of many current inhabitants of Gaza, which posed another level of danger as far as Israel was concerned. It was anticipated that they would play the security card in this instance.

It was another intractable issue which Hani wanted to treat in the same way as the border. His argument was that the best they could get was some 'token' number of returnees. Of course, if there was the ultimate settlement whereby a new Palestinian state was formed, then hopefully that would change things entirely but there was no pressure on Israel to do that. Jamal conceded that this was likely to be a no-win issue for the Palestinians, although he would like to negotiate the size of a 'token' number of returnees. This they agreed to try and do.

Last major issue. The big one. Security. With Iranian proxies still threatening, Hani recognised that Israel would never accept a well-armed Palestinian nation next door which could easily fall into the hands of Hamas as Gaza had done, or worse, Hezbollah. Jamal thought there would be a possibility that they could negotiate the creation of a limited Palestinian military with a restricted supply of defensive weapons in addition to the small arms supply they already had. In return, Israel would insist on continued military posts in the Jordan Valley that could alert them to any possible attack from the east. They could agree that these posts could be temporary and eventually withdrawn without ever agreeing any timescale.

So they had their strategy. In between the intransigence of Israel on the big issues, they hoped to achieve solid gains on a lot of smaller ones. It would be important because there was an Israeli election in three months time and they hoped to influence the Israeli voting public to back a softer line as regards the West Bank. Both men were exhausted both physically and emotionally. There was a lot at stake. They had become friends and Jamal was increasingly relying on Hani's streetwise approach to the negotiations. They had retired to Gloria Jeans Coffee House on Al-Tireh St. It was a favourite of Jamal's; he even had a loyalty card. Here they tried to relax, though not very successfully.

Jamal started to ask about Hani's family and his business, "So how did your family happen to settle in Bethlehem? Was it your father in '67 or your grandfather in '48, and who started the shop?"

Hani started to respond but he could see Jamal's mind was a million miles away. He stopped and Jamal apologised. Both men then sat in silence drinking their coffee and each eating a sugary doughnut. Will it work? Will we get anything to give to our people? What agenda will the Israelis have? These were some of the questions that were going round and round in their minds. There were no answers, yet. After just ten minutes they finished their coffee and doughnuts, got up, shook hands and each went his own way.

In Jerusalem, Medad and Dan were trying to put their strategy together as well, but were finding it difficult to have constructive discussions with the rest of the negotiating team.

Dan was getting impatient. "We don't know who is who. The whistle blower could be on the team, or they could all be involved in the conspiracy or they might all be totally innocent."

Medad didn't have an immediate answer and so Dan continued, "And how can we pressure individuals unless we know they are involved? At present, we can't usefully use any of the information we've been given. We're flying blind."

Medad was thinking. Perhaps he might know a way to get some movement, but he didn't want to let Dan know, just in case it failed. after the meeting he texted Chuck, reasonably sure that his burner phone hadn't been picked up, otherwise a move would have been made by now. The idea was that he would list the names of the Defence and Security members of the team, if Chuck would indicate if any or all of them were involved. He tapped it out and waited. He wasn't expecting an immediate reply, but he got one.

"Meet Larry at Café Café in Emek Refa'im St. at 1230 hours tomorrow."

Suddenly, the adrenalin started pumping and he began to see a way through their dilemma.

He took an early lunch break leaving the office at 12 noon to get to the café on time. He took a seat at a table in the far corner where he could see all who entered. When he had settled and ordered, he took a quick look around the place. Whoever owned it had done a nice job, he thought. It was modern, yet comfortable; youthful enough to be attractive for customers in their twenties and thirties, but still acceptable to more mature customers. There were several young mums in one corner chattering away with their pushchairs close by; an elderly couple having a coffee in another, each engrossed in their newspaper not talking to each other. He guessed that having spent almost their entire lives together, perhaps in their latter years they had said everything that needed to be said. He hoped that he and Shana never got to that stage. Two or three of the other tables were occupied by single men having a light lunch none of whom looked remotely like Larry, but more people were arriving all the time.

He waited impatiently. His frustration was mounting as the waiting continued past the thirty minute mark. Larry couldn't possibly miss him. He stared at the door of the café silently urging him to appear. Nothing. It suddenly occurred to him that the establishment might have another floor where the American might be sitting. He silently cursed himself for being so stupid. He must concentrate, be less emotional and more rational. He quickly moved to the serving counter and asked. No they didn't. He quickly re-took his seat.

His dislike of Larry was now off the scale. Although he'd anticipated a short meeting, he was now so desperate to see Larry that he felt he had no option but to stay and buy lunch. By half past one, he had eaten and drunk and, by the looks he was getting from the management, was conscious that he was taking up a valuable table in a busy café at lunchtime. He'd been stood up. Very reluctantly, he got up to leave. Disappointment was not a word that described his feelings at that moment. He slowly made his way to the door, looking at the other lunchtime customers, hoping against hope that Larry would prove to be there, smiling in his annoying way. He would have given anything for Larry to waltz in just then and forgiven him everything and anything. He trudged through the streets, blind to anyone who didn't look like Larry, bumping into people as he scoured the route for any sign of the American.

When he got back to the office, Dan wasn't there presumably in a meeting. He sat down glumly and from his jacket took out some pocket tissues, only to find another flash drive there. What the ****! How? Where? Who? He quickly put it back as if it would burn a hole in his hand if he held on to it. Suddenly conscious of himself, he glanced around the office. Nobody was looking at him or remotely interested in him. He couldn't wait to insert the stick into his desktop just to see what was on it. He quickly took it back out of his pocket and looked at it. No markings, no identification. "Calm down," he scolded himself, "Take some deep breaths." His hand was trembling as he put it into the usb port and was surprised to find an mp4 file.

Now what was he going to do? He'd got something, from someone. Was it Larry? He remembered all those bumps as he was stumbling out of the café. Could one of them been Larry? Surely he would have noticed. He took the memory stick out and pushed it back into his pocket. He was suddenly conscious that he was sweating, so much so that he had to loosen his tie and wipe his forehead. He found his collar was sticking to his neck and felt an overwhelming urge to visit the men's room which he did, using the opportunity to wash his face with cold water. He looked at himself in the mirror and tried to straighten his hair which had inexplicably lost any shape. He must have put his hand through it several times – he couldn't remember.

Back at his desk he texted Shana with his news. No, he didn't want to meet at the internet café because he needed to play the video and, without headphones for both of them, the sound might be overheard in the shop. So she agreed to meet him at her place. Since she was about to leave her studies, this was probably the last time they could meet there. They both crowded round her laptop as the mp4 file was uploaded. The video was a bit scratchy, the camera had been hidden in a place that wasn't ideal. The sound was quite difficult to hear but odd words were clear. 'Palestinian', 'Compromises', 'Never', were the obvious ones. However, it clearly showed four men in deep conversation. Gotcha! They copied the file on to the laptop and Medad pocketed the flash drive. Shana was metaphorically licking her journalist lips, but Medad cautioned her again to give it time.

Next morning Medad went straight into Dan's office and announced that he hadn't got the name of one man, but he did have the faces of four men. He handed the memory stick over. Dan loaded the mp4 file and started watching. "O my God! This is the Defence Minister, a senior General and their two aides."

Dan looked up at Medad and in a whisper, as if the whole of government was listening, expressed astonishment. "Who got this? If Mossad got a sniff of this, we could disappear for good."

Medad sat without moving. Dan looked at him. "Copies?" Medad nodded. Dan set about clearing his PC, the best he knew how. He also ordered Medad to take all the files they had received and lodge them with a lawyer, with strict instructions to release them if anything happened to either of them. He also advised that Medad, and whoever else had a copy, should scrap the laptops, tablets, phones and get new ones which would be entirely clear of incriminating data.

Medad made a mental note to dispose his burner phone and Shana said she would clear her laptop, but neither did. For her part, Shana decided to copy those specific files on to one of her flash drives, all her other work on to another one and reset her laptop to factory settings before re-installing her own files. As these files would have the same date, she would explain to anyone asking that she'd had a virus problem and re-setting and re-installing was the only way to save her device. Medad was unaware.

In the meantime, Dan was working out how to use this information to bring his errant Defence colleagues into line. Not easy. In the end, the civil servant in him got the upper hand, and he decided to do nothing until the real talks began. If they got to an impasse, then he would talk about a rumour he had heard about a conversation, secretly recorded, not that he himself had seen it of course, etc. etc. He hoped the implied threat would do the trick. If not, he would reveal a bit at a time until they came into line.

44

BOTH SIDES WERE ready. This would be the first week of talks, then a week's break before reassembling for a final week. If it went any further than this week, it meant they were really getting somewhere. If the second week didn't happen…

The fanfares had already taken place at the preliminaries so there was no media scrum this time, merely a few hardy photographers and just one TV crew. No interviews, no personalities, no political spin but quite a few large Israeli men with bulging jackets no doubt secreting Jericho .45 pistols and looking in charge. The protagonists gathered in the newly decorated lobby area of the Grand Park Hotel for refreshments at precisely ten o'clock allowing the delegates to mingle. It was either a get-to-know-you session or a first-skirmish session, depending on who you were.

The Israeli security men stayed outside, although who was to say there weren't also some on the inside competing with the Palestinian security detail who, ostensibly, were responsible for security. The Israeli delegation did have some large men amongst them who looked remarkably unlike diplomats. Among them was a certain Major General Hersch who, out of uniform, looked singularly hood-like. He was accompanied by two civil servants, his own aide and another from the Ministry of Defence, one Natan Berkowitz.

Omari had passed friendly Palestinian names to Dan and the Israeli had reciprocated, so each had been able to do a little research on the others. Dan and Hani found each other and were able to shake hands and give knowing nods to colleagues without anyone paying particular attention. Dan formally introduced Medad to Hani and, since they were of a similar age, and left them together whilst he tried to find Jamal. Sparring was the nature of the game in these forums and, although neither had been involved in such sessions before, caution was prevailing. Nothing of import was shared between shopkeeper and sniper.

Everything was civilised, after all Palestinian hospitality was a matter of honour, and the hosts made sure it was first class. Nothing had been spared and, at exactly ten minutes to eleven, a bell sounded to give delegates a few minutes to visit the cloakrooms and on the dot of eleven o'clock, they trooped into the prepared room with its layout exactly as agreed. The door was shut and wouldn't be opened until one o'clock, unless someone decided to walk out. That would be a serious sign and no-one expected that at this stage.

The agenda had already been agreed and the first item of the plenary session was security. A big one. This session would just be an exchange of views and, as positions would be well known from previous meetings, it was likely to be quite predictable. Hani's strategy was to wait until twenty minutes before the end, then suggest something new. He wasn't expecting an immediate breakthrough, but he was interested to see the different reactions of the various members of the Israeli delegation. He hoped to see some tentative splits on the Israeli side, which he knew were there. After the immediate reaction, Hani would explain it further with the advantages to the Israelis, hoping to empower the moderates and show up the hard-liners. Time would then be called and the session would end.

Both sides would then have lunch in separate dining rooms in the hotel which would be swept for bugs while all delegates were in session. Such a private lunch allowed each side to discuss the morning's progress, or lack of it, over their meal. The afternoon session would be a short, one hour session from three to four o'clock. Often this would be abandoned if one side had a lot to discuss. The leader of one delegation would simply notify the leader of the other through the agreed secretarial system. This would also be the mechanism that notes would be passed from one side to another outside of the plenary.

The afternoon session was duly abandoned following an Israeli note. The Palestinian side thought it might be rather positive if they were still discussing Hani's proposal. After four o'clock all formalities were over and delegates that wanted could meet in the lobby for more tea, coffee and some pomegranate passion cake. It gave opportunity for ideas to be floated without the weight of a formal proposition. Such a proposition would only happen when one side did not intend to change its position, so the more talking that happened in the lobby, the better.

Day followed day with a similar pattern. Rehearsal of old positions, new suggestions from one side or the other, then a break usually for the rest of the day. Formal proceedings were almost always ending after the morning session, giving more time for informal talking. As far as these active sessions went, there was no overt disagreement within the ranks of either side, although Hani and Medad knew there were fault lines on each of their respective sides.

Hani was hoping to get individual concessions secured as they went through. However, there was always a chance that the other side would want to save all concessions up until the end and then try to negotiate one against the other, to end up with a more favourable package. There was not much he could do to avoid this, except to try and get firm formal agreements in the plenary session. Then there was the strategy of leaking. This would inevitably happen by both sides through the negotiation. It was exasperating but also useful. This was where the American documents might come in useful if certain parties didn't come into line.

But the weekend was here and everyone was packing their suitcases to depart for home. Ramallah breathed a huge sight of relief since nothing had happened which could make the Israelis abandon the talks, although if they really wanted to foreclose, they didn't need a reason. Jamal had the job of briefing the PA President and Dan similarly with his Minister. So far, so good. No obvious divisions in the ranks as yet, because nothing of substance had yet been agreed. A long way still to go.

Rena was first to see Hani as he came through the front door. She wasted no time in rushing to greet her daddy. In return, he lifted her up and gave her a huge hug and lots of kisses. Ayshaa stayed at the kitchen end of the room preparing the evening meal, no welcome from her. The conversation was civilised but rather curt.

Hani offered, "How was your day?" Ayshaa answered in monosyllables, "Fine." Hani tried a more open question hoping to get to get a conversation going, "What progress do you think my mother is making?"

"Not a lot." Ayshaa wasn't having a conversation.

"Oh." Rena was still jumping on her father. He laughed and swung her round and round before trying to move into the other room to see his mother. As he was going through the door, Ayshaa asked, "do you have to go out again tonight?"

"No, not tonight."

Hani disappeared inside. There was no doubt that Ghalia looked worn out, the medication clearly not able to fully return her to health. He decided to talk to her about what he had been doing, to see if that would stimulate her interest. She was certainly happy to have Hani back and interested in how he was coping, not so much in the political issues though.

Later that evening Ayshaa, whilst she was clearing up, casually mentioned to Hani, "Your mother is getting weaker, and there's not much more I can do."

Hani quickly looked up. Ayshaa was giving nothing more away. The son was torn; he couldn't spend time at home with his mother right at this juncture, but he felt guilty. It was all falling apart. He knew, or thought he knew, that Ghalia would be wanting him to work at these talks first and not worry about her. He wanted that to be the case and desperately needed everyone just to hold on a little longer until the talks were over, then he could be back and perhaps things would get back to some sort of normal. It was feeling very strange to go from high level strategic politics to domestic issues within a matter of hours. When he was away he felt regret that he was letting his family down, and when he was home he felt he was letting down Jamal, because his attention was elsewhere and not on the talks.

He desperately needed the week's break. He hadn't been sleeping well at night for a while and the stress was showing in his face. He was a big man, fit and muscled, but beginning to look a little gaunt. If Jamal noticed, he didn't say anything but Ayshaa had. He wondered how longer he could keep all these plates spinning. Although he was not in the chair, he had produced the document they were all working to and he felt personally responsible for its success. It was all for his daughter and her generation, wasn't it? But how could he do it all? After all, he was just a shopkeeper. Surely Fatah had made a big mistake in involving him in all this. It was all a recipe for insanity.

He could only be responsible for what he could control, and he was finding that he could control less and less. He couldn't even control his own wife!

What sort of Palestinian man was he?

Dan came away relieved that no divisions on his side had been transparent to the other side in the formal sessions, but he knew the following week was going to be challenging. The weekend was going to be spent working and worrying. Although Medad had produced the draft document, he wasn't feeling the same pressure. To be able to switch off was quite easy now that there was no pressing need to produce any names. Over the weekend he took time to enjoy looking around the new apartment that Shana had now rented and accompanying her doing some more shopping. He looked lovingly at her and was really glad she was able to do this sort of stuff and that it didn't all fall on his shoulders.

This was not quite the right comment to make to Shana, but did express his delight. "This is a great apartment. You really have a gift for this sort of thing."

As he said this he was looking carefully at her not wanting to be patronising. He was learning. But she looked pleased. "Why don't we move in at the end of the month. I've said to the agents that we can sign up tomorrow."

Medad agreed and confessed that he hadn't had time to tell his mother. Shana looked up and raised her eyebrows, "Really, no time?"

"So," continued Shana, "why don't we invite her up to Jerusalem for a meal? Does she drive?"

Medad knew that she didn't and said, "No. I'm sure she can make her way here but she might have to stay over and go back the next day."

He promised to call her and hope his father would be otherwise engaged. He really didn't fancy a military lecture in front of his fiancée, especially as he hadn't told either of them exactly what was occupying his attention currently, but he might tell his mother in general terms, if there was an appropriate moment. Then another weekend, they could invite Shana's parents up from Tel Aviv as well. Not both sets of parents together, at least not yet.

Shana was working on her Ultra-Orthodox article. She had decided to write under a pseudonym in order to protect Medad and any stories that might come out of his work. A hundred word précis was written with some positive interest from a few overseas publications, including the UK Guardian. She decided not to approach any Israeli media although they might pick it up depending on how she framed it. Because there was no immediate pressure on income, she could go about preparing for her career without any time pressures. She set herself up as a media company with a 'dot com' ID, disguising the fact that she was located in Israel as much as she could, hopefully to distance her private life from what she hoped would become a successful public one.

In Bethlehem, Omari was getting on with building his charity. Ayshaa and Lara were finding plenty of current community issues which he could help with, but in reality, he was more concerned with the future. He was planning a purpose-built building within one of the refugee camps. It would be an education centre, a meeting place and also a guest house on the top floors with beds for visitors. This would be a profit making operation as well as a training opportunity for youngsters wanting to go into hotel management etc. To raise funds for this he was also planning a US tour. Although there was a strong Israeli/Zionist lobby there, he had also found strong, if less vociferous, support for the Palestinian cause on campuses, among peace groups and amongst some Hollywood celebrities.

Hani had just come off the phone giving him a brief summary of the proceedings. He had promised to keep in touch, but there was really nothing much to report except that he had met Dan and Medad. Omari detected the tiredness but encouraged him both to take care of himself and to have offline conversations with Dan and Medad if he could. He might be able to agree on some points and outmanoeuvre hard liners on either side. Hani agreed that there were definite opportunities and had plans to do that using the American intelligence.

Oddly enough in Lebanon, Angra Mainyu was thinking a similar thing. He also was working a plan with two strands. He now had Hani's document which he proceeded to doctor, and he also had the Jenin ingredient. His Iranian masters were pleased and Angra Mainyu could see advancement coming his way in the near future. A decision had been made that he could not, would not, place his whole future career in the hands of Abd Alraheem. He didn't like the man who, in his opinion, was puffed up, arrogant and promoted way beyond his capability. He needed another person. Abd Alraheem had mentioned someone in the Palestinian President's office whom he had used to get the document, a woman.

The question was how could he contact her without alerting Abd Alraheem. An untrained Hezbollah agent blundering about could do real damage and the Iranian would not risk his network. He gave the matter some thought. What they might be able to do, however, would be to merely confirm the identity of the woman, if done with care. Hezbollah had a number of supporters embedded in the PA, and one of them was a woman who worked in the Finance Minister's office and not known to Abd Alraheem. She was happy with her lot, not just because she got paid by two employers, but because for her it was a crusade.

Th order came to 'bump into' all the females in the President's office until she found the right person whom Abd Alraheem had duped. There weren't that many. Easy. Angra Mainyu gave the go ahead. Striking up a friendship with Nada then positioned her to help out financially when Abd Alraheem reneged on his promises towards her husband. Blackmail could always be used, but carrot was always better than stick in her book. An offer to exact revenge on the one who had cynically used, then discarded her and her husband without a moment's thought, yes Nada was definitely up for it.

In Washington DC, Chuck was in his office despairing of the American system, which purposely seem to pit agency against agency. He took off his glasses and rubbed his eyes, not out of tiredness, but frustration. With co-operation, a good result would surely have been assured. But not a bit of it. How had he got caught up in this? Yes, he could remember. 'Liaise' with the CIA had said his boss. Maybe it was serving his country, but he had not signed up to be a pimp to groom Medad for someone else to abuse. That's how he felt and now he was quite powerless to pull back. Yet he was a servant of the government, under oath to execute those government's policies without fear or favour. That meant they owned him and his morality until he resigned, and he was not ready to do that yet. Squaring the circle, viz. executing his job fully and at the same time being honest and wanting to maintain a relationship seemed impossible. For the moment, he had decided to keep quiet.

He prayed that Medad would use the data sent to him appropriately. He knew that Shana, although still at University, was aiming to be a journalist and he didn't want Medad to jump the gun by letting Shana have the story. If she were to publish, it would have ripples right around the world and especially around the White House. It would be uncontrollable, and if there was anything the government disliked, it was an uncontrolled media.

He just had to allow the chips to fall where they might.

45

IN JENIN, THE two trackers were following four young men going home from the mid week meeting at the mosque. Each went their own way and the trackers almost imperceptibly signalled to one another who each should follow, hoping they had made the right decision. They had little idea as to who these men were and no notion of who might be the leader. Two buildings were identified as each disappeared inside their own house. Photos were taken which would clearly mark out the dwellings for future reference. Once done each tracker made his own way back to their hideaway. After a quick call to Jamal to report in, they all headed back to Ramallah.

Unbeknown to any of them, the young men of the village had finalised their plans that evening at the mosque and were intent on regrouping that same night. At three o'clock early morning, blacked up and armed, they clambered up the hill to infiltrate the settler camp before the whole fence could be completed. No-one was watching. They had equipped themselves with just wire cutters and the silenced pistols, other equipment being left for another time. This was to be a quiet operation. No-one was to know anything until the morning when pandemonium would break out, but two of them would then be miles away with their package.

In Ramallah, the two trackers were blissfully sleeping. Jamal was having a dream about the success of the Israeli conference. The President was congratulating him on a good result and he was basking in the adulation. He was happy and everything was under control. Except that it wasn't. No-one in Ramallah had a clue what was going on in Jenin and the devastating potential that it posed. The news broke at about seven o'clock the following morning that a young IDF soldier had been kidnapped from a new Israeli settlement near Jenin.

Jamal was on the rampage, but there was little he could do except threaten all sorts of torture to his two trackers. It was now clear that they had all been too late. The role of Abd Alraheem had been the final piece in the jigsaw puzzle, not the first. As he calmed down, he began to think. It wasn't his issue theoretically, but that of the Chief of Security. However, the proximity of the talks meant that regardless of that he needed to make it his issue.

Where had the young soldier been taken? Three possibilities: West Bank: possible, but where? Gaza: not likely. Gaza was a long way from Jenin and there was no way in unless they knew of a tunnel that was still open. Tunnel! Tunnel! Lebanon! Abd Alraheem must have given directions to the northern tunnel, the kidnapped soldier to be delivered into the hands of Hezbollah. Curses poured out of his mouth. "I'll strangle him with my own two hands if I have a chance," he pledged.

He made a phone call and ordered his two trackers to get to the tunnel, if necessary go through it and try to track the soldier down. A tall order, he thought, but he had to try. He sent others up to Jenin to find any accomplices and wring out vital information.

The kidnappers had done their reconnaissance well, knew where the military outpost was and that there would be a single soldier on duty in the early hours. It was still only a small settlement, with the outpost building some way from the first houses that had been built. No doubt others would follow as the settlement grew. The Palestinian young men had arranged that two of them would get the Israeli soldier, a third, having stolen Israeli plates for the car, would drive it as near to the outpost as possible and the other would be the look out. They would bundle the soldier, tied and taped, into the boot of the car and drive it up north from Jenin to the Lebanese border by a series of back roads, avoiding military checkpoints.

It all went to plan. Simple. By the time they arrived at the tunnel, it was getting light. The Deputy had given the Imam a rough location sketch and he passed it on, and it proved to be very rough. They left the Israeli soldier bound and gagged in the car whilst they scoured the place. After an hour of looking for the entrance, they were beginning to panic until they came upon it by complete accident.

They hid their car in the scrub which had covered the area around the entrance to the tunnel and half dragged, half carried the Israeli out of the car and into the small passageway. Abd Alraheem had warned that the tunnel was very low in parts and they might have to crawl.

"He wasn't joking," said one kidnapper to the other. "We'll never get this guy through." The fact that the Israeli soldier was resisting made progress very slow and hard work.

The other kidnapper told the soldier to stop resisting or else. He didn't, so he was hit hard at the back of the head. "That felt good," said the Palestinian kidnapper. The rest of the journey was a little easier.

Angra Mainyu had arranged for a car on the Lebanese side of the border to pick up the Israeli and take him deep into Hezbollah territory. The two men waiting for them had almost given up when the Palestinian young men staggered through the tunnel exit with their human cargo. No words were exchanged. The Israeli was handed over and the Hezbollah car drove off at speed. The two Palestinian kidnappers sat down exhausted from their efforts and lack of sleep, but could only risk ten minutes. The possibility that the car might be found spurred them on. They made their way back, picked up the car and drove down to Nazareth where they planned to hole up with friends until the inevitable clamour died down.

Jamal wanted to try and handle this within the PA if he could. Although he was desperately regretful that he hadn't chosen to expose Abd Alraheem, that mistake wasn't known to the Chief. As he thought more, he could see some opportunity if the Palestinians themselves could facilitate the return of the Israeli soldier. The incident was all over the news and the Israeli army was all over Jenin. A violent backlash against the innocent citizens of Jenin was in prospect so he contacted the Chief of Security saying that he had some intelligence from Jenin which might lead to identifying at least some of the kidnappers. He needed a little time, and the IDF to pull back from Jenin.

The PA always had channels to communicate with the Israeli military but normally they were ignored. This time the Chief had a call back from a senior Israeli commander within minutes. The Chief handed the phone to Jamal who repeated his intelligence and asked for twenty-four hours.

"You've got eight hours from now," was the curt reply and the call was terminated. The Chief looked at Jamal and said nothing. Jamal knew his career was on the line. The Chief was about to inform the President that Jamal was going to find the Israeli soldier and save the day.

Jamal was working really hard to do just that. However, the IDF commander in charge of finding their soldier had already ordered a large detachment of soldiers to arrest twenty Palestinian young men at random in Jenin. No-one was going to mess with the Israelis without fear of retribution. A cohort of IDF soldiers simply went to the mosque as men were leaving, sealed the immediate area and took the required number into custody. Enough prisoner transport had been brought to make the operation quick and easy. With heavily armed soldiers everywhere, they met with little resistance bar shouts and curses. Done and dusted!

These prisoners were immediately driven north, past Nazareth, past the Sea of Galilee and through Rosh Pinna, one of the oldest settlements in Israel. North west of the village was En Honi. On the map, it was blank; nothing seemed to be there. However, if anyone happened to be driving along the track to En Honi – this non place – they would inevitably come across a military checkpoint and circular barbed wire enclosing acres of land. If drivers got through the fiercely guarded gates and drove another two miles, they would find a small collection of buildings, some dwellings and others which looked more like an industrial trading estate.

Israel had many interrogation centres and this was one. The newly arrived detainees were hauled out of the vans and dragged into one building where they were stripped to their underwear, shoes removed and blindfolds attached. Each was thrown into an individual cell so designed that each prisoner could not possibly hear anyone else. Isolation was total. There they were left. There was no immediate intention of interrogating them because it was presumed that they knew nothing. They were simply pawns in a larger game, hostages whose lives would mirror the life of the Israeli captive. If he died, they died. If he lived, they lived, but not without a retributive cost to send a blunt message to the Palestinian population.

Back in Jenin, the watchers had identified the two other conspirators. They promptly alerted the local Palestinian security commander, but before they could be arrested one of them had been grabbed by the IDF in their raid and taken away with the others from outside of the mosque.

Nevertheless, Palestinian security men began searching for the remaining conspirator. He was eventually found hiding in a mechanics pit in the mosque's garage. Both he and the Imam were driven away to Ramallah secretly, because once the IDF commander knew there had been some arrests, they would demand the prisoners be handed over, which the PA might not be able to resist for very long. Jamal wanted keep it all quiet for as long as possible to give themselves maximum time for questioning.

The interrogation facilities in the newly built Palestinian police barracks in Ramallah were in the basement of the building. They might have been rarely used but they were certainly ready for these occupants. It was the usual method. Each of the two interrogees had their own cell and initial interrogations were handled there. Get one story and test against the other, not just to find the inconsistencies but to identify who was the weakest link. In this case, it wasn't difficult to guess. Overawed and completely out of his depth, the young man didn't really know how to play the game. The story eventually came out about the new settlement, the anger of the locals, the Imam, the weapons, the plan, the night it happened, everything. He had hoped that this would be sufficient to set him free but, with only a little further persuasion, the names of the two who had driven the Israeli away were confessed.

The Imam, however, was another matter. He refused to talk at all and, for the time being, was left in his cell. He was of little concern to Jamal who now had most of what he wanted. The Ministry of Religious Endowments and Affairs had been waiting a long time to pin something on this Imam that would stick. Now they had it. The Imam was handed over to them. It wouldn't look good to the faithful if the PA handed over a Muslim Imam to the Israeli military, and the Imam knew it. But Jamal would have had no qualms at all in handing over all of them to Israel including the Imam, except that he knew nobody in the PA would allow it. Politically, it had the potential to split Fatah if the news got out, and Ramallah was one of the leakiest place on earth. It would be a major public relations own goal, one which Hamas and Hezbollah would play to the maximum. But the Israeli army might yet try to force them to do it but they would face that if and when that happened.

Jamal now knew where the Israeli soldier had been taken, the details of the car, and the fact that the remaining young men were planning to hide in Nazareth. The car could be traced, the kidnappers tracked down, but there was little chance he could make any progress in Lebanon even though he had dispatched two of his security guys. To him, it was a clear attempt by Hezbollah to cause disruption to Israeli-Palestinian relationships and scupper the upcoming talks. He could not expect any help from either Hezbollah or Hamas, in fact quite the reverse.

A serious but discreet manhunt got underway in Nazareth with quiet promises to key people of rewards for information leading to their capture within twenty-four hours. Nazareth was an Arab city within Israel itself, not part of the West Bank, so Jamal was having to be very careful. The eight hours given to him were nearly up, but he calculated that detail of the Hezbollah connection and the location of the tunnel would satisfy the Israelis in the short term and give him more negotiation room. He wanted to insist that the tunnel be watched rather than blown up since his own men needed a way back.

Good news from Nazareth. The car had been found. Surely it wouldn't be long before the two men would be discovered and captured, but it took another ten hours before they were found in the Old City near the Old Muslim Cemetery. They were taken under lock and key to Ramallah where details of the kidnapping were confirmed. But they now had details of the Hezbollah car which had taken the Israeli soldier away in Lebanon. Although Jamal was out of time, with this information also passed to the Israelis, he hoped that relationships would be mended sufficiently to go ahead with the second week of talks.

Without the return of the soldier alive, however, he feared the hawks on both sides would be emboldened, but he could do no more.

On the periphery of all this activity but unable to help to any degree except to offer encouragement to his boss was Hani. His mind was also firmly on the talks and trying to save them. He suggested that they might open another front of dialogue with the Israelis privately through his go-between in Jerusalem. Jamal trusted Hani and gave his consent.

A day later Hani and Omari met at the offices of Ghu-sin Zay-tun. Omari listened as Hani told the story behind the news that everyone had been watching. The request was simple. There and then Omari messaged Dan in Jerusalem and arranged a meet again at the Al Karawan Restaurant near Rachel's tomb in Bethlehem. It was Saturday, *Shabbat*, a rest day for Jews and an ordinary business day for Muslims. Jamal, Hani and now Omari wanted to do everything possible to strengthen the hand of the 'doves' on the Israeli side.

Dan listened respectfully. He indicated that he had not been notified that the talks had been cancelled or even suspended. He personally hoped they would go ahead after the break, but it was a political decision, not one for him. Omari closed the brief discussion by thanking Dan and reminding him that even civil servants have a great deal of influence over their political masters. They shook hands and departed their separate ways.

What Dan hadn't admitted to Omari was that Major General Hersch had contacted him and requested a meeting. On the agenda was the kidnapped soldier and the talks process. Dan knew he was going to come under some pressure to immediately cancel the talks. Leaks to the press from the Israeli security side had mobilised the more vocal of the Israeli population who were all for cancellation.

Sure enough, as Chair on the Israeli side, Dan was invited by the General to 'postpone' the talks until a more favourable time. Hersch made it clear that he was speaking for a number of others on the delegation and, while much preparatory work had been done by many good people, the situation had now dramatically changed. The country would never understand if talks with the Palestinians continued. There would be questions in the Knesset. Implication: it would all land in Dan's lap and his career would be over.

If Medad had been party to the meeting, he might have been tempted to force Dan's hand and revealed the contents of the video. As it was, Dan decided not to reveal his hand yet but to acknowledge the seriousness of the situation and promised to take soundings from other members of the delegation. He thanked the General for his input and trusted that he, and indeed others who might have a different view, might coalesce around his final decision and so provide a united front to the Palestinian Authority.

46

HANI WOULD HAVE bet a considerable amount of money that the talks would be suspended. It was now some days since the Israeli soldier had been kidnapped and there had been no claim of responsibility and no communication at all, either publicly or on back channels. No-one knew whether he was still alive or not. It didn't bode well for any concessions from the Israeli side, but here they were back in Ramallah. A huge sigh of relief on the Palestinian side. Dan had, for the time being, managed to out-manoeuvre the General.

The Israeli delegation had re-booked into the Millennium Hotel on Emil Habibi St. A modern five star hotel, it had everything one could expect including fine dining at the Al Riwaq Restaurant, a gym and a selection of indoor and outdoor pools where Israeli delegates could take off the weight they put on in the restaurant. The Palestinians were in the Grand Park on Rafat Street, also a five star hotel providing for the wealthy and politically connected. Having been moved up from the hostel he was staying in, Hani now felt embarrassingly out of place. There were hotels in Bethlehem but not like this one. They were aimed at tourists, but this was a degree of luxury targeted at those on governmental expense accounts, specifically the Palestinian Authority's expense accounts.

His embarrassment was turning to anger at the flood of money pouring into these foreign owned hotel chains until he realised that the Israelis weren't going to check into a three star tourist hotel. Nevertheless, to compare where he was to be sleeping this week with what he was used to was… well, there was no comparison. So instead of enjoying it, he felt intensely guilty.

At ten o'clock all were in the lobby of the Grand Park. The air of expectancy at possible breakthroughs had dissipated. Some delegates on the Palestinian side were anxiously looking at the Israelis anticipating angry outbursts at any moment and were doing their utmost to be friendly and conciliatory. Regardless of the huge issue that they had been struggling with, Jamal and Hani had business to do and they wanted to do it. Privately, though, they had serious doubts whether there was going to be much give on the Israeli front on anything with the hard-liners having lots of ammunition at their disposal.

Hani saw Medad over the other side of the room on his own, so he made his way across. Both were wary of each other and others who might be watching them, but Hani wanted to get to know this young Israeli a little better. His open face looked honest and trustworthy. Hani helped himself to a cup of arabic coffee and started by asking about the hotel that the Israeli delegation were staying in. Medad was happy to talk in generalities. Both wanted the talks to succeed, albeit success meant rather different things to each of them.

After the small talk Hani asked him, "what did you do before joining the Israeli civil service?"

Medad saw no issue in saying, "I was in the IDF, as everyone is my age."

Conversation revolved around the role of the IDF before Hani asked, "Where were you posted?"

"Barracks were near Jerusalem, but we tended to look after southern districts such as Bethlehem and down as far as Hebron."

Hani knew all this through his research and wanted to know more details. But before they got any further, the gong sounded and they all trooped in for the start of the formal session. Once they were seated, Jamal immediately put on record their sorrow about the kidnapped soldier and he ordered his side of the table to stand for a minute's silence. The Israelis looked to Dan for direction. Then he stood as well so all stood in a show of solidarity.

Once they had sat down, Dan expressed his thanks. "We appreciate your gesture but I would reminded everyone that it was Palestinians who perpetrated the kidnapping."

Jamal inclined his head in acknowledgement, "Indeed, but we have provided and will continue to provide critical intelligence to your security commander as regards relevant activities in Jenin and Lebanon. At this very moment we have people in Lebanon chasing down the car and I hope that we can pin down the soldier's location."

Dan acknowledged the intelligence, "We are grateful and would ask that the origins of that intel would also be shared with us."

After the game of verbal ping pong, the talks moved on and seemed to follow the same predictable pattern as every day had done so far. Hani was still compiling small victories here and there, but was yet to make a breakthrough which they could point to as a real success. This morning was to be about Security and he had plans to notch up further concessions.

Then it happened.

Almost at the end of the session, Abd Alraheem suddenly moved away from the Palestinian script he had notionally signed up to and began to shout at the Israeli delegation using rather undiplomatic language. It was in response to a derogative comment that Dan had made about the Palestinian Security Services. The whole room was silent, mesmerised for a moment before hard liners on each side erupted into shouting, and violently gesticulating at each other. For a moment, it looked like a threatening situation might turn into actual physical violence. Jamal, who could hardly be heard for the anger and bitterness that was being released in the room, banged the table hard several times before he got attention and called for a break. Everyone was happy to oblige.

The Israelis marched out of the room in unison whilst Jamal grabbed Abd Alraheem by the arm and with sheer weight wrestled him into a small side room. He threw him across the room and got out his phone. Abd Alraheem was then forced to look at pictures of himself crossing into Lebanon through the tunnel and coming back out again.

"I have the times and dates of each one of these pictures. Look at them." He pushed Abd Alraheem's face into the phone. "I have more!" Jamal was well into his stride and was now nose to nose with the Deputy. "Traitor!"

Jamal didn't really have to talk much about Iranian and Hezbollah contacts or bank statements or indeed Jenin. He just mentioned them as if he knew a lot more than he really did. It worked. Abd Alraheem paled and sat down heavily into the nearest chair. His head flopped on to his chest. He was already a defeated man.

"But you have a chance at redemption." Abd Alraheem looked up hopefully. A deal, perhaps all was not lost.

"Stay on the delegation, toe the line and apologise to the Israelis." What Jamal didn't say was that this deal only lasted until the end of the talks and there would be 24 hour surveillance on him until at least week after the end of the conference, just in case. The Deputy nodded.

Jamal's face was red with anger, and he was enjoying kicking the Deputy, if only verbally. "And I want to know the where the kidnapped Israeli soldier is. Now!"

Abd Alraheem began to protest his ignorance. "I don't know. I wasn't told. I don't know who took the Israeli."

"Do you want me to show pictures of you at the back of the police barracks in Ramallah, driving into Jenin and meeting with Ahmed al-Fahd?"

Jamal didn't have these pictures, but it did the trick. The Deputy said he didn't know for sure, but on the phone the Imam had mentioned a city in the Beqaa Valley.

Baalbek had a population of about eighty two thousand, situated in the northern part of the Beqaa valley about 80km north east of Beirut. The Beqaa valley was an upland valley about seventy five miles long and ranging between five and nine miles wide, and was one of the most fertile farming regions in the Middle East. However, in spite of this fewer and fewer farmers worked the land there because it had become the go-to place for terrorists and freedom fighters to hide away, train and plan their violence in the thick woods and tall peaks that bounded the valley.

The whole of the Beqaa Valley was a religious mix of different branches of Christianity and Islam. The majority of the inhabitants of the northern districts of the Beqaa were Lebanese Shia Muslims with the exception of the town of Deir el Ahmar whose inhabitants were Christian. The western and southern districts of the valley also had a mixed population of Muslims, Christians and Druze. (The Druze faith originally developed out of Ismaili Islam, although they do not identify as Muslims.) Baalbek itself was Shia Muslim reflecting the overwhelming Shiite population of Iran. This had uncomfortable resonances for Jamal as he knew it would have for the Israelis.

Back in 2006 the war in Lebanon began with Israelis crossing the border and the subsequent capture of two soldiers, Ehud Goldwasser and Eldad Regev. On the evening of August 1, hundreds of Israeli soldiers raided Baalbek and the Dar al-Hikma Hospital in Jamaliyeh to the north. The operation was called 'Sharp and Smooth'. It was anything but. They were transported by helicopter and supported by Apache gunships and unmanned drones. They were acting on information that Goldwasser and Regev were at the hospital and were determined the find them. They weren't there and it transpired that their kidnappers had killed them and refrigerated their bodies.

Jamal left the Deputy in the side room to ruminate on his sins and rushed out to see where the Israeli delegation was. They were nowhere to be seen. Hani said they had left the conference centre and gone back to their hotel. Jamal needed to act fast, for if they packed their bags and left town, they would not come back. Hani was dispatched to the Millennium to seek out Dan and/or Medad. He would have been forgiven for thinking his world was spinning out of control but to Hani, now a consummate apparatchik, it was simply another problem to be managed. He thought he saw an upside.

Hani, witnessing the débâcle, suspected that Dan, knowing that an Iranian mole was somewhere on the Palestinian delegation, had subtly orchestrated the situation to clear him out. He suspected that Israel might be ready to make a concession, but did not want it thrown back in their face by whoever that traitor was. So why not use a technique to force his exposure and get him either on side or off the delegation? Quite a risky move which could have easily got out of hand, but it considerably strengthened his stance with the hard liners on his own side.

Hani expected a reasonable hearing from Dan but he recognised that Dan might not necessarily be in charge now. The whole environment had changed. The Israeli delegation was ensconced in their hotel lounge. All other hotel guests, and there weren't that many due to security considerations, were barred. Hani was only in the hotel lobby but he could hear the noise of violent disagreement. The two factions were heatedly debating whether to wait or to go back to Jerusalem. General Hersch was adamant that they were not going back to the negotiating table and he was backed up by his acolytes. Dan was trying to hold the delegation and the meeting together.

Dan saw Hani as he timidly put his head around the lounge door and immediately saw an opportunity to change the mood. He invited the Palestinian over and the room immediately hushed. Hani did the abject apology bit, said that Abd Alraheem would apologise personally at the next session while Dan did the statesman bit. Both acts seem to diffuse the tension a least temporarily, and return control back to Dan. He agreed that they would be there the following day, but they would not countenance returning that day. The delegation then broke up and delegates went off to enjoy the amenities that the hotel had to offer. Hani then drew Dan apart and whispered the updated intelligence, trusting that it would lead to the freeing of their soldier. Dan was immediately on the phone while Hani left the building.

The General, his aide and Natan weren't enjoying the hotel amenities but were ensconced in the General's room discussing their own strategy. They had been gifted an opportunity to collapse the talks, but it had foundered. Now they had to make their own opportunity, and that had to revolve around the kidnapped soldier. Although they were unaware of the latest intelligence from the PA, they didn't need it. As far as they were concerned it would all be lies and the PA were desperately trying to cover up their incompetence and double dealing. The General was determined to throw his weight around and it was aimed at the Palestinian Authority. He knew he had the majority of the Israeli population on his side who did not want anything to jeopardise their security.

On the Palestinian side, Hani and Jamal were locked together in Jamal's room after dismissing their own delegates for the rest of the day. Hani reported his conversation with Dan, but also began to outline what he thought might the Israeli agenda. Jamal was thoughtful. He didn't yet know about the mp4 file showing the hard-liners on the Israeli side. Hani was now wishing he had confided in Jamal and was thinking about how he could bring Jamal up to speed without compromising his own role and his source.

He decided to speak with Medad in the lobby area the next morning, if they turned up. Hani had thought there was an outside chance that they wouldn't turn up, but there they were chatting amongst themselves over coffee and *shawirma,* slivers of meat cooked on a vertical spit and sliced off. This was served in *markouk*, vast tasty rounds of very thin bread cooked over a big metal dome.) It was meal in itself, and clearly going down a treat with the Israeli guests.

Medad spotted Hani and made his way over and greeted him. After polite exchanges, Medad apologised for any part played by his own side yesterday. This was unexpected, but welcome for the Palestinian.

Hani thought he might pursue the matter further and asked, "Why did your leader stir things up yesterday?"

Medad looked around casually to make sure none of his colleagues were in earshot. "We had a document." Hani looked at him and nodded his head slightly as if to say he knew.

"It was necessary for us." Medad was nothing if not terse. Hani turned, so his back was against the feasting delegates and revealed to Medad that he knew of another document.

Medad now looked at him directly and nodded slowly. "We have it covered." He then moved away slowly towards the tables to refill his cup prior to the gong sounding for the morning session. Hani watched him go, wondering how this was going to work out. The import was that the Palestinian delegation needed to do nothing to provoke the hard liners on the Israeli side. Jamal sidled over and Hani repeated what Medad had said. He shrugged and pursed his lips.

The gong sounded and in they trooped. Jamal and Hani kept to their strategy. This morning it was about IDF roles in the various areas of the West Bank and also the role of the Civil Administration. By the end of the morning there were some significant concessions on the table, which made Jamal and Hani quite suspicious because the hard liners on the Israeli side did not object. Their silence was either due to the threat of exposure or they knew it would never get implemented.

It was the Palestinian delegation that decided there would be no afternoon session. They wanted to consider the Israeli proposals and prepare any clarifications that might be required. If genuine, this amounted to a real win for the Palestinian side but, as yet, the Israelis hadn't asked for any quid pro quo. Hani tried to anticipate what this might be and when they might demand it. His instinct told him it was a gain offered up early, enabling them to refuse further concessions at the end of the week.

Jamal was feeding all this information back to the President, the Chief of Security and relevant Palestinian Ministers through the President's office as he had been ordered to. Unknown to any of them, it was all going to Tehran via Beirut thanks to Nada. Abd Alraheem had remained compliant and the surveillance team had reported no midnight escapades as yet, but Abd Alraheem himself, was wondering why he had not been contacted by his Iranian handler for updated information. He began to speculate as to whether they had another mole and he had been dispensed with. He checked his bank account. His expected balance was still there and his agreed monthly payment was not due in for another two weeks. He would know then for certain.

Dan, on the Israeli side, was also reporting back to the government in Jerusalem through his own Minister's office. He was congratulated for the intelligence he passed on but was not getting any feedback about the concessions on the table. This told him that there was still a debate going on within government about what they would or would not approve and whether it might positively influence global opinion, especially the US and possibly Europe.

He kept Medad out of the detail of what he thought was going on because he wanted Medad totally focussed on the talks themselves. In their discussions together though, they were both now of the opinion that there was no need to release the video or the transcript in this round of talks.

Dan was quite optimistic. "I anticipate that by the end of the week, we might have a package of measures which both sides would be happy with. Of course, it will then up to Ministers whether they wanted to sign it off. Then, I think, would be the opportunity to play the video card if needed, to get the agreement through."

Medad agreed. "It's all getting a little tricky, though. The election is now only two months away and electioneering is well underway." They both knew that the deal done in these talks would be an important background to the various Israeli parties, either to support or condemn, as would the status of the kidnapped soldier. Dan pulled himself together and re-focussed his energy on the remaining few days.

Hani had been right in his assessment. Although Dan and Medad were wanting a softer line with the Palestinians, they knew they had to tread a careful line between the tough stance of those at home and allowing the Palestinians to think they could get more. Dan was not going to give anything else away this time. Each time they would ask, he would say they already had a major gain. Implication: be satisfied this time and maybe there will be more the next time.

From conversations with Hani, Medad was sure this was good enough for the Palestinian side. They wanted a win, but also a foundation for the next set of talks, and the next, and the next after that. So that was it. Friday of the second week came. No further breakthroughs. No further concessions or wins. This stage was over. Whether any of this actually happened on the ground, was now up to others.

47

THEY ALL RETURNED home, except Abd Alraheem. He had received a message from Angra Mainyu through the usual channels. Instead of meeting in Lebanon, the 'request' was to go to Nablus, a northern city of some one hundred and thirty thousand inhabitants. Nablus was a cultural centre hosting the An-Najah National University, one of the largest Palestinian institutions of higher learning and also the home of the Palestinian stock-exchange such as it was. But none of this was of interest to Abd Alraheem.

His sole concern was to conceal his recent exposure from the Iranian and maintain his lucrative lifestyle. He was keen to meet Angra Mainyu, although he did wonder what had made him change his mind about venturing into Israel, then the West Bank. He knew that forged papers would not be a problem for the Iranian, so he dismissed suspicious thoughts. Even as he was driving, he was conjuring up further information which would cement his loyalty to his handler and his treacherous position within the Palestinian Authority.

He would be shortly passing through the main thoroughfare of Nablus towards a side street where the market stalls were parked overnight. As his car weaved through the deserted streets towards the meeting point, he had already finalised his Ramallah action plan in his head. He would go for Jamal and accuse him of selling out to Israel. With him out of the way, his position would be secure. Hani was a novice and would prove no trouble.

It was very dark and the Deputy was beginning to feel a little uneasy. There were no shops open, no houses with lights on, just the light of the night sky, such as it was. He pulled his car into the side where he thought the rendezvous was. Nobody around. He flashed his headlights. No response. Perhaps he had got the wrong street. He didn't know Nablus as well as he knew other cities on the West Bank. He checked the street. Yes, he was in the right place but his security antennae were on full alert. He told himself as long as he stayed in the car he was safe. Where on earth was Angra Mainyu? As the minutes passed his unease morphed into alarm. He ordered his lungs to take in deep breaths and his body to stop shaking.

At last. He saw a torch signal up ahead and breathed a heavy sigh of relief. The Iranian was probably just making sure no-one had followed him. Quite right. Now he could find out why he had to come to Nablus. He quickly got out of his car and managed to get a few yards away from the car towards the torch light when a shot rang out. Just one. For a moment, he froze thinking he should take cover. By the time he hit the ground, he was dead.

It had been all too easy. Two men came over to him, lifted his body into the boot of his own car while the other made a quick phone call to Lebanon. One drove Abd Alraheem's car away whilst the other followed. The Deputy's car and it's human contents were never found, not that there was much of a search, nor much mourning.

Jamal, still quite shocked at the reach of the Iranians right into their back yard, was alerted to the fact that Abd Alraheem was missing and felt he could not hide the truth from his bosses any longer. The Deputy was no longer being monitored, so it was possible he had fled to Lebanon for refuge or maybe he had realised all was lost making him a target both for Hezbollah and the PA. Maybe he was already dead. Jamal discussed it with his right hand man by phone and Hani agreed he had to alert the President and the Chief. They needed to know the extent of Iranian infiltration. If it was they who had taken Abd Alraheem out, their intelligence must be alarmingly good. Since the Deputy Chief wouldn't have admitted his exposure, there was only one conclusion: there was at least one other person working for Iran/Hezbollah in an influential position within the Palestinian Authority.

While Jamal was having his conference, Hani was making his weary way back to Bethlehem. The adrenalin had run out. He was quite ambivalent about what they had achieved. Because of the links with the Israelis via Omari, he had been expecting more, but he was happy that they made some progress and relieved that the whole exercise hadn't been derailed. Even if the Israeli Ministers ratted on the deal their delegates had made, the PA could go public and say what had been agreed and thus what the Israelis had torpedoed. Shame them into accepting something. Jamal and Hani had agreed such a strategy if Dan and Medad couldn't get their hard liners on side.

Even before Hani came through the door, Ayshaa had determined that she wouldn't ask him how his project was going until he asked her how her work was progressing. But almost immediately he came through the door, Hani headed for the sofabed and was asleep in seconds in the middle of the afternoon. The rest of his family looked at him, Rena wishing he would play, Ghalia wishing he would talk and Ayshaa wishing he would go. None of that was going to happen tonight. Ayshaa would wait until the morning. She wanted a face to face talk with her husband about where they were going and what their relationship actually meant to him. She was feeling trapped, not an unknown position for a Palestinian woman. As with all other Palestinian wives, she depended on him for income, for a home and crucially for respectability.

Divorce was rare and family law in the West Bank was governed by the system of Islamic Shari'a courts known as the Jordanian Personal Status Law (JPST). This was an inheritance from the annexation of the West Bank by Jordan after the establishment of the state of Israel in 1948. The Hashemite Kingdom immediately unified laws on the east and west banks of the River Jordan. Under this system, any marriage could be dissolved extra-judicially by the unilateral repudiation of the husband; by court decision on specific grounds presented by the wife, or by mutual consent involving a final termination of the marriage (*talaq*) by the husband in exchange for a financial consideration by the wife (*khul*).

Ayshaa had no specific grounds. Although she had given it some thought, it was not a serious proposition for her, after all she had a daughter to bring up with no independent income. Maybe she had to be the one to make the effort and begin to step back from the isolation she was creating between them. But in her eyes, she was always the one making the effort. How long was this supposed to go on for? If this was how it was going to be, she couldn't hack it for much longer. She slept on the floor that night. She was not getting into the same bed as Hani, and there was nowhere else.

The next morning she was up first. Not surprising since she had hardly slept at all and had been lying awake since early dawn. How much did Ghalia know about her deteriorating relationship with her son? Probably a lot more than Ayshaa wanted to admit but she knew her mother-in-law wouldn't interfere. It would be down to Ayshaa to raise the subject with Ghalia if she wanted to. She didn't know whether she really wanted to or not, but it was becoming the elephant in the room and staying silent was getting quite difficult. Even Rena was subconsciously aware that something was not right.

About seven o'clock, Hani started to stir. Ayshaa was already up and making breakfast for them all. She didn't ask about his work, but unexpectedly he began to talk and she listened to his opinions without commenting on them herself. He never asked for her views, and she pretended not to be interested, not wanting to comfort him in any way. She knew he was a cautious man and unused to having things go his way. Neither did he consider himself a lucky person and, as far as he knew, no Palestinian considered themselves such. They all had to fight for everything they had. Yes, sometimes it was in the wrong way, but now he hoped that even the young zealots would see there was hope politically.

He recalled this was in part how the Good Friday agreement was sealed in Ireland. However, power-sharing between the Israelis and Palestinians was not the target, rather a self governing land with no outside military or civilian interference. He knew it could not be achieved in one giant leap, but rather had to be in progressive small steps. If the PA could continually tell good stories to its population of the West Bank and, more importantly, if they could see changes in day to day life, then there might be some hope that violence could be curtailed. Maybe even Gaza would see sense, but Hani thought that was likely to be a step too far. All these thoughts and more came pouring out. Ayshaa had started listen but still said nothing.

On his way back from Ramallah, Hani had stopped to get more medication for his mother. As he dug it out of his bag now, his thoughts turned towards her. She was sitting there in the living room with them, but without them. She wasn't entering into any discussion or offering any opinions. Even when Hani invited her to comment, she simply waved her hand and shook her head.

Medad looked around his home with pride. Without thinking he said out loud, "You are an excellent home-maker" As soon as he said it he regretted it. Shana bristled and said, "I'd make a better journalist! And speaking of journalism..." Medad knew where she was about to go.

He explained, "we need to hold the Israeli video and document for a little longer, until we see whether the Minister ratifies the agreement we've made. But..." Medad quickly moved on to avoid a critical remark, "I might have another story for you, if Dan agrees."

Shana looked at him, "I'm not totally relying on you for my stories – I'm quite capable of getting my own".

Medad decided that a tactical retreat was in order and said nothing. She changed the subject and announced that they needed to go out shopping and yes, he had to come. "We need a table, some chairs, and other general furniture."

She had already bought the bed with most of the money they had available, so it was budget time. "The bed," Shana explained, "was the most important acquisition they would make," and he couldn't disagree. The apartment deposit had come from both their savings and Medad's salary would be adequate to cover rent and their living expenses in the short term. If necessary, Medad thought, I'll sell the bike.

Dan was looking alarmed. He was sitting at his desk and just finished a long conversation with his Minister trying to keep him on side, accentuating the positives and minimising the negatives. He looked up as Medad walked in and stared at him as if he'd gone mad when Medad made his suggestion for releasing the story of an Iranian mole within the PA.

"Have you gone mad? How would that help?" Dan was immediately dismissive but Medad had done some thinking about it.

"I think it could be written up as a good news story. You know, congratulate the PA for flushing out an Iranian mole, signal that they are now looking for other sleepers and put the Iranians in the firing line for infiltrating both them and us." Israeli citizens were not immune to their attentions, as everyone knew.

"Ummm." Dan thought about it for a moment. It did have some merit. "Write it up and show me, but don't include the name for the moment... and I must have final editorial say over it."

Medad agreed and by the end of the day, Shana had written her first draft which Medad looked over. It was good; not quite the right tone, but certainly getting there. Shana was a little indignant, "Since when did you or your boss get editorial skills? I'm not sure that government civil servants should have the final say over my story."

Medad patiently explained again that it wasn't her story, and she shouldn't forgo a great source for future stories. Shana reluctantly agreed and continued to work on it. Medad made some further observations late that evening, and took the fifth version into Dan the next day.

A few minor points to ensure there was no way he could be connected to it, and it was a go. Dan thought he would meet with Omari so that he could let his Palestinian contacts know what was coming. He didn't want to burn these contacts, as the story was likely to be picked up in both Israeli and Palestinian press.

Chuck had largely been sidelined in the US as far as Medad was concerned. He wasn't allowed to pro-actively contact him or receive any messages from him. The CIA had taken over, and Chuck was only to be brought in if Medad proved difficult. Since the mp4 file had been delivered, there had been no need for any contact. That is, until Shana's news story broke.

The Americans had their own mole inside the PA, exclusively so they thought. It was Nada and it was she who had originally alerted the Americans to the Iranian infiltration inside the PA. Now it looked as if it could all become public knowledge and Langley needed to know if any names were going to be made public. As far as they were concerned, it was useful to have Abd Alraheem there because at least they knew who they were dealing with. If he was publicly exposed, they would have to start again in discovering who else the Iranians had in the PA. That could take a long time.

So Larry was told to 'get his ass' up to Ramallah and meet with Nada. He arranged to meet her at the Vintage Café on Jaffa St. In the corner was a settee with a British Union Jack cover on it. That's where they would meet. As a naturalised Israeli, it was quite easy for him to get access to Ramallah, although he had to pass large red road signs which said, in three languages, it was 'forbidden, dangerous and against Israeli law' for him to enter. "What utter nonsense," he said aloud.

Nada had always given the Americans a reasonable amount of useful information. However things had changed. She was now a different woman and working for the other side. But Nada wasn't stupid so she continued to leak sufficient information to keep the Americans interested, and paying! Just as the meeting with Larry was about to end, her phone vibrated. It was her husband from Security with the news that Abd Alraheem had been reported missing and there was a general rumour around that he was the Iranian mole that the news story had fingered, and that Tehran had ordered his demise. The news was about to go public.

Nada saw an opportunity and absolutely no reason not to tell Larry. It was only a rumour, of course, and Ramallah always abounded with rumours. But this information would put her in a good light with the Americans, without her having to risk anything. If it turned out not to be true, well it was only a rumour. Larry was excited as he too liked to give good information up the food chain to cement his own position. She vaguely promised to try and substantiate the rumour either way. Larry reported back to Langley who immediately contacted Chuck. They wanted to know if the story had been deliberately leaked by the Israeli government. Medad was his man. Find out who released the story. No answer from Medad's burner phone. Understandable. So Chuck called Hagai, his journalist friend in Jerusalem.

After greetings and some family small talk, Chuck was getting to the point but Hagai was ahead of him. "I don't know who wrote the story. The editor of the Jerusalem Post is a friend of mine and all he knows is that it came from a freelance, part of a small media company, not necessarily based in Israel. Probably two or three hacks who want to write controversial stuff and don't want to be found. And, by the way, you're not the only ones sniffing around."

48

IT WAS THE turn of Ministers to make a decision. The Palestinian side weren't exactly ecstatic at the package of measures that had been negotiated, but after some arm wrestling by Jamal they had finally bought into Hani's step by step plan. The main debate was on the Israeli side. The big question here was not about concessions given at the talks, but the kidnapped soldier. As far as the Israeli public knew, the Palestinians had done it 'en masse'. The corporate guilt card was being played for the national and international media and Jamal didn't like it.

Dan was pushing his Minister to accept the deal and get world opinion on their side, whilst the Defence side was for playing hard ball with a great excuse. The exposure of Iranian penetration of the PA was being spun both ways and, despite the article being complimentary towards Ramallah, the PA didn't like it. Dan thought there might be a chance that if Israel didn't agree the concessions, the PA would pre-release the draft proposals that the delegates had agreed, and have Israel on the defensive. It would show very bad faith and strain the relationships he had worked so hard to gain.

The Israeli military commander was concerned that time was running out to find his kidnapped soldier and decided to put the twenty Palestinian detainees through an interrogation process to see if any of them knew who the conspirators were. When they came to prisoner sixteen they sensed that here was someone who knew more. Immediately he was taken away to a special room where there were all sorts of devices for making prisoners talk. He was stripped naked, hung from the ceiling and beaten with rods. Then a black bag was put over his head and alternative beatings and interrogations for hours on end. Overnight they released hungry rats into the cell to discourage him from sleeping.

The young Palestinian was literally wetting himself and at about midnight confessed his part, but he didn't know where his friends had taken the soldier. Unfortunately for him although he was telling the truth, his captors didn't believe him.

The residents of Baalbek didn't know that an Israeli Musta'ribeen unit was searching the place for a car and hopefully a kidnapped Israeli soldier. The plan was that this unit would locate the place and make a determination as to whether they could quietly free their fellow soldier themselves, or it needed a full-on IDF operation. Baalbek was a large city and it was a major task to track down this Peugeot 306 which more likely than not was carefully hidden. But it was their only lead.

They were vaguely aware of the talks and the deadline but to them it was much more important to get their man than sign any agreement with the Palestinians. Dan had stressed to the commanders the political importance of trying to find him before the talks deadline came, but he knew he had no real leverage. They wanted to get their man as soon as possible for other reasons completely. It was well known that Hezbollah was not shy when it came to interrogations, and they had all the tools the Israelis had, and some. The soldier was definitely in danger.

The search had now been going on for four days and there had been no sightings. They had begun to wonder if it was bad intelligence, and the soldier wasn't here at all. Perhaps it was all a setup by the Palestinians to waste their time, even to get them caught by Hezbollah. No, they didn't trust any Palestinian. And even if he was here initially, he might not be here now. Yet all they could do was to carry on. They needed a breakthrough.

Dan was still fixated on ensuring that his hard-liners didn't sabotage the whole conference. It was all on a knife edge. He wanted to push the button on the video, if only to show the Palestinian side that he had muscle too, but he knew that the kidnapped soldier trumped all cards. Until that was sorted, he could do very little. But if it was, and there were some good reasons for thinking it might be, then the video was back on the table. He had worked out how to do it. A single frame of the video sent anonymously clearly showing the faces of the four to the Defence Minister's aide with an accompanying message saying there was much more where this came from.

He began to think through the implications. How might the Defence Minister react? The aide would immediately take the photo to his Minister and if the Minister came into line, well and good. The video could then be in play for the rest of his career. If he wanted to brazen it out, thinking it a bluff, Dan would leak it little by little and so build up a media storm. The Minister would lose his job no question and then the video's power would be gone. The next move would be to do the same job on the General. If a Minister was out of office, even temporarily, it would be much easier to control a General, who was used to taking direction from his political masters.

Dan didn't want to use it for a relatively small return; he wanted many happy returns from the mp4 and these men under control for as long as possible. If the soldier was returned unharmed they had no reason to rebel and if they tried to, he could use the video. If the soldier wasn't found, it would all go up in smoke, the hard liners would win the election by a landslide and there wouldn't be any talks with the Palestinians for a long time to come.

Dan asked Medad about how to leak the video. "I think we need a third party to release part of the video and threaten to reveal more unless they come into line." Medad replied, "I've been giving it some thought and I think I know how it could be done with plausible deniability for the department."

Dan looked at Medad. The boss's advice was ringing in Medad's ears as he walked out of the office. "If you keep swimming with sharks, it's only a matter of time."

In Ramallah, Jamal was getting more and more impatient. He was desperate for news from Lebanon. His own men had returned with nothing so he was entirely reliant on the Israelis. He knew from the terse conversation with the Israeli commander that the PA were not trusted, yet the IDF were acting as if they had no intelligence of their own. This was causing Jamal real alarm. He was terrified at the thought that the Israelis might also come back from Lebanon empty-handed. It would be seen as entirely the Palestinian's fault and there would be serious and violent repercussions. His career would be over, and that would just be the start of the blood-letting. He daren't even think about it.

*

In Baalbek, the Israeli unit had a report from a friendly informant that a car similar to the one they were looking for had been seen. Exhilaration was tempered with scepticism since, as one of them said, "there must be hundreds of those cars here". Nevertheless, they switched their search to another district and there it was, parked outside the general trading shop, Nagi Magasins on Route Douris Baalbek. They parked their own car across the road behind a truck, but where they could still get a visual. And waited.

It didn't take long for two men to come out of the shop, get into the Peugeot and drive off. The Israelis followed three or four car lengths behind. They were thinking that another car would have helped to help disguise the surveillance, but as they had just the one extreme care was needed otherwise the whole operation would fail. The car pulled up ten minutes later in a run down district and outside a disused shop front. The two occupants got out without even bothering to look up the road to see if they were being followed. They disappeared into the building and the pursuing car carried on past the property, stopping a little way down the street in front of other cars.

After a short reconnaissance, the Israeli unit determined that it was a possible place where someone could be kept hostage, though without a thorough search they couldn't be sure. A decision was taken to search the place themselves. There had to be no trace of their entry or exit for if they had got the wrong location, there would be no second chances if news of their existence was transmitted across the region. They would come back when it was dark to hopefully complete the mission.

It was two o'clock early morning when their car quietly moved up to the shop front. The Peugeot was still parked where it had been earlier. It was a clear night and visibility outside was good. As the unit exited their car, they paused to assess any movement or noise. There was none. One soldier stayed outside as watch, the others moved towards the door they had chosen to gain access to the building. The presence of the car indicated the probability that they were all inside. Even though the kidnappers seemed relaxed, there was always the possibility that there might be more than two. If they were lucky, they would be sleeping on a rota basis and only one awake. However, they had prepared for the worst scenario. The lock on the door was the easy part, moving through the building to clear each area without immediate detection was going to be the challenge.

After a couple of minutes working on the lock, they were in. No sound from anyone; either kidnapped or kidnappers which was good, or possibly bad. Each area was scanned with night vision goggles – no torches. "Clear," whispered the leading Israeli as he quietly pushed forward room by room.

"Clear," was the reply from another soldier as he passed a room on the left. Then the sound of faint moaning from further in. The leading soldier raised his hand to indicate absolute quiet. They immediately stopped, straining their ears. Another moan. The exhilaration soared. They knew they were in the right place and the moaning indicated that the young soldier had indeed been tortured. It had only a few hours earlier that the Israeli had finally broken his silence with screams muffled only by a cloth stuffed into his mouth. A lighted burner suitable for getting a bar-b-que going had been applied under his arms and on his back. It had then been applied to his abdomen with the intention of going lower, but that was to be tomorrow's entertainment. For the moment, he was lying prostrate on a cold stone slab in a metal cage groaning.

Both captors were sleeping, completely unaware they had been penetrated. They were quickly shot where they slept with silenced pistols which, as one of the rescuers said, "was a much kinder way to go than they had in mind for their prisoner." Whilst the outside soldier was securing the premises, they spent a little time giving the prisoner some pain killing drugs and treatment for his body wounds.

The Israeli commander got a brusque call at three in the morning from Baalbak to say two Hezbollah agents were dead and one Israeli soldier was freed. Success. There was no whooping or slapping on the back in the control room, just relief that this time they had managed to recover the soldier alive. Next time, and there would inevitably be a next time…

Jamal heard the good news from the Chief the next morning. He hadn't realised exactly how much stress he had been under until now. He sank to his knees in relief, put his hands over his eyes and wiped them. Now, he thought, they have to do a deal with us.

*

Medad didn't head to his apartment, but spent the rest of the day walking, taxiing and ensuring that anyone trying to follow him couldn't. He wasn't a professional but knew the general idea of evading surveillance. He needed to talk with Shana without phoning and without going to the apartment. She had an appointment at Sara's Hair Salon in Nachlaot at two o'clock so he made his way there and started walking back from the salon along the route she would normally use. There she was, window shopping as she walked. He slipped into a shop, let her go past, then caught up with her, putting a message to meet him in her pocket and disappeared without her noticing. He had at least learnt something from Larry. It was not as slick, but then Medad hadn't had CIA training.

This has to stop, he thought. It might be fine with Shana, but a mistake elsewhere might prove fatal. Life over. He had to admit, though, part of him enjoyed it. "But it isn't a game," he said sternly to himself, "and you are an amateur." He knew his mental processes were changing and his attitudes and approach to people were hardening. Shana was the only one he trusted and he began to wonder whether he would, could, really trust anyone else ever again. Yes, of course he trusted his mother, but not his father or brother. Was that bad? Who was he to make such judgements about people. Did he trust Dan? Not very far, was the honest answer.

Perhaps this is the price you pay, he thought as he walked on. There were certainly instances of high excitement when a plan came to fruition, when the adrenalin pulsated through his body as he calculated and dissembled. But was this really what he wanted? This was a game of high stakes. The debate was still lingering on in his head when reached Café Bezalel-Jerusalem and at four o'clock Shana arrived, hair highlighted and looking cool. A quick compliment and he began to outline the job that he'd agreed with Dan. Shana sipped her coke listening quietly, but inside her level of excitement was rising sharply.

She quickly became businesslike. "The approach must sound like it is coming from a reporter. The Minister's aide needs to be contacted for a comment about the photo prior to possible publication, that would be recognised as typical journalistic practice. That's how it must be done."

Medad explained, "It would need to be a bluff at this stage, but depending on the response you might have your story early."

"So when do you want this done?"

Medad was clear. "As soon as we get word that the soldier has been recovered, contact the Minister's aide immediately. The Minister will be in his office. Use your burner phone for a possible call back, then destroy it."

While they were there in the café, the TV began to broadcast the news of the successful operation in Lebanon. They looked at each other and Medad nodded. By ten o'clock the next morning, Shana had made her phone call and had received one back from the Minister's aide. "Yes he had spoken to the Minister and he wanted to know what he could do to help."

Nicely put, thought Medad, who was by Shana's side. She made the demand which had been agreed with Medad. "Initially we want support for the agreement your delegation made with the Palestinians. Once that's done, we will hold off publication."

Quiet on the other end of the phone. A suspicious voice questioned whether this was actually from a reputable journalist or a front for the Palestinians. Shana quickly said in Hebrew that there was no doubt that if they didn't comply, it would be published, bit by bit and that would be the end of the Ministers career, and his own. She then hung up.

Shana looked at Medad. Time would tell. Medad then called Dan and said the photo had been sent, a call had come back and the 'request' made. The relevant Ministers were diaried to meet in Ramallah the following day to sign off the agreement. Shortly after this, Dan had a message from his Minister saying that the Defence side had decided to compromise and agree the proposals that the delegates had thrashed out. Dan was delighted. It had all worked. He called Medad with the good news, though not so good news for Shana who looked like any investigative journalist would who had just lost a big story, maybe one of the biggest.

In Ramallah, amid a flurry of cameras, TV crews and journalists, elected Ministers gathered to spin their stories of epoch-making moments and the 'hand of history', as they queued up to sign the agreement. Both Palestinian and Israeli Ministers looked pleased and willing to have their photos taken and give interviews to anyone who wanted to listen. This was a moment when everyone wanted to be in the spotlight.

Suddenly, a myriad of different ring tones rang out, not only from the main protagonists but from the assembled press. Each took their phone out and held it to their ear. For a moment, no-one moved or said anything. Everyone was quiet, concentrating on what was being said to them on their phones. Then absolute chaos broke out. Israeli Ministers forgot all about the up-coming ceremony. They and their aides rushed towards their cars through the throng of the international media shouting, "No Comment" to anyone who dared to verbally accost them. Within three minutes of the phones ringing, there were no cars, no Israeli personnel and no signatures.

Palestinian Ministers and their delegates stood like statues in the lobby. Their phones hadn't rung. No-one had called them. They looked vacantly at each other and it was left to the press to inform them. Hamas, no friend of Fatah, had released a flurry of rockets towards southern Israel, and the Israeli military was already bombing targets on the Gaza strip which, they claimed, housed rocket launchers.

The Palestinian President took some steps towards a microphone and called for order. "I wish to make a statement. I want to thank the delegates on both sides for all the hard work done to achieve this agreement. I particularly want to thank the Israeli Ministers for coming here today and being ready to sign our agreement."

He paused in his speech, visibly upset at the loss of the agreement and very angry at Hamas who had chosen to deliberately scupper the deal.

"I think we all know why Hamas has done this. We all know too that they are not representative of the Palestinian people. I trust the integrity of Israel in this regard and trust that the agreement will be resurrected swiftly."

It was a good speech, dignified and statesmanlike, especially as it was unrehearsed and in the middle of great confusion.

In the Iranian embassy in Lebanon, Angra Mainyu was smiling. He had lost his soldier, but he had gained what he had always wanted. He had a copy of both agreements in his hands. The authentic one, courtesy of Nada and the doctored one for Hamas, from his own fair hand. He looked at each and, with some ceremony, fed them both through the shredder.

In Bethlehem, Omari had been watching the television output and could hardly believe what was happening. With tears in his eyes, he called Hani. It went to voicemail. He sent a WhatsApp message to Dan expressing deep regret and suggesting a meet at his convenience. By the end of the day, there had been no responses. Lara tried to comfort him without much success.

In Ramallah, Jamal had disappeared with the President and Chief of Security immediately after the speech so Hani had no chance to talk. The rest of the Palestinian entourage were gradually dispersing in subdued mood. No-one wanted to watch Hamas at work on any radio or television set. They had been robbed and they didn't like it. If there had been the slightest thought of any moves for a rapprochement with Hamas, it was now dead. This impact of this moment would likely last a generation.

Hani grabbed a driver and got back home by mid afternoon to find Ayshaa still at one of her women's empowerment sessions. She got home at about four o'clock to find Hani sitting on the step outside their home head in hands. Ayshaa had heard about the rockets, but didn't know that the talks had all come to nothing. But Hani didn't want to talk…yet. There was a lot bubbling up inside, and he thought that was the best place for it at the moment. He was coming off a high into the lowest low there was.

In Jerusalem, Medad was in despair. He had been swept away with Dan in the cavalcade of limos from Ramallah to Jerusalem. He went straight home to be with Shana. The whole country was watching endless re-runs of rockets falling on farms, houses and roads in southern Israel. No fatalities, not many injuries. Some minor damage to the roofs of a few houses. However, most of the damage was not physical but had been done in Ramallah, miles away from Gaza or where rockets could reach. There hadn't been much talk in the limos on the way back and he didn't bother calling Dan. They were all in shock.

Medad would see him in the office tomorrow, no doubt.

Meanwhile the politicians, including their Minister, were publicly re-spinning their positions in front of cameras and reporters towards a more hard line stance against Palestinians in general. They were all the same. Totally untrustworthy. We were ready to compromise, and look what they have done.

It was a get-out-of-jail card for the Defence Minister and the General. The former revealed to the latter the photo he had received and both now moved on the offensive letting it be known that they had met prior to this Hamas attack to begin to plan a strategy in case of just such Palestinian action. They had been proven correct. By doing so, they completely nullified both the document and video. Neither could now be used. Every leverage that Dan and Medad thought they had, vanished in an instant.

In Langley, the Director was on the warpath. Heads were likely to roll. He had been called to the White House along with the Secretary of State to brief the President. Even as he was travelling into the city, he was forming his own narrative, to demonstrate how he was following the President's policy towards Israel. Not difficult to do, except that the President knew his CIA Director could be quite critical of Israel especially when it came to relations with Ramallah, in contrast to the President's hawkishness towards the Palestinians. It was going to be awkward for him personally, but not fatal.

Chuck had been called in to see the Secretary for a full explanation prior to his journey to the White House. He wanted to know what Langley knew about events and what role, if any, his department had played. Chuck was truthful about his grooming of Medad, but explained that running him had been the CIA's role.

On a nondescript street somewhere in Jerusalem, Mossad was opening an investigation into the whole fiasco from the Iranian's influence in Ramallah and Gaza City, to the Defence Minister's claim of a blackmail attempt on him and a senior General and the kidnapping of an Israeli soldier. No stone would be left unturned.

49

SAMIA, AFFECTIONATELY KNOWN as Sami, was twelve years old. Next year she would be a teenager and a cause for celebration in her family. If she had been a boy, that would have been a cause for a much greater celebration, for a boy meant another wage earner for the family, a girl on the other hand... But it was a close, loving family and Sami would have her celebratory birthday. Living in Gaza meant there wasn't much else to celebrate so Sami's parents would make as much as they could with the little they had. Although her family was Christian rather than Muslim, they were still Palestinian. Traditional attitudes and values were part of their life.

As young as she was, it was her role as the eldest and a daughter, to take on significant household responsibilities as well as looking after her younger brother, Jalal. That's just how it was. Girls had to grow up a lot quicker than boys and being taller than others of her age, she could easily have been mistaken for fifteen. Her parents did their best to provide a secure home for their growing family but nothing was really secure in Gaza.

The Strip was home to approximately 1.9 million souls, including some 1.4 million Palestinian refugees who had done nothing wrong except their farms and homes were in what was now Israel. They had fled, some in 1947 and others in 1969. Sami, along with everyone else, lived in the bleakest of conditions surrounded by poverty and violence, but at least school was available for her for half of each day. This was nothing to do with her staying at home to do chores or skipping classes, rather schools in Gaza operated on a double-shift basis, with one cohort of students occupying the premises in the morning and a different group in the afternoon. It was the only way. Education was a luxury and schools were scarce.

As a result, children's learning was acutely curtailed. But school did provide them with a place of relative security where they were able to learn the skills which would hopefully make for a better future. At least, that was the mantra, and 'relative' was a relative term! Sami was quick to learn and her teacher had already marked her as one of the brightest in the class. However, family came first and school came second.

They existed just above the poverty line as did many others. It was difficult to know why her father found work hard to get, even though he was a skilled carpenter. It may have been because there was little paid work available, or it may have been because he was known to be part of the Christian minority. Who would trust a Christian? Running his own business was not practical, since most people didn't have any money to pay him. He needed a regular weekly wage of some sort.

So the family was part of the 80% of the population who depended on social aid payments, mostly through UNRWA, the United Nations Relief and Works Agency. Gaza was less a country, more a rather large open air prison so the economy just could not function properly. Unemployment was 44% and youth unemployment 60%. Few people went in and even fewer came out.

At one time it was an Israeli -occupied country, but since Ariel Sharon had pulled the Israeli settlers out of the south, it was its own country yet totally powerless to control its own destiny. Hemmed in by land, sea and air, nothing moved without Israel's say so. There were only two crossing points for people: the northern Erez Crossing into Israel and the southern Rafah Crossing into Egypt. Both heavily guarded and restricted.

As a majority Islamic country, Sunday was an ordinary working day in Gaza, except for the Christians. The congregation at Gaza Baptist Church were gathered as normal, although 'normal' was hardly a word that could be used in Gaza for anything. Jalal, Sami's younger brother, was with his parents in the main congregation since he was too young to join his sister in the Sunday School, which was held in an annex to the rear.

The church was one of only three Christian churches in the Gaza Strip, and the only one that was Protestant. It's membership was about two hundred although attendance at Sunday services fluctuated wildly due to the general chaos that constituted life in Gaza. Because they were Christian, they came under some scrutiny from many of the warring factions that operated on the Strip. Some of their members including a church leader had been killed and their pastor had been forced to flee and now lived in exile, only able to visit occasionally.

They had little idea of what had been going on in Israel, much less the unfolding story in Ramallah. Nor had they any idea of the role of the Iranian or the reaction of Hamas to his doctored document, but they had heard rockets being fired into Israel and the leaders calculated that Gaza Baptist church would be one of the safest places to be when the inevitable happened.

The church's building was six stories high with the first two floors housing a dedicated public library and the top floor used as a worship hall. In the annex on the ground floor at the back, Sami was the first to stop and raise her head. The pencils on her table had started to vibrate. Then as the windows also began to rattle. They knew. Get under a table quickly. Sami was already under her table when the teacher shouted, "NOW!" The word was hardly out of her mouth when there was an ear splitting howl, a mighty crash and the whole just roof folded in like cardboard and each successive floor of the building collapsed under the weight of the ones above some of them spilling over onto the annex. There was no time or breath to scream and shout. The F16 fighter had unleashed its load and Gaza Baptist Church, its libraries and surrounds were totally decimated.

Even as the masonry was settling, there was an erie silence about the place. The billowing dust from the rubble and shattered glass hid the catastrophic damage for at least ten minutes. Nevertheless, after three or four minutes when it was clear that there were no more missiles, local people emerged from nearby undamaged buildings. With masks, towels and anything else to cover their mouth and noses, they set about pushing through the dust trying to clear the tangled mess of steel rods and concrete with just their bare hands to see if anyone had survived.

It was a well rehearsed process without any mechanical assistance. All available diggers were in use at other target sites. No-one had expected a Christian church to be a target. It was only after twelve hours that a single digger arrived, and then another twelve hours later when they pulled Sami out alive, just. No-one else had survived. In all sixty adults, four babies and ten children had died, among them little Jamal.

It was the final Israeli strike of a retaliatory mission against Hamas for firing rockets into southern Israel. According to a document the Hamas leadership had received, Fatah had wanted to do a deal with Israeli at the expense of Hamas. No-one in Israel was hurt even though over fifty rockets had been fired. Such rockets were peashooters compared with F16 GPS guided missiles. Over one hundred and fifty men, women and children had been killed and many more injured in the brief fifteen minute air campaign. These souls were not Hamas party members neither did they necessarily support Hamas, but that made little difference. They were just ordinary people living in Gaza.

It was true that the population of the country had voluntarily elected Hamas in 2007 after Hamas had wooed them with their social service wing, *Dawah*. They had provided food, medicine and support to a population taken for granted and ignored by Fatah who thought they had a divine right to rule the whole of Palestine. It was no surprise to any impartial observer that the people of Gaza collectively decided that a change would be better. It couldn't be worse. Hamas thus had a democratic mandate, of sorts. But there would never be another election.

To make their mark, they refused to abide by previous treaties made via Fatah and the PLO which immediately put them outside accepted world opinion. Proscription by the international community as a terrorist organisation swiftly followed. It was said that they had their origins in the Sunni Muslim Brotherhood movement which was a pan-Arabic collection of Sunni-Islamic organisations, but they also had ties through Hezbollah to Shia Iran and even Saudi Arabia. It was complicated. All, up to this moment, opposed Israel's right to exist and specifically their right to the land they occupied citing passages from the Quran which apparently said that any land that had been under Muslim rule could never be removed. Israel also quoted passages from their Torah which also appeared to give them a similar claim.

It was well known that the Israeli government rarely commented on their military operations but, on this occasion unusually, there was a succinct apology coupled with a warning that nothing would deter them from defending their land and people. It was their right. Intelligence sources, they said, pointed to the church building as a Hamas weapons base. If it was, the pastor and congregation didn't know, and now they didn't exist.

There was a decent amount of airtime given to the 'incident' on CNN and just a brief mention of the incident on the BBC. Equal air time was given to both sides: Israel blamed Hamas; Hamas blamed Israel and the news cycle moved on. In the BBC's case, the newsreader then announced a much more important item: the latest Euro-millions lottery winner who lived in Sunderland, UK. Apparently, the winning couple wanted to travel round the world but insisted that the money wouldn't change their lives. It was highly unlikely they had Gaza on their travel itinerary.

Sami slowly woke up from sedation... again. She felt groggy but she was already familiar with that sensation, having undergone several surgical procedures since she arrived at the Al-Quds hospital. She had been brave this time and there had been no crying when she had entered the operating theatre yet again. From her room in the hospital, she could see the Mediterranean in the distance and hear the voices of children coming from a nearby school. But her eyes were always looking elsewhere, staring at objects and people in the room, as if there was still something to worry about.

Her thirteenth birthday was celebrated in Al-Quds hospital. Initially she had occasional visits from her uncle, aunt and other members of her extended family, but they were Muslim and weren't very keen to do more than the minimum to help. Even they didn't know it was a special birthday.

"Some days are better than others for her," explained a counsellor to them. She was responsible for providing psychosocial support in the hospital.

"Some days she just bursts into tears and keeps asking to see her family. Other days, she's more reactive; she smiles and chats with me. At the moment its very difficult for her to accept that her parents and baby brother are dead. She has flashbacks of the explosion when they were killed and she was buried alive in the rubble."

The extended family soon stopped visiting. Sami knew that would be the case and wasn't too surprised. But surely her parents and maybe the pastor or members of her congregation would come and visit her. Probably tomorrow, if not later that day now she was out of surgery. It would be so good to see them, especially little Jalal. She often looked after him, playing his favourite games. They had fun together. Sometimes she would sneak him out of the house and they would play on nearby waste ground – totally forbidden by her mother. He was under strict instructions not to tell.

But they were all dead, weren't they? There was no-one else coming to visit. She still hadn't fully accepted that they were never coming back, even though the nurses gently told her. What did they know? They were great but overwhelmed with the need. Demand was hugely outstripping supply. They struggled with everything; lack of drugs, training and secure, clean buildings in which to work and operate. How could they possibly know about her family?

But there was no celebration, no party, no congratulations. No-one except her seemed to know that she had just turned thirteen, and what was the point of celebrating anyway? In her moments of reality she remembered the initial gentle shaking of her pencil on the desk, the ear-splitting noise of the F16, the fearful sound of masonry crashing around her, the inhaling of lungfuls of dust, then nothing. She remembered coming to and hearing people shouting faintly somewhere in the distance. Her attempts to shout only caused her to breathe in more dust, stimulating a bout of coughing that seemed never to stop. Then she became conscious of a dreadful pain in her abdomen and leg. The stifling claustrophobia caused her to try and get out, but then immense panic as she found she couldn't move any part of her body. She was going to die.

Consciousness lapsed for seconds, minutes, hours, who knew? Then dragged out of the rubble by friendly faces assuring her everything was going to be all right. But it wasn't. They were all dead. Yes, she remembered. She burst into tears again, but no-one came to comfort her. After a few minutes some willpower deep within her kicked in and she counted herself lucky that she had survived at all. It was a miracle. She had a broken arm, a broken pelvis and a seriously damaged left leg. The surgeons had done what they could but whilst the arm was healing well, the injured pelvis meant that future children for her would be nigh impossible and her left leg would be two inches shorter than the right for the rest of her life.

She heard the words but was too young to realise the impact these injuries would have on her life. As the days dragged by and reality firmly set in another emotion began to take over. Anger. It would erupt in her at the slightest inconvenience. Most children her age would have been sad, traumatised and pitiable. Maybe she was all of these things as well, but over and above, she was angry: angry firstly at her parents, the church, even at those who had pulled her out of the concrete. Yes, she knew it was irrational, but it was there. In her more lucid moments, if a thirteen year old has those, she was angry at Israel, angry at Hamas and angry at God. She wanted people to know what had happened to her and her family. She didn't want pity or flowers, she wanted change. Writing to God was a bit of a problem but she could certainly write to the Israeli Prime Minister and to the leader of Hamas, and she would.

Her teachers had told her about Malala Yousafzai, the 14-year-old Pakistani girl who had been shot by the Taliban, how she had stood up to them achieving global attention and helping to change attitudes in her country towards the education of girls. Also Greta Thunberg, the 15-year-old Swedish girl with mental health issues, who had decided to go on school strike at the Swedish parliament and started a whole new movement of school pupils to leave lessons and take to the streets to protest about the non action on climate change.

If they could do it, so could she. Couldn't she?

The letter to Hamas spoke of her family, the fact that they were Christian and what had happened to the church and the congregation. She thought she might as well say it how it was and not mince her words. She asked for a meeting and some answers; for example, did Hamas have weapons near the church building? Was that deliberate? Were there other similar caches near other churches and mosques?

Her letter to the Prime Minister of Israel was similar but asked different questions: how did he know there were weapons near the church building? Was he completely sure? Was any consideration given to the fact that it was a Sunday when the church would be full of families? Did he take any responsibility for innocent deaths?

It took quite a while to put all this together between operations and she did have help from some of the hospital staff. They understood what she wanted to do and saw it as therapeutic for her. They made lots of suggestions when Sami told them what she wanted to do but all felt it was to be her letter and her questions. They didn't want any personal kickbacks from Hamas. When she was finally satisfied with the letters, Sami asked one to post them. She wasn't expecting much response, but she felt a whole lot better.

Both letters actually reached their intended offices which was rather miraculous, but truly the easy part. The question was, would the gatekeepers see the potential here for their masters such that it got passed up the pay grade? In Jerusalem, it was the government press office which first reviewed the letter. The Director passed it on to the Chief of Staff with a recommendation to ignore, saying it would be a grave mistake to get involved with specific individuals in what was a defensive military operation. It could lead to all sorts of precedents, none of which were to Israel's advantage.

In Gaza City, Hamas didn't have such a bureaucratic civil service so it got through to the Hamas inner circle quite quickly. Khalid, one of the leaders' right hand men read it. He was not a PR expert by any means, rather a 'fixer' who was dispatched to do any number of tasks, but he passed it on and a decision was made to get an interview with the girl and use it to take another swipe at Israel.

The Israeli PM was getting considerable flack from the American Baptist lobby with its 1.3 million members and over five thousand congregations. They were appalled that the Israelis had bombed Gaza Baptist church and wanted to know what the Israeli government were going to do about it. Since they were a considerable part of the fundamentalist evangelical movement in the US that supported and funded Israel, the PM was beginning to feel the pressure.

It was eventually decided that Sami should be invited to Jerusalem for a private meeting with the President, though not the Prime Minister, followed by a no-questions photo opportunity. This, they reasoned, had the benefit of taking the issue seriously, but keeping it out of the political/military arena. However the President, a figurehead with very limited powers, had some considerations of his own and only agreed if he could offer funds to rebuild the church. It was agreed. They all hoped that this would stem further international criticism and go some way to neutralising any positive publicity Hamas could get over the incident.

50

ISRAELIS WERE GLUED to their television sets whilst aircraft bombed Gaza, but it wasn't so on the West Bank, even for those who had television sets. Although Fatah and Hamas had been bitter enemies for decades, ordinary Palestinian people on the West Bank still felt a solidarity with their cousins suffering in Gaza, especially when Israeli fighter aircraft were in action. There was nothing they could do but wait for the backlash in their part of Palestine. It would come as surely as night followed day.

Families in the south of Israel were not watching television either. They were in range of rockets from Gaza and were temporarily holed up in bunkers. They had no sympathy for any Palestinian wherever they were from. Their attitudes were always hard but the general electoral mood had hardened dramatically over the whole country. Those Israeli politicians who supported the talks quickly changed tack, concentrating rather on broadcasting their security credentials to the electorate. Dan's Minister was no different, and so he also felt anxious to 'prove' his credentials and disguise his previous advice. There was no doubt that Dan felt utterly betrayed and although he saw a message from Omari, he was in no mood to meet him, ever.

Neither he nor Medad were aware of the impending Mossad investigation, but leaving nothing to chance, both were hurriedly deleting and destroying everything which linked them to the leaked American files, although Medad had already lodged copies in a safety deposit box. Shana was ahead of them. As soon as she heard about the Hamas action, she knew everything was lost. Hours before, Medad had told her what had happened in Ramallah and she had already dismantled not only her burner phone but also her laptop. Reconfiguring to factory settings somehow didn't seem final enough. She cancelled her business domain and with it her web site and, hopefully, all trace of her involvement. She would have to begin her journalistic career again.

Hani was doing nothing. He was moping and getting under Ayshaa's feet. She wasn't easy to live with at the moment. Everything he had ever said was being twisted and shouted back at him so that he was the bad guy. He decided to go over to the shop to clear his head and think, his domestic issues would have to wait. There was a Bethlehem meeting with his men that evening and the agenda was already beginning to build in his mind together with the possible reactions of both loyalists and critics. Without Jamal he was feeling a little abandoned and annoyed with himself because he hadn't realised how dependent he had become on him. He determined to become more his own man in future.

A car was pulling up outside the shop and Jamal entered. They greeted one another but there was a little detachment in Jamal's presence this time. He took another look around the shop and shook his head. Hani pre-empted the comment he knew was coming, "It's important to maintain your roots otherwise it would be easy to become disconnected from the ordinary people."

Jamal stared at him as if it was a personal insult aimed at him. But Hani's face was as honest and straight as always, so he smiled. This was the Hani he knew. He had not changed since his entry into the political maelstrom that was Ramallah. Something inside Jamal envied Hani his simple approach; he knew it didn't come from a simple mind. On the contrary, Hani was one the brightest and sharpest men he had recruited. His reputation among the higher echelons of Fatah was intact, even enhanced because of what had nearly been achieved.

Jamal's, on the other hand had not, even though he had been responsible for the intelligence that let to the release of the soldier. He confided in Hani, "It seems I'm being moved."

"Why," exclaimed Hani in surprise, "You've done a superb job, even got back the Israeli soldier."

Jamal smiled, "It isn't always about what you've achieved or not achieved that counts."

"What then?" asked a puzzled Hani.

"Who is on your side and who isn't." Jamal was sanguine. "It seems that the Chief of Security is blaming me for his embarrassment over the treachery of his deputy, and the Chief still has the President's ear. Not a lot of brownie points for the intelligence on the kidnapped soldier, I'm afraid."

So that's that, thought Hani. He stared at the outstretched hand before shaking it. Jamal turned to leave as Hani stumbled over his attempt to express thanks to Jamal.

Before leaving the shop, he turned and smiled at Hani. "You've still got a good future ahead of you." And with that he left the shop, got into his car and drove off.

Looking back, Hani was thanking Allah that he had decided not to reveal the second American document and the mp4 video to Jamal. That information would die with him and Omari. Omari! He suddenly felt guilty that he hadn't met up and given his friend a de-brief. A quick WhatsApp and they were both sitting having mint tea at the Walled Off. Hani looked around the place. This might be the last time I come here, he thought.

He turned to see Omari eyeing him strangely. "You look as if you've given up." Hani made no comment. Omari started asking his questions and Hani was giving inadequate answers.

"You invited me," reminded Omari. Hani jerked himself out of his emotional slumber and apologised. It was all too painful, but he recognised that Omari had put almost as much work into their negotiation document as he himself had done so Hani felt duty bound to try and answer his questions.

When it came to "where do we go from here?", Hani fell silent again because he knew it didn't depend on him. He was just a cog in a much bigger machine which had its own values and priorities. He confessed to Omari, "It's not a question for me anymore. I'm just going to be thankful to be a leader in Bethlehem and forget Ramallah."

Omari was quick to urge him, "No. You must not think in such terms. Feelings now are understandable, but they should never be the basis for such significant decisions. Give it some time."

Hani didn't answer. He understood what was being said, even acknowledging to himself that Omari was probably right but he hadn't yet got to that place. In reality, he was mourning. And, as his mother had quietly pointed out days earlier, there would be many other times of mourning before any lasting celebration happened, if it happened at all in their lifetime.

*

Shana and Medad, on the other hand, talked a lot about what had happened, who was to blame, and what life might now look like. Medad was quite concerned about Dan's change of tone. He understood the desire of a top public servant to fall into line with the political mood of his masters. The situation was not impacting him in the same way, at least not yet. He supposed he had not been in a public role long enough and was still a man with his own opinions. Not yet a true civil servant perhaps, but no doubt that would change if he stayed there long enough.

He was only too well aware that it was he alone who had been in receipt of the incriminating files. It was he alone who had supplied them to Dan, and it was he alone who had taken the decision to conceal the source from his boss. If Dan ever wanted to cement his own position by sacrificing someone else, those actions alone probably placed him as number one contender. In fact, Dan might come under real pressure to do that very thing. For days now, Medad had been wanting a private word with him but Dan was making himself scarce. Until he had cleared that down, Medad felt he was still vulnerable.

As it happened, he needn't have worried. Dan emerged in his office a few days later and Medad got his chance. Dan explained, "No, no, no. I have no intention of placing you in the firing line. On the contrary I'm going to give you access to my Palestinian source if that person agrees."

Medad didn't quite know what to say, so he said nothing. Dan continued, "I'm still personally committed to a peace process with the Palestinians, but for me now is not the time to push that point of view. I'm going to back away and leave the field open for you, should you want to continue."

"Yes, I think so, but do I still have a job?" Dan assured him, "Of course. First rate analysts are needed now more than ever. And by the way, I was speaking to the Minister yesterday and the Cabinet have agreed that if, and that is a big if, we ever agree to meet with the Palestinian Authority again, they must run a new election on the West Bank to ensure legitimacy."

Medad was thinking quickly, "How will that work when our government is pushing to legally absorb swathes of the West Bank into Israel proper?"

Dan shrugged. "Sounds to me like it's upping the stakes and clearing a path for integration." Medad agreed, "The PA won't want an election and I'm not sure we really want one... better the devil you know?"

But the conversation was over and Medad wandered out of Dan's office with a jumble of questions arising in his mind. His boss hadn't said he was moving, so how would that work? This Palestinian contact whoever that might be... was it a set up? All Medad's cynical instincts were coming into play, he was still finding it difficult to entirely trust Dan. Would he now be in control, or would he still be playing second fiddle to Dan? And what about this new demand, how will that play in Ramallah?

The whole office was subdued and everyone was taking the opportunity to go home early. There wasn't much to do until the election was over, then it would be a mad house. Medad trudged home with the rest looking forward to talking it all over with his wife. Shana saw some positives. "If this Palestinian contact consents, go and see how you get along. This could be what you have been waiting for. There's not much left to lose. But you'd probably better hint about the election demand rather than allow it to come as a surprise otherwise that could be the death-knell of any peace process."

It's getting a lot more complicated, thought Medad.

Chuck was anxious to get back to Jerusalem and re-awaken his relationship with Medad, if he could. He didn't know how much damage the whole Hamas débâcle had caused, but instinctively knew that Larry was not the person to restore confidence or smooth ruffled feathers. Chuck's family really didn't like him being away and he did try to keep it to a minimum, but the fact that they had all met Medad and Shana helped in that regard. Chuck explained that following the trouble in Israel, Medad might need some support within the government. He didn't elaborate further.

Another long plane journey, another diplomatic entry into Tel Aviv and another diplomatic car to Jerusalem. He would see Hagai again for his take on what was going on but at the end of the visit this time, rather than at the beginning. He had meetings scheduled at the embassy but they were cover, his only priority being to sit down with Medad and secure the relationship. How to do it? Bump into him on the off chance? No, that would be Larry's tactic and would give all the wrong signals. Call ahead and plan a meal? Yes, but perhaps he should have done that from the US. That was his plan but he had bottled it because he desperately didn't want Medad to decline. No, he wanted to be in Jerusalem, to make it personal.

An official invitation was sent for dinner at the Embassy. He wouldn't talk business, but just be friendly. If Medad was a little frosty, he would work his charm on Shana, talk about their trip to the US, remind them of his family, give them kind regards of his wife and children, invite them back again etc. etc. He was hopeful Medad would come round.

Not a lavish affair where Medad might be embarrassed at other Israeli government guests, but a personal and private dinner. Chuck would arrange for the US Ambassador to make a quick appearance to welcome them, but then leave Chuck to give them a quick tour of the building and to end the tour in the Ambassador's private dining quarters with the full service of his personal chef.

That was the plan.

51

RACHEL WAS SOME twelve years older than Sami, now in her mid twenties and acclimatising to being part of the UNRWA contingent in Gaza. She had graduated in History and Politics at Bristol University and had stayed on to do an MA in International Development. Part of this was due to a boyfriend who was also at the University and staying on in Bristol, but mostly because she had joined the United Nations Society at the Students Union. As the boyfriend relationship waned, so the interest and commitment to the work of the UN waxed.

As she was doing her MA, several UN employees came as speakers at the society meetings talking about their work overseas, and Rachel determined that this was what she wanted to do. However, her Scottish Presbyterian parents weren't at all keen. She was an only daughter and they were fearful that she might be seconded to some dangerous place on the planet and not return. But whilst Rachel understood her parents' worries, she was going to live her own life. It was clear to her that for far too long, she had lived according to the desire of her parents. No risks. No excitement. Not a lot of pleasure.

University had helped break the chains that she felt around her, especially as she had chosen one that was miles away from the Scottish Borders. She had completed her extra year, but now they wanted her to get a 'proper job' with a 'proper organisation' and the UN just didn't fit that category. For Rachel, however, it fitted perfectly. Opportunities from UNRWA were on her mind even before she finished her MA and, having applied early, she received an internship offer fairly quickly. As a bright and personable graduate with good IT skills, it didn't take long for promotion to come her way. And here she was in Gaza.

It wasn't a place that she had ever thought of serving in, and her parents were definitely not in favour of her going to 'that place', with all those 'terrorists'. But Rachel, determined to be her own person, weighed up the opportunity and it just seemed to her to be the right thing to do. Someone had to go to Gaza, why not her? She knew it was a difficult place where UN personnel were not excluded from the general life restrictions that the Strip presented.

But what a place! Just three hundred and sixty five square kilometres or one hundred and forty one square miles, housing multitudes of people with nowhere to go and no hope of that ever changing. It was the third most densely populated country in the world, and it was growing at nearly 3% per annum which, according to some analysts, would make the place unliveable within ten years. Most countries in the world that mattered had designated Hamas as a terrorist organisation, and with that designation the whole population suffered.

Most countries included Egypt. The southern Egyptian border checkpoint with Gaza at Rafah was just as strict on movement as the northern Israeli border. The Egypt army had deposed a democratically elected Muslim Brotherhood President who had threatened to tear up established norms, and the new army President was not going to allow a Muslim Brotherhood offshoot like Hamas to infiltrate back into Egypt. Both organisations were Sunni and both wanted the state of Israel to be destroyed. Egypt, along with Jordan, had signed peace treaties with Israel and there was a degree of cooperation between the states, particularly on Gaza.

The UN quarters were slightly better than most of the population. Nevertheless, the electricity supply coming from Israel was extremely restricted. Back-up generators were available, but these could rapidly consumed their limited supply of fuel and so were confined to emergencies. Yet the UNRWA 'family' were a close knit bunch and all tried hard to get along with each other. They had to, for there was no escaping. Occasionally there would be an emotional explosion by someone. It was almost expected, so no-one took offence. Either the person got over it and apologised, or they left. Simmering emotions between individuals were just not tolerated. The director in charge had been there long enough. He knew the cancer that this could be.

Rachel had never seen such an episode, although one of her best friends had, and the protagonist had been quickly transferred. Gaza did that to people; it chewed them up and spat them out. Nevertheless, the population of Gaza needed humanitarian help and that's what the UNRWA was there for. To give it its full name, the United Nations Relief and Works Agency for

Palestine Refugees in the Near East was an UN agency specifically created in December 1949 to support the relief and human development of Palestinian refugees who fled or were expelled from their homes and farms during the 1948 war and the 1967 Six Day War.

The organisation set out to provide education, health care, and a variety of social services to this refugee population of over five million people located in five jurisdictions: Jordan, Lebanon, Syria, Gaza and the West Bank, including East Jerusalem. It was unique among UN agencies in being dedicated to helping refugees from a specific region or conflict. It was the UNHCR which was responsible for supporting all other refugees, but their mandate included a responsibility to eliminate that refugee status by local integration in current country, resettlement in a third country or repatriation when possible.

The UNRWA had no such mandate. Rather its priorities were to help Palestinian refugees to acquire knowledge and skills, lead long and healthy lives, achieve decent standards of living and enjoy human rights to the fullest possible extent. Whilst Rachel agreed wholeheartedly with these objectives she, along with many others on the ground, were frustrated at the limited role they could play in changing peoples' lives. It seemed to them it was merely a never-ending holding operation.

Rachel wasn't responsible for the remit or policies of UNRWA. Her role was to get involved at the grassroots helping the people in the Relief and Social Services Programme. She had specific responsibility for the community-based organisations (CBOs) which helped women, the disabled and children. These organisations were supposed to have their own management committees staffed by volunteers with UNRWA just providing them with technical help and small sums of targeted financial assistance. However, a larger mentoring role often had to be played due to a lack of education of those she was helping. Her promotion meant that she now oversaw a number of CBOs, ensuring they had food aid, cash assistance, and that special hardship families had help with any shelter repairs. Children from these families were given preferential access to vocational training centres, whilst the women were encouraged to join UNRWA's women's programme centres where childcare was available.

One of the reasons why Gaza depended on UNRWA was because its economy didn't work. Business infrastructure on the West Bank might have been bureaucratic and inefficient, but in Gaza it was non-existent. Gaza City's roads were cluttered with cars, bicycles, pedestrians, and donkey carts moving at a snail's pace, all with little regard for each other's prescribed place on the road. The telephone, electricity and water systems were no better, often just not working. Raw materials, components and other supplies needed to be imported either from or through Israel, and border checkpoints opening and shutting at will meant there was little or no guarantee that anything could be imported or exported for possibly weeks at a time.

Debt levels could be very high because it was normal practice to give credit for people to purchase items and debt easily spiralled out of control, so that even the credit-giving businesses went bust. The one rule of business in Gaza seemed to be 'have faith that everything will get better'. It rarely did. Without UNRWA, life for most Palestinians in Gaza would have been very precarious. Even with it, life could be unbearable. Law and order, for example, was a basic tenet of any stable society yet although there were policemen, enforcing the law did not seem to be a priority, unless it was a very important person who had suffered some criminal damage.

Fortunately, Rachel hadn't any need to call on the police for assistance and if a problem did arise, she would go to UNRWA's security first. At just twenty five, Rachel had grown up immensely in the eighteen months she had been in Gaza. She was now quite confident moving around and getting what she needed. Gaza was Gaza, and she now accepted it as it was. The only change she was looking for was in the women she mentored. Her occasional letters to home painted a bright picture of what she was doing and how she was helping. She hoped it would help her parents come to terms with what she was doing and make them proud of her. The letters she got back, however, didn't give her that impression. They still seemed to be full of fear and dread, cautioning her about this and that, especially men.

There was no intention on her part of looking for a man; obviously, that didn't mean that a man wouldn't find her, but she would take things as they occurred. She knew that most young people were more worldly wise than their parents gave them credit for and, as an only child, she understood her parent's anxiety but determined she was not going to let it take over her. She was living her life in her way and most of the time she was enjoying it, helping people who needed help when there was no-one else.

She was not expecting Sami to enter her life. To come alongside a thirteen year old girl with such a traumatic history and disabilities to go with it, had not been on her radar, but it had been mentioned to her that the girl needed some help and so she visited the hospital. Instead of finding a girl who was lost, distressed and sorry for herself, she found someone who had initiative, enthusiasm and a plan. The help needed was not the help that Rachel had assumed. Sure, Sami had some down times, who wouldn't after what she had been through, but her spirit was remarkable. She risen above her circumstances and was trying to make a difference. She looked and acted years much older than she was.

Rachel introduced herself to Sami as she lay in her hospital bed and they talked for a couple of hours about what the teenager wanted to do. Rachel was impressed that she had already written to the Israeli Prime minister and the Leader of Hamas asking questions about her experience. She found herself making suggestions and getting involved with her ideas but, although she was enthusiastic about what Sami was wanting to do, she had to point out to her that she could only act in a personal capacity and not as an employee of UNRWA. Getting directly or indirectly involved with Hamas would be construed as political activity and that was not part of the UNRWA mandate.

Although Sami didn't fully understand what that meant, Rachel promised to work with Sami as much as she could, even getting time off work if possible. It was clear that an unlikely bond of friendship had been made between the two.

52

AYSHAA FOUND OUT she was pregnant again. She had her suspicions as most women do but now it had been confirmed. How did that happen? She tried to think back without much success. As far as she could remember, they hadn't slept together for ages. Nor had she ever slept with anyone else. Whatever she thought of Hani, she would never be unfaithful for that would be totally against her religion.

Pregnancy was definitely not what she wanted because it was going to stifle her BWP activity and making her more dependent, just at the time when she wanted to be more independent. There was no shortage of women wanting to come to BWP sessions and although Lara continued to offer a full day each week and Ayshaa two days, it was still not meeting the demand. The mums and toddler session was helpful for Ayshaa since Rena could be there and Ghalia was just about up to looking after Rena on the other morning. Having shadowed Lara for a while, Ayshaa was now fully competent to lead sessions on her own, but was also training up Israa to be the BWP lead on the women's empowerment programmes which would help to take the strain.

But Ayshaa's vision was so much more than just training and life skills. She wanted now to concentrate on building a strong leadership team for the organisation and felt that it needed to be in place and competent within six months. Ethar had some computer skills, so Ayshaa had her as head of communications which Ethar thought sounded really grand. Under Ayshaa's direction, Ethar had composed and printed off a sample free newspaper from her laptop. It was limited to a couple of double-sided A3 pages and modelled on what she saw the mainstream papers doing.

In order to make it acceptable to Fatah, it featured issues that Fatah held dear. The plan was that when their funding became more assured, the balance would subtly change and feature more of what they wanted to communicate. There also were some BWP and Ghu-sin Zay-tun success stories and, although these had to be anonymous, there was the tag line to 'come and see' for yourself. Having tested out the sample on some of the groups she led, the reaction had been positive, but no further progress had been made.

Whilst the Israeli-Palestinian talks were going on, Ayshaa thought it not appropriate to push the idea, though the truth was she didn't want to ask Hani for a favour. "The less I depend on him the better", she thought. But the money men in Ramallah would need someone to cajole and push them if they were to provide the finance, and that someone had to be Hani. So for the moment, the project had stalled.

In the meantime, one of the mums in her group who had a cousin in Hebron, began talking about a women's cooperative in Hebron who were making fair trade handicraft items. Rabia suggested that perhaps they could start something similar? It provided much needed additional income for the Hebron women and enabled them to show *sumud* – steadfastness – in the face of the Occupation. It was in itself an act which strengthened community and honoured the role and contribution of women. She explained that whenever and wherever possible, they bought materials, and used services from suppliers in the Hebron district to help support their local economy.

Ayshaa was not keen. "Isn't there enough 'tat' in the souks without adding more?" she asked. "And it seems a lot of effort and organisation for very little return."

They were discussing it at one of their leadership team meetings and Rabia had joined them. She understood Ayshaa's point but had a bigger vision.

"What if we were able to produce goods for overseas markets?" she asked. "If we just did traditional Palestinian patterns, I agree the local market and tourists would be our only customers. But I would like us to export to America and Europe."

Ayshaa began to see the idea in a new light although Ethar was looking rather sceptical.

Rabia continued her presentation.

"I believe design is the key. I've already done some on-line research on Ethar's computer." With that she showed the group some designs from other web sites which marketed their goods both through Amazon and their own web sites.

The others began to look impressed for Rabia had done her homework well and was presenting a good case. She explained that she knew someone who could take these traditional designs and use them as a basis for her own modern designs.

"There are plenty of women who can produce fabric to a prepared design, but we don't just want to do shawls, rugs and scarves. For example, there's a UK website called Rags to Bags which takes end rolls of cloth and transforms them into lots of really useful items. It seems to be run by a single person and it's her personality and designs which are attracting buyers as well as her items. They seem to sell well."

Rabia seemed to have the group nodding their heads, even Ethar. "I think we should also sell our goods as 'Made in Canaan', rather than 'Made in Palestine'."

Wow! That sparked off a really heated argument much wider than making and selling cloth items. Canaan, strictly speaking, was an ancient term for a region approximating to present-day Israel, the West Bank and the Gaza Strip, plus adjoining coastal lands and parts of Lebanon, Syria, and Jordan. Canaanites were mentioned in Mesopotamian and Ancient Egyptian texts, as well as in the Bible.

Ethar was definitely not in favour. She thought they would be selling out their heritage and that they ought to produce Palestinian products made by Palestinian women. Israa was of an equally strong contrary opinion. She thought that they ought to move away from selling items as a way of supporting the wider Palestinian movement.

"It smacks of 'begging' and reinforces a 'victim mentality' which we are often accused of." Israa's continued to support Rabia's idea.

"Surely items ought to be able to stand on their own in the marketplace without the unsaid request to support the Palestinian cause, which might alienate a large part of the American population in particular."

The dissent was threatening to get out of hand and Ayshaa had to calm the team down, pointing out that this is how the men carried on and that the women ought to be different. They took the point. The Palestinian mum wasn't sure how to tackle such divided opinions, and certainly didn't want to ask her husband for any advice. Listening to the arguments, she knew the issue couldn't be ducked. She was the leader and had to make the decision. It was the first controversial decision for the BWP team.

Strong leadership had to be shown and a clear decision made, but at the same time she didn't want to splinter her new team. So she began by talking about 'team', how difficult decisions would have to be made as they grew and that this one might turn out to be one of the less difficult ones!

Ayshaa asked each of them a crucial question. "If it happens that a decision doesn't go your way, will you accept it or will you walk away?"

Everyone could see that Ethar was struggling silently with making a decision. She felt strongly about this issue but, just as strongly, wanted BWP to succeed. Almost grudgingly she said she would not. The others indicated the same. Ayshaa made her decision.

"OK. Initially we will make items in both types of design and see what sells in the wider marketplace under the Canaan brand. What doesn't sell abroad, will be sold locally under the Palestine brand."

Ayshaa knew that some initial funding would be required and predictably, this was the subject that Rabia raised next.

She turned to Rabia. "This is your responsibility now and you should explore all options, including establishing a cooperative similar to that in Hebron." She added, "and you will need to demonstrate your ideas and work out an initial set up cost, as well as a trading budget for the next two years."

Rabia shyly replied, "I've already made some progress in this area. If our website also carries some personal stories, not the whingeing type, but uplifting stories of success etc., which is constantly updated, we could begin to get a following and then we might be able to sell advertising space."

Ayshaa cut off any further discussion. "It's a good idea, but work it up and we will discuss it again when you've got something to show us."

The meeting broke up with Ayshaa wondering to herself how on earth she had managed that. But everyone seemed satisfied, at least for the moment. It was a significant moment for the fledgling organisation. Ayshaa had no intention of making team decisions on a majority basis. That would be a recipe for chaos in her culture. It was her organisation and her team needed to have confidence and trust in her regardless of whether they liked the decisions she made or not.

Ayshaa was due to meet Lara the next day and decided to share what they had decided to do, but not the fact that she was pregnant. In fact, she hadn't even told Hani yet. Lara was enthusiastic about the new venture, explaining that it was a path they had also chosen to go down. They had some thirty women who were either widows or whose husbands couldn't get work either because of disability or visa restrictions. The women made what they wanted, with the charity providing some initial start up funding, then further help to sell the products. When Omari went on his tours, he took samples with him and received orders which the women fulfilled.

Ayshaa expressed some concern over getting the business and finance side of things set up properly. Rabia had good ideas and great enthusiasm but no bookkeeping skills whatsoever, and anyone who wanted to invest, or any Trust that wanted to donate funds, would need to be assured of absolute propriety. Lara thought about this.

"I can't commit any of Ghu-sin Zay-tun's staff, but my mother-in-law works in the finance department at the University. If you like, I'll ask if she would be interested to help. She would probably prefer to meet up with you to know more and see if you could all work together. No guarantees though." Ayshaa nodded her thanks.

The conversation inevitably moved on to their husbands. They knew that they had worked together and both wives agreed that it was good that they had become friends and hoped that the ups and downs would serve to strengthen rather than strain the relationship. They paused, both wondering what the immediate future held for relationships between them and the Israelis. Ayshaa wondered out loud, "What about trying to establish a women's Israeli connection?"

Lara looked up, "That's an interesting idea. I agree it would be good, but perhaps avoid the myriad Israeli peace movements and organisations which are very busy on social media, but seem to get nowhere."

Ayshaa wondered, "Should we do it independently of our husbands or in tandem? Or maybe both. Perhaps have a separate set of relationships, but keep the men informed? What do you think?" No answers, but more to think about. After hugs and promises to keep in touch, they both went home.

After a deal of procrastinating, Medad had finally decided to contact Omari. Using Dan's burner phone, he messaged Omari to see if he wanted to meet up. Of course he did. It was arranged for two days time in Bethlehem at the Star & Bucks on Manger Sq. Omari had heard about Medad from Hani but this was the first time that there was an opportunity to meet him. He was reassured that it was Dan's phone that had been used but, nevertheless, Omari sat some way from the café, waiting and watching. Medad had agreed to wear a certain type of hat so Omari would know him and sure enough, there he was. Now, was there anyone else following? Omari carried on reading his paper and looking up to see if anyone was watching. A couple of men caught his eye, so he waited a little longer. They moved on, and he thought it safe to go inside.

It was quite crowded with tourists having their lattes and cappuccinos. Omari approached the table where Medad was having his coffee and asked, "Perhaps I might join you? That's a very nice hat you're wearing."

Medad removed it, "It was the best I could do at short notice. What do you want to drink?"

Omari answered, "I'm fine thank you. I thought I'd get here a little early, so I've had mine. Thank you."

There was no outward show of friendship for the benefit of anyone who might be watching but Medad expressed his appreciation for the meeting and explained that Dan had decided to step back for the time being.

Omari nodded, "The whole episode must have taken a great deal of strain and stress on him, on both of you."

Medad didn't comment directly but took another drink of his coffee. "Of course, I've already met Hani at the talks and I would like to keep the channel between us open." Omari also waited, looking directly at this young Israeli and wondering whether he could push forward the peace agenda on his own. Medad didn't want to have a discussion about any Palestinian election because it wasn't his business, so he just mentioned the Israeli election.

"Of course you know that our election is now just a week or two away and it looks a slam dunk for Likud."

Omari agreed, "Yes, it looks that way."

Medad then asked, "When will you have a general election?"

"That," pronounced Omari, "is a good question. Who knows?"

Medad left it at that and nothing else of substance was discussed, each man expressing satisfaction to have met and sharing some tentative optimism for the future. Omari gave his burner phone number to Medad so that he could WhatsApp him directly and said maybe Hani might want to come next time, if that was acceptable to Medad. It was.

53

RACHEL HAD BECOME not only Sami's closest friend but her advisor in chief. They had laughed together, cried together and hugged each other over the past few weeks. But now Rachel was serious. She tried to outline how things might develop if Sami really wanted to open Pandora's box by allowing Hamas to interview her if the opportunity came. The teenager listened but was intransigent. Within a matter of days, a letter was released to the press together with an announcement that the Leader himself would go to the hospital to visit the orphan. Hamas clearly saw some propaganda material in prospect.

A job for Khalid. It was his task to go to the hospital and pave the way ensuring that Sami was willing to cooperate fully. The Leader did not like his time being wasted or any chance that, having made the trip, a thirteen year old girl might stand him up. That would not do. She had been warned that someone would be coming to check her out, but even so she flinched when he came into the room. He looked every bit as dangerous as he was. A big man in every sense, with deep set eyes and very large hands that looked as if they could strangle anyone without a moment's thought. He smiled a creepy smile as his interrogation began and Sami began to wish she had not written her letter. As a thirteen year old, she really had no idea who these men were or what they did. She just knew they were in charge.

The 'fixer' took Sami through the conversation that she was going to have with the Leader, coaching her with the type of points she might want to make. He wasn't overly concerned because it was not going to be broadcast live. It would be recorded and, with careful editing, would then be broadcast on state television. The result would say what Hamas wanted it to say. At the end of the encounter, Khalid simply asked whether Sami would cooperate as he had indicated. She would.

Rachel didn't want to meet Khalid in person. She had been advised that her presence might be taken as UN support for Sami. That, as Rachel again patiently explained to the teenager, would be outside the remit of UNRWA. Whilst the UN had no official political views about Hamas, Rachel had her own views which were not altogether complimentary, but she had done her best to re-coach Sami on the main talking points to cover in the Hamas interview, and how to answer potential difficult questions.

The eventual arrival of the Hamas delegation was seriously disruptive for the hospital, despite assurances given by Khalid on his reconnaissance visit, but the hospital was happy to be in the limelight thinking it might get more funding. However, the delegation showed little care for patients or staff. For Sami, it was a major ordeal. She was still in bed with a further operation just a few days away. But the Hamas delegation totally ignored that.

A make-up artist had been commissioned by Khalid to do Sami's hair and make up, to ensure that the camera had the best possible picture of her. In the mirror, Sami thought she looked years older than she was. That part she enjoyed, but was not looking forward to the real interview. Sure enough, it was quite intimidating to start with and she stuck to the line 'suggested' by Khalid. As she warmed up, though, she began to take full advantage of her position and began to make her points as any naïve but opinionated thirteen year old might. Khalid remained in the background leaving the limelight to his boss, but Rachel had been at surreptitiously filming everything on her phone from besides a cupboard at the back of the room just in case any subsequent Hamas editing put Sami in a bad light.

After the film crew, Hamas leaders and hangers-on had left the hospital, Sami looked totally spent. Adrenalin had kept her going during the filming, but as soon as it was over she closed her eyes and slept for twelve hours solid. Nurses popped in when they could to check on her, after all she was now a celebrity. It would do the hospital no good if she didn't recover well so from now on she would get the best possible treatment.

Rachel checked back in at UNRWA and got on with her job. Today was an admin day. Paperwork had to be done, plans made for the next period and all submitted to the bosses. When she got home that evening, she uploaded the video from her phone to her laptop and went through it a few times noting particularly the sections where she thought Hamas might edit something important out. She didn't want them to get away with anything.

The next morning she looked in on Sami to see if she was awake and ready to see it. She was out of bed when Rachel arrived and having her daily wash in the communal washing area, but wouldn't be long. Whilst waiting, she had a look around the adjacent orthopaedic wards. It was still chaotic from the recent Israeli attack. One young man was lying on his bed with bandages on both legs with what looked like his mother weeping inconsolably on a chair in his room. A young woman arrived, could have been his wife, girlfriend or sister, but it didn't matter. She was very animated and clearly frustrated at the slowness of the treatment and started shouting at the medical staff.

One of the nurses came over to her and tried to explain that their surgeons were working nonstop and had been since the attack. The hospital was overwhelmed, with all their operating theatres working at maximum capacity. Forty orthopaedic operations had been carried out in the last twenty-four hours, with fifty others still waiting their turn. The verbal decibels decreased slightly but nerves were understandably frayed as relatives, worried about wounded family members, feared their conditions might deteriorate whilst they waited. But there was nowhere else to go.

Rachel looked further afield in the hospital and saw the injured stuffed into rooms and lining the corridors with the same commensurate noise from relatives and patients alike. It was bedlam. This was nothing like she knew back in the UK. How on earth can these people work in this environment? She looked at the walls; some walls had bullet marks in them, others holes big enough that you could poke your head through. So much for a sterile environment, thought Rachel. Just as Sami appeared there was a corridor full of high octane grief coming down towards them; men, women and children. Somebody had died. Rachel guessed this happened on a daily basis, but would do little to encourage other patients or relatives.

Rachel didn't want to watch any longer. Sami was back so they could view this video together and discuss how it had gone. Sami was in a talkative mood and so went through the recording a few times talking over the good and not so good bits, which all served to cement their relationship further. Rachel was trying not to influence Sami in her views, but they found themselves agreed on most things that affected their daily lives. They were almost sisters.

Now Sami had recovered from her latest operation – only one more to go

– it was time now to talk about the Jerusalem visit. Apart from the obvious first meeting with the Israelis, it would be the first time Sami had gone out of the Gaza Strip and the first time Rachel had been to Jerusalem. In the time they spent together, Rachel reviewed the questions Sami wanted to ask, limiting them to the most important, "you won't get a lot of time, so let's make the most of it."

Then it was a matter of thinking of supplementaries on the basis that the responses would be 'politicians' answers. Yes, they felt they were getting better at this. They took a taxi to the Erez crossing where they were expected and an Israeli car was waiting for them to take them non-stop to Jerusalem. Security searches for them were waived and they waltzed through totally unhindered much to the chagrin of the long queue – another first! On the way Sami took out her papers again and started to review their questions. She was getting a little nervous. Rachel told her that in comparison to the Hamas encounter, this would be a lot easier and she might get some reasonable concessions from them.

In Jerusalem, the Presidential staff had laid on a small private reception for lunch with just a few civil servants from the relevant ministry, including Medad but not his Minister. It enabled Sami to rest before the audience with the President and subsequent photo opportunity, but also provided the opportunity for Medad to meet her. He had requested this opportunity to meet her and assured her that not all Israelis were hardliners. There were many who wanted peace and were working for that end. Confidentially, he gave her his card and invited her to call him if she thought he could do anything for her. Rachel was suspicious, but kept her counsel for the moment.

Diplomats often refer to difficult conversations as a 'polite or frank exchange of views'. Perhaps during the interview with the President, Sami wasn't altogether polite but she was quite frank. Why shouldn't she be? Her family had been murdered by the Israelis … for what?

The President decided he should be presidential. "On behalf of the government of Israel, I would like to apologise for the bombing of your church building. We are checking our intelligence as we speak." Sami looked at him but didn't answer.

He smiled at her, thinking she was overwhelmed by the occasion. "Of course we will earmark funds to rebuild the church."

Sami asked directly, "For who?" The President looked lost at the unexpectedly blunt question. He quickly glanced around for any of his aides who might be able to help. Unfortunately, he had been so confident in his ability to undertake a meeting with a teenage girl, that he had dismissed all help and sent his staff away.

He stuttered a little, then regained himself, and looked back at Sami, "I'm afraid I don't understand."

"There isn't any congregation anymore. They're all dead."

"Ah yes. I'm very sorry."

She was looking directly at him and the President couldn't avoid her stare, for that was what it was.

"Gaza isn't a place where people are free to convert. We don't publicly discuss faith issues. Proselytising is not acceptable. So building a new church sanctuary might be nice, but building a new congregation is not going to be possible... and anyway after what has happened, I'm not sure I'm even Christian anymore." Rachel had quietly positioned her phone towards the two of them with the movie facility on.

The President coughed and began to realise his mistake. He was half way out of his chair ready to suggest they go outside for the assembled photographers when Sami began to talk again. He sat down again and once more looked around for anyone who might be able to rescue him.

"I still have another operation to go through but supply of medication is very limited, not only for me, but also for all those in similar circumstances after your attacks." The President was now feeling a little ambushed and readily agreed to provide some unquantifiable funds for medication. Before any further requests could be made, he jumped up to help Sami out of her chair and escorted her through the door into the Peace Garden to meet the waiting press. After the brief photo session, he looked very relieved to be saying goodbye to this young girl and thankful there was to be no press conference.

On the way back from Jerusalem, Rachel and Sami reviewed the footage. They found the picture quality was not great and sometimes no-one was in shot, so only a few frames could be used here and there but the sound quality was good. Rachel thought she could make something useful out of it. So what had been achieved? It was clear to both that it would all be a forty-eight hour wonder unless Sami continued to reach out to the audience she had gained from these interviews. She wanted to hold the Israeli government to account both in terms of what the President had promised and their professed 'defensive only' intent. But how to make this exposure last and, more importantly, count for something in the long run?

On the way back to Gaza they talked at length about how Sami could continue what she had started. The question was, what did Sami want to achieve?

She thought about it. "Well, I definitely want to release some of the pressure on the population of Gaza, whether that be from Hamas or Israel, or both."

As they discussed back and forth, Sami began to develop a larger vision. "I think I want to be part of the overall Palestinian peace movement that encompasses both the West Bank and Gaza." Rachel began thinking about how to achieve this. "Maybe a daily blog might be a good idea and build up a following of people who wanted to know what daily life in Gaza is like and what they could do to push forward the peace agenda."

Sami's enthusiasm was kindled. "Maybe a YouTube channel to speak directly to the audience which would maintain the momentum we've established through the interviews."

Rachel nodded. "Great idea. That would give you increased international exposure you want for your cause."

They lapsed into silence as they left Israel and crossed once more into Gaza. In the meantime Sami had to undergo her final operation.

54

ANGRA MAINYU WAS not surprised to be re-called to Tehran. He was pleased with himself and had carried out his mission with total success. He was a short, thick-set man who tended to wear built up shoes under his traditional thobe. Not that he cared what others thought of him, but he disliked being looked down on by inferiors who were taller. His many meetings were usually held sitting down, with him behind a desk on a higher chair, and if anyone of his aides even thought of joking about it, they were dead meat.

He was expecting a promotion and he was not disappointed, but a little disgruntled when he learned that he was being sent back to Lebanon. But, as he rationalised to himself, he was the one with all the contacts on the ground and he had successfully penetrated not only the Palestinian Authority, but the Israeli government as well. With Hezbollah taking his orders and Hamas pliable, he ruled supreme.

But Tehran wanted more. It was one thing to sabotage Fatah's treacherous policy of cosying up to Israel. That was easy. It would be quite another to begin to weaken Israel diplomatically, militarily and economically and this was the major tenet of Iranian foreign policy towards Israel. It had many strands, but the whole Middle Eastern strand was now Angra Mainyu's responsibility. Other strands were not in his domain but he would be kept informed in case of overlapping issues.

There was a time in the past, during the presidency of Mohammed Khatami, that Iranian policy vehemently denounced violence and terrorism. Khatami promoted détente and pressed for "dialogue among civilisations," to improve Iran's relations with its Persian Gulf neighbours. He reversed Ayatollah Khomeini's *fatwa* against author Salman Rushdie, bettered relations with Europe, softened Iran's adversarial attitude toward Israel, and above all, offered an "olive branch" to the United States. It was said that his foreign policy restored the tradition of *hekmat*, (wisdom) to Iran's statecraft. But those days were long gone.

Israel, unsurprisingly, had a mirror image foreign policy focus on Iran. Although they had interacted since Israel's birth in 1948, their competitive regional interests had largely shaped their subsequent relationship. That had been relatively close until the Iranian revolution in 1979, but even after Ayatollah Ruhollah Khomeini was installed, arms sales from Israel to Iran continued until the mid 80s, ceasing only after Iran kept delaying payments.

But it was the 1982 Israeli invasion of Lebanon that mobilised the Shiites. Iranian troops were deployed inside Lebanon and they sired Hezbollah to fight Israel on their behalf. Albeit through a proxy, Iran now faced Israel across a common border. Not content with one, Iran also armed and funded another proxy, Islamic Jihad, which was tasked with carrying out terrorist attacks within Israel. Thus there was a lot of history but that paled into insignificance compared with the potential of Iran's nuclear program, a barely disguised attempt to obtain an equality with Israel. It raised the stakes for both sides in their regional rivalry. Israel therefore believed that their security justified all options being on the the table to ensure Iran did not acquire such a device.

Now Angra Mainyu was tasked with pulling the various strings at his disposal, one of which was to ensure Israel was always tied up in Palestinian matters. He reviewed the viability of these strings and concluded that they were inadequate for the task. He needed to penetrate Israel and Fatah in more depth in order to succeed in his mission. The penetration of both the Israeli political class and the Palestinian Authority didn't come as a shock to Israel's secret services who knew that people could be bought or coerced quite easily provided the right subject was picked: either sex or money, occasionally both.

But these victories were nowhere near substantial enough for his new responsibility. He needed to considerably strengthen his network and could no longer rely on just one agent in Ramallah. Although he had replaced Abd Alraheem with Nada, he wanted more and was now turning his attention to Gaza. The Strip was Sunni linked to the Muslim Brotherhood whereas Iran and, consequently Hezbollah were Shia. Thus, there was an enmity between the two and, although they had a 'common enemy' in Israel, that didn't mean that they naturally worked together. However, since Iran largely financed their military wing, Hamas was obliged to listen and sometimes act on their intelligence. This is precisely what had happened when they had sent their rockets into Israel to scupper the Palestinian talks process.

The Iranian 'diplomat' had been working on a plan for some while and smiled grimly to himself as he treasured its *taqiyya*. This was an old Shiite practice of displaying one intention while harbouring another. Deception was Angra Mainyu's forte. That was not entirely evident to Hamas when the message came through from the Iranian to The Leader. He wanted someone from Hamas to come to Lebanon for a face to face meeting. There was not a little disquiet around the leadership table at this request.

"It sounds like an order," said one. Hamas were proud of their independence and took orders from no-one. Whilst Angra Mainyu had direct input into Hezbollah in Lebanon, Hamas could usually only be handled at a distance, but for this task he didn't want any written, digital or telephonic evidence. He had hinted to Hamas that there was a prize worth having at the end. So the decision was taken to humour the Iranian and send someone.

Everyone knew it was virtually impossible to get in and out of Gaza through legitimate exit points, the Egyptian government were just as firm policing the Rafah crossing as the Israelis were the Erez border. So illegitimate routes had to be found. Many of the tunnels that had been built under the Wall from Gaza directly into Israel had been discovered and blown up by Israeli forces, but one or two still existed into Egypt near the Rafah crossing. Such a journey from Gaza to Lebanon was fraught with danger but, the Hamas leadership had concluded, there was not much to lose by agreeing to the meeting requested, except possibly the life of the envoy. Khalid was dispatched from Hamas to make the hazardous journey to Lebanon via Egypt.

He groaned when he heard what the Leader wanted him to do but his was to obey. A car dropped him off about a mile before the actual crossing and began to make his way to where he remembered the tunnel entrance was. He had used it before but that was a few years ago. There were specific natural markers, he recalled, which would guide him to the spot and he was sure he could follow them. It would all come back to him, he thought. Actually, a lot had changed in those years; small shrubs had become larger, sand had shifted its contours and outcrops of rocks which were bare then, were now covered with vegetation.

At one point he was ready to admit defeat before suddenly coming face to face with a twin rock face that he remembered. He raised his face to the sky in thanks to Allah and knew that the entrance was only a few minutes away. Then he was in. It had been pitch black right from the beginning and he was having to feel his way with his hands. He knew it would be this way, and he also knew that if he precipitated a roof fall, it could be very dangerous. This could be his grave. He broke out in more sweat as he hurried to get through. Claustrophobia was not normally a problem, but this was not normal. It took almost two hours to get through, many times tripping over fallen rocks or piles of sand, and by the time he saw light, he was bloodied, bruised and swearing like a trooper. As he was trained to do, he paused for five slow minutes before exiting both to increase his oxygen intake and accustom his eyes to Egyptian daylight.

A Muslim Brotherhood car was waiting for him at a pre-arranged spot about a mile away on the other side and, once he made contact, he was whisked away to a plane that would fly him to Lebanon. Khalid was not expecting an airport, but thought a tarmac take-off and landing strip would be standard. The driver made a phone call and within ten minutes a single engined plane landed on the sand and taxied towards them. No runway, no buildings, nothing. The driver assured him that the sand was harder than concrete. I hope so, thought Khalid.

"But we must hurry," urged the driver. The pilot started down the runway almost before Khalid had closed the door. He was just as anxious to get away. After take-off, the plane kept low, obviously to avoid radar, Khalid thought, and went out to sea a long way right into international waters. He hated these small planes and his hands gripped the sides of his seat and prayed to Allah for a safe landing somewhere, anywhere. Before very long, the plane circled over what looked like a field. On closer inspection, it definitely was a field and a quite bumpy one. Khalid had no idea if he was in Lebanon, but he could see a car a few hundred meters away. The moment he got out of the plane, the aircraft was back down the grassy runway and into the sky. Beirut, it turned out, was only an hour's drive away and his Hezbollah driver lost no time in trying to get there in record time.

The Albergo Hotel on Rue Abdel Wahab El Inglizi, in Achrafieh district was a five star hotel and not used to having guests show up looking dishevelled. He had spent most of the time in the plane hanging on for dear life so much so that, embarrassingly, his hands were blotchy red and rather swollen. The Palestinian had tried to clean himself a little in the car, but there was still sand and bits of debris in his hair and on his coat. He cursed himself for not bringing a small toilet bag so he went straight passed reception and headed for the ground floor men's room, where he washed and tidied himself as best he could.

Angra Mainyu had taken a suite on the top floor. This was in addition to his tiny office in the Iranian embassy, which he rarely visited. Nothing but the best for him. It also added a certain style which served to intimidate others who couldn't afford such luxury, especially someone from Gaza. The receptionist indicated the lift and said the top floor. Even though the Gazan had only been in a lift a few times in his life, he tried to look as if he did this everyday. The security at the door of the suite roughly frisked him and Khalid glowered at him as he unwillingly submitted. The contents of his pockets, including his phone, were taken and placed in a basket. He was getting riled at these silly procedures. He was supposed to be an honoured guest, the one who was invited, not a potential hit man trying to force his way in. Anyway, if it came to it, he knew he was a match both for the Iranian and his security detail. He was shown towards a seat opposite Angra Mainyu's table, where the Iranian was sitting. Khalid knew that how well one treats a guest is a direct measurement of the kind of host a person is. *Karam*, the Arabic term for 'generosity' is an incredibly important part of the host's Islamic faith.

Angra Mainyu was not that religious although he observed the outward forms in public, so Khalid was just invited to sit and have tea. He was well aware of what hospitality should have been, especially when the Iranian will have known the difficult journey he had made It fell far short so he declined the tea. Khalid was not one to be intimidated by anyone, even Angra Mainyu. But the Iranian was in no hurry and not a word was said for at least two minutes while the man himself took tea. Eventually, he asked Khalid whether the supply of rockets was sufficient? Did they need more? What about some surface to air missile launchers, with missiles of course? This was all aimed at emphasising Hamas' dependence on Iran.

Khalid understood the game and responded tersely that finance was always a problem. Angra Mainyu nodded. He already knew the answer, then went on to reveal that there was a 'Plan' for the freedom of the Palestinians that did not involve munitions or weaponry, so there would be little or no impact on Hamas' finances.

Khalid was taken aback and sceptically asked, "whose plan?" Angra Mainyu didn't answer, almost as if the Palestinian had asked the wrong question. So Khalid also said nothing and waited. He had come a long way and he wasn't going to be trifled with. If there was something to take back, then he would wait until this man said it or gave him something.

Then the Iranian said it.

55

CHUCK'S TRIP TO Israel to woo Medad and Shana was on hold. He had been called into Langley with the State Department's reluctant agreement. Chuck needed to be at the meeting because he didn't want another mess up with Medad. The CIA had a Station Chief in Jerusalem, but she had not been used to liaise with Medad because, for some reason unknown to Chuck, they had used 'Larry'. However, it had been decided to begin to use proper channels and so yet another person was going to have to strike up a relationship with Medad. Unfortunately for her, Medad had 'burned' his burner phone and was uncontactable through that means.

Chuck was angry. He expressed his exasperation in no uncertain terms with the usual American anglo-saxonisms. He was reminded that he was a guest at Langley and invited as a courtesy. He reminded them that it was he who 'recruited' Medad, and that since he had handed responsibility over to them, it has been a complete ***k up from start to finish. The point was conceded and shortly after the Deputy Director closed the meeting as far as Chuck's involvement was concerned.

As he left the room, the others stayed. The Under Secretary for Middle Eastern Affairs at the State Department had purposely neglected to disclose that he possessed Medad's personal mobile number, so contact for him was possible in theory. But Chuck suspected that he was persona non grata as far as the Israeli was concerned and probably with all at the CIA. We are really good at mucking things up, he thought.

Medad's days had become somewhat boring. The routine of a civil servant was dull when there was no specific objective. He was depressed and even more so as he saw the direction that the electioneering was going. Another day had been completed and he was wearily climbing the stairs to their first floor apartment, when his neighbour heard him unlocking his door and came out on the landing. They had exchanged pleasantries before, but didn't really know each other. She seemed agitated.

"It was the police or security of some sort. They came up the stairs, banged on the door and, as your wife opened it, they grabbed her and dragged her down the stairs and into a waiting car."

Medad couldn't believe what he was hearing. His neighbour went on, "Oh, she didn't go without a struggle. No. Kicking and screaming she was, struggling to free herself and shouting abuse. She has quite a vocabulary, doesn't she?"

Medad stood for a moment, open mouthed. My God! Police! Mossad! The documents, the video! They've discovered everything. He was ashamed to admit later that his first thought was, me next. He quickly got a grip, thanked his neighbour and went into the apartment. Who had done it? What could he do? Who could he speak to? He was walking up and down the apartment his thoughts completely jumbled up. He needed a drink. He poured himself a large arak. Originally from Lebanon, it's made by distilling grapes into alcohol to which anise is then added. Medad mixed his with lemonade.

He knew he had destroyed all his electronic devices but he didn't know for sure if Shana had. He rushed into the bedroom and saw her new phone and new laptop, so assumed she had. Then he remembered the stuff he had deposited in the safety deposit box. Was that the source of the leak and the kidnapping? Unlikely, he thought. He sat down, calming himself and trying to think it all through. Any normal person would notify the police if such a thing had happened so he did.

He left the apartment and made his way to Sur Bahir where there was a newly opened Israeli police station. He didn't know where else to go. They seemed uninterested – just another domestic with the lady deciding she'd had enough. More paperwork! He couldn't tell them any of the details his neighbour had given him, and feigned ignorance about why she might have disappeared. Predictably, they advised that he go home and in a day or two she might return.

He should have called Dan to warn him, but something held him back. He would wait until morning. What else could he do? It was an uncomfortable night, tossing and turning, dreaming that Mossad had found all the evidence and both were going to gaol. Next morning, he was in no fit state to go into the office so he called in sick. He stayed in the apartment and waited and waited. No Shana. By lunchtime, he was getting quite paranoid when he thought of Chuck. He decided to text a simple 'hello' message via WhatsApp. If he got a reply, he planned to outline the situation and challenge the Americans to do something. He knew Chuck was an early riser and would be up, but probably not left for the office yet.

Sure enough his phone pinged within a couple of minutes. A WhatsApp call was coming through. Chuck listened, calmed Medad and said he would investigate and get back to him. In the meantime, he should go about his normal routine. Easier said than done. His journey to work the following morning time was circuitous and took twice as long as he tried to determine if he was being followed. He wasn't, at least he didn't think so.

This was a dilemma for Chuck. If he or even Langley contacted Mossad, they would have to reveal their 'off the books' association with an Israeli government contact without their knowledge. That could become more problematic if Mossad in turn talked to any friends at Langley who wanted to embarrass him in particular and the State Department in general. The whole Medad relationship would be exposed with trouble for him and a devastating result for the young Israeli.

So Chuck decided not to involve the CIA or Mossad directly, but instead contact Hagai who had his own contacts. He advised Hagai that a fellow journalist, a lady, had been seized by security services of one hue or another. Could he sniff around? Of course, Hagai wanted more information, but Chuck resisted his pressure for the moment. He didn't want Hagai to know that he too had been by-passed.

Medad had no option but to trust Chuck. Chuck had no option but to trust Hagai.

Hani was also finding life a bit dull after the excitement of the talks. Ayshaa was pushing on with her work, but he was left looking after Bethlehem for Fatah, and sorting through the minutia of issues that was being brought to his attention. Important to those bringing their problems of course, but Hani was wanting a larger stage and Ramallah seemed a long, long way away. He hadn't been invited there for months.

Omari had mentioned to Hani his meeting with Medad, "I think he genuinely wants to keep in touch." But Hani was delaying. He didn't know why except that he felt becalmed and rudderless. He had no momentum, no strategy, no objectives, nothing to stir him.

Hani responded, "But there's nothing to talk about, is there?" Omari said, "Not yet, but he did ask an odd question about Palestinian elections, and when they might be."

"Yes, we'd all like to know that," Hani rejoined and there the conversation ended.

Ayshaa had noticed Hani's negativeness and wondered out loud whether he was depressed. That seemed to jerk him out of his 'pity party', so the following day he decided to make contact with Medad. What was there to lose? He asked Omari to arrange the meet at the WalledOff. As it was immediately adjacent to the Wall, it would certainly make an impact on Medad and shock him.

It did. Coming into Bethlehem was not an issue, even if the checkpoint soldier with the M16 did strongly advise him to turn back; it was dangerous for Israelis apparently. Medad stared at the Wall and the military guard towers. He had heard of it, seen it on the television, but never seen it from the Palestinian side. He looked at the graffiti and the mess. The UN had the responsibility for cleaning up the rubbish in the refugee camps, but whoever they contracted with were fleecing them, because it didn't look like any had been cleared up for years. Yes, he was shocked.

He was to meet Hani in the exhibition section. Deliberately staged by Hani to put Medad on the backfoot, it was working. The James Balfour exhibit at the entrance served to prepare guests for what they were about to view. They spotted one another, but both continued to walk around and exit into the piano bar. No handshakes, but Hani did offer to order a drink and both settled on tea. The conversation was a little stilted until Medad disclosed hesitantly that his partner, Shana, had been picked up by the Israeli security services and it had been three days since it happened and he still had no news of her. Hani was immediately contrite, and began to realise what risks Medad and his boss had been taking. But there was nothing he could do, except express his concern and his hope for her safety. Medad didn't mention the Americans, but did offer the opinion that once Israeli elections were over, maybe somebody else would put their head above the parapet and talks would start again.

56

MEANWHILE, LIFE IN the West Bank went on… and on. Ayshaa gave birth to a little boy, much to Hani's delight. He decided it was time to try and mend bridges with Ayshaa although he had no idea how to do this, or certainty it would be successful. What he did know was that with this birth the next generation of Palestinians would probably continue to live just as his parents and grandparents had – under Occupation. Hani knew he had failed and he felt bad about it but he continued to gratefully receive Fatah's money and tried to content himself with his responsibilities in Bethlehem. He had given up on Ramallah where, it seemed, everything had moved on. New people, new policies, and not to his taste.

Ayshaa was relatively content and her BWP team was functioning well. Rabia, true to her word, had put together a little presentation showing other websites which carried advertising. "Apparently, it's quite easy to monitor the traffic on your site, see what products different types of people are interested in and if traffic reaches a certain consistent level, advertisers will want space."

"But how do you find advertisers?" It was Ethar trying to bring Rabia down to earth. She was a practical person and found Rabia's visionary approach difficult. She was going to play devil's advocate.

"An agency does this. They do take a cut, but it would still be an income stream for us." Ayshaa didn't want Ethar and Rabia to keep crossing swords so she asked Rabia, "Do you have some agencies in mind?"

Rabia produced a list four, two based in Jerusalem and two based in Ramallah. "All are willing to have a conversation with us, although the Jerusalem ones would have to meet with us in Bethlehem unless there is someone who has a permit to get through."

Hagai was singularly unsuccessful in tracking down Shana for Chuck. Then about a week after she had been taken, she re-appeared late at night. Medad heard a knock on the apartment door and there was a teary reunion on the doorstep. He held her close and they stayed that way for some minutes just feeling each other's familiar presence not speaking. Then as Shana's knees began to buckle, Medad drew her in and helped her to the sofa. He didn't want to pound her with lots of questions, desperate as he was to understand what had happened. Shana tried to talk, but wasn't making much sense after what had been a shocking and traumatic experience. She was certainly frightened by what had been said and what her captors, whoever they were, had threatened. Medad lifted her off the sofa and carried her to her bed where she immediately fell asleep. However, Medad who lay beside her didn't sleep at all, asking himself the questions only his wife had the answers to. About three o'clock in the morning, Shana began to toss and turn muttering, "No, no, please don't." Medad put his hand across her back and tried to comfort her as best he could whispering that she was safe now.

It was nine o'clock when she woke up. Medad was already up and, over a drink in bed, she told her story at least as much as she knew. She didn't know who had taken her but they, whoever they were, seemed angry about her article about the ultra orthodox. They accused her of perpetrating conspiracy theories and of being anti-Semitic. Medad felt a swell of anger rising in him but for her sake, kept it under control. Then he asked to main question he had been wanting for ask ever since she got back.

"Was there any mention of the American documents?" Shana shook her head. "That's what I thought too, but no."

Neither of them could really understand it, but were mighty relieved that it was over. The rest of the day was spent in the apartment, Shana sleeping on and off with Medad looking after her. The office could wait.

Later that afternoon when Shana was well enough, they debated between each other whether to accept the invitation to the American embassy. Shana was a little more positive than Medad who was really fed up with the whole business. On balance they decided not to take up the invitation. Unsurprisingly, their relationship with Chuck and the US spying machine quickly died. Medad wouldn't take Chuck's calls and eventually he stopped calling. Part of Medad was a little regretful but both he and Shana wanted to draw a line under the past and start over. It wasn't that they had changed their beliefs about peace with the Palestinians, but that it now had to be someone else. They had done their bit and had come perilously close to disaster. They now had a life to live.

Omari, on the other hand, was anxious that the relationships that had been birthed continued so that when another chance came it would have the best chance of success. He met with Hani and tried to facilitate another meeting between him and Medad, but both declined. Omari understood the responses but was saddened. It was almost as if the status quo was destined to go on and on; at least it felt like that to him. The machinery of Palestinian-Israeli politics seemed to eat up a lot of good people, leaving only those who were self interested to continue to live well. The vast majority of his people continued to live as they had done for seventy years. Those who had experienced the days of 1948/49 were now no longer alive and even of 1967 were few and elderly. For the rest, this was it. Life. How long could it go on for? Omari didn't know. Perhaps forever.

So many people had fingers in the Palestinian pie; the United States blundering about without any real objective that didn't include the next Presidential election or oil; Iran gradually increasing its regional influence through Hezbollah, Islamic Jihad and Hamas and certainly more powerful now Syria and Iraq were weak; other Arab states with their own problems and some beginning to make deals with Israel which, the Palestinians claimed, stabbed them in the back.

Omari knew that the West Bank had many intelligent and well educated community leaders who continued to proclaim hope when those looking in from the outside could see very little hope. Up to now he had continued to hope that the arts, sport, education, mediation would keep a lid on the frustration of the growing young population, and maybe do more than that. Now, he wasn't so sure. Ayshaa and her BWP certainly hoped so. Regardless of the political situation, the women who attended BWP classes were benefiting and it was the women who had the opportunity of influencing the younger generation, at least up to the age of eight or nine. After that, well the street took over.

Omari recalled the 'starfish on the beach' story. Maybe that was the way forward. This apocryphal story, told in many different ways, was of a young boy walking on a beach after a storm which had stranded hundreds of star-fish. He was throwing some of them back into the sea when an older man had come up to him, commenting that there were hundreds of starfish and the youngster wasn't making much of a difference. As the boy threw the next one into the sea, he retorted that he had made a real difference to that one.

Maybe it was at the micro level rather than the macro level that change was going to come. The macro scene, after all, had produced yet another failure, to add to all those past failures. Maybe Palestinian politicians and officials might begin to target finance to community organisations like BWP, rather than starting more prestige construction projects. In any event, Ayshaa would continue to focus on her micro projects with as much funding as she could lay her hands on, from anyone who would listen and Omari would continue growing his charity.

Maybe Ramallah would eject unscrupulous and corrupt officials including politicians, and allow honest, upright leaders to represent their community and work with Israel. Maybe they would stop the in-fighting with each other and, with Hamas, and present a united front to the world. He knew that Hani, like his wife, would not give up planning how to achieve those goals both by example and by argument. But now...

... now Omari didn't know what the future held.

Natan was cock a hoop at what Hamas had done. He was at another meeting of the twelve. "We couldn't have organised it better ourselves. Brilliant."

Shai concurred. "Not only do we not have to give any concessions to the Palestinians, but everyone's attention is now on security and a government sympathetic to our views may even get an outright majority."

There was a murmur of assent around the table, not the clapping of hands and brash congratulatory reactions of Americans. The meeting went on to discuss plans that had been previously been voiced but put on hold when the talks had been mooted.

As was their practice, the group dispersed separately over a period of about an hour, the last to leave were the two old friends, the originators of the group, Natan and Shai, the latter being the General's personal aide. They sat down together for a separate meeting before leaving. Natan was clearly upset and had decided that Shai was the only one he could trust.

"One of the others must have arranged for that photograph to be taken and until we find out who, I will not be able to trust any of them." He was walking up and down the room expressing his displeasure, while Shai sat silently, thinking quickly.

He thoughtfully suggested, "Surely there must be another explanation. All of them were carefully recruited and screened by both of us."

Nevertheless Natan wouldn't shift. "We need a better plan to ensure what we want, and I think I know just what to do."

And with that he left the building leaving Shai as the last one to leave. He left it for ten minutes then went home himself ruminating on what his friend had said. He was beginning to feel quite uneasy. Natan had a lot of power which he could wield with or without the Minister's knowledge and, as he had said before to the twelve, no point in having power if you don't use it. He intended to.

Shai spent much of the rest of the evening speculating on what Natan might do, what his ambitions might be and who might be in the firing line. For all his words when everyone else had left, it had not gone unnoticed to Shai that Natan had not revealed any of his thoughts to him. "Perhaps I'm in the firing line," he said to himself, "and his little act at the end of the meeting was intended to put me on notice." Shai finally decided that he was now at risk and would call Larry. He had no idea that Larry was also the go-between for Medad. All he knew was that this was the way to get the attention of the Americans, which he certainly got.

There was a considerable amount of to-ing and fro-ing between two of the pillars of the Washington establishment. Larry had duly called his CIA contact who then passed it up the line for a decision, which was a call to Chuck's boss at the State Department. The decision was finally taken with some reluctance from the State Department, to dispatch Chuck although they had previously decided that future liaison should be undertaken locally, but the CIA prevailed mostly because Chuck had the background and the personal contact. However, he was ordered by his boss to meet first with the

Ambassador and a few selected attachés to bring them up to speed, but not to meet with Larry.

Chuck was happy to go, especially as it gave him a second opportunity to mend fences with Medad. Gloria was not so happy. "Not again!" was her response. Departure from Dulles airport was that evening so that he could arrive the next day reasonably refreshed. The rest of that day in Jerusalem was taken up with the requisite Embassy briefings.

It was just a day later that Medad heard a soft buzzing noise as he sat in his office doing nothing in particular, just going over and over again the events of the last week in his mind. In his daze, he wished someone would answer their phone until he realised with a start that it was coming from his own jacket hung over the back of the chair. It was his own burner phone which, he was ashamed to say, he had never thrown away. He wasn't in any mood to answer it but, as it wasn't stopping, he fished it out.

He looked at the display and noted that it was not one of the limited numbers he had added to his contact list. He quickly debated whether to answer it or not, then decided to on a whim. In a very tired voice he asked who it was. It was Chuck. Before Medad could say anything, the voice said, "I have a name." For a millisecond it grabbed Medad's attention before he realised that Chuck was days too late.

"Don't they listen to the news," he said to himself. Before he could sarcastically answer the American, Chuck had said, "It's not all over." and the line then went dead.

Now he had Medad's attention. What on earth did he mean? Of course it was all over. Even if he knew who the name of the informer was, it was still all over. He quickly glanced around the office to check that no-one was paying him any attention. They weren't. He put on his coat and quietly exited the building to get some fresh air and think. Just as he went through the outer door, his phone pinged; that meant a text. He walked some way from the building and looked at the message. It was an invitation to meet. Evidently Chuck was in Jerusalem and thought that some sort of progress was still possible.

Medad had been extremely doubtful about any further meeting with Chuck, but he had decided he would meet the American this one time, even though he had determined with Shana that he wouldn't. Interesting, he thought to himself. Perhaps deep down I still want to believe progress is possible. This meeting wasn't to be at the new Jerusalem embassy as was the previous invitation, but for lunch at Café Café in Emek Refa'im St. He laughed sardonically as that was the exact place that Larry failed to show, but somehow managed to place a memory stick in his coat pocket. He wondered whether Chuck knew this. It was almost lunchtime, and Medad made his way to his unexpected lunch appointment.

Larry had been instructed to invite Shai to the Café Café the following day for lunch. Shai had duly arrived and waited for Larry, but it was Chuck who turned up recognising Shai from the video pictures and introduced himself. Medad arrived almost immediately and not surprised to find Chuck there but certainly taken aback to discover there was another lunch companion, a fellow Israeli, whose face was familiar.

Chuck quickly took charge of the situation and motioned them both to sit down and not react. "Let's order first." It didn't take long, for no-one was going to be fussy about their food. Chuck formally introduced each Israeli to the other and took a little while to explain his own lack of communication to Medad, giving each of the other men a chance to catch up with what Chuck was doing. It seemed that Shai was just as surprised to have another lunch companion as Medad. The food arrived as Chuck was finishing his apologies and explanations. The three men lapsed into silence as they ate their food and tried to grasp the significance of their meeting.

Just as they were finishing and about to start their conversation again, Chuck announced he had to go to the bathroom, leaving both Israelis together. They both followed him with their eyes as he disappeared down the stairs in the corner of the restaurant and then glanced at each other awkwardly.

Shai was first to speak. "Chuck says that you are trustworthy?" Medad, still a bit shaken, nodded. Shai explained, "I am the Name." Medad opened his mouth, but no words came out. "If my actions were widely known, I would lose my position and the opportunity to guide Israeli policy in the direction of peace."

Medad looked at Shai as a few of the jigsaw pieces began to fall into place. He quickly assured Shai that he had the same objectives, but sadly observing, "it was all too late."

"Perhaps not," said Shai.

57

RACHEL HAD STARTED her life in Gaza by wanting to right every wrong she saw, treading in the footsteps of many who had gone before. And there were a lot of wrongs in Gaza that had been there for a long time. At first she couldn't understand why her UNWRA colleagues turned a blind eye to so much of what she saw around her. There were so many people who needed help, so much deprivation, neglect and poverty. Yes the children seemed happy, but weren't children always happy? Surely it was the Mums and Dads who had to provide for their families who were the touchstone for judging a society. If they looked oppressed and downtrodden, something was surely wrong.

But Rachel saw something far worse; this hopelessness had become ingrained in the DNA of the people. It would take more than a mentoring programme and some food parcels to change. Rachel was not a psychologist or social scientist, but she was a human being and on that basis alone she was appalled.

This was apparently her major test and her superiors were watching to see her reactions to what she saw. If she could pass this one, she would survive in Gaza. If not, she would have to leave otherwise a breakdown wouldn't be far off. That was how it was, because there was no answer to what she saw, certainly not within the remit of the UNRWA. They did good work, but no more than a set of sticking plasters on some serious gaping wounds, and psychological wounds were far worse than physical ones that might take generations to heal, if ever.

It wasn't long before she recognised that her older and wiser colleagues weren't amoral or blind to what was around them; UNRWA wasn't deficient in some way. It had a non political mandate and hence couldn't make fundamental changes to Gaza. All they could do was to relieve some of the worst excesses of what existed. Her colleagues just tried to keep to their mandate and reduce their expectations of change to what they knew they could deliver. Unsatisfactory, but wise nonetheless.

Rachel had successfully gone through that process and now she could see newer colleagues going through the same turmoil, which seemed to affect women more than the men somehow. Perhaps it was the male gift for compartmentalisation, or perhaps they were happy just doing their job and didn't look beyond. She didn't know.

Sami didn't need to go through any process to understand Gaza. She knew it wasn't really normal, but it was natural. This was her life everyday. She had no ideas about trying to right every wrong, but she did want to tell the world what was going on, then it was up to the world. Rachel was trying to encourage her on the one hand, but keep a professional distance on the other not always successfully. She had to admit, though, that Sami had chalked up some amazing accomplishments in a short time, although they hadn't amounted to any real change yet.

Sami's latest upload with its challenge to Hamas for another interview had its desired effect. Hamas had replied and another interview was on. As Rachel had suspected, Hamas didn't waste time. It was to be in two days time and Sami was invited to their compound to do the interview, "because all the necessary equipment is here." Rachel spotted the subtext. In their environment Sami, just a thirteen year old girl, would probably find it more intimidating than the hospital and thus not want to embarrass her host with questions that went too far. Sami insisted that Rachel come with her to video an unedited version of the interview. Hamas knew that they had both been to Jerusalem to meet with the Israeli President and they wanted to win the PR game that was being played, so no objection was made to her presence.

Because Rachel didn't want Hamas to know where they were living, (they could find out easily enough) it was arranged that they both be picked up outside the hospital. Rachel would be there to video the pick up on her phone and the entrance to the 'studio'. The latter didn't exactly go to plan because as soon as they arrived at the compound, security insisted the phone be confiscated, a problem that Rachel had foreseen. She had borrowed Joe's phone which she still hoped to use unobserved. It fitted neatly into one of the chest pockets of a jacket she had brought with her from the UK. She made a hole in the pocket just where the camera lens was and hoped the bulge didn't show too much.

Whilst all this was going on at the Hamas compound, there was a top level meeting at UNRWA. Rachel's immediate boss had been very forgiving of her taking time off to help Sami but the Director, who didn't know either girl very well, was becoming very concerned that his organisation could be targeted by Hamas if the relationship with Sami went badly and Rachel was known to be their employee. Up to this point he had not reported the situation to his superiors at the UN, but he decided that he needed to do it before things went too far and, in his opinion, it was just about to.

He made it clear that this interview, once loaded up on YouTube, would be accessed by the world: United Nations, governments in Israel, Europe, the US and the Middle East, not to mention regional NGOs, secret service agencies and the like, all wanting to see what nuances they could deduce from what Hamas said. This was going to be a make or break for Sami and Rachel and he was not going to have the paramount work of his agency in Gaza put in jeopardy by anyone.

Meanwhile Rachel and Sami had arrived at the 'studio'. Although they were not technical experts, the equipment looked new and impressive which helped to partially explain how good the editing had been of the original video.

"They must also have some good technicians," whispered Rachel. In the middle of the room were two chairs with microphones and just three static cameras to take different angles.

"And doesn't look like they want many people in the room." responded Sami. As they were still on their own, Rachel found an inconspicuous place at the back of the room so she could surreptitiously tested out the zoom on Joe's mobile whilst Sami got herself settled. The teenager got out her folder of questions which they had painstakingly put together, and sat down on the chair with its back to Rachel hoping that the Leader would take the chair facing Rachel's camera.

They were kept waiting for about ten minutes before the Leader came in with two security men. With profuse but rather insincere apologies, he sat in the vacant chair, indicated that the cameras could be switched on and invited Sami to ask away. She did the introduction as per their script and asked the few easy questions they had planned to settle him down. The questions and follow-ups gradually got tougher but he maintained his composure well, deflected where he wanted to and answered straight where it was easy to do so. He painted a rosy picture of the future of Gaza without the Israeli block-ade, placed the blame for all the ills of their society at the Israeli's door, was scathing about Fatah, even more deprecating about the US ... and on and on it went.

It all lasted about an hour and Rachel was fearing that the memory on Joe's phone was going to be found wanting if it went on much longer. But Sami was looking tired and although the Leader looked as if he could go on forever, he was gracious enough to see how tired the teenager was. His last comment was to congratulate her on what she had achieved and he looked forward to following her blog and YouTube channel closely. Subtext again – don't upload stuff that criticises me. As Sami and Rachel were packing up, Khalid came into the room and had a hurried conversation with the Leader even though Sami was not more than three feet away and both quickly departed.

"He's a real smoothie," said Rachel of the Leader once they were back outside the hospital and clear of listening ears. After explaining to Sami what a 'real smoothie' was, they both agreed that 'smoothies' could also be quite dangerous and never to be underestimated. Back at Rachel's place they viewed the video several times after some rest and food. Although it was tantalising to do a bit of editing, they decided not to in line with their promise. They would wait for Hamas to put their version out first. If they had edited it in their favour, Rachel said she would immediately put out the unedited version. Privately, she hoped they would.

There was bad news on Rachel's desk when she went into work the follow-ing day. It was a written note from her immediate superior asking for a formal meeting about her on-going work with Sami. Rachel had been fearing the consequences of asking whether it was possible to put Sami on the payroll to ensure her security. She was now kicking herself for flagging up what she was doing outside UNRWA hours but there was no regretting it, her view being that as long as it was outside working hours, what she did in her spare time was her own business. The boss was located in another part of the building and following a timid knock on the closed door she entered. She anticipated a difficult conversation, and it was. Her boss was sympathetic but explained how the Director was looking at the situation.

"I think," she said, "that if you were in his shoes, you might do the same thing." Rachel's argument about out of hours activities was completely washed away by her boss.

"Hamas don't bother with niceties like that. As far as they are concerned you're UNRWA and whatever you do will have an impact on all of us. You're not back in the UK. Normal rules don't apply in Gaza!"

She had forty-eight hours to either desist from associating with Sami or resign.

58

WITH NOT MUCH else to do, Hani was constantly looking at his phone desperately wanting it to ring, but it stayed annoying silent. Nothing from Ramallah,
nothing from Omari and nothing from Medad, although he was not really expecting anything from the Israeli. He thought Jamal might have called or even
emailed but no, and he couldn't find it in himself to initiate anything because
he could think of nothing to say.

It was one morning about ten o'clock when his phone did unexpectedly
ring. He saw it was Medad and wasted no time in picking up to receive a curt
request to meet him at the WalledOff, with Omari if he wanted, that afternoon at four o'clock. After just a moments hesitation, Hani rang his friend
who agreed to drop everything and be there. He thought about a pre meeting
with Omari but decided that there was nothing to say until they had heard
from the Israeli. Maybe a post meeting would be better.

There was no doubt, Hani felt a buzz of excitement run through his body.
When he had got up this morning he had felt listless, depressed and of little
value to anyone. Now something had changed, he was sure of it. The last
time he and Medad had met it was perfunctory and stilted. The man wouldn't
phone unless something was in the air, but he couldn't imagine what. There
were many hours to go before the meet up and Hani's mind was working
overtime with invented scenarios. He tried to steady himself without much
success, after all this is what he did. This was his real value.

Ayshaa was out for the day with Lara at some BWP event. He didn't even
think about ringing her with the news. This was his appointment – she was
busy with hers. Maybe afterwards he would talk to her depending on what
Medad had to say. He left early and arrived at the WalledOff early, as had Omari, their outward calm belying some inward excitement. They made straight
for the piano room and Omari bought the teas. Then Medad was slightly early
as well. Clearly he was as impatient as they were to discuss the news.

Medad reminded them, "Do you remember how we had received a document indicating an Iranian mole within the PA?"

They nodded. He went on to explain that in addition to that document, another had been received showing them the splits that they had on their own side. Hani and Omari exchanged glances.

Medad explained, "This was for our side alone to sort out and we had a strategy in place before Hamas fired their rockets." Medad saw eyebrows being raised on the other side.

He continued, "We had a video of two of our own senior people and their aides planning to sabotage the talks. So we knew who they were but we didn't know who the mole was, who had secretly planted the camera that captured the details of the meeting. Of course, as things turned out we couldn't use it."

Hani and Omari looked at the young Israeli enquiringly, Omari asking, "So why does it matter now?"

They waited for Medad to explain himself. The young Israeli was a little vague on some detail and sparse as to any names and many of the facts, but the Palestinians got the gist. An unknown influential group had been working together to plan the destabilisation of the talks and, although that had happened thanks to Hamas, weren't content to leave it at that. Medad outlined their objective: to rid the land of Palestinians and have a pure Jewish land only for Jewish people. A hard line right wing government was required to deliver that and it was their belief that government progress to date had been slow and ill thought out.

Hani and Omari, who were very well aware that there were such groups, were dubious as to the danger. They didn't think these people represented the whole Israeli population and therefore wouldn't get much traction for such policies. Medad held up his hand.

"What's new, is that this group has splintered and that, following the leaking of the video, the leader now doesn't trust any of the other members of the group." Medad looked upset, "I'm afraid he is going it alone and, believe me, he is very well connected with considerable authority in the security field."

He paused before delivering a final point. "He was on our delegation at the talks and knows the two men who were clearly masterminding those talks from your side."

*

Natan had gone home after the meeting in a cold and calculating mood. Gone was the angry rage, now it was all about rational planning and execution. As he approached his house, he could hear his Canaan dog, Babka, barking. This was unusual and he was on his guard. He went carefully into the house to be almost bowled over by the affectionate dog, full of energy. A note on the table explained that his dog walker had been called away and couldn't take Babka for his afternoon walk. He was relieved and annoyed at the same time. No message, no call from her and whilst he was normally home at six o'clock ish now it was late. The dog was desperate.

So out into the darkness they both went, Natan not taking much notice of the dog, more working up some ideas which others might implement. No, he was not going to get his hands dirty. He recalled there used to be someone in the Civil Administration who would, but he couldn't recall his name for the moment. His mind switched and started to wander over the meeting he had just been in. He reviewed every man in turn trying to work out whether any had the motivation and means to secretly film the session with the General. They all knew the meeting had been set up, so it could be any one of them or possibly any other staffer in the General's office. He gave up deciding to ask Shai to screen again each person who may have had access to details of the meeting. But it could wait until the current plan had been executed, because he wasn't going to share his plans or meetings with anyone now. He just needed to finalise what he was going to do.

The Civil Administration, established in 1981, was the part of government that was in charge of the West Bank which comprised not only of Palestinian villages and towns but also the 'illegal' Jewish settlements. The CA sought to protect the Jews and confine the Palestinians on the West Bank, and they had the authority to do this because, unknown to many, this organisation was subordinate to a larger entity known as Coordinator of Government Activities in the Territories (COGAT) which itself was a unit in the Ministry of Defence. So while formally separate, the Civil Administration was actually subordinate to the Israeli military and Shin Bet, the Israeli Security Agency.

East Jerusalem, although occupied at the same time as the rest of the West

Bank in1967, was different. It was run by the Israeli Mayor of Jerusalem but the Municipality and the Civil Administration cooperated closely. East Jerusalem used to have its own Palestinian City Council with Ruhi al-Khatib as its Mayor but that was hurriedly ended by the then Deputy Military Governor, Ya'akov Salman, who sought to depose the Palestinian Council. He did this simply by summoning Khatib and four other members of the Council to the Gloria Hotel restaurant, and reading out a short statement in Hebrew to them.

"In the name of the Israeli Defence Forces, I respectfully inform Mr Ruhi al-Khatib and members of the Jerusalem City Council that the Council is hereby dissolved."

Ruhi al-Khatib looked at his four colleagues and began to protest. "You have no authority. We are representatives of the people."

Salman replied, "You are no longer."

"This is outrageous. I demand the order in writing." An Arabic translation was written out on a napkin then and there in the restaurant and thrown across the table at them. There was nothing they could do. It was a fait accompli.

Both authorities, the Civil Administration and the Jerusalem Municipality began to integrate their general planning and building policies aimed at preventing Palestinian development and at the same time dispossessing them of their land. So while the planning and building laws benefited Jewish communities, they served the exact opposite purpose when applied to Palestinian communities in the West Bank. There, Israel exploited the law to prevent development, thwart planning and carry out demolitions. This was part of a broader political agenda to maximize the use of West Bank resources for Israeli needs, while minimizing the land reserves available to Palestinians.

Natan had worked for the Civil Administration early on in his career and knew that security issues were a top priority for them so that these planning objectives could be achieved. The civil servants, of which he was one back in the day, only had to make an order and the IDF would be there to carry it out. His immediate task, therefore, was to find out if any of his former colleagues were still employed at the CA and if they were, hopefully, they would now be in senior positions. He ruminated on how to do this without raising any red flags. True his current position afforded him great influence and he was certain if he approached formally he could make something happen, but he wanted to stay in the shadows if at all possible.

He started to look through his office filing system for documents which came from the CA to ascertain whether any names looked familiar. He was interrupted several times with current business in the Defence Ministry, but as soon as that was sorted, he went back to work on the files. After a couple of hours, he was beginning to tire and wondered whether there was anyone left from his era when he suddenly came across a name he recognised. Ares Heiman. Yes, there it was. He remembered him, partial to a few Fullers IPA pints of an evening. Fullers brewed their beer in Chiswick, London and exported to Israel. What was important to Ares was that it was certified as kosher.

Natan hadn't picked that up before, but it told him that Ares had a religious streak in him and thus, might have similar views to his own regarding the Palestinians. Hopefully, he was the man. Firstly a dummy official meeting was set up for Natan to visit the CA, so while he was there he would seek out or 'bump into' Ares. Over a couple of beers after work, Natan would try and establish whether Ares would be able and willing to cooperate.

The official meeting was set up for three o'clock in two days time, rather short notice for the CA but Natan was conscious that days were passing and he was making slow progress. After his diaried appointment had finished, he asked where Ares Heiman worked, as he was an old friend. He was directed to another building and there he was. Already with a coat on ready to depart for the day. They greeted each other professionally until Natan offered to take Ares for a drink and natter about old times. That did the trick; barriers came down and off they went, Ares explaining that he knew a great place which served excellent beer.

The conversation quickly confirmed Natan's hopes and, after a few beers, Ares was unashamedly pronouncing his right wing views on the Palestinian problem to anyone who would listen. Natan had no problem extracting from Ares a commitment to look into something for him, but his loose tongue after a few beers caused him some concern.

59

KHALID HAD NO idea that certain Israeli and Palestinian officials were shortly going to be making enquiries that might affect him, or that one Israeli official would be meeting with a senior military commander with some responsibility for Gaza. He didn't know either of them, neither did he care; they were irrelevant to him. He was only concerned with one thing and that was pleasing his boss by carrying out tasks given to him because that was the source of both his money and his future. The decision-making processes within Hamas were pretty simple. It wasn't a large organisation with lots of staffers like Fatah on the West Bank. From Hamas' perspective, Fatah took money from anyone, spending it on themselves trying to look like a real government. As far as they were concerned, Fatah were collaborators looking to ingratiate themselves with Israel, the US and with anyone else who would give them more money.

Khalid's life in Gaza was certainly more privileged than most, but that could always change and he was anxious to get back from his Beirut trip. Nothing lasted forever; you could be in favour one minute and out the next. Because there was no trust between him and the Iranian, Beirut had become a place of vulnerability and that ensured a swift exit. He picked up the car outside the hotel and invited the driver to get to the plane as fast as he could. As the driver swerved through the outer suburbs at speed, he began to puzzle over the message he had been given. No doubt it would mean more to others for it meant nothing to him.

The journey back to Gaza was just as tortuous as the first leg. He got back to near the Egyptian border crossing without any hitch but his guide to the tunnel entrance on the Egyptian side didn't show. He cursed the Egyptian repeatedly as he scoured the area on his own where he thought the tunnel was located. He couldn't afford to wait, but on the other hand, he couldn't afford to be found just wandering in desert scrub. Someone would certainly spot him and it would arouse their suspicions. The Egyptian military were just as strict as the Israelis when it came to who they let in and out of the Strip.

After a couple of hours his guide turned up with abject apologies for his belated arrival, which Khalid dismissed angrily. In fact, there was a moment when the Palestinian grabbed the guide by the shoulders and was on the point of smacking him hard, but just managed to control himself remembering he still needed the Egyptian to show him the entrance to the tunnel. The man wasted no time in doing so and the Palestinian began clambering through the tunnel. Once again he vowed to himself, without any real optimism, that this would be the last time. He hated it. The last part of the tunnel into Gaza was uphill and, although he thought he was quite fit, he was beginning to breathe the stale air heavily.

It had been originally excavated from the Gaza side in an undulating landscape which was a mix of rock and sandy soil. The place had clearly been chosen carefully for it started in a strip of soil between two areas of rock. Those who excavated the tunnel had an easy job at the outset allowing them to penetrate inside the hill some twenty yards before rock was reached. Thus the chipping away of the rock would have not have been heard outside, even though it was only half a mile or so from the road which went to the Rafah crossing.

Khalid had no idea who had done it nor how it had been done without various authorities discovering it, but he didn't care. He was just coming to the exit point when he paused to breathe in some fresh air and to let his eyes adjust to bright daylight outside. It also gave him time to survey the immediate area and assess any danger. As he stood motionless, he could hear his heart pumping vigorously and made a mental note to achieve a better level of fitness before the next time for, despite his vow, he knew this was the only way in and out of Gaza for him.

He could faintly hear the traffic on the road approaching the crossing as he tentatively climbed out and dusted himself off. He trusted there would be a car waiting for him in the pre-arranged spot on the road and sincerely hoped there was no mix up on this side. He had to move away from the tunnel entrance immediately for if he was spotted it might have been discovered, and he couldn't be responsible for that. He would be toast. Much as he hated it, Hamas depended on it. So he zig-zagged his way from the tunnel entrance to the rendezvous site.

No mix up. Relieved, he quickly jumped in and the car headed away from the crossing back towards Gaza City and, for the first time for a while, he allowed himself to relax. As the car made its way through The Strip and he used the time to rehearse for the debriefing and the questions that would certainly follow. When they eventually arrived at the outskirts of the city in the late afternoon, speed slowed considerably. There were people everywhere, from toddlers and teenagers to old men and women, all out on the streets living life, not to mention horse and donkey carts moving at a pedestrian pace.

Eventually the car passed through at the heavily guarded buildings that Hamas used and they were waiting for him. Khalid had already sensed they would be disappointed that he had not brought back the whole 'Plan', so at the start of the meeting he defended himself.

"I have to admit my own disappointment at what the Iranian had to tell me." He decided not to tell of the disrespect he had received. He explained to me that, "we will only be given each step one at a time." There were murmurs of dissent round the table.

"The Iranian is treating us like children," one muttered. Another said, "Who does he think he is?" The one at the head of the table said nothing except, "What is this first step?"

Everyone stopped their antagonistic whispering. Khalid took a deep breath, "we need to make contact with an Imam in Jenin." He paused.

"That's it?"

"That's it."

The silence in the meeting room was palpable, then there was uproar. When it was clear the Leader was not joining in, the silence returned and the meeting dismissed. Khalid alone remained. The Leader moved slowly up and down the room digesting the news and thinking. After a few minutes, he turned to Khalid expressing his thanks and directing him to Jenin. Khalid was not feeling as if he wanted to make another secretive journey, especially to the West Bank. Nevertheless, his was not to question orders.

He made his move to leave the room when the Leader turned to him and said, "From now on, it's just between us. Understand?"

Khalid nodded his head. He was given no timetable but it went without saying that he should depart as soon as possible and that meant within the next day or so. It was now well into the evening, so he went home to his family.

He, his wife and their three children lived in a nice neighbourhood, as far as nice neighbourhoods went in Gaza. His family and neighbours knew that the big man was a government official, but in what capacity no-one knew or dared to ask. He greeted his wife, but there was no explanation about where he'd been or why, and she knew better than to ask. A standard conversation started every time he returned from a trip.

"Where are the girls?"

"Somewhere outside playing. They'll be in soon."

His wife brought him some food and he lowered himself into his chair, ate it and nodded off to sleep again. As soon as the children came in, they were cautioned to be quiet which they were, and were sent to bed. His wife also went to their bedroom later, whilst Khalid continued to snore in his sleep in the living room.

He was obviously used to sleeping on the sofa for he woke up early, quite refreshed, though not looking forward to the trip to Jenin which meant another Egyptian crossing. He had determined that he needed a day off so he had made arrangements to make the journey to the West Bank on the following day. The children were upstairs playing noisily – perhaps that was what woke him up – so he washed, dressed and was out of the house before either his wife woke up or the children came downstairs.

The blue sky and warm sun would have been welcoming if he had not been in Gaza, yet he couldn't complain. As long as he did what he was told, he figured he was safe. But there were always younger men coming up fast as he had done those years before. Normally as physique faded, experience and intelligence took over. Well, he had the experience, but he was never sure that it was enough, for he knew he wasn't the sharpest tool in the box. However, the boss trusted him so at the moment he could relax.

He headed down towards the centre of the city to a little backwater called Al Eilah St. Halfway down the street he disappeared into a doorway and up the stairs to the top room. Here was his second family; his mistress and her young son, now a toddler. He embraced Jodell and turned his attention to Achim his son. A son was very important to Khalid, it somehow reinforced his masculinity. That did not mean to say he didn't care for his daughters, he did, but… they were different.

Khalid couldn't risk going out with them because he didn't want to disgrace his wife, so he stayed there all morning talking and playing with Achim. Maybe he would spend the night there; he hadn't decided yet.

60

HANI AND OMARI left their meeting with Medad wondering what this new information might mean for them. Medad deliberately hadn't spelled out any implications for them. He had just given them the facts leaving the Palestinians to judge the situation for themselves. As they walked back through Bethlehem together, they floated to each other various scenarios that might occur but nothing really struck them as probable. All Hani could do was to brief his men to keep a look out for anything unusual around Bethlehem, but he couldn't elaborate much more to them. It sounded a little weak because it was; in Occupation-land there were unusual things happening all the time.

He emailed the information to Jamal as a matter of course but as he had been forced to move on, he suspected that he would just copy it to the Chief to cover his backside, but that was all. Hani reckoned he could then expect an email from the Chief of Security or the new Deputy (whoever he was) to do the same ass-covering exercise. That would put him alone in the firing line. Well, so be it, thought Hani. He'd had enough of Ramallah politics and didn't want to play the game anymore. As it happened, he was at the bottom of the food chain anyway with no-one else to take the blame. He couldn't exactly blame an Israeli informer, but it was not in his nature to pass blame or duck the consequences of his own actions.

Having done all that he could do, Hani headed home wondering how much to tell Ayshaa, if anything. He decided he would, just to see what her reaction was but he might preface that by asking her how BWP was going. A little peace-offering perhaps. When the children had gone to bed, he did so and they had the longest peaceful conversation they had had for a long time. No answers, and Ayshaa made it clear that one conversation did not make a marriage. Hani didn't answer and let her have the last word – not forgiven yet then. But he felt better and some weight was lifted off his shoulders. At least, he thought, she didn't throw it all back in my face. It's a start.

Omari, on the other hand, shared most of what he had heard with Lara on a confidential basis knowing she would respect that. He valued her insight and often she had 'left field' ideas that cut through his straight line, lawyer-type thinking.

The first thing she asked was, "Do the Israelis know about you and the role you played in the abortive talks."

He had to admit they did, "But only the good guys."

"But," she pressed him, "who is to say who are the 'good guys', who are the 'bad guys', and who are just Israelis."

Omari thought a bit harder. Lara continued in this vein by asking whether he knew if his 'good guys' had passed on his name to anyone else. Omari was now becoming a little concerned and admitted that he didn't know. Perhaps he had let the role of intermediary between both sides go to his head without taking suitable precautions. Her riposte was that he needed to find out.

Although Shai was glad to have met Medad, he had decided that this was as far as he was going to go with the Americans. He was concerned that he may have put himself and his family at risk and wanted out. It was Chuck received the message and passed it on to Larry who was tasked with 'running' Shai. He reported back to Washington including a warning about what Natan might do, also mentioning Shai's position and that he had passed that issue to Larry. The official job done, now for the personal job.

Chuck's concern now was Medad. Having discharged his immediate official responsibility, he wanted to follow up the lunch he had with Shai and Medad with a personal meeting with his friend if he could. He wondered about resurrecting the Embassy tour and meal with Shana, but decided perhaps there needed to be a further thawing between the men before such an invitation would be accepted.

He messaged Medad, hoping the meeting with Shai had been useful and inviting him to a follow-up lunch just for the two of them. Medad discussed with Shana whether to accept the overture from Chuck seeing that they had previously said to each other that they had wanted to draw a line under the past.

"The problem is," Medad rationalised, "the past is still with us and now, very much alive again." Shana agreed. "You should go."

So he decided to accept Chuck's invitation. The American booked the Philadelphia Restaurant in Al-Zahra St, just half a mile from the Old City. He had not been there before, but it sounded American. It happened to be Middle Eastern cuisine with excellent food, although the area in which it was situated was quite run down. After they had shaken hands and sat down, Chuck's small talk was about the drabness of the local area to which Medad replied that there were many different parts of East Jerusalem. He and Shana lived in a new apartment block only a mile or so away. Chuck refrained from making a political point about settlements in East Jerusalem.

He moved the conversation on to safer ground, about family, their US trip, future plans and non-controversial stuff to try and re-establish their relationship. But before they could order food, Medad's burner phone rang. That was unusual. Only a few people had the number and normally it would be a text. He quickly debated whether to answer it and as Chuck was looking at him quizzically, he decided to. It was Hani. He had just heard from Jamal that his East Jerusalem house where his family had lived for generations had been demolished that morning and his whole family were just sitting outside in the rubble, homeless. Jamal himself was not being let through the military checkpoint into East Jerusalem – something about his residency status not being in order. Hani hurriedly gave an address and cut the connection.

Medad quickly got up and motioned Chuck to follow him. They left the restaurant and set off at a quick pace, Medad explaining to Chuck what had happened and who Jamal was. Medad had no idea that Jamal had family in East Jerusalem, but understood the bureaucracy that Palestinians had to go through to keep their Jerusalem status. Twenty minutes later, they were standing on a corner opposite a demolished house, belongings scattered everywhere, the woman still crying and children wandering around looking bewildered. Twisted steel rods and concrete rocks were strewn everywhere. Kitchen appliances and children's toys were among their possessions, now scattered everywhere. It wasn't a pretty sight but someone had ordered it, and others had done it. Just obeying orders! All heavy machinery which had done the deed had gone as had the IDF security detail which had inevitably accompanied it.

Chuck looked on in horror. This was the first demolition he had witnessed in person. He had seen videos but they did not, could not, convey the raw emotion and brutality of it all. There was still the occasional noise of falling debris, the faint smell of gas and lots of dust. He was truly shocked, especially as Jamal was a senior official of the Palestinian Authority and the leader of the Palestinian delegation at the recent talks.

"This is no coincidence," muttered Medad and Chuck nodded his agreement. Chuck took a few pictures with his phone, but there was nothing else they could do so they quietly slipped away. Neither of them felt like lunch anymore so they both went their separate ways quite despondently.

Hani received a message from Medad saying what had happened, suspecting that it was Natan's work and advising that he should take some precautions himself. Hani already knew that Jamal was vulnerable because of his status in a way in which Hani was not. Nevertheless, Hani now knew for sure that he was on a list of some kind, possibly a hit list and he had to take that seriously. He messaged Omari with the news and suggested that he too, might need to take some further precautions. It was a troubling development because it seemed this man could reach anywhere he wanted, and Medad seemed to be sure that he had not yet finished.

Hani took Medad's warning to heart. He knew that part of the population of Israel wanted peace but not at any price, it had to be with security. But there was another part of the population that wanted all the land to themselves. He had seen with his own eyes that every time the status quo was threatened by the opportunity of peace, the security card was played. Hani could see plainly how it was not only in the interests of the Israeli right wing, but paradoxically Hamas and Iran, who also wanted the Israelis and the Palestinians to be at continual loggerheads.

Hani shared his thinking with Ayshaa. She knew that the people of the West Bank and in Gaza had no real power, influence or say in their future. They were at the mercy of Israeli policies since no international group shown any signs of doing anything to bring Israel to account. She also knew that well heeled Palestinian leaders were also quite happy for the status quo to continue and that the often quoted phrase 'our suffering is our strength' was only quoted by those who weren't suffering.

Well, she thought, maybe one day there would arise another generation in both of the two countries who would 'get it'. We didn't manage to do it for our children, but maybe our children will succeed for their children.

61

IT WASN'T A surprise to Ayshaa although a big shock for Hani. Ghalia was moving around their home one day admittedly quite slowly with a stick, and the next she had died. Ayshaa had gone in to her room when she hadn't come out for breakfast. She gently shook her and immediately realised she had passed away. She shouted to Hani who hadn't yet gone out. He rushed in, "No, no." He started to pump her chest with tears trickling down his face.

Ayshaa put her hand on his shoulder, "Hani, she's cold. She will have passed peacefully during the night."

She had never really recovered from an illness a few years previously, only in her early sixties, but not an untypical age of death for Palestinians. Hani was very upset, feeling guilty for not looking after his mother, but the funeral had to be within twenty four hours of the death and so arrangements were made. There was a particular ritual to be observed when a Muslim died. The body is washed to physically cleanse the deceased and then wrapped in a simple plain *kafan* to respect their dignity and privacy. Collective prayers for forgiveness of the dead person were offered. In the Sunni tradition, grief at the death of a beloved person and weeping for the dead was normal and acceptable, but loud wailing by the women frowned upon. The grave had to be perpendicular to the direction of Mecca and the body placed in the coffin so that the body lying on its right side facing the holy city.

Both Hani and Ayshaa wanted a quiet funeral without hordes of people joining in but this was not the Palestinian way. Ghalia was known as the wife of a previous Fatah leader and so the governing party was out in force, if only to show its subjects that it was still there. Young men waving flags, old women weeping, Israeli troops in the distance filming, just another funeral; but no trouble, no stone throwing and no tear gas this time. Hani's orders were obeyed for the most part. He was able to lay his mother to rest peacefully, trying as best he could to keep his head down to conceal his face from the cameras. The little family made their way back home for the three days of mourning. After that, life went on.

Practically, it had left a little more room for the family, until Rena his daughter was joined by a baby brother, who they named Sahail. This birth was a source of both joy and frustration for Ayshaa. It was the traditional Palestinian woman's role to be in the home, but Ayshaa already had an important life outside of the home. She had founded Bethlehem Women for Peace (BWP) and had been working with others on delivering programmes to empower Palestinian women, against the backdrop of major domestic violence in her community. It was a constant struggle to keep these two competing interests in balance, so much so that there was still a reservoir of resentment against her husband who, it seemed to her, could still go and do what he liked, when he liked, with whom he liked.

It was true that Hani was spending more time at home these days and Ayshaa had noticed but refused to acknowledge it to him. In her eyes, he was still making up for his past absences. As far as Hani was concerned, he would probably have preferred to have the excuse to go to Ramallah more often, but the administrative capital of the Palestinian Authority had not really settled down since the recriminations over the failed talks. Lots of people continually jockeying because a good position meant a good deal of money. Hani was not interested in getting his nose in the trough, just wanted to make progress with the Israelis for the benefit of his people and his children. Much as he wanted to keep out of Palestinian Authority politics, he had to partially play the game but regarded many of his fellow officials as corrupt, although that was a word never to be used.

His focus always reverted back to Bethlehem and relations with the Occupying Power. He continued to chair a meeting with a group of Fatah men in Bethlehem once a fortnight to review what the IDF were doing in their area. They had now developed a system for notifying each man where the meeting was to be held and they had experienced no further security leaks. In addition to the normal minutia of business that they tried to deal with, Hani had his men keep a watch for the Musta'ribeen who were back in the Bethlehem area.

Today though, he had received an urgent call from Talal, his new boss in Ramallah. Hani didn't know much about Talal, but he quickly responded in the affirmative, wanting to make a good impression. A 'company' car had been made available to him so no more sitting in the shop waiting for a lift. The old Toyota was hardly the Mercedes that used to pick him up, but at least it was exclusively his to use. Hani was quite relieved to be away from the family for a bit and have something else to think about, Ayshaa still distant and domestic life still fraught.

Ramallah was only eighteen or so miles from Bethlehem, but could take two or three hours. He had to stay within the West Bank, since the licence plates on his car were yellow and thus would not be allowed to go into Israel. He arrived just after midday to find Talal not in his office but out at lunch. Hani was a little annoyed, obviously the meeting was not as urgent as all that! He himself had not eaten but rather had gone straight to the office as soon as he had arrived. He decided to get a bite to eat as well and so made his way to Boaz for a lamb kebab with spicy *moutabel* (eggplant-based dip). Boaz, also the name of the owner, was located across the road from La Grotta, close to the Old City and down the hill from Al Manara. Hani was happy to sit at plastic tables and eat his kebab with hummus and Arabic salad. Posh restaurants weren't for him.

He got back to Talal's office at about two o'clock where the boss was waiting for him. It was the same office, but Hani noticed it had a brand new desk and chairs and the smell of a plush oriental carpet. Clearly no expense had been spared.

"There are rumours that Hamas is planning something." No pleasantries. No small talk. Hani said nothing but thought that this was hardly news.

"Something big and something in our direction." Talal, a tall lean man with a scraggy beard, leaned back in his chair, surveying his underling, and casually asked, "Have you, by any chance, kept in touch with any Israeli delegates you met during the aborted Palestinian-Israeli talks?"

"No, I haven't." Hani replied, wondering what this was all about.

"Could you get in touch?"

"Possibly, but not directly." Hani wanted more information. "Although there is an intermediary that might be able to help, if I knew what you wanted."

There was a pause in the conversation. Talal was clearly a man who didn't like giving much away so Hani completed the thinking for him. "So maybe the Israelis know what we don't know?"

"Exactly." Talal finished the meeting with, "See what you can do."

With that Hani was dismissed. He stared at Talal for a moment before slowly getting out of the chair and leaving the office, not a happy man. All that way for something that could have been done over the phone in two minutes. A weak man, he thought.

Just as he was leaving the building to return to Bethlehem, a thought occurred. His old boss, Jamal, was still around somewhere. He pulled out his phone and called him. If you have a moment? He did. They met back at Boaz for a coffee and after the preliminaries, the discussion centred on Talal.

Jamal snorted. "A jumped up little squirt, but his sponsor and protector is the Head of Security, so you'll have to play along."

The conversation then moved on to Hamas. Hani wondered, "What about this rumour that Hamas is planning something?"

Jamal confirmed that he had heard them, but no-one he had spoken to knew either where it had originated or what it pointed to. Hani was inclined to dismiss it as propaganda designed by Hamas to disrupt and cause confusion. Jamal turned the conversation back to Talal, and what he wanted of Hani. When he heard about the Israeli request, Jamal's jaw dropped a little.

"That sounds as if it came from the top. Somebody is clearly very worried, we don't wash our dirty linen with the Israelis."

They finished their coffee and Hani set off home now slightly more concerned than he had been.

62

MEDAD HAD FELT 'burnt' after the failed talks and, despite meetings with Chuck, Shai and Hani, his depression was not lifting. Even the demolition of Jamal's house had not changed his mood. He had lost his desire for the fight. People were going to do what they wanted and he couldn't stop it. What was the point? He talked long and hard with Shana, now a freelance journalist, about what he should do. As an ardent supporter of a peace process, he had done his best to see the Israeli-Palestinian talks succeed. But now? Now he felt that perhaps his time inside the government machine had come to an end. Maybe he could work with one of the Israeli peace organisations, of which there were many. There were a host of them, but B'Tselem was an organisation high on the consideration list.

Eventually, however, he decided to take Shana's advice and stay with the Israeli civil service until an alternative opened up. She was thinking that there might be another opportunity for peace one day, and someone needed to be there for that. Medad wasn't thinking any such thoughts but he did get a promotion now that Dan had moved on, reporting directly to the same Minister. It was a quick promotion over the heads of others who had served longer, but even that didn't serve to lift his gloom. Not much was happening in the office and, since Shana was freelance, they were both able to think about wedding plans and book some time off. Both of them wanted to settle down a little after the excitement and danger of the previous few months and this would be the perfect time.

The wedding ceremony had to be a religious affair, even though both of them were agnostic. The newly-weds thoroughly enjoyed the day although predictably Medad's father and brother had not. Both were of a Zionist persuasion and didn't approve either of Shana or her secular liberal parents. Medad's mother, however, was quietly delighted. The couple were regular visitors both to Tel Aviv, where Shana's parents lived and to the Gush Etzion region of southern Israel where Medad's parents lived, but always somehow managed to visit when his father and brother were away. Now they were settled in their East Jerusalem apartment and very happy.

Yes, married life was great. No children, but then Shana wasn't sure she wanted any, at least not yet. Medad would have quite liked to have children but recognised that their lives, their careers were also important. They were not the traditional Israeli family having lots of children to populate the Jewish state, but part of a new generation. Life at the moment was quite unhurried.

The last thing Medad was expecting as he walked home from another ordinary day at the office, was a WhatsApp message from Omari asking if Medad could come to the WalledOff. His first reaction was a rather annoyed, "What does he want?" But immediately he repented. Omari was a good man and it was he, Medad, who had been the last to make contact. At that time he was anxious to maintain some contact with Hani but time had passed and, well, things had moved on. As he thought about it a little more, he realised that it wouldn't be just a social meeting. Something must be up, so he agreed.

It had been Hani's initiative. After returning from Ramallah, he had immediately contacted Omari to discuss the situation and the task he had been given. The Palestinian lawyer was doubtful whether much would come of the meeting, but yes, he would set it up. He insisted that Hani had to be there but he was right about one thing; nothing much did come from the meeting. The men renewed their acquaintance, though the atmosphere was a little strained. Medad was a lot more circumspect than both Palestinian men had remembered. He knew nothing about any serious Hamas initiative, and couldn't promise anything.

On the way back to Jerusalem, however, Medad was thinking hard. He had been deliberately vague to Omari and Hani because he hadn't wanted to be drawn into some inter-Palestinian issue. But the more he thought about it, the more he realised that issues between Hamas and Fatah would inevitably have some impact on Israel. Yes, he would follow it up and push some doors. The question was, which ones to push without alerting those who would then squeeze him out?

His immediate thought was to contact his old boss. Whilst this was not an area that Dan was now responsible for, Medad recognised that he had many more contacts within the government machine that Medad had. This led on to another thought. He had kept himself to himself whilst he had been part of the civil service and he began to realise this had been a big mistake. Now he was not in a position to do much himself without calling in favours from others and he didn't want to be beholden to Dan forever. He made a mental note to put himself about a bit, especially in the defence, security and maybe intelligence areas.

Anyway, no alternative to contacting Dan now. He thought coffee or lunch would be better than a phone call. It was to be lunch, Dan never missing an opportunity to have lunch, especially on someone else's tab. The date was set for a few days hence at Primitivo which, at King George St, was walking distance from the Knesset. The cuisine was Mediterranean and the speciality was seafood, which Dan liked. Medad got there about twelve thirty, slightly before the time agreed so he could greet Dan properly.

After pleasantries and ordering, Medad got down to business. Dan knew both Palestinian men and would take seriously what was coming from them. He asked for details but Medad had no more than Hani had told him about rumours from Gaza being received in Ramallah that Hamas was planning something big and on the West Bank.

Dan mused. "That would be different and, if substantiated, would suggest an escalation of the conflict between the two sides."

Medad nodded. "Although it sounds like an inter-Palestinian dispute, it would inevitably have implications for us."

Dan agreed. "Yes, I think you need to get to the bottom of it." A few contacts were suggested and Medad made a note to follow them up.

He warned Medad not to leave it too long before he told the Minister. "If he was to find out before being briefed by his own staff, it could be a career-ending mistake."

Medad stared at Dan and began to appreciate the political ramifications of the pay grade he was on. As he returned to his office, Medad realised that all of his conversations with these 'contacts' of Dan's would have to be confidential otherwise his Minister would certainly know prematurely.

However, he didn't have much faith that they would be. Leaking in Jerusalem was endemic.

63

SAMI WAS GETTING lots of views on her YouTube channel and vblogs. She was astonished. "They're from all over the world," she exclaimed to her friend.

Rachel was hardly listening for she had a huge decision make. UNWRA was her life, it was where her friends were, where her career was, where her pay check came from. She had told her parents that she would be safe with the UN, what would she tell them now if she resigned? They would ask what was she moving on to do. Would she tell them that she was going to support a teenage disabled girl with no family in her quest to change Gaza single-handedly?

"I can't believe it." Sami was jumping up and down, at least as much as she could with her legs in the state they were. Then she noticed that Rachel was not sharing her excitement. "What's the matter?"

Rachel looked at the young girl. "I need to make a decision," she said.

"What decision?"

"I can't stay with UNWRA and at the same time support you. They won't let me." Rachel slumped down on the sofa besides Sami.

"Why ever not?" To Sami everything was straightforward. "We're just friends. Aren't you allowed to have friends?"

Rachel tried to explain. "It's not you they're worried about, it's what you're doing. They believe that if I'm associated with you and an employee of UNRWA, Hamas will have evidence to throw against UNRWA and put obstacles in the way of them fulfilling their mandate. They cannot allow that to happen."

Sami sat quietly. "Do you want me to leave?"

"Of course not. I just need to think what to do." Rachel wasn't sounding confident and Sami picked up her hesitation, so she went off to her bedroom. She also wanted to think.

Rachel paced up and down the small room was asking herself, "what do I really want to do?"

The truth was that she really wanted to support Sami, but how could she do it without any income or security? Then she realised the import of what

Sami had been saying about her followers. She had heard of many YouTubers who started up in their bedroom and now were making a living from their channel. How many followers did Sami have? Was it enough to give them an income and security? And how to monetise it effectively? She had no idea yet.

She got up and knocked on Sami's door. No reply. She tentatively opened it. No Sami. The window was open. She'd gone. Rachel swore in her Scottish Presbyterian way and rushed out through her front door to try and catch her. It was mid evening and there were many people out on the streets but no-one admitted to anything. There was no sign of her in any direction and she was just about to go back in when she remembered. The beach, that's where she'll be. So she set off at a pace knowing Sami wouldn't be able to go as fast as she.

Having escaped from Rachel's apartment through the bedroom window, not an easy task with a gammy leg, Sami had hobbled through the streets her eyes full of tears, feeling lonely and unloved. There were still lots of people going about their business but nobody stopped her to ask how she was or could they do anything. Even before she caught sight of the Mediterranean, she could hear the lapping of the water and just round the corner there it was. She loved it. Just looking towards the horizon gave her a feeling that anything was possible. The vista was unfettered, open and visionary. Although the air in Gaza City wasn't the best, here she could smell and even taste the salt of the Sea in her mouth. For a few moments it was exhilarating. Then she remembered her predicament. Her leg was hurting so she sat down on an old log that had been washed up some days earlier which had not been pressed into service by anybody. It wasn't very comfortable but she was too tired to move and certainly too tired to make her way back at the moment, if she ever wanted to go back. It wasn't that she disliked Rachel, quite the contrary. But she couldn't be responsible for her losing her job and her income.

Maybe she would recover some energy before it got dark and find some-where to sleep, she didn't know. This disabled life was new to her. She realised perhaps for the first time that she was not able-bodied anymore. She couldn't just do whatever she wanted. Disabled or partially disabled, what did it mat-ter? Her body had new limitations and not ones she had any control over. She thought for a moment, certainly partially disabled enough not to be able to get to her real home.

Home. She fought another set of tears welling her up in the eyes as she remembered that she had no home. Maybe she could sleep on the beach; she had heard that many people did, probably quite successfully but then there were always the perverts. Every society must have them; those who would prey on a teenage girl like her. She suddenly felt vulnerable. Very vulnerable. She looked round quickly but didn't see any threat. Of course, she said to herself, that didn't mean that there was none.

She was feeling very sorry for herself and with good reason, but she couldn't just bunk up with Rachel forever. What was she going to do? Getting a job was going to be nigh impossible. How was she going to pay for her life? Perhaps she didn't have one anymore. Thought upon thought, emotion upon emotion flooded her. At this point she didn't have the will anymore to fight back the tears, so she just sat there and cried. After about two minutes her crying had abated and settled into a sort of sniffle. She sat down totally miserable, unwanted and utterly useless.

An old man saw her and picked his way over to her from the other side of the road. As he got closer, he saw her rear up and struggle to her feet, scared.

He expressed his apologies, "I didn't mean to sneak up on you." He looked more closely at her and asked, "Aren't you the girl on the video?"

Still a little scared, she turned round and saw a man who could have been her grandfather if she had ever met him, "What video?"

He looked at her again as if to say he was sorry and had got the wrong person. But then he peered closer, checking her over. "Yes, you're the one, the one who did the video with the Hamas boss."

She paused before looking up at a kindly face sporting a grey shaggy beard, "Oh yes, that one. I suppose I am." There was little enthusiasm in her voice. The truth was that she had temporarily forgotten all about it, even a couple of days was a long time for a thirteen year old. "I'm surprised that anyone has seen it."

The old man looked surprised and replied, "Everyone I know has seen it, even me!" He chuckled, "You gave him rather a hard time."

Sami was at a loss to know how this old man had possibly seen her video. She was still a little vague in her answer, "Did I? I suppose I did." She recalled the interview and smiled as she recalled the couple of minutes when she really got stuck into him and turned to the old man saying that there were good bits that they would have almost certainly edited out.

"Did they?" she suddenly asked, finally interested in the subject. The old man grunted as he sat down next to her on the washed-up log. He looked at her more closely. "How did you manage to get to talk to the Leader? You're just a girl."

"Initially, I wrote him a letter from hospital. My family was killed in an Israeli air raid."

"Ah. Still you did well."

"So did they edit out the best bits?" Sami had temporarily forgotten her predicament and wanted to know about the video.

"Well, I don't really know, do I?" rejoined the old man. "But I saw some good bits. He even squirmed a bit at one point."

"Ah yes," replied Sami, "I do remember that bit. I thought it was going to end there, but after a pause, he carried on. I'm sure they would never have let that go out on the television."

"But you see," said the old man, "I didn't see it on television, but on my daughter's computer. She has the YouTube and, yes, apparently it was a little different to the one they broadcast."

He continued, "She says that everything is on the YouTube. She is following you and watching all your programmes."

"vblogs." said Sami.

"What?" said the old man, puzzled.

"They're called vblogs."

"Oh. Well, you're famous now."

"Really," said Sami. The old man took a last look at her, got up and started to shuffle off back to his side of the road. "Sorry about your leg." were his parting words.

Sami carried on sitting and thinking. Amazing. She smiled a determined smile to herself, and decided to start back to Rachel's with new motivation and strength.

Rachel had arrived at the nearest beach area and when she saw the teenager talking with the old man, she hung back to see what might happen but was ready to intervene if necessary. There was no need and as soon as he moved away, she saw her friend start to get up. She came up alongside and sat down next to her. She looked at Sami with an expression that mothers have when they are just about to scold their child. "What on earth are you doing here?" she asked.

"I didn't know where else to go," Sami didn't look at Rachel, but kept her face down. Part of her wanted to cry and part of her wanted to laugh. She was famous!

"Well, I've decided to stay with you instead of UNRWA," said Rachel.

"What! Why?" Sami looked up at Rachel in astonishment. "Without a job, you won't have any money coming in. My father was always talking about the need to have money coming in."

Rachel explained, "I'm going to talk to my boss and see what the best way is to leave UNRWA. They could make me redundant or give me notice, either way I get some money upfront. What I don't want to happen is to be charged with bringing UNRWA into disrepute, in which case I don't get any money. In the meantime, let's begin walking back and talk about the number of followers you're getting."

Sami perked up a bit. "How is that going to make any difference?"

"It could make all the difference," explained Rachel. "If your following continues to grow, you can attract advertising and earn money enough for both of us."

The rest of the journey back was excited chatter about the possibilities. Sami reminded Rachel that one of her followers was a lady called Ayshaa from Bethlehem. She had wanted to take the relationship further, but Sami had not replied.

"I looked at her website on your laptop," revealed Sami shyly, "and she has some advertising from companies all over." Rachel suddenly thought that getting her own laptop ought to be a priority since the one she was using belonged to UNRWA. Then an internet connection, not easy in Gaza but continuing to piggyback on UNRWA's wifi was not sustainable. They would soon find out and the Director would not be pleased.

"OK," said Rachel, "why don't we make contact with her and see how she got her advertising? It might not be the same companies who want to advertise because she's selling stuff whereas we're giving news and insights from Gaza."

They continued to talk and make plans when they got back to the apartment, Rachel on her laptop and Sami in the kitchen putting some food together. Just as the food was ready, Rachel called out, "Ayshaa has responded and is happy to help and suggested a Zoom call."

A few minutes later, "And look, Hamas have now put up the interview on their website. Let's watch it and see if it's the same version that went out on television."

It was the same. Either they hadn't seen what Rachel had already uploaded, or they didn't care. Sami dictated an update to her personal blog to go with Rachel's video which was posted on Facebook and Instagram, and became her daily update on Twitter. All three linked with each other.

"In the morning we'll see what views we've had and how many people are now following, but now I think we've had enough excitement for one day." Rachel was escorting Sami to her room, "and no more jumping out of the window."

Once Sami had been put to bed, Rachel began to think about what they needed to do. She decided that there was no time to waste in getting blogs and YouTube videos out there. Sami would record from the apartment, then she would have to upload it from her laptop at UNRWA for the moment, but the issue Rachel was keen to share with Sami wasn't so much technical as political.

The negative side of being in the public eye, especially on social media was not something to be ignored and Sami needed to understand what might, indeed would, happen. There would be many people who would agree with her but many, maybe even a majority would not, and be quite personally vehement and potentially abusive in their opinions. Before she left in the morning, she suggested that Sami look at a few bloggers on Facebook, Twitter etc. and

YouTube channels that were similar and look at the reactions they provoked. It would enable her to assess whether she wanted to put herself out there. If she did, then Rachel would certainly support her.

Sami hadn't been brought up with screens, the internet or social media as many children, even in Israel, had. It was a new world and she was aghast at some of the things she saw and heard. She had thought naively that if she just recounted what had happened to her and her family, it would just be accepted. What she now discovered was a world quite offensive and bitterly divided, especially over the Israeli-Palestinian issues.

Sami didn't see Rachel for the whole of the that day but that she would be back at about five o'clock. That evening they went through the social media discussion. There was never any real doubt that Sami was going to go ahead, but Rachel had to be sure she knew what she was doing. By the time they had gone through this discussion, they had agreed what they were going to do.

64

MEDAD DECIDED THAT his best strategy would be to choose the most likely person to know about any grand Hamas scheme, approach them and ask questions about Gaza generally. He could then pretend to his Minister that the issue had just come up in the course of that conversation, inform him and that way the door would open for him to investigate further officially. It didn't matter for Medad's purposes whether that person had information or not, they would just be his patsy. This was his strategy for covering himself and minimising any risk of leaks backfiring on him. He knew though, that once he mentioned this rumour to his Minister, he in turn, would need to mention it to the PM, if only to cover his own backside. The question was, how long would the Minister wait before doing so?

Medad was banking on a minimum of a week to chase it all down – if there was anything to chase down. He was suspicious but not convinced. He knew his Minister would not want to talk to the PM without compelling information, if not proof, which currently he did not have. But also his Minister would not want the PM to hear such a rumour from another source so Medad knew he had to move quickly.

The first person on Dan's list was inside Shin Bet. Medad thought long and hard as to whether he should mention it to anyone in the intelligence and security services, particularly someone he didn't know. The answer he would probably get was, 'don't worry your little head, we'll look into it'. He concluded that yes, they would be the best people to know, and yes, the best people to investigate. On the downside, there was no guarantee that any information they had or subsequently discovered would be passed back to him, leaving him high and dry.

He kicked himself again for not having pro-actively cultivated a list of contacts around the various government departments over the years. If he had, he could have gone to each as a friend, rather than now as an official, albeit a senior one, in Middle Eastern Division of the Foreign Affairs Ministry. Should he contact Shin Bet? He decided not. Rather there was someone in the

IDF whom he served with, knew well and might be able to get some inside military information for him.

Hirsh, one of his friends during his prescribed military service, was always going to stay on in the army. Unfortunately, he didn't have any contact details for him, but he was sure it couldn't be that difficult. Sure enough, it didn't take long to track him down and, as it happened, Hirsh was now deployed at Erez, the northern Gaza border crossing. When Medad heard this, he was delighted; his mood lifted and he began whistling quietly as he went about the office. Hirsh was totally in the right place to know what was going on in Gaza. The phone call between them was brief but Hirsh sounded intrigued with the little that Medad had said, and agreed to meet him when he was next off duty.

Yad Mordechai was a small town located about 10km south of Ashkelon, and near the border crossing. It boasted a population of only eight hundred souls but had a Joe Coffee. This was an American chain from New York, that served a lot more than coffee. Hirsh wanted to meet there at 8am for breakfast, probably not wanting to take time out of his day. Medad swallowed hard for he knew that meant a very early start for him. The coffee shop was situated on Route 4 near the intersection with Route 34, so not difficult to find fortunately.

Medad duly set his alarm and, as was often the case when an early start was called for, he woke several times during the night to check the time. There was no need to wake Shana, so the alarm was a back up and he hoped to be awake enough to switch it off before it woke her. He was, and quietly slipped out of bed, tiptoeing out to the bathroom with his clothes to shower, get dressed and hopefully leave without Shana waking. He slipped away just as she was stirring, after taking a strong coffee to keep him awake for the journey. It was still dark, likely to be so for a little while longer so roads were empty and the bike quickly ate up the miles. He was wishing he had got round to buying a car, the bike being perhaps a little rash for a senior civil servant. As he found his optimum speed, he started looking forward to a warm café and breakfast.

An Israeli breakfast usually meant eggs, Israeli salad and bread together with various accompaniments. It would never include meat such as ham or bacon, common on breakfast menus in many other countries. Even though

Israel was a secular state, many customs stayed in accordance with the Jewish laws of kashrut, the dietary laws of Judaism. So meat and dairy products were never served together in any meal and, of course pork products were totally forbidden. Mostly the Israeli breakfast was a dairy meal, with a variety of cheeses on offer. Fish was considered *pareve* indicating no meat and thus was permitted with a dairy meal. Herring, sprats, sardines, salmon and other smoked or pickled fish dishes were also common.

Hirsh was already seated when Medad arrived in his leathers and a bit dishevelled knowing he was a little late. They greeted each other as old friends with many slaps on the back, Medad playfully complaining about a breakfast meeting and Hirsch noting he hadn't progressed from his 'biker' stage. Even at just past 8am the place was relatively full, mostly civilians though a few in fatigues. The military had their own mess where soldiers ate and drank and, as a rule, they didn't mix with civilians but Medad suspected that the civilians here were linked to the military. Hirsh had chosen a table at the far end of the restaurant. It was an American diner layout with tables for four and lots of Americana on all the walls.

They ordered food, Medad ordering eggs whilst Hirsh's order was a little more adventurous since Medad was paying. After placing their orders, with the obligatory coffee, they caught up with each other's careers after they had finished their compulsory military service. Medad confessed that he was now married. Hirsh?

"You know military life. Yet to find time to survey the field." Medad laughed. "So military life is good then. But is it better than married life?"

Hirsh just smiled. For a few moments the conversation paused while both men tucked into their breakfast. Medad recalled their conversations back when they were both young conscripts. He wanted to see if Hirsh still had the same idyllic view of the military as he did then. He mentioned the suicide of a 19-year-old American woman who had been serving as a combat soldier in the army and asked whether the number of suicides was still high.

Hirsh gave a military answer. The numbers were falling each year and the Israeli army had the lowest suicide rate in the world. Medad decided to push a little. But what about those who leave after their conscription period is over?

What figures are there about those who suffer from PTSD, have flashback and nightmares ending up as alcoholics, especially the snipers?

Hirsh didn't answer but kept his head down eating his meal. Medad saw that he was embarrassing his friend, so he apologised. Hirsh decided to get straight to the point. "So what's on your mind?"

Medad paused and glanced around, as if to add a little confidentiality to the subject. Then he looked straight at his friend. "I've begun hearing some rumours about Hamas." He paused.

Hirsh replied tersely, "Not much new in that."

Medad continued, "that they might be planning something different, something big, something involving the West Bank." He was at pains to stress that he didn't believe there was anything substantial to the rumours, but his Minister wanted him to poke around. Without asking a question, Medad looked enquiringly at Hirsh.

Hirsh was now a *rav seren* or chief military commander, the equivalent to a major in NATO. He had done well. He sat back in his chair and now began to look more a military officer than a friend. Medad was expectant. When he did speak, he reminded Medad that there were chains of command in the military which also served as a chain of communication.

"Any information gleaned from covert or overt operations in Gaza will be passed up the chain for senior officers to consider."

Medad raised his eyebrows and looked hard at him. "But the military must keep the politicians in the loop surely, and in my Department which is responsible for Palestinian Affairs, all we have is a vague rumour."

Hirsh shifted uncomfortably. "All I can say is that Hamas activity in Gaza since the rocket attack that had brought the talks to an abrupt end, has virtually ceased and it has all gone quiet. And you didn't hear it from me."

Hirsh stood up stiffly and offered his hand to Medad who also stood up. They shook hands and Hirsh left expressing thanks for the breakfast and saying they must meet up again. Medad sat back down a little puzzled. He sat still for a few minutes wondering what on earth he had said that caused Hirsh to get up and go. He went over the whole conversation again in his head, trying to squeeze as much truth as he could out of what little had been said.

He decided to order another coffee and began to think it all through again, right from the beginning. Somehow he felt that since this was the place where the conversation took place, he might imbibe some more inspiration on the matter.

So what to conclude: firstly, clearly there was something going on and secondly, someone further up the military chain of command would probably know more, and thirdly, if Hirsh wanted to meet up again, might he have more to divulge? Did he know more now, or was he going to do some digging on Medad's behalf? Medad didn't know. But at least now Medad had his phone number. But why not say it now? He looked around. Joe Coffee was obviously a popular place and military fatigues were still there, so maybe he wanted a more private place. Medad didn't know.

No other inspiration came so he paid up and started back to Jerusalem. As he rode along he realised he would have to approach others since he could not be sure that Hirsh would come up with anything concrete. But for Medad, scepticism about a Hamas operation had definitely morphed into a deeper suspicion. That meant he felt he could take a more direct approach in his quest.

65

IN THE ABSENCE of anything else to think about, Hani was playing scenarios in his head about exactly what Hamas might be planning. That stretched from an all-out war with Israel having been much better armed by Iran, unlikely he thought, to a quasi peace settlement with Israel as a means of neutralising Fatah and the Palestinian Authority. In truth, he could see none of the possibilities as remotely probable. Nevertheless, round and round they went in his head. He had nothing much to tell Talal and was expecting a curt reminder any day now. If he didn't have any news, his star which was already on the wane in Ramallah would disappear into a black hole and perhaps his money with it. That would be a huge problem both for his family and his identity.

He was a little envious of his wife Ayshaa and her busyness. She had things to do, people to see, work to get done. Her BWP charity was booming, at least in terms of the number of women who wanted to meet up and learn how to feel, and be, more empowered in their lives. He didn't know about how they were financing it all. The fact was that she didn't need him anymore and that was very evident in their relationship. The centre of his life had evaporated whilst hers had burgeoned. He had even given up going to the shop since there was no-one to meet and he didn't really want to re-start his shopkeeper career. Career, he smiled grimly to himself, more like a prison sentence.

"I'll be back late afternoon." Ayshaa swept out of the house with both children, clearly going to make a day of it, leaving him on his own. She was not an unthinking woman and knew very well how her husband was feeling, but either didn't have the words or the desire to make him feel any better nor did she feel it was her role anymore. Today she had two BWP sessions lined up, one in the morning for women with babies and toddlers, and one without the nursery in the afternoon with Lara. She was positive and with good reason for there had been remarkable changes in the women she and Lara were training and supporting.

Lara was quite a discerning lady and although Ayshaa had not said anything about how she and Hani were not getting on, her positive outward demeanour hadn't fooled Lara. But she needed some sort of permission to approach Ayshaa about such a private and personal matter, and so far that had not been granted. To date, it had not affected her work with BWP but Lara could see that down the line there had to be a resolution, otherwise the charity's work would inevitably be compromised. Lara would bide her time. She made a mental note to speak to Omari about Hani and, without giving anything away, ask him to check in on him every now and again.

Hani was still finding it hard to come back down to earth and get stuck into the work that needed to be done locally. He put all that on the back burner promising himself that he would get round to it one day, but not today. His mind was still on Hamas and Gaza. The possibilities continued to go round in his head: he could call Omari, but there was nothing new to say or ask; could WhatsApp Medad, but the ball was firmly in the Israeli's court to come back to him and he didn't want to be seen as desperate, although he was certainly getting that way. Yes, he could meet up with some of his men, but most of them would be working on building sites in Israel, at least those old and fit enough to work and there was nothing urgent.

He eventually decided on a walkabout to survey his area of responsibility as far as Fatah were concerned. He would head from home down Star St towards Manger Square, and on to Shepherds Field St heading towards the Dheisheh refugee camp. This had been established in 1949 to house Palestinians who had been removed from their land to make way for the new state of Israel. Hani knew it had been built to serve about three thousand refugees initially; people fleeing from numerous villages west of Jerusalem and Hebron, but its population had grown to over fifteen thousand over the seventy years since it had been settled, and living on just 0.3 square kilometers.

Hani was so glad he didn't live there. He knew that fifteen percent of dwellings still had no mains sewage system and had to rely on communal pits. Nevertheless they were his people and he wanted to look after them and do what he could to make their lives easier, which of course, was also what his wife wanted to do. Walking through Dheisheh, he came across a demolition which had happened that very morning. The mother and four children were still crying and their possessions strewn everywhere. Women neighbours were around the family but the man was nowhere to be seen. He made a note to try and find out who and why, if there was a real why. They would need some help.

He knew the objective of the Israel Defence Forces (IDF) was to make life in the refugee camps unliveable in an effort to get them to move. Their tactics included not only demolitions but tear gas and sound bombs, with the Bethlehem Aida refugee camp apparently becoming the most tear gassed place in the world. Nightly raids of Palestinian homes were common with loud fighter jets flying over the camps at all hours of the day and "kneecapping", where Israeli soldiers aimed to shoot at the knees of Palestinians in hopes of disabling them.

Perhaps he'd visit the Aida camp another day. It was no different to Dheisheh in that they were both refugee camps 'inhabited by migrants who refused to be migrants'. Both camps had originally been made up of UN tents following the 1948 war, then converted by the UN into corrugated metal homes. Return to their original land and homes was now never going to happen, so the residents began to build themselves more permanent stone dwellings many stories high enabling everyone to be housed, but making the streets correspondingly narrow, dark and dank.

The Aida camp was adjacent to Rachel's Tomb, cut off from Jerusalem by the Wall. As he thought about Aida, Hani recalled the twelve meter high archway built in the shape of a keyhole was the camp's entrance. On top of the arch lay a nine meter long iron key, a permanent and creative symbol of the right of return that these refugees sought. The key had a *'not for sale'* sign on it serving as a reminder that the right of return was not one that could be bought or negotiated. Hani approved.

Although the Separation Wall served as a security wall for the Israelis, it was a prison wall for the inhabitants of the camp. On the Palestinian side of the Wall were the names and faces of the Palestinian martyrs who had given their lives for the cause, but integral to the design of the Wall was a blue gate which could be opened only from the Israeli side which allowed tanks to roll into the camp at any time. Hani had men who kept an eye on this ready to report if those gates opened, even during the early hours when the population was asleep, not that they could do anything about stopping them but they felt they needed to log every incursion.

66

HANI WAS BACK from his walk around Bethlehem with his legs beginning to ache. He was conscious of becoming a couch potato and not doing enough exercise. That's got to change, he promised himself. As if to prove the sedentary lifestyle that had subliminally overtaken him, force of habit made him open his computer again. I'm getting addicted to this thing, he thought. Ah, another email from his boss. He groaned inwardly, the man was becoming a nuisance. Ayshaa and the children were out so he felt able to curse the man loudly and with real feeling.

Talal was expressing some impatience at hearing nothing from the man with the Israeli contacts, especially as "I was counting on you." Hani had nothing. Nothing. He decided to message Medad, entertaining no great hopes of any useful information, let alone a breakthrough. Even if the Israeli had definite intelligence, Hani was not sure that it would be passed on to him. He pulled himself together, ashamed at letting his negative mood envelop him again.

But Medad himself was stumbling around as everyone else was. There was no hard evidence, just rumour and speculation. Any sceptic could drive a coach and horses through it all. It could still all be an elaborate stunt to confuse and waste the time and resource of both the Israelis and the Palestinian Authority. He was sitting at his desk dealing with the day to day administration of his department which, in comparison to this potential Hamas 'Plan', was exceedingly dull. He was getting through the paperwork a lot faster than he should have, handing out tasks to his subordinates as quickly as he could in order to clear his desk so he could be free to pursue any lead that came in. That would be a miracle, thought Medad despondently.

Thus the message from Hani caught him a little off guard. He had almost forgotten about the Palestinian but it was him, after all, who had brought the matter to his attention in the first place and it might be that he had more information to give. So he replied in the affirmative, texted Shana that he'd be late and duly left the office slightly early and set off on his bike to Bethlehem, reminding himself again that he had to get a car soon. He had to pass through a military checkpoint where he was told again that going into the West Bank was dangerous. He had made a rude comment the previous time but now buttoned his lip.

He got to the WalledOff early evening. As far as Medad was concerned, the meeting was a disappointment. He had travelled quite a distance and gone through a checkpoint (never quick) for nothing. It was one way traffic; he was the giving the updates, Hani having nothing of worth to offer in return, at least this time. But, Hani said more positively than he felt, he was reasonably hopeful that his contacts in Ramallah would have something more concrete soon. Medad, for his part, was open about who he had spoken to without naming any names. He was assured him that Jamal, whom he knew from the Israeli-Palestinian talks was also on the case. Hani hoped that this information would reassure Medad, after all it was Jamal who had been instrumental in recovering a kidnapped Israeli soldier. Medad nodded to show some support, but the lack of confidence was betrayed in his eyes. The meeting broke up without any shaking of hands. Medad twisted his accelerator grip and got back to East Jerusalem mid evening in time to eat with Shana.

Hani returned home after the meeting with some progress to report to Ta-lal, even if it hadn't come from him. Something was afoot that was for sure. It seemed while the 'why' was obvious, the 'what', 'when', 'who' and everything else was still a mystery. The response to Talal confirmed that the rumour was no longer just a rumour but being taken seriously by Shin Bet, the IDF and the Head of the Middle East and Peace Process Division in the Israeli Civil Service. He had thought long and hard as to whether to include Medad in his report, albeit anonymously. But he felt under pressure to report as much as he could. If Talal asked for more detail about his Israeli contacts, he would stonewall and talk about 'plausible deniability', even if his boss didn't under-stand what that meant.

He needn't have worried though. Talal was quite happy with the response and replied positively, but to "keep on it." Hani read into his tone that he was being pressured for some information from above and didn't really care what it was as long as it got someone off his back. Hani's respect of his boss, which was already low, plummeted further. By the time he got back home, Ayshaa was there preparing the evening meal and he decided to share what he had learned from Medad with Ayshaa. Instead of being dismissive as he thought she might be in her off-hand sort of way, she wiped her hands and sat down with a serious look on her face.

"If this is true", she started, "this is not going to turn out well for any of us and certainly not our children, unless it is nipped in the bud."

She went on, "There needs to be a cooperative effort between us and the Israelis, and you and Omari are the only ones who can do that from our side." Having delivered her verdict, she got up, tried to quieten the children and get on with the food.

Hani had to admit that she had a way of getting right to the nub of the issue. She was right of course, and he had been stumbling along thinking he had no real role when all the time he should have been taking the initiative and trying to make things happen. He was a little ashamed of himself, but now motivated although still no idea where to turn next. Unless… yes, he would go and see Jamal in Ramallah. That was where things were going to happen. If he liaised regularly with him, perhaps that would open up some more avenues to pursue.

He knew Jamal had been sidelined in the Ramallah hierarchy but maybe this could be a way back in for him. He also knew that because his family house in East Jerusalem had been targeted with demolition leaving his wife and children homeless and traumatised, there had been a lot to cope with. Jamal had been beside himself with fury at the Civil Administration who had ordered the demolition and the IDF who had made sure it was carried out. All he could do was to move his family up to Ramallah and say goodbye to their East Jerusalem status.

This was a major event for any Palestinian. To have to move from the family home which had been theirs for generations was like selling out those generations who had worked hard to build a future for their children. Thus Palestinians wouldn't sell their homes or land for anything, but in this case they had no alternative. Jamal knew exactly who had orchestrated it, but had yet to come up with a satisfactory way of redress. It had been another victory for the hard right in Israeli politics. Coincidentally, his sideways move in the

PA had also given him the required time and space to plot his revenge.

Hani was sure that Jamal would be wanting to get back to the front line in Ramallah. So with his decision made, he called Jamal and made an arrangement to have lunch with him. Jamal suggested that he come down to Hani because he didn't want word getting back to Talal that he was still meeting his old colleague behind Talal's back. This suited Hani who really didn't want to drive all the way to Ramallah in his old car. Neither did he want word getting to his men in Bethlehem that he was talking to a bigwig from Ramallah, although he admitted to himself that even if they saw the two together, they probably wouldn't recognise Jamal.

Not a slim man by any means, yet Hani was of the opinion that Jamal was certainly slimmer. He didn't know whether that was due to the stress of his family having to relocate or due to a much reduced expense account. They had lunch in a village just outside Bethlehem and it seemed to Hani that there was not much lacking in the man's appetite.

Hani was completely open with his old boss about his meeting with Medad and the progress he had made. He also paraphrased what Ayshaa had said about the crucial nature of finding out more, and adding his own desire to get ahead of Hamas somehow. Jamal pondered on all of this. He had nothing to add since he had not given it much thought since his last meeting with Hani. He had been tempted to think it was all down to Talal trying to enhance his position by shouting wolf.

Obviously there was much more to it and Jamal could clearly see the opportunity for him.

"I still have friends and colleagues in Security and other places," he mused. "I'll put out some feelers and see what I get back."

Business done, they got on with more personal and family matters whilst enjoying each other's company and having a good simple lunch. They had become good friends and it was an enjoyable time for both of them. Hani certainly needed it, being a little estranged from Ayshaa and his family. Conversely, Jamal was still getting used to living with his family, so he needed it for different reasons. Hani went home reinvigorated and relatively happy, Jamal with a new task to get stuck into which might yet get him back into favour.

67

MEANWHILE KHALID WAS on the move again but moaning to himself, why it always had to be him. Then he remembered what the Leader had said, "Just the two of us." He still didn't know whether that was a good sign or not. Khalid thought he was quite good at reading people but not the Leader. He was impossible to read so and, supposed the Palestinian, that's why he's the Leader. He wondered whether he himself was easy to read or not, whether his wife knew he had a mistress, whether the children knew, and whether she also had someone on the side?

Occasionally he would think about the future; how was it all going to work out, what would the Leader do if he found out, would it be a problem – perhaps he already knew, could it make him a blackmail target? He yawned a tired yawn and thought that probably the Leader had his own 'personal' life. How he wished he could have a holiday, but Hamas was not the sort of employer to give its employees four weeks paid holiday a year. Maybe when he got back from this trip he could ask for some time off, but immediately thought that if there was substance to this 'Plan', he would most likely be working harder. So his thoughts drifted from one situation to another as he made his way down through the Strip to the Rafah tunnel without coming to any real conclusions.

It was said that originally there were over a thousand tunnels between Gaza and Egypt, mostly used for smuggling goods and military supplies into Gaza. The whole area situated along the border between Gaza and Egypt was a narrow strip of land over twelve kilometers in length called the Philadelphi Corridor. Egypt had already constructed an underground barrier down the length of this strip to block out existing tunnels, prevent new ones from being built thus enabling them to control the border more effectively.

Khalid did wonder from time to time how long the particular tunnel he was using might be available before it was discovered; he was fervently hoping it wouldn't be closed whilst he was out on a mission. That would not only prove counter productive for whatever mission he was engaged on but also very annoying personally. It had certainly been open as long as he could remember and was something of a miracle it hadn't been discovered, since he knew that both the Israelis and Egyptians were always on the look out for evidence of people crossing illegally through tunnels.

Sometimes there would be a scheduled military exercise in the area and a whole squad of men with the appropriate equipment for discovering tunnels would carefully comb the area on their side of the border. Khalid guessed that this tunnel was too small to be used for goods and therefore probably only used for the occasional person, which meant it would not show up on any equipment monitoring movement unless someone was in there at the precise time they were searching. As far as he knew, it may only have been known to the leadership of Hamas. Nevertheless, he surmised it would only be a matter of time before this route was closed and he wondered what would happen then.

Anyway, here he was trudging through the Rafah tunnel yet again. He was getting too old to be crawling through this tunnel, he thought, but at least it was quicker to get into the West Bank than Lebanon. As he emerged gradually into the light, he quickly scoured the area, but saw no-one. No soldiers scouring the area that he could see, so he felt reasonably safe. It was not too far to the pick-up point so after a few minutes rest at the tunnel exit, he began to zigzag his way to where he hoped his car would be waiting.

The car was there with its Egyptian driver sitting with the window open smoking a Malboro Red. With a quick thankful prayer to Allah off they went, heading for Jenin. He guessed the route would go due south down the Sinai peninsula as far as Nizzana and then an easterly turn across into Israel. It was not a route he had done before, so was totally dependent on his Egyptian driver to get him just inside the border, where there would be a Palestinian driver to take him all the way up to Jenin. Khalid had no idea how the logistics of such an operation was possible, but he was thankful that mostly it worked. Once across the border, it was quite a way to the first major town, Beersheba, which was given a 'just in case' wide skirting and then on to Hebron. Here they could stay the night and rest from the journey.

They stayed at a two roomed bed and breakfast in the Old City where an Israeli enclave of hard line Jewish settlers was also located. There were only about four hundred of them in comparison to a local population of over six thousand but nevertheless, they made their presence felt by throwing rocks, bleach, urine and even dead rats at the houses of the locals and particularly at this bed and breakfast place. The settlers lived in the Avraham Avinu settlement, which faces directly on to this one-storey home and overlooked the narrow alleys where the souk was located. The merchants in the souk had strung up a grid-like mesh across the roof of the narrow alley to catch the plastic bottles, dirty nappies and other debris chucked down by the settlers on top of the shop owners in the souk, wryly describing them as "gifts from heaven". There was nothing the inhabitants of the Old City could do about it for the settlers were protected by the Israeli military.

Whereas the Egyptian driver said nothing the whole way down the Sinai, the Palestinian driver talked non-stop until they got safely to Hebron. Khalid put it down to nerves – maybe it was his first time in the wilderness south of Hebron but he didn't mind as long as he got to where he needed to go. After breakfast, they carried on their journey towards Jenin which was a long way from Hebron using just Palestinian roads. He trusted that the driver knew his destination but even if he didn't, Khalid had been given some basic directions. He had never yet missed a destination so far in his service to Hamas and wasn't starting now. He switched off from the inane chatter of his driver and began to wonder what this Imam had to say that was so important.

As they were passing around Bethlehem, Khalid instructed his driver to make a short detour to Manger Square as he was interested to see it having never been there. The driver explained that no cars were allowed on the Square, but he could park just down the hill and point his passenger in the right direction. The Gazan went up the hill in the direction he was given, then mounted the steps on to the Square itself. There was the Mosque of Omar on the right and the Christian Church of the Nativity further down on the left. He wandered round the square for about half an hour looking at the shops and the various pilgrims from all over the world. One circuit was all he needed and he headed back to the car, settling down for the rest of the journey.

It was another few hours before they were approaching the outskirts of Jenin. His driver, who was from Jenin, explained that the Imam in question did not belong to the main mosque in Jenin, but a much smaller, more radical mosque on the outskirts of the city. It was the same Imam, Ahmed al-Fahd, who had been arrested after an Israeli soldier had been kidnapped guarding a new local Israeli settlement in the area.

"There is a rumour," he went on, "that he is in direct touch with Hezbollah and Iran, but what do I know." For the first time Khalid began to see the connections.

It was mid afternoon by the time Khalid and his driver arrived at their destination. They were both welcomed in by the Imam and his wife with traditional Palestinian hospitality being offered and gratefully accepted, a far cry from the reception he had experienced in Beirut. While food and drink were being taken, small talk was made about the journey and the situation in Gaza which filled the time. When they had finished, the driver and the Imam's wife left the room, leaving Khalid and al-Fahd to talk.

Khalid was not one to observe conversational niceties more than he had to, so was anxious to receive what the Imam had to say. He explained to the Imam that it was he who had met Angra Mainyu in Lebanon and it was the Iranian who had said that Hamas should contact him for their next step. The Imam looked at Khalid and, seeing a mere messenger, sighed.

68

AFTER THEY HAD fully discussed the niceties of social media, Rachel had another subject to talk about with Sami. During the day at work both her colleagues and the women she worked with, talked about Sami's video of the Hamas interview and the difference between the two versions.

Rachel looked at Sami and said, "I think we had better think carefully about your security. It maybe that Hamas will not like the unedited version of the interview."

Sami was sitting on the sofa while Rachel was responsible for food this time. Neither of them spoke, both thinking hard about what all this meant and weighing up the potential cost of what they were going to do. Rachel laid out some bread and hummus on the table with a cup of tea. When food had been consumed, Rachel cleared away and, before leading Sami to her bedroom and tucking her up in bed for the night, she promised they would talk about it more in the morning. When Sami had gone to sleep, which wasn't that long, Rachel tried to make some phone calls. She hadn't thought that the video would circulate so fast, neither had she thought about Sami's security but she certainly was now.

It was Friday evening and it seemed none of her friends had their phones turned on, or they were just ignoring them. The UNRWA did have a security team and she wanted to talk with them, but decided she'd have a chance of a better outcome if one of her friends had a contact there. After twenty minutes phoning round, she finally got through to Joe.

He answered with a cheery, "Hi Rach." Rachel flinched. She didn't like being called Rach; why not Rachel? But she was wanting a favour, so she said a cheery, "Hi Joe" back.

Joe was a friend but not a prospective boyfriend, at least as far as Rachel was concerned. She had made that clear on several occasions and Joe had given up, but they were still friends and Rachel got straight to the point. After all, it was a Friday evening and the UNRWA crew did try to keep themselves amused and let their hair down a little. Life was hard enough during the working week and it was morale boosting to end their week in style. This evening was a quiz night and, if she remembered correctly, it was due to start… about now.

"Joe, I know the quiz night is about to begin – sorry I can't be there – I have a favour to ask." Joe went quiet, but the noise in the background was anything but quiet. "Can't it wait until tomorrow morning?"

Joe was anxious to enjoy his evening and not be dragged out anywhere. Rachel relented and promised to ring in the morning at about eleven. Should be enough time for him to wake up and be human, she thought.

She didn't want to go out knowing Sami was asleep, so she got herself comfortable on her sofa and picked up her half-read book. She had got through the next six pages before she realised she couldn't remember a thing about what she had just been reading. Her sub-conscious mind was still focussed on Sami and what to do, whereas her conscious mind seemed to be completely inactive. Nothing more to do than have an early night and wait until she had spoken to Joe. You never know, she thought, my brain might have thought of something overnight and I will wake up in the morning with the problem solved.

Well, if it happened like that to some people, it didn't happen for her. She slept fitfully and woke up with no further guidance whatsoever. Sami, on the other hand, had slept soundly and was very chirpy. Rachel explained that she was going to call Joe and see if UNWRA security could help in any way. As she was explaining this to Sami, it suddenly occurred to her that if she was on the UNRWA payroll, that would solve everything. It was now ten o'clock and she decided to call her boss and explain the situation.

"This is very unusual to say the least." Her boss was not going to fill her with hope. She was saying all the things she already knew. "If we 'harbour' someone who is wanted by the government, we take sides and go beyond our mandate. We risk our whole programme."

Rachel knew this but was wanting to pursue the idea to the very end. She rang off with the words, "Give it some thought, and maybe there is a way, somehow." She gave a wry smile to Sami who had listened to the conversation. Now it's time to talk to Joe.

Joe listened carefully. He knew about Sami as did most of the staff. Yes, I have a friend in the security detail, but I'm not sure he will risk his position. If Hamas are looking for her, they'll find her, or one of their gangs will. At some point she will have to talk to them. Better she takes the initiative, especially if she can go straight to the top. Rachel was listening carefully. Joe was making a lot of sense and this was a step she hadn't considered, but it wasn't her decision. Sami would need to make her own mind up, so the girls spent the rest of the morning going back and forth over the issue. Finally Rachel reminded Sami that she had a YouTube channel and a vblog… why not ask the Hamas leader for another interview? He can say then whatever he wants to say and we can promise this time it will be released without any editing.

Sami perked up and said that was a great idea, but was not sure how to contact him. Then Rachel came up with the idea that Sami should put out the invitation at the conclusion of the next YouTube video and see if he bites. If the first video is anything to go by, most of the population of Gaza will watch it. If he doesn't respond, he'll look weak but if he does, you're now a public figure and he won't be able to touch you. Even as she said it out loud, Rachel thought it sounded rather naïve, but it looked like the best solution they had come up with and it put Sami in the driving seat.

Let's do it! Sami recorded both new blog and video, both talking about her trip to the beach, what she had felt, what disability had momentarily meant to her, what the old man had said, everything. Then at the end she invited the Leader for an interview with no edits. He could say what he liked. That's the easy part, thought Rachel. We'd better start preparing for this interview, because if he says yes, it will be sudden to try and take us off guard.

69

MEDAD WAS REALLY at a loss as to who else to approach on this sensitive subject. He was feeling the pressure and consequently was also finding it difficult to sleep. Shana not so. She could sleep soundly without any problem, but at the moment she was fully occupied researching background for a new article she was preparing and didn't seem to have time to listen to her husband's moans and groans. Their flat in East Jerusalem was now completely furnished with a study for her and a corner desk for Medad in the living room; after all, he had an office to work in each day which she didn't. It was Wednesday evening and they had eaten lamb kebabs with Israeli couscous known as *ptitim*.

Shana had settled herself in her study to work for a few hours but Medad couldn't seem to stay still at his desk. Rather, he was constantly moving around the place in frustration, walking in and out of the kitchen, the living room and Shana's study at will. A sense of foreboding had come over him and after twenty minutes of this Shana had had enough. "Stop!"

Medad stopped. "Sorry," he said and went to the bathroom, retrieved two sleeping tablets, swallowed them and took himself off the bed. He awoke at about nine o'clock in the morning to find Shana out and his phone buzzing. Reaching over to his bedside cabinet, he noted another unknown number but was so desperate for something to move that he answered it anyway. It was a voice from the past which he instantly recognised and totally transformed his mood. Seth was another of his close friends in his IDF days. He was Orthodox Christian, his parents having resettled in Israel from the Soviet Union. It was Seth who had used his contacts to get Medad into The Research and Information Centre (RIC) and from there to work for the Head of the Middle East and Peace Process Division. So Medad owed him.

Although both had been around the governmental area for all this time, they had never bumped into each other nor had there been a move by either which could have brought them together, until now. A meet was agreed at half past ten. As they renewed friendship over coffee and doughnuts, personal updates took a little while. Medad married, Seth not.

"The problem," Seth complained, "is my parents and their religion. They want me to marry someone from the Christian Orthodox tradition, and there aren't a lot of girls to choose from." Medad commiserated.

"But, there is someone," he said with a twinkle in his eye.

"And you haven't told your parents," finished Medad. They both laughed.

The conversation fell into old routines and jokes. They had regressed to eighteen year olds again. Seth delved back into the past again.

"Do you know where Hirsh and Akiva are?" Medad was able to throw some light on their old friends.

"No idea where Akiva is, probably on some ultra-religious settlement somewhere, but Hirsh is now a *rav seren* stationed at the Eretz Gaza crossing." Seth was impressed at his rapid promotion, but not with the current posting. That's an awful place. They fell into silence for the first time in an hour.

Medad had decided that since Seth had phoned him, there must be something on his mind and he would wait until that surfaced. Then he might, might, mention something of his present assignment. It was as if both knew the rehearsal of the past was over – enjoyable, but both men had serious roles and someone had to kick it off.

So Seth started. "I know a little of the part you played in the abortive Israeli-Palestinian talks recently and while my views might not be exactly the same as yours, I'm not an extreme right-winger."

Medad sighed as some recollections briefly returned to him. He admitted, "I have to say it was extremely disappointing."

Seth sounded sympathetic. "I don't exactly know what deal you had come to with the Palestinians and I don't want to know, but I admire your ability to bring a diverse Israeli delegation to any kind of agreement."

Medad thanked him and said that part of his strategy was to splinter off the PA from Hamas, get some deal there, then concentrate all forces on Hamas and their paymasters, Iran. Seth was quiet. He didn't comment on the strategy Medad had outlined but was thinking hard.

Medad was watching Seth carefully wipe his mouth after the last bit of doughnut. He thought he was now going to find out what Seth had called him about.

He began, "From where I sit, I don't think it would be possible to get any deal through the Knesset at the moment. If a miracle happens and the upcoming election changes the balance of power and a centre leaning coalition was able to form a stable government, maybe. But I don't see that happening now or any time soon."

Medad said nothing. Seth must have called him for more than just to talk through the current political wrangling. Then it came.

"Actually I know where Akiva is," Seth confessed. "Apologies, I needed to know if you knew." Medad was a little taken aback at this roundabout way of approach. It smacked of a lack of trust and Seth saw it in Medad's eyes.

Seth quickly continued, "He's with Shin Bet. He's been in touch now and again but has asked me to keep his role secret, but I know that he wouldn't mind you knowing. More importantly for me, an issue has arisen on which I need advice."

Shin Bet, or Shabak was Israel's internal security service with its motto of 'Magen veLo Yera'e' which can be translated as 'Defender that shall not be seen.' Equivalent to MI5 in the UK and the FBI in the US, it was one of the three security organisations which Israel had set up, the others being Aman, military intelligence and Mossad, the foreign intelligence agency.

Medad was thinking very rapidly. "That's a surprise, I had no idea that's where he went." Seth quickly interrupted to try and recover his friend's trust.

"He knows I have taken a particular interest in Gaza and so approached me two days ago on what I might call, 'a fishing trip'."

Medad felt a heart-thump of excitement and, as calmly as he could, asked Seth what Akiva was 'fishing' for? Seth consciously looked around before answering.

"He started by casually asking me why I had made Gaza a particular interest and went on to ask if I had any contacts there who knew what was going on there at the moment... and the questions and comments went on in that vein, never actually saying or asking what it was he really wanted to know."

Medad considered this. "It sounds like he's been quite well trained and you're being sounded out for some informer-type role, to do with Gaza. Perhaps he thinks as an MK, you will have insights and knowledge which Shin

Bet don't have."

Seth pursed his lips. "That's crazy. If so, then my estimate of Shin Bet's capability has just shot through the floor."

Both men sat silently, and around them the café began to fill up for lunch. Seth suggested they walk a bit. Medad was wondering when to ask his sixty-four thousand dollar question. It might as well be now, he thought. So as they moved further away from the crowds, he asked Seth whether he had heard any rumours from Gaza about any new initiative Hamas might be taking.

Seth stopped and looked at Medad. "I've levelled with you, perhaps you ought to level with me." Medad took a deep breath and decided to spin the story a little by talking about meeting up with Hirsh and them having a conversation about Gaza and 'something big', neglecting to say that he'd initiated the discussion.

Seth was astounded. "It sounds like you and Hirsh are already all over this." Medad said that unfortunately he hadn't been able to confirm anything since and was thinking it was just rumour.

"But if Shin Bet were making enquiries, perhaps there is something to it."

Seth listened and summed it up: "so nobody knows what this is about?" Medad nodded glumly.

"Perhaps," continued Seth, "I can make a suggestion, that we keep each other in the loop because I don't think that given their positions, either Hirsh or Akiva will want to share very much. They're locked into their own hierarchies."

The two friends agreed although both went their separate ways wondering how long that might last. Medad aired his concerns to Shana that evening, who made an astute observation.

"Since you know nothing you can't lose anything, and you won't lose Seth as a friend because you haven't seen him for years. At the moment he's just a contact who could again become a friend, depending on how it all pans out."

Medad nostalgically remembered the IDF days and all the experiences, good and bad, that their group had gone through together, and how friendships had changed because of superior loyalties imposed on them from their differing hierarchies. He wished it wasn't so, but then remembered he had his own obligations. That reminded him… he probably had enough firm intelligence to meet with his Minister at least say something was afoot and that, at the moment, neither the military, the security services nor his PA contacts knew anything more. On second thoughts, he'd better not mention his PA contacts to the Minister just say that it was a waiting game, but better to be forewarned.

At least he knew where to look, Gaza.

70

PARWEZ WAS A good man who didn't do things by halves. He was a successful businessman in Nablus and, as such, was one of a relatively small group of Palestinian individuals, not because there wasn't talent. Colleges on the West Bank were churning out two thousand engineering and computer graduates a year but, according to Parwez, there were two major elements missing to turn graduates into potential entrepreneurs and business people.

One was access to investment and the other was availability of mentors. The Palestinian Authority had a plethora of institutions that aimed to provide such support: the Palestinian Ministry of National Economy, the Palestinian Ministry of Finance, the Palestinian Investment Promotion Agency, the Palestinian Federation of Industries, the Palestinian Chambers of Commerce, and so on. But, according to Parwez, bureaucracy and inefficiency stifled any initiative in the country. He had the luxury of both funding and mentoring when he was young in the shape of his father, who had started his own olive oil business when Parwez was very young. By the time the boy had grown, his father had established a number of related businesses and he mentored his son in running them. Parwez didn't necessarily have the risk-taking ability of his father, but knew how to run the businesses and expand them, where risk was not the major ingredient in success.

He had married a childhood sweetheart and she had presented him with two daughters and a son. As a Palestinian man, he obviously hoped that his son would follow him when he wanted to retire, but it was his elder daughter who grew up to be the business-savvy one. Shachna his son was more a religious boy and wanted to become an Imam, perhaps not surprising since his name meant, 'close to God'. Although his mother was quietly pleased (the name was her idea), he was rather a disappointment to his father, whose religion was more cultural than theological.

However, Parwez knew that helping the poor etc. was an intrinsic element of Islam and saw his successful businesses as a means to that end. Although he paid the going rate for the workers at his factories and sometimes a little bit more, he knew the poverty and deprivation their families experienced, especially those who had their land and homes taken away by Israeli settlers. He couldn't employ all those in need and those he couldn't take on found it quite difficult to obtain work even in a large city like Nablus. Indeed, many were unable to work due to either the physical or mental consequences of Occupation. So as well as an entrepreneur and businessman, Parwez was also a philanthropist.

In his home city, he had started a charity called *Al-khabaz*, which was Arabic for 'bread', because this was how he had started, buying bread from local bakeries and offering it to those who needed it, in and around Nablus. It was a small contribution which was never going to help everyone who in need, but it was making a difference to those who came to pick the staple up. There had since grown up a number of food banks on the West Bank which had taken on some of the basic food needs of the population probably a lot better than he could.

Parwez was content with this but his younger daughter, Raaida whose name meant 'leader', decided that she wanted to be a part of this work. Even in her teenage years, she could be found helping to organise the empty shop where they worked from and as she got to know how it all worked, she wanted to expand and provide more. Her parents could see that this charity was going to be her life and she would devote herself to it. So at twenty-one years of age, Parwez brought her formally on to the Board with himself and his wife. It was still to be a family concern.

By the time she was twenty five years old, *Al-khabaz* had expanded to provide many other things besides food and water. It now included basic medicines, women's products, clothes, even children's education classes and housing repairs teaching as well as providing basic food and water. Although Parwez had got an annual grant from the Palestinian Authority, the majority of funding continued to come from him. However, he made it clear to Raaida that more services would need more funding from outside the family.

So with the grace and boldness that comes from a visionary young woman, Raaida became the principal fundraiser and public face of the charity. She attended key civic meetings, even though most of the other attendees were men; the fact that she was Parwez's daughter counted for a lot and, in the beginning, she traded on it for all she was worth. Her vision was always outstripping her funding, but she worked at it relentlessly.

She secured additional funding from other businessmen and the more prosperous citizens of the city, even from the mosques in Nablus. It was fast becoming a social service, filling a genuine vacuum which the Palestinian Authority had failed to cater for. Even then, the services it offered were still far short of other countries but there was an explicit acknowledgement from the population of Nablus that *Al-khabaz* was serving them better than the Ramallah based government. Gradually Parwez allowing the strings of control to pass to Raaida, and she became the Chair with her father and mother stepping back in favour of Shachna. He was interested in the venture, but only as a non-executive. Happy to be part of a family charity and make suggestions from time to time, he didn't want any direct day to day responsibility which suited Raaida well. It was at his suggestion that she approached the mosques for funding as well as other businesses. Within ten years, not only did Nablus have a *Al-khabaz* but every major town and city north of Jerusalem, Jericho being the most southerly city apart from East Jerusalem itself.

Unfortunately Parwez never saw that day. His untimely death, due to a long term heart condition, was genuinely mourned by most of Nablus. It was very sudden and for a few months, it paralysed the family. They finally pulled themselves out of their mourning and the daughters quickly immersed themselves in the organisations that their father had passed to them. Shachna, more than the others, seemed to react quite radically to his father's death, almost as if he was waiting for his father to pass before vigorously pursuing his own course.

Raaida had enjoyed a good life by any standards, and she was grateful to her father because day to day she saw the misery that her people had to endure on the West Bank. She was not a party political animal, but was astute enough to understand politics with a small 'p'. She was learning fast how to make and keep connections now that her father was not there to support her. *Al-khabaz*, her staff, volunteers and recipients was all she cared about. It was down to her that the charity was beginning to be recognised as a major

Palestinian institution.

In the beginning as a volunteer she had started with a blue-eyed naivety wanting to try to solve everyone's problem. But she soon found that not only was this beyond her, but that as she solved one, another would appear. She began to recognise a 'victim' syndrome at work where people tended to consider themselves solely as a victim of the negative actions the Occupation. It was true that her people had been the victim of considerable wrongdoing through no fault of their own but she saw how pervasive this attitude had become, robbing many of initiative and the ability to do even small things to help themselves. Such people saw life as largely negative and beyond their control with life's challenges directly at them personally. Because of that they avoided responsibility, kicked back criticism and felt they deserved sympathy and other people/countries should help them out.

Maybe, thought Raaida, for the middle aged and older people it was a mechanism for avoiding feelings of anger which they could no longer express for if they did, it would surely result in more loss. She didn't have much contact with younger people who didn't worry too much about expressing anger, particularly at the IDF, loss or no loss, but they didn't usually come to *Al-khabaz*. Increasingly she felt she needed to get to the children while they were young and teach them about how to empower themselves in a situation that was not likely to change.

The charity already provided some education classes but that was more for topping up the teaching in the basics that local schools did. There were some 'empowerment' classes for the women, but nothing along these lines for children. As Raaida was thinking aloud with some of her local staff, one of them whose husband worked in the Ramallah machine, said that she had been talking about this with her husband and he knew of a group in Bethlehem who were already doing this.

71

AYSHAA HAD ALWAYS regretted the religious divide within the Palestinian community. Mostly the Muslims and Christians got on together, at least the women did. That was why she had tried to partner with Mariam and BCI. The news, now widely circulation on the West Bank, of Sami's YouTube video offered a possible way forward for Ayshaa in this area. As her parents were part of Gaza Baptist Church she appealed to the Christian population, but her uncompromising interviews with both Hamas and Israel gave her credibility with the majority Muslim population on the West Bank.

She had been giving some thought to a way forward here and, at her leadership meeting, confessed that she had made contact with Sami and had a positive response. Ethar and Israa were supportive, but Rabia who ran the fundraising side of the charity was more cautious of involving Christians in their operations.

"If it means using Mariam and BCI again then I don't think that's a good idea," she explained, "but I'd like to find a way of using her vblog as a resource."

Ayshaa agreed and said she intended to talk it over with Hani when it seemed a good time. However, after several days, it never did seem like a good time so, not willing to wait any longer, she resolved to pursue the relationship with Sami herself. She congratulated the teenager on what she had achieved, outlined what she was trying to do in Bethlehem and said many on the West Bank were following her. At this time, Sami was still trying to respond to each and every comment that she posted. If it was positive she was thankful and encouraged the respondee to do what they could to support their neighbour etc. If it was questioning, she tried to engage with them, if negative then she ignored it.

Rachel was very interested in what BWP were doing since it was mirroring what she was doing in Gaza through UNRWA so encouraged Sami to follow through with Ayshaa privately. As part of the 'get to know you' exchange, Ayshaa let it be known that her husband had been part of the PA team trying to negotiate with the Israelis a few months earlier. Rachel had heard about the talks and knew that it directly related to the killing of Sami's parents. All Sami knew was that Israelis bombed her church and killed everyone except her.

However, because the Palestinian Authority was at odds with Hamas, both girls in Gaza thought it might be best if there was a pause in the conversation, wondering if this relationship was going to cause them trouble. So Ayshaa didn't hear back from them privately, although she continued to follow the blog and in particular, the YouTube videos. To her, it certainly didn't seem that Sami was a Hamas supporter and what she wanted was a just peace deal with Israel that lifted the blockade and gave the Gazan people a chance in life. Ayshaa could certainly agree with that. She also understood the silence though and hoped it wouldn't last too long but it was over to Sami to get back in touch if she wanted to.

It led Ayshaa to consider how crazy it all was. Firstly the world community granting Israel somebody else's land which they could make a national home. She didn't begrudge their desire – she had the same desire for her own people. Secondly, she thought, the ill-conceived attempts by Egypt, Syria and Jordan to overthrow the new state which led to the West Bank and Gaza being occupied. Thirdly, how Jordan and Egypt in particular had made peace treaties with Israel, so they were safe from reprisals (thank you very much) but left the Palestinian people whose land had been put at risk, without any rights, split down the middle and at the mercy of desperate reprisals from Israel and fourthly, how no-one in the world cared! How could this happen?

And it was Christians in the US, the same people who supported Gaza Baptist Church who, in their naivety, were supporting Israel both morally and financially. Thinking about this and the power of the Evangelical and Jewish lobby in the US, didn't make her angry. It just made her depressed. What hope is there? Here we are working away, making a little difference here and there when in reality, there is no hope. Nothing is going to change.

She was sitting on the step at her front door in the dying sunlight. Inside Rena was playing with her baby brother and Hani was not home yet. It would be a quick in and out for him tonight since he had a meeting of his men later so she'd better get on with some food for everyone. Two hours later and all this was all done, the children were in bed, Hani out and Ayshaa on her own. Following the session she'd had with her BWP team, she thought she'd call Mariam at BCI and talk over her feelings about trying to bridge the religious divide again.

Mariam was delighted to hear Ayshaa on the line and after an exchange of personal and family news, she listened carefully to what Ayshaa was saying. There was no doubt that Mariam wanted to help bridge any religious divide there was, but at the same time was doubtful that she could do anything more herself after the last experience.

"I'm not sure that much has changed, has it?" she asked. Ayshaa explained that any future involvement would need to be different and, while she hadn't fully thought it through, she had been following a vblog from Gaza and had made contact with Sami, the thirteen year old girl who was doing it. Mariam immediately knew what she was talking about and confessed that she was also following what was happening over there. Ayshaa didn't like to reveal that she had made a person to person contact yet, but wanted Mariam to think over any possible relationship first.

Thinking Mariam would decline, she then spoke to Lara at Ghu-sin Zay-tun. She was also following what was happening in Gaza with Sami. Both wives mentioned to each husband what they had talked about. Ayshaa revealed to Hani that she had made contact with Sami over in Gaza. Immediately the word Gaza was mentioned, Hani got interested and as gently as he could teased out more details of who Sami was and what she was doing. He didn't want to butt in on Ayshaa's relationship, but he could see some opportunity. Omari was having the same thoughts, as his wife Lara outlined what she and Ayshaa had talked about.

So the next morning Omari sent a message to Hani to meet at the WalledOff. Whilst the women were interested in using Sami's blog to impact the Christian-Muslim divide in Bethlehem, the men had different things on their mind.

72

MEDAD'S MEETING WITH his Minister went better than expected. He listened without interrupting (a first) to the whole story from the initial rumour to Medad's various attempts to validate it. Medad omitted to mention his Palestinian contacts, but there was just something in the raised eyebrows which suggested to Medad that he knew more than he was letting on. However, he gave Medad the green light to pursue it at full speed, one hundred percent of his time and if he needed any doors opening, to just ask.

He didn't say what he was going to do, although Medad was confident he would seek a brief meeting with the Prime Minister, no doubt looking forward to more details from Medad and a career plus for himself. He expressed the hope that the PM would leave it with him for a few days at least, but he knew there was a high probability that he would alert Mossad and Shin Bet. There would then be competition not only between the two agencies, but also with his department as to who could get to the bottom of it first and stop it. The PM believed that competition was a great motivator but, thought the Minister, it didn't promote teamwork but rather led the various organs of government to become silos where information was held tightly rather than shared.

However, Medad emerged from the meeting with a passport from his Minister to go anywhere and ask anybody. The question Medad had to face was whether to approach Akiva. Which loyalty would win out? He was sure it would be Shin Bet but, on the other hand, if Akiva thought that Medad could get an inside track on this thing, then that wouldn't harm Akiva's career either. So the question was, would his erstwhile friend be ready to give some intelligence to him on the chance that he might get a lot more back by 'cooperating' with Medad?

Since nothing was coming from Hani and the Palestinians, the only leads he currently had were his two friends, Hirsh and Akiva. Having already met Hirsh, he felt he had to have something to give him before he got anything else back, so maybe he could play one against the other by passing on the information that one gave to get more from the other, then vice versa. That is, if between them they did have any intelligence that was worthwhile.

As he travelled home that evening, he wondered how to approach Akiva. On the 'dove-hawk' spectrum, Akiva was or had been a 'hawk', very nationalistic and very against a two state solution with the Palestinians. He remembered him saying,

"As far as I'm concerned this land is our land. We were bequeathed it by God. We lost it, but now have regained it. And we will never lose it again. We want a Jewish land for the Jews. No-one else."

Medad was at the 'dove' end of the spectrum and they both knew each others positions. Looking back, he reckoned it was something of a miracle that they had become such good friends. The chances were that Seth had already mentioned to Akiva that Medad was also on the case, so with that in mind, he decided to approach him professionally, rather than as a friend. The friendship would come into play anyway, if Akiva wanted it to. Approaching him this way would give him respect and move it out of the 'favour' arena.

Shana hadn't kept up with any of her university or IDF friends. Her sole focus was journalism and becoming a successful freelance. As she heard what Medad was coming back with each evening, her keen journalistic nose was already smelling a story and she was asking about updates each evening. They had both been here before and Shana suspected she would have to wait until the right moment to release the story. She knew that Medad would keep her in the loop because when she had been given a story previously, she had done a professional job.

Subsequently, she had written an expose of the whole Israeli-Palestinian talks débâcle using some privileged information from Medad. But again serious steps had been taken to anonymise her identity and location both to protect Medad and to be more acceptable to foreign papers and news websites, but it had got her both national and international coverage at the time and her journalistic persona had become well respected. There was no doubt that she was intrigued by what was beginning to play out and had already sketched out in her head how she might approach the story.

After talking over dinner, they both agreed the way ahead. The next day in the office, Medad called the number he had for Shin Bet, asking for Akiva and giving his own name and title. He waited and waited. It must have been four or five minutes before a lady came back on the line and said that Akiva was out but a message had been passed on and he would be in touch. Medad was not happy. It could be genuine or it could be a powerplay type response. If the latter, Akiva had changed and he would have to watch his step carefully.

Medad received Akiva's response later that day which, in friendly terms, suggested that he would come over to Jerusalem from their Tel Aviv HQ if that was acceptable. Medad messaged back that it was and suggested Café Café on Ephraim Street since it was becoming his regular meeting place. That message from Akiva told him two things: firstly, the fact that he was willing to come over to Jerusalem meant he was keen, but secondly, a coffee meant a relatively short business-type meeting rather than a longer more friendly meeting over lunch. Not a problem for Medad.

He knew that Shin Bet had been involved in Gaza for a long time. They had three separate divisions: the Arab Department looked after Gaza and was responsible for uncovering criminal activity; the Israel and Foreigners Department (the Jewish Department) looking after issues within Israel and counter terrorism, and finally the the Protective Security Department, responsible for protecting senior individuals and locations in the country such as embassies, airports, and research facilities.

Occasionally they would work alongside Aman, the Military Intelligence agency. Medad recalled them working together to discover tunnels into Gaza some years back, although there had been criticism from some that there had been a lack of cooperation initially. That wouldn't surprise anyone, just another confirmation that every arm of the government tended to operate independently when it came to information. The other episode he remembered was the uncovering of a 'spy' network in Israel by Shin Bet. Israeli Arabs, who had family in Gaza and thus were allowed to use the Erez crossing had agreed (been coerced?) by Hamas to carry out reconnaissance in Israel of sensitive sites and take it back with them over the border. Such activities constituted terrorism according to the Shin Bet.

Medad didn't know for certain where Akiva was deployed, but after his chat with Seth, he thought it was odds on that he was directly concerned with Gaza. His suspicions were vindicated as they met each other again.

"Yes, now attached to the Arab Department with some responsibility for Gaza, and I gather from Seth that you have some as well." Medad explained his position, and they danced around each other for a bit.

He then decided to break the stand-off, but still be businesslike. "Look Akiva, I understand lines of command and hierarchies just as we had during the time in the IDF. I have my reporting structure and I appreciate you have yours."

Akiva nodded as Medad continued. "I think we are both interested in what might be happening in Gaza and it might be worth cooperating, at least as far as each of us can go." He waited for Akiva's response. He didn't respond directly but referenced Medad's role in the Palestinian talks a couple of years ago where he was one of the lead negotiators. Medad knew that Akiva was wanting an agreement to pass on any information he had from his Palestinian counterparts.

Medad was thinking that being a little 'economical with the truth' might be called for in this situation.

So he explained, "Unfortunately, these have largely been burnt thanks to Hamas but I am trying to resurrect them."

He passed the baton back to Akiva and directly asked him what his contacts in Gaza were saying. Akiva thought for a moment and asked, "Do we have a deal?" Medad offered his hand across the coffee table and Akiva shook it. Both men relaxed a bit and sat back in their chairs. "Fancy another, with a doughnut?" Akiva signalled for refills and pastries, and added, "It's on me." The ice was broken but it remained to be seen how long the partnership would last. When the necessities had been served, Akiva began to explain his role.

"I have two 'agents' running in Gaza, one a member of Hamas and the other one of the other para military groups. There's not much from either so far although I am pushing them hard. Yes, I think there is some grand scheme, but only a few know of it and even fewer know any detail."

Medad sat back to hear what intelligence Akiva might throw him.

"There is a man called Khalid who seemed to be the leader's right hand man, his fixer. He has recently been away for some days from his family, twice that we know about and once was to Lebanon via the Rafah crossing. We don't know who he saw or what was said, nor do we know where he went the second time. The only other firm information I can give at the moment was that it involved an Imam somewhere, and he could be anywhere."

Medad felt as if he had been holding his breath while Akiva had been speaking but he gradually relaxed as he assessed Akiva's information. "That's excellent intelligence. I'll see if I can get hold of the Fatah men. There's little love lost between Fatah and Hamas, so if they have anything, I'll get it and you'll be the first to know well, maybe the second."

They laughed, shook hands again and promised to keep in touch.

73

SHACHNA HAD BEEN busy. He had already got his sister Raaida to agree to accept funding from mosques and have an Imam or two on the Board to represent their investment in *Al-khabaz*. One of these Imams was from Jenin, one Ahmed al-Fahd. There was no reason why this should have raised any red flags for Raaida. As Chief Executive, she was totally focussed on keeping *Al-Khabaz* running and expanding where she could. Whilst she had a manager in each place, she like to be in control of everything that was going on. With operations now in every city and every major town on the West Bank, it consumed both her time and her mental space. It was her life.

She failed to notice how her brother was subtly changing the membership of the Board. Because of her busyness, Shachna had suggested some time ago that he could relieve her of some pressure by managing the occasional meetings of the Board. Nothing usually came of these meetings which Raaida found rather tiresome and, in her opinion, did nothing to further the cause. She had stopped attending them for she had better things to do.

Al-Khabaz was certainly a success and depended upon by many, many people. It had their vote, and even those who did not depend on its services regarded it as a great institution. In fact, more than once the Palestinian Authority had tried to annex the organisation to itself, but Raaida had consistently refused which hadn't brought her any plaudits from them.

It seemed that Fatah and the Palestinian Authority had not learned the lesson of Gaza. Although they controlled the West Bank, they continued to ignore the ordinary people. Hani was one such and had made his views known to his previous boss, Jamal. Unfortunately, he was so part of the Ramallah infrastructure that he couldn't see any need to rock the money-boat. Hani didn't even bother to have any such a conversation with his new boss, Talal. A complete waste of time. He knew there was an *Al-Khabaz* in Bethlehem; in fact he and Ayshaa had used it in the past. Although it was a privately run charity, he knew it did good work but he had no idea how large it was or how it was gradually being infiltrated.

Having had the 'Sami' conversation with Ayshaa, his immediate priority was to meet with Omari and decide whether this connection could be used in their quest. It seemed to him too much of a coincidence that this relationship had cropped up at this time. But he had to admit that perhaps he was clutching at straws. Omari, though, had gone one step further. He had looked at Sami's YouTube channel and saw the link with the leader of Hamas. As they talked together they went round and round trying to get a handle on what action they could take that would move things forward. They finally settled on setting up a meeting with Medad and giving him the information they had.

Medad was making progress of a sort but despite the intelligence from his former IDF colleagues, he was no nearer understanding exactly what Hamas had in mind. His next step was to challenge the Palestinians to come up with some intelligence of their own, after all it had been one way traffic so far. Omari surprised him by WhatsApp-ing him first and offering to come to Jerusalem, obviously without Hani who would not be able to get a pass.

This time they met on an anonymous park bench. The café was beginning to become too regular and he wanted to maintain the secrecy of the Palestinian relationship. Hidden in an open space! Omari opened by explaining about Sami, the beginnings of a relationship with Ayshaa and her links with the Hamas leadership. As soon as Medad heard the name 'Sami', he knew he had met her and already had established a link by giving her his card.

"Ah. I've met her."

"When?" asked Omari.

"After the Hamas interview, the first one, she was invited by the President to come to the Presidential Palace as an attempt to head off some bad press in the US."

"Yes I saw bits of that on the television, but I didn't know you were there."

"I was representing the Ministry and had a chance to have a quiet word. I gave her my card and said she could contact me any time."

It had been during the visit to Israel of Pope Benedict XVI in 2009 that President Shimon Peres had inaugurated a new custom that all visiting world leaders would plant an olive tree in the *Beit HaNassi* Peace Garden. Sami was not asked to perform such a task but the Israeli government thought it was a suitable place to meet her and try to sooth the American Baptist Churches over the destruction of Gaza Baptist Church building.

Medad mused, "It's another contact, but I'm not sure whether she will have any further information than any other contact we have. But I can try."

Omari agreed, "It's all very nebulous. I'm still hoping the whole thing is a hoax."

Medad was firm, "No no, it's real all right. There's too much activity for there to be nothing."

Omari was quiet for a moment. "Hani suggested that Ayshaa could tentatively ask Sami to be alert for any signs, but Ayshaa was not keen, since the relationship has hardly started."

Medad said, "Yes, I can see that. But perhaps she could start by talking about the peace process that Hani and I have been involved with and seeing what her reaction is. It would also give me an opening to contact her as well."

They had got as far as they could so they left the park and both made their way home in different directions each thinking and hoping for a breakthrough. Hani did make the suggestion to Ayshaa but, in retrospect, it would have been better if someone else had done so, for she was not in any mood to take orders or even suggestions from Hani which affected her BWP.

"Absolutely not." And there was no further conversation on the matter. Hani was sorely tempted to go on Sami's blog himself and make contact as a preface to asking the question, but thought better of it, since it would almost certainly rebound and that would scupper everyone. It looked like the Israeli was on his own, as far as Sami was concerned.

Medad was under some pressure to meet again with his Minister and was ready to do almost anything to move it all forward. He decided that he would message Sami directly that evening, introduce himself again and talk simply about the peace process, his Palestinian contacts and how she might help. He spent nearly frustrating three hours trying to get the right form of words which would settle her but also get a quick response. Shana was out and he would normally have asked her to scan the text and give her approval or not.

He couldn't wait until she got back, so he pressed the send button, and waited.

It was about an hour later when Shana came in and Medad was pacing up and down because there had been no reply.

"I think I've blown it," he moaned.

"What are you talking about?" said Shana as she was hanging up her coat.

"I've messaged Sami over in Gaza and I've had no reply."

"When did you send it?"

"Over an hour ago."

"My word. A whole hour and no response! How dare she?" Shana had a very sarcastic tongue when she wanted.

"But it's vitally important."

"To her or to you?"

"To everyone."

"Sit down for a moment. Think about it. First she might not be in. Second, she might not have her computer on and seen your message, and third, have you thought how dangerous this might be for her, if Hamas were to get access to her account? Remember, she's a teenager."

Medad was insistent. "But she has a friend with her who is probably in the twenties. Surely she can see the importance of what I'm asking."

"Did you say how urgent it was?"

"Well no, but surely that's obvious." Shana shook her head in disbelief. But there was nothing he could do until she replied.

74

SAMI HAD LOOKED at Medad's message but didn't know what he meant by his 'Palestinian contacts', since none had mentioned his name. However, she did remember him as a quietly spoken man who had seemed quite friendly and not the normal arrogant Israeli. She discussed it with Rachel. "Do you remember this man from our visit to Jerusalem?"

"Not really," she replied. "How did you meet him?"

"As I remember, he was part of the Israeli delegation and whilst we were all waiting for the President to appear, he came up to me, said he was working for a peace process, gave me his card and said if he could help in any way, to contact him."

Rachel looked at Sami, "Have you still got it?"

"Yes, somewhere, I think."

"Did you believe him, was he genuine?"

Sami nodded, "Yes, I think so."

"What kind of message should we send back?" Rachel was still not wanting to take over decision-making from the teenager. Sami considered for a moment,

"I think we should find out what he wants. It may help us to have a contact within the Israeli government. But let's sleep on it and see if we still feel the same in the morning."

Rachel nodded, "I agree."

Over breakfast, they both agreed to send back a positive message to Medad but also asking who the other 'Palestinian contacts' were."

The text came through as Medad was just about to leave the apartment and as Medad read it he was encouraged to push further in his next message. He mentioned BWP and Ayshaa explaining that it was her husband Hani with whom he was currently working because there were rumours of a 'Plan' that Hamas were developing which might set back the peace process for a long time. His final question was, "In your meetings with Hamas, did you ever hear anything which might relate to this 'Plan'?" Medad thought it was a bit brusque but he felt he needed to move quickly.

Sami and Rachel were still together in the apartment when the message came through. Both looked at the message together, then at each other. Rachel began to feel uncomfortable. "This is getting very political. What if Hamas can hack our private messages and they find this?"

Sami was more blasé, perhaps because she was younger and maybe a little over-confident. "But what we are doing is political, isn't it? I mean, we are not doing this to make money. We want change, don't we?"

Rachel squirmed a little, "Yes, but I also want to stay alive. We can't just waltz up to them and ask them about this 'Plan'. If it's that secret, we would be clapped in irons immediately. No we can't do it."

A rather tense conversation began between the two of them that looked as if it would run and run. Meanwhile, Medad was impatiently scouring his messages looking for an answer, which was not forthcoming. After an hour of not speaking, Rachel suddenly remembered Khalid coming in to the recording studio and having a conversation with the Leader. She asked Sami,

"Did you catch anything of what he said? It looked very secretive."

Sami shook her head, "I was busy looking at my notes ready for the next set of questions."

Rachel was persistent. "But you were right next to them. Think."

Sami started to think and run through exactly what happened before Khalid came in. "Yes I remember, I looked up when he came in and wondered what he was doing so I did look at them together for a split second."

"Think."

"He was whispering something… now you come to mention it, I did hear something although I assumed it was someone waiting outside for him."

"What did you hear?"

"It was only one word, 'Imam'. I'm sure it means nothing. I mean there are hundreds of Imams about." Rachel considered this.

"You're right, I can't see how it means anything. But it's all we've got. Let's send it and then we've done all that we can. We can forget about it."

It was late morning when the one word message eventually went off.

75

NATAN NO LONGER trusted any of the original Twelve. He had never discovered who had leaked the video of the meeting between the Minister of Defence and a senior army general, and it rankled. They still met from time to time, but Natan never mentioned any of his personal plans to anyone, not even Shai his long time friend. He would confide in no-one, but it was clear that his desire for Palestinian blood had not been assuaged by the demolition of Jamal's house in East Jerusalem. He wanted more, and with an insider within the Civil Authority he was in a position to get more.

Ares Heiman, he knew, was rather garrulous especially when he had put away a few. So Natan had to tread carefully. He could not afford to be exposed or blackmailed if Ares blabbed what was happening to a fellow boozer, or suddenly decided to become belligerent and demand money himself. He thought he could get away with one more hit at Fatah. After that he would have to take steps to ensure Ares remained quiet. He arranged another meeting at the Civil Administration HQ with an opportunity to buy Ares more beer after hours. This time he would have to offer the man some 'expenses' as well as appealing to his patriotism. But first a little research was called for.

In Gaza, the Leader now understood what the 'Plan' was and what his role would be. He set about making his preparations.

In Jerusalem, Medad had retired for the night but had put an alarm on his message system so that if there was an answer from Sami, he would immediately receive it whether he was asleep or not. The alarm was set to play Aviv Geffen's song, *Achshav Meunan* but very softly so as not to wake Shana. Just as he had got to sleep, it started playing. He reached over, turned the alarm off and swung his feet on to the floor. He crept into the other room and excitedly read the message. It was just one word. Surely not. There must be more.

He checked to see if there were other messages, but there were none. That was it. He checked again; yes it had come from Sami. He couldn't believe it.

He checked a third time with the same result. If Shana hadn't been asleep in an adjacent room he would have thrown his phone across the room in despair. Instead, he trudged back to bed disconsolately knowing he had just drawn a blank from every source he had. In the morning he told Shana what the message was but she was no help at all.

"No idea," she said. "What's an Imam going to do? Perhaps it's a spelling error, you know, predictive texting? See what other letters it could be. Or maybe Sami and her friend are trying to be helpful and it's in code in case Hamas have bugged their computer. Sorry, that's the best I have." And with that she left. Medad grunted and, having called the office to say he was working from home, he set about working the problem but by lunchtime he was nowhere. His head was hurting. A ping from the phone signalled a WhatsApp coming in. It was Shai looking to meet up; would he come to the Café Café at his earliest convenience. He had not expected to see Shai again since the meeting with Chuck at the Philadelphia. It sounded like he had some news and as no-one else had, he responded immediately that he could meet in a few hours that day.

Both ordered tea and Shai began to confide in Medad about Natan and his frame of mind, particularly with regard to Palestinians involved in the talks.

"You remember Natan?" Medad said that he did.

"Well," Shai continued, "our little group still meets from time to time, but he shares nothing. I know him. We've been colleagues for many years, and I'm anxious about what else he might be planning after he got that Palestinian leader's home demolished in East Jerusalem."

Medad pursed his lips, "What else could he do?"

Shai explained, "He used to work for the Civil Authority, so he must still have contacts there. I'm sure that's how he managed to get the demolition order through before. If he's done it once, he could do it again."

Medad suddenly woke up and swore. Hani. He quickly got up, muttered thanks to Shai and dashed out. As he went he was furiously WhatsApping Hani to meet him at the WalledOff in two hours. He didn't want to put details in even a WhatsApp message and two hours was the quickest he reckoned he could get to Bethlehem.

Hani was doing nothing in particular when Medad's message came through. It was clearly urgent so he messaged back immediately and set off for the WalledOff. He walked excitedly thinking that Medad must have got a breakthrough on the Gaza problem. He was looking forward to some new information which might serve to get Jamal back in favour and Talal off his back.

The Israeli wasted no time when he met Hani. Gone was the reserve and hesitancy as he quickly explained about Natan and the warning he'd just received from Shai. Hani was inclined to dismiss the idea, but Medad was insistent. "Look, the man is a lunatic of the far right. He has the contacts to make it happen at any time and you need to take precautions."

Hani thought, "I don't exactly know what I can do. I live in a flat on the ground floor of a terraced building. He can't demolish that without the whole block coming down."

Medad relaxed a bit, "Well, better to be forewarned. Natan doesn't know about Omari, so you are the only other leader from the talks that he would know." Hani expressed his thanks and he would talk it over with Ayshaa that evening. "By the way," Medad asked, "Did you or her ever contact Sami over in Gaza?" Hani looked a little crestfallen,

"I'm sure she will have done, but it will be to do with BWP. I don't know if she has mentioned you. I haven't done so myself."

Medad looked puzzled, "BWP?"

"Bethlehem Women for Peace. It's her charity to do with empowering women and training them to cope with life. I'm afraid I don't have much of a role there."

Medad looked impressed. "That sounds great." He got up to go and both men moved towards the door. Hani once again expressed his thanks to Medad and held out his hand, which Medad took. It was the first time the men had actually shaken hands.

"By the way, I did contact Sami myself about our little problem and all she said in her reply was 'Imam'. It means nothing to me and I have no idea if it means anything to anyone."

Hani still thinking about what he would say to Ayshaa that evening shook his head and they went their way.

76

NATAN HAD DONE his research and had found out where Hani lived but it was as Hani had said to Medad. Demolition would be messy even for the Civil Administration. So he had switched his immediate attention to Hani's wife. He also noted from the reports he was getting that they had two small children. His informers told him that Hani and his wife were rarely together; he had his work and she had hers. Maybe they wouldn't miss each other.

Those around the Palestinian Authority's President eventually persuaded him to call a general election on the West Bank. Although he hadn't announced his retirement, it was assumed by many that he would hand over to the next generation. The reaction in Jerusalem was more amused than serious. The Palestinians could play with democracy, but everyone knew democratic processes in Ramallah were a fiction.

Hani heard the news and wondered whether it had implications for him in Bethlehem. Would he still have a job? He didn't know, although he would like to think that he was part of the up and coming generation. It was a shame Jamal was still sidelined but that led him on to think about Natan and the threat he posed. He had mentioned it to Ayshaa the previous evening and she immediately put the responsibility back on Hani's shoulders.

"That's your job, your only job; to keep us safe," was all she said and carried on with what she was doing.

Suddenly Hani remembered, "Imam!" he shouted out loud. He swore and, ignoring Ayshaa's protest about his language, jumped on his phone to call Jamal. His erstwhile boss picked up and before he could exchange greetings, Hani launched in.

"It's the Imam from Jenin."

Jamal was taken aback, "What?"

"It's Ahmed al-Fahd"

Jamal tried to slow Hani down, "What about the man?" Hani tried to get a grip on himself and explain.

"I was with Medad yesterday and he has been in touch with that girl in Gaza who has interviewed Hamas. He asked her if she knew anything about any plan which they might have to disrupt any peace process and she answered with one word, 'Imam'. It has to be him."

Jamal was quiet at the other end. He was quickly thinking through the probabilities. It was quite a leap, but not entirely implausible. He came to a decision.

"Let's suppose you're right."

Hani jumped in, "I know I'm right. It all fits."

Jamal continued calmly, "If you're right, the only way of testing that is to put him under surveillance and see what he's up to, who he meets etc."

Hani asked, "Can you do that where you are?"

"No, but I'll call in some favours without mentioning why and you mustn't mention this to anyone yet. Let's give it a few days."

Ayshaa was listening but not saying a word. Hani ordered her not to say anything to anyone about what she may or may not have heard. She didn't respond.

Sami and Rachel had moved on from Medad's message and were planning the next YouTube video. Followers were growing and they already had some advertising interest through the agency they had appointed. A single contract had been signed and some were yet to be signed and, more importantly, money was starting to roll in. Rachel's last salary from UNRWA was due any day now, so within a month they needed an income to keep a roof over their heads. She had decided not to inform her parents about her career move, thinking it would only make them worry.

The next video was to be about the children of Gaza as Sami still thought of herself as one of them. They had done a 'vox pop' exercise around where they were and Rachel had edited it with Sami writing her narrative around what the kids had said adding in some of her personal experience. As far as any 'Plan' was concerned, they knew nothing.

However, they had underestimated the technical capability of Hamas.

Their computer had not been bugged, but they already had access into UN-RWA's wifi in order to monitor the agency. It was also the wifi that Sami and Rachel were still using. A coincidental conversation between one of their bright young software geniuses and Khalid drew the latter's attention to the messages sent and received by the girls. The young man had been asked to keep a watch on what UNRWA were doing when he came across the girls' blog and messages. He was interested to see what they were saying about Gaza and Hamas as he had heard their story. The IT operator had no knowledge of any Hamas 'Plan', but in general conversation with Khalid mentioned that Sami had been in touch with an Israeli. This had perked Khalid's interest and he wanted more. That's when he found it.

Shachna was persuading Raaida that *Al-Khabaz* could have a bigger impact if it entered the political arena. She was not persuaded. He was thinking that it would be easier for everyone if she agreed to the strategy, but even if she didn't, they could go ahead because he had the votes on the Board in his favour. He did his best, but she was steadfast. "This was not what our father had in mind, and I'm sure he would disagree."

Shachna tried one last time, "But the situation has changed. You know that Fatah was been worse than useless for our people. Now we might have an election. If *Al-Khabaz* stands as a political party we will have a significant voice in changing things."

But Raaida didn't want to get mixed up in the dirty world of Palestinian politics. She was so busy with the day to day that she failed to see the mirror image of what Hamas had done in Gaza. It was their social services organisation called *Dawah* that won Hamas the election in Gaza. Fatah used to govern Gaza but had paid a minimum of attention to the social needs of the Gazan Palestinians. So, while they largely ignored the ordinary men and women, the population of Gaza turned to the only organisation that was helping them – *Dawah*. Hamas had created credibility at grass roots level and that was crucial in winning the trust of the population and thus the vote. The people rebelled against Fatah and embraced Hamas in disguise.

Shachna shrugged and left it at that.

*

Medad had to tell his Minister that there definitely was a 'Plan', but he had yet to get specifics. As a sign of his desperation to convince his boss that he was getting somewhere, he went into some detail, including names about his contacts in the military, Shin Bet and Palestinians he'd known during the talks, all of whom agreed with him. None yet had any facts but were working tirelessly to uncover the truth and felt there would be a breakthrough very soon. He avoided mentioning Sami because depending on a teenager in Gaza for serious intelligence seemed like stupidity. Perhaps it was.

His Minister was not best pleased. He had nothing to go to the PM with and was not blind to the race between agencies and ministerial departments to be the first to get details into the PM's hands and after all, Palestinian Affairs was what his Department was all about. Medad left with his tail between his legs, his previous track record now blotched.

Natan was working on plan B as far as Hani was concerned, but he happened to bump into Major General Hersch at some reception and after a conversation about past and future Palestinian talks, Natan intimated to the General that there was intelligence that cast Hani as a danger to Israeli security. Hersch was reminded that Hani was a Fatah leader in Bethlehem who operated also in Ramallah and had played a pivotal role in getting dangerous concessions at the recent abortive Palestinian-Israeli talks. As the General was on the Israeli delegation, he knew who Hani was and agreed that IDF filming should pay particular attention to locating him and passing that information to their snipers.

This wasn't going to be an immediate reprisal, so he continued to target his wife. He now knew about BWP, the women's training sessions that she held and where she held them. Natan didn't want to kill, maim or disable a woman, even a Palestinian one. No. He wanted to destroy BWP, a double whammy to hurt Hani through his wife and prevent Palestinian women resisting Occupation. Ayshaa had developed a routine of meetings which was easily mapped and allowed Natan to prepare his plans.

Every week Ayshaa would meet four other women for two or three hours much longer than the other training sessions. Each was followed to her home and in this way the leadership team was identified. First step: send each husband, excluding Hani, a threatening letter. Second step: for those who continued to meet, mug them in a quiet place. Third step: send an anonymous letter to Ramallah claiming that BWP was anti-Fatah and should be closed down and Hani investigated. That should do it, thought Natan, at least for the moment. He didn't believe it would be the end, but it should cause sufficient disruption until IDF snipers could do their job.

Jamal was now more desperate to prove his capability to the President than he was about the actual Plan he was trying to investigate. Even though he was not wholly convinced, he went about the task with zeal. Being at the centre of things for so long had given him many contacts and many favours owed that he could call in. Thus getting some surveillance on Ahmed al Fahed wasn't that difficult, especially as he was a known Hezbollah sympathiser.

After a week of watching, the report which Jamal received didn't look hopeful. The only place he went other than the mosque was to the HQ of *Al-Khabaz*. Everyone knew the charity and the good work it did, so no red flags were raised. Provisionally, he came back clean. Jamal was disappointed by not surprised. He messaged Hani with the results.

77

SHACHNA HAD THE Board's vote to register *Al-khabaz* as a political party for the upcoming Palestinian general election with him as the leader. Being the son of the founder made him the natural choice. Whether he would maintain such a position if they won was another matter entirely. He would campaign on the basis of what the charity did in helping ordinary people and the good name of his father. Within days someone who had masterminded the Gaza election which brought Hamas to power arrived to advise the campaign. He had used the same route that Khalid had used and brought with him not just expertise, but funds.

Raaida was furious especially when she found out that she had been out manoeuvred on the Board. Shachna changed his approach. No more was he the pleading brother trying to reason with his sister. Now he was aggressive towards her.

He got close to her face, "You had your chance and you blew it. You just get on with your job and I'll get on with mine."

Leaflets were produced and distributed at every *Al-Khabaz* centre. They offered the people a new start. Food, jobs and support for all. 'For the many not the few' was the strapline borrowed from campaigns in the UK and probably elsewhere. It was a startling proclamation and one which Fatah could not match, having had decades to do it and failed. Every media available was used to ram the message home until every person on the West Bank knew it by heart. Everyone wondered what Fatah's response would be.

Jamal had never thought of *Al-Khabaz* as a potential political force. Now they had announced themselves, he thought privately that it was a brilliant move. Publicly, he and everyone in Ramallah now saw the parallel with Gaza and the establishment began a negative campaign accusing Hamas of funding and directing operations. As yet though, there was no evidence. Yes, Ahmed al Fahed was on the Board of *Al-Khabaz*, but they needed more.

Hani's private thoughts were similar to those of his old boss, but if Hamas ruled the West Bank as well, there would never be a two state solution and Israel would have to declare war in order to defend the thousands of illegal settlers living. The whole of the West Bank would be filled with Israeli soldiers and hundreds if not thousands of innocent people would lose their lives. This was the reality as he saw it. He had to inform Medad.

For his part, Medad had parked the idea of an Imam being the key to 'The Plan'. He didn't get it. However, an emergency meeting with Hani at the WalledOff quickly convinced him and he hurried back to Jerusalem to talk to his Minister. The threat was never going to come from Gaza. It was a cunning deception. No wonder neither Hirsch nor Akiva were getting anywhere. They were looking in the wrong place. He laughed at the simplicity of it, but then his brow furrowed as he realised the implications if Hamas gained control of the West Bank.

If only the recent talks had come to a successful conclusion. Fatah could then claim significant concessions from Israel and might have stood a chance of staying in power. From Israel's point of view, better Fatah than Hamas. He didn't need anyone to tell him that this was a powerful challenge to Fatah and their history would not save them. Israel would need to do something, but how could it interfere in the Palestinian elections, which they had demanded, without more international condemnation.

Medad knew his Minister would want a recommendation. He didn't like having problems dumped on him without solutions. For advice on possible solutions, he reached out to Dan who had more experience than he did.

Ayshaa got a series of hurried short calls from Israa, Ethar and Rabia saying that their husbands had received threatening letters regarding their involvement with BWP and had refused them permission to meet anymore. Ayshaa was dumbfounded. She was just about to go out, but quickly sat down in a chair to compose herself for tears were forming in her eyes, not for herself but for her team. She didn't want any harm to come to them. As she sat her anguish began to turn to anger, firstly directed at Hani. Surely it was because of his involvement with Fatah and it was unacceptable. She would tell him to his face.

She called Lara and told her the news. Lara could hardly believe it. "Who would want to do this? What is there to gain? Who are they getting at?"

Ayshaa started sobbing again, "I think it may be something to do with Hani and Fatah. Maybe something to do with this election? Perhaps they just want to hurt us."

Lara could her the tremors in Ayshaa's voice. "Look, I know it's a terrific shock but just take care of yourself and your little ones for the moment. It may be that BWP will be resurrected very soon. Don't blame Hani, I'm sure it's not his fault. I'll talk to Omari and see what we can find out."

It was now late afternoon so Ayshaa decided that busyness was needed. So she began to make the evening meal and get the children to bed. Then she was going to bed herself. Maybe things would look better in the morning.

Natan was pleased with how Plan A had worked and was deciding when he might launch Plan B. He would leave it for a few days. His paid agents in Bethlehem wanted to lie low for a while to avoid detection.

Hani was, however, not lying low. His anger was off the scale and he WhatsApp'd Medad with what had happened. He wanted answers: who was it, where were they, what were they likely to do next? Usually these details were never put in a message but revealed at face to face meetings, but Hani was beyond it.

Medad contacted Shai to see what could be done. "Natan has started," he told Shai. "We need to stop him."

Shai was doubtful. "If I know anything about Natan, nothing will be traceable back to him. He will have recruited local thugs and probably paid them through another third party."

Medad was insistent, "But surely there's something we can do. I'm guessing he's not finished yet."

Shai explained what he thought Natan's strategy was. "If it gets out that Fatah leaders and their wives are being deliberately targeted, it isn't the Israelis who are going to be blamed, but the opposition in the upcoming Palestinian elections."

Medad thought for a second. "If that opposition is backed by Hamas and Fatah is weakened by this activity, then we are interested because the last thing we want is for Hamas to take over the West Bank."

Shai responded, "Then you'd better talk to your Minister." Medad retorted, "Maybe you ought to do something about Natan." Shai hung up.

It was the following day when he managed to get some time with Dan. They took a walk in Rose Park, near the Knesset. It took a while to explain everything but Medad thought it important to give Dan all he had.

Dan was thoughtful as he listened. "My advice is to try to meet him out of the office where he can be relaxed and not jump to conclusions. Then say you've uncovered a lot of inter-related bits of the jigsaw puzzle, and you are going to go through each one saying how they fit together."

He paused as if expecting Medad to be taking notes. "Of course, it's a gamble but my advice is to go all in. Begin with showing him that video of the General and the Defence Minister – say it just came into your possession as you were following leads, or something. Say you have witness evidence that Natan Berkowitz, the Minister's aide has now gone rogue; that he was responsible for the demolition of that Fatah leader's home in East Jerusalem and now is going after another of the Palestinian leaders at the talks. Link it to the election, explain the Hamas plan and conclude by expressing a view that Fatah might be preferable to Hamas."

Medad was quickly assessing this approach. "Some of the evidence I have, some I don't have. Shai, the aide to the General will never surface."

Dan responded, "As long as your argument holds together, he won't want chapter and verse for everything, but he will need something to show the PM."

Hani had spoken to Omari about what had happened to Ayshaa's team members. It was Omari's opinion that, "Whoever it is really wants to hurt you but not directly, not yet anyway. They want you to suffer as they hurt Ayshaa. It may be that there might be a direct attack on her next."

Omari was looking closely at Hani whose face was hardening. "I know who it is and he couldn't do this without Palestinian help. Some of our countrymen are getting paid to do this."

"Be very careful." cautioned Omari, "this election is turning a lot of things upside down. You may not be able to count on those you've counted on in the past."

Hani made up his mind. He was going to call an emergency meeting of his men in Bethlehem. He wanted to face down anyone who showed any kind of disloyalty, including his two dissenters.

Sami and Rachel were oblivious to the panic in Israel and the West Bank over their single word answer. They were also unaware that Hamas had been alerted to their messages, but not for long. It happened the next evening. Sami was proving to Rachel that even with one leg shorter than the other she could still walk faster than her friend. Rachel was playing along and pretending she was going as fast as she could but allowing Sami to get ahead of her.

It all happened very quickly but with practised precision. A black Mercedes with black tinted windows drew up alongside Sami. A burly man jumped out, grabbed the teenager, pushed her into the back of the car, climbed back in himself, and off it sped before Rachel knew what was happening. By the time she had processed what had just happened, the car was gone with a screech of its wheels and a whole load of dust. She ran down the road after the car waving and shouting to no avail. Nobody did anything or saw anything, even though there were plenty of passers by. The car disappeared round a corner and Sami had gone.

All she could do was to sit down at the side of the road and replay in her mind what had just happened. She thought of Sami, a young teenager with the whole of her life in front of her. What kind of society was this? Tears had been flowing down her face for some minutes but she didn't care. She was guilt ridden because she was her friend and her security, and she had failed. She felt empty, bereft and, after what seemed an age but was actually only ten minutes, she got up and walked slowly back to her flat wiping her face.

In an ordinary country, she would have called the police, but not here. She knew it was either Hamas directly or one of the many militias who would do

Hamas' bidding. She had an idea to call UNRWA security, not that they could intervene, but surely they might be able to give her some advice or help in some way. Nothing was forthcoming from them. The individuals were apologetic and hoped Sami would be found unharmed, but since neither she nor Sami were part of the organisation…

She sank to the floor of her kitchen helplessly thinking she had no-one to turn to. The laptop pinged with a message. Rachel dragged herself to her feet to look at it thinking it may be from Hamas, saying what they had done and she should desist from any further blogs or YouTube videos. It wasn't Hamas but rather Medad with a simple thank you message. Rachel suddenly realised that if they knew about Sami, they now knew about Medad. But he was in Jerusalem and probably safe, but nevertheless he should know what had just happened. The question was how should she get that message across without getting it flagged up.

Finally she decided just to tell Medad in a straightforward way what had happened, and to hell with it. The message ran, 'Compromised. Sami gone. Closing down.' Even as she wrote this, she felt an upsurge of anger and rebelliousness. No she wouldn't close down. Those words were deleted and the message sent.

Let's see what they do, she thought.

Epilogue

HANI, THE EX-SHOPKEEPER, had done the maths. He was tired and his anger was now being replaced by a simple desire to grab his wife and family and be safe. He was through with it all; his best just hadn't been good enough. He knew he'd been beaten and even his wife was against him. Would Fatah would win the election? Probably not. In his mind they didn't deserve to, in which case he had no income. The shop was now virtually derelict with little chance of resurrection.

The meeting with his men had been set up so he had to go through with it, but his heart wasn't in it anymore. It was the worst session he had known. Everyone knew how strong *Al-Khabaz* was proving to be among the ordinary people. They all, including the dissenters, realised that this might be their last meeting and the payments they received from Fatah might suddenly end. In fact, it could be worse, for whoever came into power might want to track down Fatah supporters and punish them. Thus, they were all now looking to their own futures and no-one was remotely interested in what was happening to a few women. For some, this was a sign of what might be to come.

Hani got back home and unburdened himself to Ayshaa who listened impassively.

"Well, if your role is ending, mine isn't," she declared passionately. "I don't care whether it's Fatah, Hamas or whoever, my work is still needed and I'm carrying on."

He looked at her as he had done at the beginning. A firebrand. Yes, he still loved her, but he knew he'd blown it. There was no more he could give. She and Lara got on well when they worked together, he thought, and maybe they would be successful. Another thought flitted across his mind. Perhaps Omari might be able to use him in some way in his charity. He owed him another meet, so with some renewed vigour, he determined to explore the option with him.

Then, perhaps unsurprisingly, Fatah called off the Palestinian election so that they could "more accurately compile a voter register ensuring every Palestinian on the West Bank had the opportunity to vote". In reality, of course, they didn't want to lose to *Al-Khabaz*. Ordinary Palestinians had little difficulty in seeing through the propaganda and felt, once again, they had been kicked hard by their own side. The ageing President and his entourage, however, took little notice. Whilst the Israeli media poked a great deal of fun at them, their government ministers were quietly relieved that the Hamas-backed group did not have the chance to win control of the West Bank. But there was little chance of a peace conference or any concessions to the Palestinian Authority. The fig leaf remained the demand that Ramallah had an election to ensure authenticity, and so far that hadn't materialised and probably wouldn't.

Hani remained the Fatah man in Bethlehem if only for the salary. He tried half-heartedly to advocate more help for ordinary people, but he knew that cry would still fall on deaf ears in Ramallah. Yes, Omari had offered him a role in his charity which, had Fatah lost the election, Hani would have accepted, but at least he seemed to be almost his own boss in Bethlehem for the moment at least.

Ayshaa, true to her word, kept her BWP work growing and, apart from the occasional minor backlash, the group grew and played a major part in the lives of many women from the refugee camps. Their marriage continued in name only and, in spite of gentle offers of help from Omari and Lara, the relationship remained estranged. Somehow, however, they continued to live in the same rooms for the sake of their two children, so maybe all was not lost.

Omari continued to travel in and out of the country tirelessly explaining the Palestinian cause to anyone who would listen. His charity at home grew in scope and gained the deserved respect of certain Israelis as well as many of his own people. He failed, however, in persuading Dan to answer any text, WhatsApp or call so that relationship quickly fizzled out. He was not surprised. But he remained friends with Hani although they rarely met, since there was nothing to discuss and Hani didn't want to talk about relationships with women.

Lara never became the leader of Bethlehem council but was instrumental in a number of initiatives which helped the lives of the women who had voted for her. She wasn't unhappy at that since now she had a growing support base in Bethlehem as an established political leader of some standing.

Medad, the ex-sniper, was at home pondering Rachel's message while Shana was ensconced in her office writing furiously, as she did.

"This is all getting out of hand," he said aloud to himself. "It's all falling apart."

A sudden depression came over him. Would it ever end? What was the point in trying further? Would there ever be a day when Israelis and Palestinians would live together in a just and sustainable peace? Only in his most upbeat moments did he think there would be a good and righteous solution. The status quo might flex here and there but he knew in his heart that it wouldn't change.

If it wasn't Hani and Ayshaa being persecuted it would be someone else. If it wasn't that Imam plotting with Hamas and Iran, it would probably be another seeking Israel's downfall. If it wasn't Natan, it would be right wing settlers who would seek to stoke fear and dread in the Palestinian community. If it wasn't Hirsch and Akiva, there would be other military/intelligence personnel who would continue to follow orders seeking to cement the Occupation and uncover security concerns, real or imagined.

His wandering mind turned to Sami – ah! Would there ever be another Sami? Medad had met her once, had watched her videos, followed her vblog and was in awe of her courage in Hamas' backyard. Just a teenager, but what an impact in a few short months. Nevertheless, he told himself, now that she had apparently been silenced, Hamas would continue to exploit their people for their own ends and send rockets over southern Israel whenever they wanted. And Israel would continue to harass and bomb them in the name of security.

He shouted out to Shana to get her attention. "You know, would it really matter if Hamas gained indirect control of the West Bank?"

She didn't reply. Medad pushed on. "Israel's right wing politicians and their supporters would never move their settlers back into legal Israel whoever purported to govern what might be left of the land. What do you think?"

No answer from Shana. Maybe, he thought to himself, they would finally have the excuse to deploy their considerable military might to drive the remaining Palestinians completely off their land and demolish all their houses. They would finally have a full Jewish state with their quasi biblical boundaries solely for Jewish people.

Medad let out a long sigh. He instinctively concluded that such a solution would never provide real security for Israelis. They would always be looking over their shoulders. They had sown to the wind, and inevitably would some day, reap the whirlwind. Their leaders had sold them on a false prospectus, and he was part of that government machine.

He suddenly made a decision. He was done with it all. It wasn't a place where he would want to bring up his children, that is if he and Shana ever had them. He felt alienated from his own country and his own people. If truth be told, he had always felt alienated from his father and brother, but not his mother. He recalled what she had said about his Old Testament namesake, "a leader and a prophet". Well, maybe he had some prophetic leanings. He thought he could see the mistakes his country was making and what future that would lead to, but seemed powerless to do anything about it. Not much of a leader either then.

Shana finally emerged later that evening taking her ear buds out as she walked into the lounge. Medad looked up, "You know, I seem to have more in common with Hani than with most of my own people."

Shana was sympathetic, "You're a bridge-builder, maybe a visionary. We don't have many of either in this country. I agree we're in a mess but we're also in a minority with these views. Most people who want peace think they will achieve it by higher and higher security, meaning more and more oppression for the Palestinians."

She paused and reflected. "I am finding that most of my stories about Israel are being taken up by foreign news organisations. Here people don't really want to know what it's really like of the other side of the wall. They're just thankful they're on this side. But I don't think they realise what's coming."

Medad looked at her, "Why don't we get out and settle in the US? We could still do our bit for peace from there. It might be a much better place for our kids."

Shana raised her eyebrows, "You're thinking of having kids?" Embarrassed, Medad tried to backtrack. "I was just thinking ahead a little," he said hesitantly, not wanting to say the wrong thing.

"Have you talked to your friend Chuck recently?" Shana asked.

"No," Medad replied, "but now you come to mention it, perhaps I ought to."

The Israeli election went ahead of course, producing another Likud right wing coalition which meant a steady continuation of the policies of previous decades with regard to subduing the occupied population of the West Bank. Israeli schoolchildren would still be taught that all Palestinians were terrorists and the security card would continue to be played to reinforce this as and when deemed appropriate. Natan Berkowitz certainly approved. Even Hamas was happy to have a Likud government in Israel for it gave them the propaganda ammunition with which to cajole their civilian population into protest.

However, the PA in Ramallah were not happy. They were smelling treachery in the air as some other Arab states besides Egypt and Jordan had decided to begin a process of recognising the State of Israel. Whether persuaded or bribed by an American President desperately wanting an anti-Iran foreign policy success to help justify a second term was immaterial to them. It was also a coup for the embattled Prime Minister of Israel also desperately clinging on to office to prevent a slew of corruption charges coming his way.

Shana was happy, though. This was money in the bank for her. She was saying to her readers that in the longer term, if ever those Arab countries agreed between themselves (unlikely given the history), they could present a united front to Israel finally resolve the Occupation justly or threaten to break off relations. That could hurt Israel.

She thought about the move that Medad had proposed. Her writing could be done from anywhere in the world although it was always good to be where it was all happening. She then thought about children. No argument there, so they finally decided to emigrate. Medad's letter of resignation didn't come as much of a surprise to his Minister who had always suspected his civil servant's passion for a peace process. In spite of Chuck's gentle persuasion, they finally settled for New York rather than Washington. Medad didn't want to be dragged directly into another political sphere, at least not yet. Over the next few years they came to love the city that never sleeps and to prove it, brought up four children there. Medad immersed himself in the charity work of Jewish Voice for Peace but kept in touch with Chuck on the 'off chance', as he explained it to his wife. Shana's journalistic career ticked over in between children with a column in the New York Times and the occasional splash in the Washington Post or UK Guardian. She also had contacts with Middle East Eye and Middle East Monitor so there was always the opportunity there. But it was all about Israel in one guise or another. It was in her blood.

Lebanon remained in turmoil and the Iranian 'diplomat' continued his task of infiltrating all aspects of Israeli society with a growing number of informers in Israel itself, on the West Bank and now in Gaza. In spite of severe financial and commercial sanctions on Iran itself, there still seemed to be an open purse for Angra Mainyu to fulfil his mission, which was going very well, thank you.

In Gaza, Sami was being held in a cellar somewhere not very far away from where she was kidnapped. She thought she had only been in the car for ten minutes or so, but since she had a hood over her face she didn't know whether they were driving in a straight line or going round in circles. They were treated her fairly well so far; food twice a day but no washing facilities and a bucket in the corner. It must have been Hamas, she thought, but she had no idea what their plan was. Her captors didn't bother hiding their faces so confident were they, which confirmed to her that they had some authority to kidnap her. She wondered how long was it going to last.

She thought about Rachel and what she was going through, but there was no way of getting a message out. Indeed if she had tried, it might have put her in danger as well. Reviewing what she had done over these past weeks she found that, despite her present circumstances, she didn't regret anything and hoped Rachel would continue posting and videoing. Now there was an international audience, she knew Rachel could do it anywhere there was an internet connection and if necessary, she would have enough money from the advertising to move around. Perhaps she would contact Medad and see if he could use his influence to get her out of Gaza.

Sami tried to comfort herself with thoughts that her work would carry on even if she couldn't do it herself. She had done what she could, more than she could have imagined a few years ago. Yes, her parents would have been proud of her, she thought, she hoped.

Rachel did continue for a some time to maintain Sami's vblog from various place within Gaza itself, but after many weeks of not hearing from the teenager, she got back in touch with UNRWA, who accepted her back into their employment and the vblog petered out. Sami, tragically, was never seen again.

There are some stories which have happy Hollywood-type endings: the guy gets his gal, the detective catches his villain, the defence lawyer gets his innocent client off, and so on. Sadly this cannot be one of those stories.

In many areas of the world, governments of left and right come and go. With each, policies often change and sometimes outcomes change, occasionally for the better. But that doesn't seem to happen here. As far as Israel is concerned underlying policies and sought after outcomes never have really changed. Occupation of the West Bank had been a fact for over fifty years and remains a fixed way of life for both sides. Most observers are certain it isn't going to change any time soon.

Acknowledgements

All the main characters in this story are purely fictional and pulled from my imagination. Some come from recognised institutions such as the *IDF (Israeli Defence Forces)*, the *PA (Palestinian Authority)*, *Hamas*, *CIA (Central Intelligence Agency)* etc.

Others such as *BCI (Bethlehem Christian Institute)* and *Ghu-sin Zay-tun* are loosely based on existing institutions but have been re-named and re-imagined. I trust this re-imagining is acceptable to them.

Still others, notably *BWP (Bethlehem Women for Peace)* have been invented. Gaza Baptist church is also referenced and does exist but, as far as I am aware, has never been bombed but its pastor has indeed been exiled.

I have received a great deal of help and support from many of my friends for this first novel. Specifically, my wife Sandra for getting my time lines sorted, John Chapman for his early advice and Simon Porter for his unwavering encouragement. Also Dr Andrew Wilson and Philip Everest for their detailed and invaluable comments on the many drafts of the manuscript. It is much the better for their expertise.

Lightning Source UK Ltd.
Milton Keynes UK
UKHW011059210621
385897UK00003B/298